A Star to Wish Upon

By
Alexa Bervid

cover illustration by Ally Bertapelle

For all the girls who dream of
finding their true love

Prologue

Once upon a time in the small, quaint town of Annapolis, Maryland, there lived a little girl named Cecilia Margaret Hartley. She was a sweet young girl, very bright, funny, and had a big heart. She was rather tall for her age, with golden auburn hair, sapphire blue eyes, soft peach skin, and a merry smile. She was a dreamer, growing up fascinated by Disney, particularly the princesses, all her life. Cecilia had also grown up writing stories and dreamed of becoming a writer.

Our story begins in 2005. Cecilia was seven years old. It was the first day of summer and Cecilia and her best friends were celebrating at the fairgrounds. The girls had spent the whole time running around, going on rides, playing games, and eating a lot of junk food. At this point Cecilia's parents, who were chaperoning the girls, were exhausted of their hyper behavior and craziness. And the crowds full of people, especially other children, did not help at all.

Later on in the night, around 7:30 p.m., the girls were playing some carnival games. They played a ring-tossing one where they had to throw some rings onto some wood sticking out in the ground. Your prize that you won depended on where you ended up throwing your ring.

Esperanza Lopez, one of Cecilia's friends, was struggling. She grunted every time it would land on the ground. Esperanza was very creative, bubbly, and a true kid at heart. Sweet in nature, she was a total optimist, and always tried to find the best in every situation. Her father was an immigrant from Spain and her mother was from

Brooklyn, resulting in beautiful tan skin. Esperanza's hair was raven black and her eyes were emerald green.

Meanwhile, another one of Cecilia's friends, Grace St. Valentine, kept getting so close to throwing a ring on a wood thing, but she would always miss. Grace was one of those people who tried to be the smartest person in the room, and many times she was. She was wise beyond her years and by far the most intelligent in the group, and considered as "the mom." She had blonde hair which was darker in the winter and lighter when summer came, with dark brown eyes.

Cecilia's third friend, Nicole Grey, had given up after throwing and missing a ring about three times. Now she was standing there and cheering on her friends. Nicole--she was---a character. She was certainly the most free-spirited of the four friends, always looking for adventure and to try new things. Still, she always had the courage to defend her friends, even if her hot temper could get out of hand. She had distinctive aquamarine eyes and wavy buttery blonde hair.

After a few throws, Cecilia landed on a marker. Her eyes opened wide. She wasn't usually very good at playing games like this. But now she had finally won!

"I won," she mumbled to herself in surprise. Then she jumped up and down cheering in excitement, "I won! I won!"

All of Cecilia's friends congratulated her on getting the prize. And her parents, who had been watching from the sides, walked over to them and also offered their daughter congratulations. Cecilia turned around to see the ring again, and she noticed she had landed it on a stick that had a giant purple question mark on it.

"What's that?" Cecilia pointed to the stick.

"Looks like a question mark," Esperanza guessed, looking at the stick.

"Must be a mystery prize," Grace inquired. "It's a surprise."

"A surprise?" Nicole groaned, disgusted. "Who likes surprises?"

Cecilia asked the teen boy who was working the game: "Uh, excuse me." The teen heard her and went up to talk to her. She continued, "What does the question mark mean?"

"That means you are going to get the mystery prize," the teen smiled. "It's a surprise!"

"Told you," Grace bragged.

"Want me to get it for you?" he asked all the girls.

"Yes, please!" they replied in unison.

"Ok," the boy chuckled. "Be right back." And so he went back to get the prize.

"What do you think it is?" Grace excitingly whispered to Cecilia.

"What if it was a nail polish kit?" Nicole squealed.

"Or a music box," Esperanza guessed.

"Or something that is for both girls *and* boys," Grace pointed out.

Before anyone could reply to Grace, the teen boy was walking out with the prize, and Cecilia's smile dropped. It was a tiny Beanie Baby plush toy of the superhero Serpent Boy. He was every little boy's favorite superhero these days, or perhaps after Batman. The plush, polyester toy could easily fit into someone's hand. Serpent Boy had a full-on dark green and black-colored suit, including a mask that had round white circles for eyes. Cecilia, who had never been fond of anything related to superheroes, was not impressed.

"Here you go," the teen handed the toy to Cecilia, who just stared at it. She held it with both hands, feeling the polyester material against her skin. "Have a nice night," the friendly teen smiled. Everyone said goodbye, with Cecilia mumbling a "thanks," and they all started walking away.

The group went to go sit at some benches and eat popcorn. When they sat down, Cecilia's father went to go get popcorn. Cecilia didn't say anything, she just stared at her new Serpent Boy plush the whole time.

"I can't believe I got this toy," Cecilia whined. She shook her head, "I hate Serpent Boy."

"What did I tell you about the word 'hate' honey?" Cecilia's mother kindly corrected her daughter.

"I strongly dislike Serpent Boy," Cecilia answered.

"Would you rather have a Disney prince plush toy?" Nicole teased her friend.

"Why do you not like Serpent Boy?" Esperanza asked curiously.

"I don't know," Cecilia shrugged. "I just don't."

"Maybe someday you will like him," Grace suggested.

But Cecilia certainly didn't think so. "No! There's no way ever ever ever ever in a million years I will like Serpent Boy!"

"Is that so?" Nicole wiggled her eyebrows.

"I'm making a promise," Cecilia crossed her shoulders.

Meanwhile, approximately 3,632 miles away from Annapolis, there lived a little boy named Elliott Parker in the London borough of Kingston upon Thames. He was small for his age, a trait he inherited from his family, and had only just turned nine. He had very curly brown hair with skin like snow, which came from his Irish background, and eyes the color of his hair. He also had a very distinctive mole on his chin that would magically disappear one day when he was eighteen.

It was one of the last days before the school year ended during the children's recess period. Elliott, however, was not eating in the cafeteria with the other students. He was in the school gymnasium, wearing tights, and practicing with a ballet teacher. His mother had enrolled him in ballet classes a year prior after seeing his potential, and one of the many ways he trained was this way.

The only downside to practicing in the school's gymnasium was that there were children peeking through the windows, snickering and making fun of poor Elliott. But Elliott didn't let it bother him. By this time, he was used to it. He just kept dancing and pretended as if the bullies weren't there.

On the way back from school that day, Elliott was walking home with his best friend Teddy Graham (which earned much teasing, for obvious reasons). Despite the bullies, Elliott had a lot of friends, but none like Teddy. Teddy was slightly taller than Elliott with messy blonde hair and sparkling blue eyes. Teddy had noticed that Elliott had been wearing sunglasses ever since school ended, but he didn't think to say anything.

"I can't believe in just a week, we'll be on vacation!" Teddy said excitedly, swinging his lunch box around. He turned to his best friend and asked, "Are you and your family going on holiday to Ireland again this year?"

"Mhhmm," Elliott nodded, still thinking about the bullies.

Teddy then got concerned. "What's wrong, Elliott?" he asked, stopping on the sidewalk to face his friend.

Elliott didn't say anything for a moment. He turned to his best friend. "The nurse gave me these to wear after school today," he told his best friend.

At this point, Teddy was confused. "Why?" he asked.

Elliott let out a heavy sigh. He slowly took off the glasses to reveal a black eye given to him by some of the harshest bullies on the school yard.

Teddy's eyes opened wide. "Holy sh..." he stopped himself from saying the word he often heard his father say. "Who did this to you?"

"Pauly Wilkes and Hugh Morgan," Elliott murmured, mentioning the two boys who targeted Elliott the most. "I just---" Elliott started to tear up and couldn't find the words to say. "I have to go," he started running, trying to hold back the tears.

"Elliott! Elliott!" Teddy called to his best friend. But Elliott didn't listen. He just kept running as if he was being chased by a hungry wolf.

When Elliott finally reached home, he saw the front door was open and just went inside. He creaked the door open slowly and saw his mother, Phoebe, in the living room. She was a photographer, taking pictures of Elliott's three-year-old brother Ryan dressed in a sailor outfit. She had a full photo shoot with a miniature sailboat, cameras everywhere, and everything you could imagine in a photographer's studio. Phoebe was a beautiful woman and very artistic, with strawberry blonde hair that was often in a loose ponytail or a messy bun or braid, and hazel eyes.

She had noticed the door was open and turned around. She didn't see the black eye right away and when she saw Elliott she said, "Hello darling, how was---" but as soon as she saw the black eye, her face dropped. It was at that moment that Elliott burst into tears, from the bullying and that his mother, who had just been so happy taking pictures of his little brother, was now concerned about him. "Oh my, Elliott, sweet pea. What on earth happened?"

She reached over to hug Elliott tightly. He cried into his mother's shoulders, "Bullies, again. Teasing me about being a dancer." Elliott choked on his tears and struggled to get his words out.

"Oh, my poor sweetheart," Phoebe soothed her son. She ended the motherly embrace to look at her son. She was down at his level by now and had put her warm hands on his cheeks. "Let's get some ice on that and you can tell me what happened. Okay?" Elliott quickly nodded. Phoebe stood up, gently wrapped her arms around her son's shoulders, and went to get ice.

Hours later, Elliott still lay in bed, his ice pack covering his eye. He was still upset about what had happened earlier. He heard a knock on the door and murmured, "Come in."

The door opened to reveal Phoebe and George, Elliott's father. He was a man who could go from fatherly, reserved, and humourous every now and then. He looked very much like an older version of his son, and worked as a carpenter in London.

"Hello, Elliott," he whispered.

"Hi, mum. Hi, dad," Elliott replied back.

Phoebe and George slowly made their way to the end of the bed to see their son and comfort him. "We just came in to check on you," Phoebe said in a gentle tone.

Elliott just shrugged, "My eye is okay. And I've decided I'm going to quit ballet."

"What?" George asked in confusion as if he didn't hear his son right.

"I thought I could deal with the bullies, and I did for a while," Elliott said, trying not to sob again. "But after this, I'm going to quit."

"But sweet pea---" Phoebe started to say. She took a deep breath, "Don't let those bullies get to you. Just because you have different dreams than them doesn't mean you should stop trying to achieve them." Elliott sat up slowly and Phoebe leaned in closer to her son, caressing his cheek with her fingers.

"And, if you ask me, it's good to be different," George told his son. "I mean, think about it. Most of those lads at your school play rugby, correct?" Elliott nodded. George continued, "It's good that there's at least one person in that school that does ballet. If every child at that school played rugby, it would be pretty boring if you ask me."

"And you can always join dad in the carpentry business if dancing doesn't work out," Phoebe reminded her son. This made the three of them chuckle, as young Elliott wasn't the best at dealing with tools despite the mentoring from his father and grandfather, who were both carpenters. In fact, most men in the Parker family were carpenters, and they wanted Elliott to learn the trade. But Elliott promised he would try harder when he got older.

"Can I ask you two something?" Elliott asked in genuine curiosity. His parents nodded. "Will dancing help in getting interest from the ladies?"

This made both George and Phoebe burst out laughing at their nine-year-old son's comment. George, still laughing, finally said, "In a few years it will."

"And who knows," Phoebe said, "maybe you'll want to try acting down the road. Miss Frost told me you did really well when the class performed a play."

"Nah," Elliott shook his head with some kind of disgust on his face. "Not really my thing."

"You never know, Elliott," George patted his son's head. "You never know." And after that, the family went down to have dinner.

At around 8:30 that night, Elliott couldn't fall asleep. So he went out to the ledge by his windowsill to look at the stars. Soon, his eyes caught the wishing star, shining and glittering from above.

Elliott smiled as brightly as the star itself, closed his eyes, and whispered: "Star light, star bright, first star I see tonight. I wish I may, I wish I might, have the wish I wish tonight."

He took a deep breath and whispered, "I wish."

Meanwhile back in the states, a few hours later (because of the time difference between Annapolis and London), Cecilia had gotten home from the carnival around 9 p.m. and went to sleep around 9:20 p.m. But she couldn't fall asleep. She lay there in her bed with the

14

Disney princess covers, her eyes wide open. She sat up in bed and crawled to the window right beside it. Opening the cream white curtains, she looked outside.

Seeing all the beautiful stars scattered across the night sky made Cecilia smile. She especially smiled when she saw the most important star of all: the wishing one. She closed her eyes and whispered softly under her breath, "Star light, star bright, first star I see tonight. I wish I may, I wish I might, have the wish I wish tonight.

She took a deep breath and whispered, "I wish."

Little did Cecilia Hartley and Elliott Parker know that they wished for the same thing: to find someone to love and truly make them happy. Also, little did they know that they would fulfill the other's wish. Although at the time it seemed unlikely that the two would ever meet, since June 3, 2005, it was written in the stars.

Chapter 1: Wishing For A European Adventure

For as long as I can remember, Disney has been a big and important part of my life, and in a way it's made me who I am. I've always wanted to be a Disney princess. I wanted to have a fairy godmother like Cinderella. I wanted to be a mermaid like Ariel. I wanted to be smart as a whip like Belle. And like all of the princesses, I wanted to find true love, that one person I wanted to spend the rest of my life with. I had promised myself I would find my prince charming and that we would live happily ever after. However, if you told my seven-year-old self who my true love would be, I would never have believed you.

It all began the summer of 2019, when I was twenty-one years old. It was the summer right before my final year at Washington College. A bunch of my friends, who I had gone to school with from kindergarten to college, decided to go on what we called "a European extravaganza" before we began the final part of our college journey. All of us were different, but that didn't stop us from becoming friends. We wanted to do something fun for the summer before school started and before we would begin to think about the rest of our lives. Eighteen days in Italy, Austria, and Germany with my best girls.

The night before we would be leaving from Dulles Airport, I was packing up the last of my things, and about to weigh my bag to see if it was at the limit. I looked around my room thinking this would be the last time I would see it for a while. The color was still green, the bed was still only half made, my bulletin board with all the family photos and movie posters and Disney memorabilia still remained. Hopefully it would still be there when I got back, unless my psycho puppy Jane chewed on one of the posters or photos.

Just as I was finishing up, there was a knock on the door. "Who is it?" I called.

"It's me!" my mom's voice said from outside. "The woman who gave birth to you!"

"Come in!" I chuckled, having sat down on the bed after organizing clothes and packing them for several hours.

When my mom answered the door, she had a bright smile on her face, her platinum blonde hair put together neatly in a braid and wearing her pink flowered pajamas and matching slippers and robe. Just then, good old Jane, being the crazy dog she is, rushed in and jumped on the bed. She was a border doodle (cross between a border collie and poodle), or as we call her, goater doodle, because of her love of paper. She jumped up and down on my bed, and was running around like a maniac.

"Jane!" I shouted as she laid down on my suitcase. I couldn't help but laugh and say, "Get off my suitcase, you crazy thing!" Jane heard me yelling at her, and she knew she had done something wrong and that she had upset me. She rushed over to me and licked my face all over, and showered me with kisses. "Awww, I can't stay mad at my baby!" I said with affection.

"She really does love you, Cecilia," my mom put a hand on my shoulder.

"I'm gonna miss her so much!" I said, falling over from the kisses. "Eighteen days without her seems too long! I'll miss you and Dad too!"

"We're gonna miss you too, sweetie," Mom replied. She sat next to me on the bed and hugged me tightly, and I hugged her back as Jane tried to get in on the hug.

"I can't believe I'm going to be out of the country for more than two weeks. Then right after that I have to worry about senior year and what I'm going to do later in life," I said, still embracing her.

We finally let go, and Mom said, "I know! But you're going to have so much fun! And don't worry about next year. Enjoy yourself! You're going to get some inspiration for a story, you're going to see new places, meet new people, get a hot European boyfriend..."

"Woah! Since when do you want me to get a boyfriend?" I asked.

"Well, they always say travel inspires romance. You know when I spent the summer in South America, I met this GORGEOUS boy in Argentina, and we fell in love and dated for a little bit."

"What happened?"

"Well, I went back to the U.S., he stayed in South America, and we parted ways. Then the next year I met your father." She joked, "Biggest mistake of my life!"

"Hey!" I said, pretending to be offended.

"At least I got you," she shrugged. "I'm just kidding. I'm glad I met your father, *and* that I had you."

"I'm proud to be your daughter," I said, then kissing her on the cheek, which made her smile. Then I quickly changed the subject back to boys, "I think we'll be too busy sightseeing and everything to really go looking for boys, except Nicole who will probably have a new boyfriend in every country." We both laughed, as we both knew my friend Nicole's flirtatious, wild side really well.

"If you say so. But you never know, you might meet the love of your life on this trip," she added, and I just nodded. She then changed the subject, "Anyway, are you finished packing? The girls will be here any minute!" Mom said. My friends were coming to spend the night before we left for Dulles, so we could all go to the airport together.

"Yup! All done! I'll be right down!" I said. "Love you Mom!"

"Love you too, honey," she kissed me on the cheek and left the room with Jane following behind.

As I was picking my passport off the bed, I looked around the room, thinking about how I was growing up and how I used to call this place my room, but since going away to college I had begun to think of it as my *childhood* room. Out of the corner of my eye I saw the Serpent Boy beanie baby plush toy hidden in my opened closet. I groaned, but then chuckled to myself. I remember that day when I won the toy at the carnival and I was made. I'm not sure why, but I hated Serpent Boy at the time. Now I don't mind him, but he's not my favorite. It cracks me up that we always said we were going to give that toy away, but we've always kept it. It's funny how things work.

I sighed and looked down at my passport in my hands. "Cecilia Margaret Hartley," I read aloud. "This little girl is growing up. She's about to go on a trip of a lifetime!"

******

Later that night, my friends and I were all settled in, hanging around the living room talking and finishing up the pizza we ordered. We were talking about our upcoming adventures, how they would be scary but exciting, nerve racking but daring. Just then my dad, who my friends had long ago dubbed as "the cool fun dad," came in.

"Hey girls! Just making sure everything's ok," he said, wearing his gray robe, plaid blue pajama pants, and white T-shirt shirt.

"Hey Dad! We're doing great thank you!" I said, wanting him to get out of the room so we could have some "girl talk."

"Okay,fine I'll leave, if you need us we'll be up in our room, but you may not want to bother us because we'll be busy if you know what I mean," he said, as he winked. He loved making dirty jokes.

While Grace, Nicole, and Esperanza laughed at my father's joke, I just rolled my eyes because no one finds their parents' talking about their sex life particularly funny, so I just responded with, "Oh brother!"

"What brother, Cecilia?" Dad said in reply, continuing to use his dry humor. "I thought you were an only child!"

They all laughed once again at the sarcastic comment, and this time I joined in.

"Anyway, I'll leave you four to it, good night, love you guys, see you tomorrow, and please, no sneaking boys in," Dad finally said.

After giggling, my friends said, "Good night, Mr. Hartley," in unison.

"Good night, Daddy," I replied. "I love you." I then blew him a kiss, and he blew one back. He smiled and then he left us.

"I love your Dad," Esperanza said, giggling lightly, once he was gone.

"Try living with him," I sarcastically replied.

"At least your dad is funny," Nicole quickly said back, and she then said disappointingly, "My dad is grouchy."

"It's like if our dads were the seven dwarves, mine would be Happy and your's would be Grumpy!" I said, once again making a Disney reference.

"Your love for Disney just doesn't stop, does it?" Nicole said.

"You know, if you want, we can go to Disney World for eighteen days instead of Europe," Esperanza jokingly said.

"Oh, come on, Esperanza," I responded quickly. "I've been to Disney World ten times, I want to go someplace different, and I've never been to Europe before! I just think Grace is disappointed because we can't go to Ireland. I bet she wanted to show her older sister she's better than her by doing Irish dancing in Ireland."

"For your information," Grace said, getting defensive and responding quickly, "we've *both* done Irish dancing in Ireland at World's, and she came in second and I didn't even place, so that doesn't help me. But don't worry, one day I *will* beat her!"

"There's Grace, showing off her type A personality once again," Nicole said sarcastically.

"Hey guys, can I ask you something?" Grace said, clearly trying to change the subject.

"Sure, Grace," Esperanza said, and she had our full attention. "What's up?"

"Okay, so you know how I've told you I have four British cousins, right?" Grace said. We nodded, having heard stories about her four British cousins *plenty* of times before. She continued, "Well, I know that this was supposed to be just a girls' trip, but it just so happens that they are going to be in Rome when we are. So, I hope you don't mind, but I invited them to come along on the rest of the trip with us. They are all very sweet boys. Is it okay if they come?"

"Oh of course, Grace," Esperanza said in a motherly tone. "We would love to meet your cousins! We have heard *so* much about them!"

"Plus, I bet Cecilia is more than excited," Nicole said, targeting me. "Remember how she's always said that British accents are sexy, and they turn her on?"

"Oh yeah!" Esperanza said, remembering how I feel about British guys. "There was that one British guy at our school! What was his name?"

"Oh," Grace said, trying to remember his name. She finally remembered: "Henry Stone!"

"Yes! Henry Stone!" Esperanza said excitedly, now remembering the name. "She was *crazy* for him! She had this whole plan where she was going to marry him, move to England, and have seven kids with him!"

"And when we were playing a game of who would you do in Mrs. Franklin's Honors Lit class and she said," Nicole continued, and then mimicking me as if I was a Disney princess said, "Oh, of course! Henry Stone! I would love to have lots of sex and babies with Henry Stone!"

All three of my friends started laughing hysterically. Esperanza was crying because of how hard she was laughing. And Grace snorted as a result of her laughter, and snorting was not something she usually did. And Nicole went into a whole laughing fit and fell on the floor collapsing in giggles. Yes, I did have a crush on Henry Stone, a transfer student from England who came in our sophomore year. Gosh, was he handsome! He had long, wavy strawberry blonde hair, meadow green eyes, about 5"11, and the most perfect dimples you've ever seen! Unfortunately, at the end of sophomore year he went back to London and I regretted not having the nerve to even talk to him.

"Okay, okay, okay, okay," I tried to calm down the non-stop laughter. "It's over. He's gone, back in England, I'll never see him again. I'm over him. He's ancient history."

"Oh come on, Cecilia," Nicole said annoyed. "There were times where he was *clearly* interested in you, but you were worried about your 'no dating in high school' and 'vow to save yourself for marriage' policies to even go out with him! I love you, Cecilia, but you're such a goody-goody! You let go of a really good guy when you actually had a chance with him!"

After that, all was silent. I've been friends with Nicole since kindergarten, but we were just so different. She was more of the rebellious, flirtatious wild child and I was the typical Catholic goody-two-shoes stereotype. I think she felt bad for what she said, and after about thirty seconds of silence, Nicole sighed and said, "I'm sorry, Cecilia. You know I am. I shouldn't have blown up at you like that."

"No, it's fine Nicole," I assured her. "You're right, Henry was the one who got away."

Esperanza, being the mother hen she was, said, "Okay, I think this is a sign we should get some sleep. We've got a really busy day tomorrow."

"You're right, Esperanza," Grace agreed. "We could all use a good night's sleep."

After saying good night, we all went our separate ways. Grace slept in the guest room in the basement, Nicole slept on the couch in the family room downstairs, and Esperanza slept on the bed in the room we called

"Jane's room," or the office. Meanwhile, I went to my own room, hoping to sleep soundly like a baby. But I didn't because I realized something.

Nicole was right. I let Henry, a guy who I liked and who liked me back, go and I didn't do anything about it before it was too late. Nicole was right, I had to let my goody-two-shoes self go and become stronger. If I met a boy in Europe that I liked, I would tell him how I felt, and I wouldn't let anything get in the way between us! I was a strong, independent, confident woman. With that decision, I went to bed, ready to begin my European adventure which, little did I know, would change my life forever.

Chapter 2: Wishing For A Movie To Watch

Around 6 a.m. we got past security, and we still had a whole hour before we had to begin boarding. We were still really sleepy, after getting up at 3:30 a.m., for a flight that wasn't even till 7:46 a.m. As someone who usually sleeps in till 10:30 or so, I was not a happy camper.

"So what should we do?" Grace asked after we took the tram from security to the gate. "Get some breakfast?"

"I could eat!" Esperanza said. She suggested, "How about *McDonald's*?"

"You guys can go," Nicole, who was clearly in a bad mood because she was up so early, said. "I'm on a diet so I'm going to go to *Jamba Juice*."

"Um, Nicole," Grace corrected her, "they don't have *Jamba Juice* at Dulles. You must be thinking of BWI."

"Oh my gosh, Grace!" Nicole snapped. "Why do you have to correct me every single freaking time?!" When she realized how much of a you-know-what she was being she said, "Yeah, I'm sleeping on the plane."

"I know!" I said, trying to make the situation better. "How about we go get some *Starbucks*? That way we can get some coffee and a scone or something!"

Everyone agreed, and we all went to *Starbucks*. We each got a frappuccino and a scone. I got a cinnamon roll frappuccino, Esperanza a vanilla bean one, Nicole a peppermint mocha one, and Grace a caramel one. Nicole and Esperanza got blueberry scones and Grace and I got vanilla bean ones. Afterwards, we went to the gate and just sat there and ate our breakfast and talked.

"Can I just say," Esperanza said, taking a sip of her frappuccino, "I'm *so* glad we're not going to London Heathrow and then Rome. It would be such a pain to switch flights like that!"

"No kidding!" Grace agreed. "If I had to go on two planes just to get to one place, I would shoot myself." We all stared at for her joke. "What? I wouldn't *actually* do it!"

"You can't talk about weapons in an airport!" I told her. "Haven't you ever seen *Meet the Parents*?!"

"That was different," Grace responded. "He used the word—"

"No! Don't say it!" the rest of us said in perfect unison, not wanting our friend to get in trouble for saying the word "bomb" at the airport.

"Anyway," I said, quickly trying to talk about something else. "Speaking of London Heathrow, when are your cousins joining us?"

"You'll actually meet them in Rome today," Grace said. "They will already be there, and they will meet us in the hotel lobby."

"Better keep an eye on your cousins, Grace," Nicole warned her friend. "I think Cecilia is clearly interested in your cousins. She's asking all these questions!"

27

I stuck out my tongue at her, then turned to Grace and said, "So how old are they?"

"What did I tell you?" Nicole pointed out.

"Well, little Oliver is the youngest. He's seven," Grace started.

"Oops, sorry, Cecilia. He's too young for you," Esperanza, who was usually not one for sarcastic jokes, said.

"Then Connor is eleven and Ryan is seventeen," Grace continued.

"Wait what about the oldest? How old is he?" I asked. I would have to admit, I was very interested. "Is he younger or older than us?"

"Wow, Nicole, you're right!" Esperanza said. "Cecilia is totally interested in Grace's cousins!"

"What did I tell you?" Nicole asked, clearly feeling proud that she was right.

"Well, the oldest, the one I have such a special bond with, is in fact twenty-three, only two years older than us," Grace responded to my question.

"Hmmmm," I said. "Name?"

"His name is..." Grace said. She suspiciously paused and I was concerned by the worried look on her face. "Eli!"

"Eli," I repeated his name. "What a nice name." I still remained suspicious at the way she hesitated to say his name.

"I feel it in my fingers, I feel it in my toes." Esperanza and Nicole started singing the song from *Love Actually*, which we watched every year as a tradition on Christmas Eve.

"Love is all around me," Grace joined in.

"Okay, okay, okay, okay," I interrupted. "That's enough." And we kept waiting and waiting for boarding to commence.

******

After the flight got delayed till 10 o'clock due to some "bad windy weather in the ocean," we were finally on our way. The good thing was that we could spend those hours between then sleeping, and we all decided to watch movies.

"What movie shall we watch?" Nicole asked, scrolling through the collection of movies.

"How about *A Star is Born*?" Grace suggested. "I've never seen it you know."

"No, trust me, you don't want to see it," Esperanza warned. "I saw it in the theaters with my mom, we came out of the theater balling our eyes out. We were crying the whole way home and it wasn't until an hour later that we finally calmed down."

"Ok. *Crazy Rich Asians*? That's a good movie," Nicole said, trying to pick something they all liked. "We saw it in the theater together, remember?"

"Yeah we did," I said. "And after that time I watched it twenty more times."

"Okay, we're not getting anywhere," Grace said. "Let's keep looking."

After about ten minutes of browsing through different movie options, I suggested, "How about *Serpent Boy 2*?"

"*Serpent Boy*?!" Grace exclaimed, "Oh my gosh I love that movie!"

"Oh wait," Nicole realized something. Turning to me, she asked, "Are you going to be okay with this? Do you still hate Serpent Boy like you did at the fair fourteen years ago?"

I chuckled and told them, "No, it's fine. I've changed a lot since then."

"Let's watch it!" Esperanza sighed, "Finally a compromise!"

"Oh and the actor!" Nicole said, fangirling. "What a cutie! I don't know about you, but I would totally do him." I noticed Grace shifted uncomfortably in her seat when Nicole said this.

"He's super hot! What's his name? I'm totally blanking!" Esperanza said, trying to remember the *Serpent Boy* actor's name.

"Elliott Parker," I reminded her.

"That's it! Thank you!" Esperanza said.

For those of you who don't know, the actor they're talking about now is Elliott Parker, the British boy of every girl's dreams. He had medium length, curly hair and eyes both the color of Hershey's milk chocolate (or as he would probably prefer, Cadbury). He was not the tallest, about 5"8, but that didn't stop any girl from being charmed by his bright smile that could light up New York City and his adorkable humor and heart of gold. Every girl wanted to marry Elliott Parker and every boy wanted to be him. Whether he was stopping bad guys as the super hero Serpent Boy or showing off his acting chops in a variety of comedies and dramas or dancing and singing his heart out in plays, Elliott Parker was the total package. I personally thought he was cute, but not *that* cute, despite my love for British guys.

"I bet he's Cecilia's type," Nicole said. "British, sexy, sweet..."

"Whatever happened to her being interested in Grace's cousins?" Esperanza asked.

I turned to Grace and joked, "Yeah Grace, would you rather have me date your cousin or Elliott Parker?"

"Neither!" Grace responded quickly. "My cousin means the world to me and if you ever hurt him I would kill you. And Elliott Parker..." She didn't finish.

"What about him?" I asked. "What about Elliott Parker?" There was complete silence for a while. "Grace, is everything okay?"

"Nothing," Grace responded quickly and with a frantic look all over her face, from her worried eyes to her slightly red cheeks. "Let's just watch *Serpent Boy*, ok?"

So we watched *Serpent Boy 2*, took naps, watched some movie called *Pompeii* about the infamous city destroyed by the volcano, a place we would visit on our trip. I'm a huge fan of the Bastille song, the movie not so much. But throughout my time on the plane I still kept thinking and thinking about lots and lots of things. Why did Grace hesitate when she said her cousin's name? Why did she sound weird when talking about both her cousin and Elliott Parker? Questions kept racing through my mind on the 8 hour and 40 minute flight to Rome.

Chapter 3: Wishing For An Autograph

Phew! After a long flight and a two and a half hour delay, we had finally arrived in Rome! We sleepily got off the plane and as we stepped off the plane, we took a deep breath of the Italian air. (Well, the Italian *airport* air).

"Who else feels jet-lagged?" I asked the group. Right after I asked that, we all raised our hands at once and in sync.

"What time is it at home?" Grace asked.

Esperanza looked at her Apple Watch. "6:55 p.m."

"And here?" I asked.

Nicole looked at her phone and said, "12:55 a.m."

"Ugh!" Grace groaned.

"Anyway, let's go get our bags," Nicole said.

And so we were off to get our bags. We got off the plane at 12:55 a.m., and didn't get our bags until 1:23 a.m. I hadn't been this tired since my Girl Scout troop and I went to lock-in at the Annapolis Mall. We were locked in the mall at 10 p.m. when it closed, and the event went until 5 a.m. The experience of staying up all night was fun. The beaten feeling you have after pulling an all-nighter? Not so much. I felt like I was going to collapse on the floor and all of a sudden turn into Sleeping Beauty, but without pricking my finger on a spinning wheel.

It took *forever* to get a cab! All of the cab drivers either already had someone or some jerk stole our cab just about we were going to get one. Finally, at about 1:39 a.m., we finally got a cab, and we arrived at our hotel, *The Hotel Orange*, at about 2:04 a.m. It was a cute hotel, rather quaint and small. I was rooming with Grace and Esperanza and Nicole were rooming together.

When we got into our room, it was tiny, with two cute little beds close together and a mini window on the side. There was a bathroom next to the front door, and in between the beds and bathroom was a tub!

"Um, why is there a tub in the middle of the room?" I asked after noticing the tub.

"Must have thought we were a married couple on a honeymoon and gave us a special room," Grace joked.

I giggled and said, "I don't know about you, but I am dead tired!"

"I don't blame you at all," Grace agreed. "I don't know about you, but I'm going to bed."

I made my way to the bed and practically collapsed on it, not even bothering to take off my shoes or change into my jammies. After a second or two I asked Grace, "By the way, will we meet your cousins tomorrow?"

"Who?" a sleepy Grace forgot for a minute, but then she remembered, "Oh right! Yes, you'll meet them tomorrow...or later," we chuckled at the fact that it was actually the 23rd and not the 22nd. "Would have introduced you guys today, but I figured they didn't want to get up at 2 in the morning."

I giggled and said, "I wouldn't blame them!"

"Anyway," Grace, who was clearly eager to get to bed, said, "Good night sleepy head. Love ya!"

"Love you too, Grace," I replied. "Good night." And just like that, we each fell into a deep sleep.

******

The night before, we had all agreed to sleep in and have an easy day, then start exploring the next day. As a result, we did not get up until about noon, and we were proud of ourselves for sleeping for ten hours. The sun shone brightly through the window and into our hotel room, acting like a less noisy, definitely less annoying alarm clock to get us up.

Grace had got up before I did, me being the heavy sleeper I am. She whispered in my ear, "Wakey wakey. Rome awaits!" And I tiredly, slowly opened my eyes and saw her standing there, already showered and dressed, wearing a lavender floral romper with her shoulder-length sandy blonde hair tied neatly in a French braid, ready for the day.

"You're ready?" I said, shocked at how she was so prepared to begin her adventure when I hadn't even gotten out of bed yet.

"Yes!" Grace said in her adorable, yet very perky voice. She quickly and excitingly said, "I took a shower, brushed my teeth, changed, and put on sunscreen! And I

35

am ready to go!" Oh that Grace Valentine. She was such a little bean. (Which, if you don't know what that is, is a petit, sweet, adorable person).

"I'm not even out of bed yet," I said groggily.

"You're good," Grace assured. "Take your time! We don't have to be anywhere at any time just yet."

I nodded, then slowly got out of bed. I had been in these clothes for nearly twenty four hours and felt so disgusting wearing them. I took a long shower (not too hot, not too cold), changed into a blue and white-striped tank top with cream colored shorts, brushed my hair, put on *lots* of deodorant, put my hair in two ponytails, and was ready!

Grace and I went down to the lobby to meet Esperanza and Nicole. They were already there, sitting and waiting for us. Esperanza wore an orange sun dress paired with a white hat and her dark hair was in a side pony-tail. Nicole had donned a pink crop top with a flowy black skirt and her light blonde hair was in a perfect ballerina bun. They smiled at us, and looked as excited to explore Rome as we were.

"How did you guys sleep?" Esperanza asked.

"Like a baby on a soft cloud!" I said to describe my wonderful night sleep.

"Are we going to meet your cousins now, Grace?" Nicole asked.

Grace replied, "Yes. We are meeting them at *Bar Del Cappuccino* right now. So excited to introduce you guys!"

"We can't wait to meet them!" I told her. Finally, after hearing all these stories about Grace's English cousins, we were finally going to meet them. She always described them as sweet and great fun to be with. Would she be right?

"First, I've gotta go to the bathroom," Esperanza stood up and said. "Anyone else have to go?"

"I do," Grace said.

"I might as well," Nicole agreed.

Esperanza turned to me and asked, "Cecilia?"

"No, I just went," I assured her. "I'll just stay here."

"Alright," Nicole said. "We'll be right back." And the girls all went to the bathroom together, and I waited patiently for them.

Suddenly, a young man came running into the hotel. He was running so fast I couldn't quite see his face. He dashed behind a large plant and looked worried. I felt like I should go and help him, so I walked over to the plant and saw him hiding behind it. He looked so familiar to me, brown hair covered with a backward baseball cap and pale skin, dressed in a white t-shirt and jeans.

"Uh, excuse me sir," I whispered to him. "Is everything okay?"

"Shh," he responded. I could tell he had a British accent. "I'm hiding."

"Hiding?" I asked in curiosity and shock. "From what?"

"Get down!" he whispered, and pulled me down behind the plant. I squatted next to him. Where had I seen him before? I couldn't quite make out his face. I peeked from behind the plant and saw a whole group of girls running and screaming passing the hotel's door. As soon as they were gone, the stranger sighed with relief. "Oh, thank goodness." As he got up, he politely offered me his hand, and said, "I-I am terribly sorry, miss. It just kind of gets scary with those girls out of control and everything."

I accepted the offer for him to help me up, and as he pulled me up I said, "Oh no, trust me, it's fine. Really. But if you don't mind me asking why they were chasing—." And before I could finish, I could finally see his face clearly, and knew exactly why those girls were chasing him. "Oh my gosh," I said, totally starstruck. "Are you, are you Elliott Parker?" I was in complete utter shock. I was meeting Serpent Boy himself. I had to admit, he was much cuter in real life.

"You guessed correctly," he politely responded. "I'm here wrapping up a movie and the fans spotted me and started chasing me, and here we are!"

"I can't believe it, I'm actually meeting Serpent Boy," I said, still star struck. "I've never met a celebrity before. How does one address a celebrity?" I asked myself. Then I bowed down to him and teasingly said, "Your royal highness, Elliott Parker. It's a pleasure to meet you. I am Cecilia Hartley of Annapolis, Maryland."

Elliott Parker politely chuckled and gave me his hand and said, "Oh no, no, no, it's fine, please get up," I took his hand, got up once again and he smiled, "You can just call me Elliott." I smiled back. The teen magazines didn't lie at all. He was very, very charming. "Anyway, I best be on my way, actually. It was very nice to meet you—" He couldn't remember my name for a second, biting his lip as he thought. He pointed a finger, and was about to say a name, but he couldn't think of one.

"Cecilia," I finished for him.

"Cecilia," Elliott repeated. He said to me, "That's a pretty name."

"Thanks," I smiled. "My parents named me after Cecilia, patron saint of music, you know?"

"I do know," Elliott nodded. He smiled, "She's a cool saint. My parents named me after—," he paused to think for a minute. I waited for his response. Elliott thought out loud to himself, "Why *did* my parents name me Elliott?"

"Dunno," I shrugged, "I never met them."

Elliott chuckled, "Well it was very nice to meet you. Are you staying in this hotel?"

"Yeah," I nodded. I sadly said, "We're leaving Thursday."

"Me too," Elliott said. "My brothers and I—" before he could finish, he looked at his watch and exclaimed to himself, "Oh sh-." Before he could finish he looked up at me, he quickly said, pointing to the elevator, "I've gotta go. I have to meet some people. It was nice meeting you,

Cecilia, and I hope to see you soon." He awkwardly smiled at the last part.

I smiled back at him. "It was incredible to meet you, Elliott," I responded. "Hope to see you soon too." And he quickly walked away, still looking at me and smiling as he got on the elevator. Just as he was out of sight, the other girls came back.

"Hey, Cecilia," Grace waved. "Ready to go?"

I was still in a happy daze as I nodded and said, "You guys are never going to guess who I met in the lobby!"

"Pope Francis?" Nicole guessed. I shook my head.

Esperanza guessed, "The President?"

I shook my head and said, "Thank goodness I didn't."

"Who?" Esperanza gave up.

"Elliott Parker," I said excitedly. The other girls just stood there blank staring. Still very excited, I explained everything but really quickly, "He was running from some fans, and I didn't realize who it was, and we hid behind this plant..." I looked at their faces and they still looked completely confused. "Well, it's a long story."

"Elliott Parker? Really?" Grace asked almost worryingly. "What did he, what did he say?"

"Not much," I responded. "He was filming a movie here, got chased by some crazy fangirls, then went back up to his hotel room. He seemed really nice." I found myself smiling.

"Elliott Parker?" Nicole said in disbelief. "Get real, Cecilia."

"Hey, I've actually met him, believe it or not!" I said in defense.

"Prove it," Nicole crossed her arms.

Before I could say anything, Esperanza said, "Okay anyway, let's go." Then we left and walked to the café where we were supposed to meet Grace's cousins. The whole walk there I kept thinking about one thing and one thing only: my brief meeting with Elliott Parker.

******

We finally reached the quaint little *Bar Del Cappuccino*, which was everything you could imagine a café to be. When you walked in, there were small round tables with a bakery and coffee brewery and cashier on side. In the corner there were three young boys, one about seven, one about eleven, and one about seventeen. Must be Grace's cousins! They all looked similar, all with curly brown hair and very pale skin, although they were all different heights.

"Gracie!" they all shouted.

"Kids!" Grace excitedly ran towards them. They all hugged each other and were all so happy to see each other. As soon as they were done reuniting, she introduced us, "Guys, these are my cousins," she pointed to each one as she said their name, "This is Ryan, Connor, and little Ollie." They all smiled and politely waved and said hello.

41

"Boys, these are my best friends. Nicole Grey, Esperanza Lopez, and Cecilia Hartley."

"Very nice to meet you," I said.

"Hey, kids," Nicole said.

"We've heard so much about you," Esperanza said.

The boys all ran up to us and clearly took a liking to us, as they all gave us warm and tight embraces as if they were old friends who hadn't seen each other in ages. Little Oliver, or Ollie, in particular took a liking to me, and he tightly wrapped his arms around my leg.

"You're my new best friend!" he cheerfully told me. It reminded me of the time when I was a counselor at Vacation Bible School and one little girl in particular who was quite fond of me, had wrapped herself tightly around the leg in the same way, and wouldn't let me go. Too bad that little girl is probably about twelve years old now, as I think she and Ollie would make quite a cute couple.

I couldn't help but feel warmed by what Ollie said, and I embraced him back and calmly said, "I'm happy to be your new best friend, Ollie."

Finally, after a bit of hugging, Esperanza said, "Now where's your oldest brother? Eli, is it?"

Ryan politely corrected her and said, "I'm sorry, you mean Elliott."

"Elliott?" a confused Esperanza asked. "Who's Elliott?"

"Our brother of course," Connor said.

Nicole spoke to the boys, although her words were clearly to Grace as well, "I'm sorry, but your cousin told us his name was Eli."

Ollie, who had let go of me by then, ran up to Grace and asked, "Do you not remember our brother's name?"

In a motherly but frantic tone, Grace assured him, "Oh no, no, no, Ollie. Of course I do!" Embarrassed, she turned to all of us, and she turned beet red as she saw the puzzled looks on our faces.

"Grace," I said, "is there something you're not telling us?"

Grace gave a heavy sigh and said, "Okay, fine. There's something I need to tell you guys. Before I tell you, I just wanted to say I'm so sorry. Yes, I lied, and my cousin's name *is* Elliott, I didn't tell you guys because—"

And just as she was about to explain herself, the bell on the café's door rang and everyone turned towards it. And you're never going to guess who walked in, but Elliott Parker. Esperanza and Nicole were surprised to see him, but I was even more surprised to see him because in a big city like Rome, how is it possible that he would come to the same café we did? With a smile on his face, completely oblivious to the confusion happening among us, he quickly walked over to Grace with open arms.

"Gracie!" He gave her a big hug, and Grace awkwardly hugged him back. I felt my jaw drop at that exact moment. He was so happy to see her. "I missed you so much!"

43

"I missed you too, Elliott," Grace awkwardly said.

I looked around at the different faces as this was going on. Esperanza's jaw had dropped almost to the floor and she was clearly trying to process everything going on. Nicole had her arms crossed in disbelief and had a mixture of anger and puzzlement on her face. And Ryan, Connor, and Ollie looked just plain confused. Me? I was still trying to figure out why Elliott Parker was hugging Grace.

After they finally broke apart from the hug, Elliott saw Grace's face. "What's the matter? Your face is red!"

Grace, who looked like she was on the verge of tears, said, "Guys, this is Elliott, my oldest cousin. Elliott, these are my friends Nicole, Esperanza, and Cecilia."

Elliott turned to look at all of us. When he noticed me, he said, "Oh hello, Cecilia! I didn't know you knew my cousin." Biting my lip, I nodded.

Nicole finally lost her temper, and said through her gritted teeth, "Your cousin is Elliott Parker?" Grace slowly nodded. "Why didn't you tell us?"

Grace, who had by now started tearing up, replied, "I was going to tell you! I really was, I promise. But I knew you guys wouldn't have believed me."

"You're right," Nicole admitted. "We wouldn't have believed you." But then she said, "But at least it's better than being lied to."

"I thought we were your friends," Esperanza said.

"But we *are* friends!" poor Grace said. I turned to Elliott, then to his three brothers. They all looked as uncomfortable as I was.

"Well, friends don't keep secrets and lie to each other," Esperanza said, losing her temper, which I've never seen her do. With that, she angrily stomped out of the café, and a just as angry Nicole followed her. And when they were gone, the rest of us stood there in awkward silence. Grace was in tears at this point, with a concerned Elliott's arm around her shoulders. I turned to the cashier, who had some sort of an embarrassed smirk on her face. I turned to Elliott's brothers. Connor and Ryan looked frustrated that their cousin wasn't feeling well, and poor little Ollie looked just plain confused.

I sarcastically muttered under my breath to myself, "Well, this vacation is starting out *beautifully*."

Chapter 4: Wishing For Peace And Quiet

I lay in the hotel room, by myself. Just me. And the walls in this hotel were so thin that I could hear Nicole, Esperanza, and Grace arguing from next door. I couldn't make out what they were saying. I had the feeling I didn't want to know, but I think I had a pretty good idea as to what they were saying. I just lay there silently. I had nothing to do, and I didn't feel comfortable venturing off into Rome by myself. My stomach growled, because I hadn't had anything to eat all day, besides some mints from the hotel lobby. I felt like I was on the brink of starvation. This trip sucks!

Just as I was about to call my parents for comfort, there was a knock on the door. Hopefully it was one of the girls, saying they had made up and were ready to take a walk around Rome. But I could still hear the yelling from the other room, so I quickly ruled that one out. Perhaps it was housekeeping, but I remembered I had put the "do not disturb" sign on the door handle. I went to answer the door anyway, unsure who I would find on the other side.

"Coming!" I shouted as I got out of bed. I slowly walked over to the door, and I was so anxious for the company that I didn't even bother to ask "Who is it?" or look through the tiny hole. I opened it to find Elliott there with a concerned look on his face.

"Hello, Cecilia," he said softly.

"Hi, Mr. Parker," I said, then I quickly corrected myself. "Elliott." After a brief moment of silence I said, "What are you doing here?"

"I just wanted to check on you, see how you were doing," he said. "I could hear the other girls arguing."

"Yeah, no, I'm fine," I assured him.

He looked around the hall, left then right, then turned back to me and whispered, "They're talking way too loud!"

I agreed with him and whispered back, "I know, right?"

Elliott lightly chuckled and said, "I bet you that you could hear their arguing all the way to California."

With that, I laughed and he laughed with me. I then asked him, "So how are you doing?"

"Alright, I suppose," Elliott shrugged his shoulders. "At first I was a little offended that Grace lied to you girls about me, but then I saw her point of view and if someone told me their cousin was a celebrity, I most likely would not have believed them either." I nodded my head in agreement and Elliott said, "I'm sorry you have had to stay cooped up in this hotel room all day. It is not fair to you at all."

"Oh no, it's fine, really," I tried to convince him, but I could tell by the look on his face that he knew that I was not okay. Noticing he had been standing out in the hallway this whole time, I said, "So, do you want to come in? I've been alone all day."

"Oh no, thank you," Elliott told me. "I actually also came to ask you if you wanted to come out with us. We're going to get dinner and gelato, and take a night walk, if you want to join. I'm sure you would like to explore Rome a little bit."

I was very excited and quickly responded, "Yes! Please! If I have to stay here or listen to them fight for one more second I'll die!"

Elliott smiled and nodded his head. "Oh believe me, if *I* have to hear the contentious fighting for one more second *I* will die."

"Thank you so much, Elliott! You are a lifesaver!"

"Of course, anytime," he said smiling. "Meet down in the lobby in twenty minutes, alright?" I nodded. "See you then." He walked back towards his room, and I shut the door. Finally! I would get to see Rome!

******

Twenty minutes later, I got down to the hotel lobby where I saw Elliott and his brothers sitting there, waiting for me. They were sitting in perfect order from oldest to youngest, and it kind of reminded me of the Von Trapp kids from my favorite movie, *The Sound of Music*. Later in our trip, we would be visiting Salzburg where they filmed and would be visiting the locations on a special tour, and I was more excited than any of my friends.

Anyway, as soon as they saw me, Elliott smiled and waved, "Cecilia! Hello!" And he stood up right away and his younger brothers all joined in unison.

48

"Hey guys!" I waved back as I walked over to them.

As soon as I met them, Connor complimented me and said, "You look very lovely, Cecilia."

"Thank you, Connor," I said, appreciating his compliment. "You just made my day."

"We all think you look splendid," Ryan smiled and said. Man, these British kids loved to pay compliments! "I know Elliott certainly thinks so. And he's very shy, you see, and told me to ask for your number."

I giggled lightly. I never had any siblings, but from what I've seen in TV shows and movies and from my friends who had siblings, they could be quite a handful and embarrassing at times. I looked over at Elliott, who was slightly blushing from his brother's embarrassing remark. "Ryan," he whispered to his brother. He then turned to me and, still blushing, he tried to convince me, "I'm so sorry, that was all just a complete joke, I promise." I nodded my head, but I wasn't convinced that Elliott was bothered by it even a little.

Then Connor and Ollie wanted to get in on the teasing. They started singing, "Elliott and Cecilia sitting in a tree, K-I-S-S-I-N—" and before they could finish, Elliott quickly covered their mouths. I was trying my best not to burst out laughing and blush at how cute Elliott looked when he was nervous.

"Okay, okay, okay, okay," he told his brothers. "Shall we go to dinner?" We all agreed and he said, "I know a *splendid* place from when I was filming *Chariot Racing* here."

As we walked out of the hotel lobby, I asked him, "You mean that gladiator movie?" Elliott nodded. "That was a really great movie!"

"Thank you," Elliott replied as we started to walk. "I don't think Rotten Tomatoes, with their 45%, would have agreed."

"Don't listen to them!" I told him. "Hey, they gave *Pompeii*, this horrible movie we watched on the plane, a 27%, and I think that deserves a 5%."

"I don't think I ever saw that movie," Elliott told me.

I warned him, "Don't waste your time!" I quickly changed the subject, "You know, I've never met a celebrity before. I have so many questions!"

Elliott smiled and nodded his head, "Oh my goodness, I'm sure you do. That's what people *always* say when they first meet me."

"Really?"

"Yes. They are always questions like 'Who are you dating?' or 'What's your favorite movie you have been in?' or 'How did you get jacked to play Serpent Boy?' And I'm always like, can't these people ever become more creative in their questions?"

I couldn't help but laugh. Not only was Elliott very charismatic and quite handsome, but he also had a really good sense of humor. "Okay, I'll try not to ask any of those questions."

He grinned, "I appreciate that."

"But I think your brothers are way behind us," I pointed back to where Ryan, Connor, and Ollie were walking several feet behind us. "I'll ask you when we get to the restaurant."

"Alright," Elliott agreed. "Sounds good to me."

And so we waited for the three boys to catch up. Then we were on our way to a restaurant called *Il Pomodoro Speziato* (or The Spicy Tomato), a cute little restaurant in an alleyway. We were seated at a round table for the five of us. We were given breadsticks and olive oil and the menu to start with. All the rest of us ordered water, except for Elliott who asked for wine. I could have ordered an alcoholic beverage, but I've hated the bitter taste of every drink imaginable, ever since my twenty-first birthday. And technically Ryan, being seventeen, could have had one because the drinking age was 16, but he had said that he tried some while he was here, and was not a huge fan. Anyway, as soon as we got our drink order and had decided what we wanted to eat (I decided to have traditional, Italian cheese pizza), we got to talking.

"So," I said once the waiter had taken away our menus. "Where are you from?"

"London!" Ollie replied, excitedly as if he was happy to be from London.

Then Elliott added, "But if you care to be more specific, Kingston Upon Thames."

"I'm not going to lie, I had never heard of that place. "I'm sorry, I don't think I know where that is. What's there that may make me recognize it?"

"Have you heard of Bentall Centre?" Connor asked referring to the shopping mall there (as I found out later).

I replied, "I'm sorry, no."

"Kingston Bridge?" Ollie suggested. I shook my head.

"All Saints Church?" Ryan added.

"I'm really sorry," I said. "I'll make sure to look it up later!" I gave a thumbs up. "Anyway, what else can I ask?" I thought, then turned to Elliott. "What do you like to do besides acting?"

Connor, thinking I was asking him this question too, said, "Well, I don't really act very much. I'm more of a rugby player, you see."

Ryan corrected his younger brother and said, "She was asking Elliott, you bloody dimwit!"

"Hey!" Ollie said. "What did Mummy say about using those words?"

"Stop trying to act like her," Ryan said back to his brother. Ollie just stuck out his tongue at Ryan.

Elliott, being the big brother he was, tried to calm everyone down. "Alright, that's enough. We're in public you know!" He then turned towards me said, "I'm terribly sorry, Cecilia. What was the question again? Oh right, besides acting!" He thought. "Hmm, I've always enjoyed gymnastics. And dancing has always been a big part of my life."

I never knew this about him before. "Really? That's really cool! What kind of dancing?"

Elliott replied, "Oh any kind, really. Especially ballet." He started to get really excited when talking about this, it was really freaking cute. "Ever since I was about ten or so I took dance lessons. And now I could pretty much dance anywhere if the time called for it!"

I chuckled, then replied, "That's really amazing, you know when I was about six or so Grace, Esperanza, Nicole, and I took a beginners' ballet class, and we had a recital and everything. After that, we never really danced again. Guess we weren't as cut out for it as you were." Elliott nodded and smiled.

All of a sudden the talk became more serious when Connor asked me, "Did you get bullied for being a dancer like Elliott did?"

"Connor!" Elliott whispered to his brother. When I heard the word "bullied," I was stunned. Elliott Parker, the idolized UK actor, had been bullied as a child?

"I'm sorry," I said after a very brief moment of silence. "You got bullied for being a dancer?" Elliott, with a saddened look on his face, slowly nodded. I was shocked. "But why? All the girls go *crazy* for you! You have such a huge fan base! You're a terrific actor! Why?"

Elliott, who was looking down, gave a heavy sigh, looked up at me, and said, "Now I guess I do, but not always. When I first started taking ballet lessons, I got bullied badly. The whole idea that says that men and boys who do ballet are feminine you know. It was a rough time. Got so bad I had to switch schools."

I said, "I'm so sorry, Elliott. That's terrible."

He replied, "Thank you, Cecilia. But it also helped me. I found solace in acting in productions at the West End, where I eventually got discovered by a Hollywood casting agent for *Disaster Earthquake*. Remember that movie?" I nodded. Who could forget Elliott Parker's debut film? "Landed some other movie roles shortly after that, including Serpent Boy, so I guess without the bullying I wouldn't be where I am today."

I had always seen the lighthearted side of Elliott Parker in interviews and everything, but I had never seen this more serious side of him. To me, after hearing his story, he didn't seem like a celebrity at all. He seemed like a real human being.

"You know, I got bullied too," I told him.

"You did?" Elliott asked. I nodded. "What for?"

"For lots of things. Going through puberty early, for being considered ugly and unattractive compared to the other girls, for needing braces. I was in middle school, everyone's *favorite* place to be. But it also helped me discover writing. I would write down the thoughts I was feeling, make stories about what happened to me, and I soon began to love the idea of writing."

"So you're a writer?" Elliott asked.

"Yes," I said. "I hope to be published someday."

"Well, I've never read your work," Elliott said. "But I can assure you, you can show those bullies that you can do anything you want."

Elliott's kind words made me feel really good. I don't know what it was, but I could feel for a very brief moment my heart making one soft pound. I don't know what it was, but whatever it was, it was brief. That moment was interrupted with Ryan, Connor, and Ollie teasing and singing, "K-I-S-S-I-N-G!" Silently laughing to myself, I turned to see Elliott become a little red from blushing.

From that time until when we got our food, I learned so much about the Parker boys. They had a pit bull named Elizabeth after the Queen herself and the whole family, especially Elliott, were huge advocates for pit bulls being considered safe and not harmful. I also learned that they had a charity called *The Parker Trust Foundation* that raises money to help children with cancer. And I heard the hilarious story about how Elliott found out he was Serpent Boy. He had gone through several rounds of auditions for over six months. After that, they told him that he would find out whether he got the part the next day and he would start work on Monday. Six weeks went by and Elliott still hadn't heard from the studio, and he was feeling really depressed and disappointed. Then one day, he was sitting on his bed, looking at Instagram on his phone and the studio's page announced that they had cast Serpent Boy and to go look at the website to find out. When Elliott went on the website, he saw his name and beaming with excitement he ran downstairs screaming, "Oh my gosh! Oh my gosh! I got Serpent Boy! They cast me! I'm going to be playing Serpent Boy!" And Ryan couldn't believe it because after they hadn't contacted Elliott for weeks, and he suggested that maybe the studio had been hacked or something. A few hours later, the head of the studio called to congratulate him on getting the part, to tell him that he would be flying out to Los Angeles to start work in a week.

After we got our food, Elliott said to me, "Alright, you've heard enough about us. How about you?"

After taking a bite of my delicious pizza and putting it down, "Oh okay. Ask me anything!"

"Okay" Elliott thought for a second. "Where are you from?"

I replied, "Well, I was born in Philadelphia and have lived in Annapolis from when I was two until I moved to Chestertown to attend Washington College, of course."

Then Connor asked a question, "What's your favorite color?"

"Green," I said. "It's always been green."

"Favorite movie?" Ollie asked.

"*The Sound of Music* for sure," I said. "That's why I'm so excited to go on the tour when we get to Salzburg."

"Do you have any pets?" Ryan asked.

"Yes," I replied. "An adorable, crazy puppy named Jane."

Then all through the night they asked me all these questions about my hobbies, family life, love of Disney, etc.

We shared funny stories and had a really great time and a delicious meal. Not too bad for a first night in Rome!

******

After we left the restaurant, we were ready to get some gelato. Luckily there was a little place in a nearby piazza that sold it, and we filled ourselves with delicious gelato. I got two flavors: chocolate and cookies and cream. I thought that this was a pretty good combination. As we made our way back to the hotel, the three younger brothers were on a sugar rush. So they ran ahead of us, and Elliott and I took our time and talked while walking.

"I don't think I ever got to ask you," he said, "what are you studying at Washington College?"

"I am studying creative writing," I told him. "Someday I'd like to write novels, maybe even plays or film scripts."

Elliott replied, "That's amazing! And this is going to be your last year in college, correct?" I nodded. "What do you plan to do after? Continue schooling or go off to get a job?"

I briefly paused, took a deep breath, and said, "That's kind of complicated. You see, my parents want me to further my education and become a more experienced writer. But I don't want that! I don't want more years of schooling. I want to see the world, become my own writer. I can't do any more years of schooling."

Elliott asked me, "Did you tell them that's what you want?"

I shook my head. "No. They would probably freak."

As we continued walking, Elliott asked, "What makes you think they would freak?"

I paused. "I don't know. I just feel like they would I guess."

"But they also might do the opposite," Elliott said. "Now look I've never met your parents, but if you tell them that you don't want to go to grad school, they might understand. I mean, even if you don't do what they want you to do, they'll still love you and support your decision. I think they just want you to be happy."

Wow! Not only was Elliott funny, charming, good-looking, and easy to talk to, but he gave some pretty good advice. We finally got to the hotel at around ten o'clock, but I didn't want the evening to be over. I had gotten to know Elliott, and he was so sweet and so fun to be with! And while I loved his little brothers dearly, I found myself wanting to spend time with Elliott, just the two of us. What did this mean? Was I developing feelings for Elliott Parker? What kind of feelings were they? Ones of hidden deep love? Infatuation? Lust? Or was it just a silly celeb crush that would be over in a few days?

In the lobby, Elliott told his brothers, "Why don't you boys go upstairs. I'll be right up, alright?" The boys nodded, we said good night, they went to the elevator. It was just me and him. What did he want? "Are you going to be alright? Do you need me to walk your room with you?" he asked.

At first I said, "Oh no, thank you. I think I'll be fine." But then, when I realized that him walking me back to my room means I would get to spend more time with him, I changed my answer. "Actually, you know what, why not? Better safe than sorry! You never know what could happen in a city like Rome!"

"True," Elliott said. "Alright, let's go."

Gosh was he perfect! His charming smile, his muscular body, his sexy accent, his good-hearted personality. I didn't want him to leave me. "No!" I kept telling myself. "He's your friend's cousin *and* a celebrity! You can't date him!" Despite me telling myself this, I kept wanting him to stay with me.

Elliott pressed the "up" button on the elevator and we got inside. Because the European elevators are smaller than the American ones, and there were four other people on it with us, Elliott's shoulders were touching my shoulders. I found myself smiling at that, and I turned briefly to see a smirk on his face, as if he were happy we were touching too.

Luckily we were on the same floor, and not that many doors apart. So he walked me back to my room. "I don't hear any screaming," I said, noticing the hallways were quiet and we couldn't hear the arguing like before.

Elliott lightly laughed and said, "Yeah, probably because the hotel staff told them people were trying to sleep, and they had to keep it quiet." I laughed. Man, this guy was too perfect for this world.

"Anyway, I'll see you tomorrow," I said. "And thank you for inviting me."

"Of course," Elliott said. "I had a very nice evening."

I smiled and blushed, "I did too." After a brief pause, I said, "Anyway, good night!"

Elliott replied, "Good night, see you tomorrow."

With my room key, I unlocked the door and went inside. I closed the door slowly, but not suspiciously, so I could continue looking at his smiling, adorable face. When I finally shut the door, I could feel the small, soft pound in my heart once again. "What are you doing Cecilia?" I had no idea what to do with my feelings. I turned to find Grace in bed. She smiled and waved when she saw me, completely oblivious to the fact that I was feeling some sort of attraction or infatuation for her cousin.

"Hi, Cecilia!" she said, looking more relaxed and cheerful than she had earlier.

"Hey," I said. "What's going on with you, Nicole, and Esperanza?"

A relieved Grace said, "Oh don't worry, we made up! I agreed to never keep a secret from them again and agreed that we should just enjoy the trip."

I was just as relieved to hear this and, as I made my way towards the bed, said, "Oh thank goodness! I thought this would last the whole trip!"

"So," Grace asked. "How was the night out with my cousins?"

Collapsing on the bed, I said, "Oh really great, thank you for asking! We had a delicious dinner, gelato, and excellent conversations!"

"That's fantastic," Grace said. "Anyway, we should probably get some sleep."

"True," I agreed. "After all, tomorrow is our first full day exploring Europe!"

Chapter 5: Wishing For A Prince Charming

The next two days were super busy! We went to the Vatican, St. Peter's Basilica, the Sistine Chapel, an audience with the Pope, and various churches that I can't even remember the names of because we saw so many of them. We did so much walking, spending hours in the beaming sun. At the time there was a heatwave going across Europe, which was so bad that people in France were swimming in fountains to get cool. Although I am someone who is really sensitive to the heat, I had been fine thanks to all of the water I had been drinking. I was fine until the fifth day of the trip and our last day in Rome.

We had just had a really hectic day. We saw many historical relics such as part of the cross that Jesus Christ carried; we had knelt down and climbed the steps he walked on when carrying the cross, and saw so much more. The experience sent chills down my spine. Then around 3:45 pm we got to the Colosseum. On that particular day, not only did I not drink enough water, but I had also been served the most disgusting, bland pasta on the planet at lunch and hadn't eaten anything else all day after my breakfast of scrambled eggs.

So when we got to the Colosseum, I wasn't feeling the best. But I really wanted to see the place where gladiators fought each other and chariot races were held, so I tried to hide the fact that I was feeling kind of queasy. Luckily, it all seemed to go away when I saw the former stadium. It was so much bigger than I expected! I had always loved history, and it was really cool to see a significant historical building in person as opposed to in a history book.

After taking pictures of the Colosseum and in front of it, we started to head inside. "The Colosseum is *so* cool!" Esperanza said, still in awe of its architecture.

"Except the fact that people were slaughtered here, both by humans and lions," Nicole added with a sarcasm that trailed off.

"Lions ate people here?" a shocked Ollie asked.

Grace lowered herself to Ollie, comforted him, and told him, "No, of course not, Ollie." While hugging him, she said to Nicole, "Way to traumatize a seven-year-old, Nicole!"

After we had gotten past security was when I started to feel dizzy. I think the heat had gone to my brain because I felt as though the world was blurred. Everyone had been looking around the Colosseum when they noticed I looked out of it.

Esperanza was the first to notice. "Hey, Cecilia," she said concerned, "are you okay?"

"Yeah, I'm fine," I assured them. I was lying, I was *not* fine.

"Are you sure?" Nicole asked. "Cause we can stop if you want."

"No, it's fine, really," I tried to convince them. "I can go on. Just kind of hot that's all."

All of them, with concerned looks on their faces, decided to trust me when I said I was okay. So we continued walking around, seeing the middle area where the fighting and racing happened. After a few minutes, Elliott looked especially concerned with my health.

"Cecilia, you really don't look good," he said, putting his hand on my shoulder. "Are you sure you're alright?"

Queasily, I nodded. Then I admitted, shaking my head, "Elliott, I don't feel so good."

Elliott started to worry. "Do you have water?" I held up my water bottle. It was empty. Thank goodness Elliott had some. "Here you go," he handed the bottle to me, I drank it. "I have a fan too." He took his electronic fan out of his sling bag, turned it on, and put it near my face. "Are you doing alright?"

"No," I finally admitted. "I want to go back to the hotel, but I can't." I felt so queasy.

"No, you have to go back to the hotel," Elliott insisted. "I'll go back with you." By then the rest of the group had stopped and looked concerned, and Elliott told them, "Alright, Cecilia is not feeling well, so I'm going to take her back to the hotel. But you guys continue, and we'll meet you later."

The group nodded. They looked concerned, but kept walking. Elliott put his arm around my shoulder and helped me get out of the Colosseum and go to a nearby taxi waiting place. We sat down on a bench. I felt like I was going to be sick.

Still feeling queasy, I said, "You don't have to go back with me."

But Elliott assured me, "No, it's fine, it really is. Don't worry. You've got to remember I filmed a good amount of *Chariot Racing* in there so I've seen it lots of times. And it gets boring after a while. Also, it's more important that you don't get a heat stroke than seeing inside a silly Roman building." Handing me his bottle once again said, "Here, drink some more water."

Desperate for water, I gulped it down too fast and, as a result, I vomited everywhere. Elliott comforted me. He put his hands on my back as it continued. "It's alright. Let it all out."

After I had finally stopped, I burst into tears. Why did I not drink water? Why did I not eat more of that pasta even though it tasted like garbage? Now I was sick. Elliott, seeing I was hurting, put his arms around me and gave me a huge, warm embrace. "Shhh. It's alright. Don't cry." His voice was so calm and, with his muscular arms wrapped around me, I felt safe.

"This day sucks!" I said sobbing. "Why am I so sensitive to the heat? Why didn't I drink water or eat my food?"

Elliott, continuing to comfort me, whispered, "Shhh. It's not your fault. Don't worry. Calm down. We're gonna get you back to the air conditioned hotel where you can rest." He then looked up and saw no taxis were coming. "And since there are no taxis in sight, we are going to have to walk."

He unwrapped himself from me, stood up, then offered me his hand to help me up. Still dazed and tired as he pulled me up, I said, "But—but I feel too weak to walk back."

"I know," he nodded. "That's why I'm going to carry you back." Then he scooped me up in his arms rather easily, carrying me bridal style.

"But—" I said. "How can you carry me? I'm 5"6 and a half and you're 5"8, and in this heat?" Secretly, I wanted him to carry me because I really did feel like a Disney princess with him as a Disney prince, carrying me off into the sunset. Or in this case, out of the sun.

He convinced me by saying, "Two things. One, the hotel is really not that far. Two, you've got to remember that I've had years of training in gymnastics, ballet, and working out to play Serpent Boy, so I think you're in pretty good hands. I may be small, but I can lift all!" Despite the fact that I was not feeling good, Elliott made me laugh. He then said to himself in surprise, "Oh hey, that rhymes!" We both laughed and then, his deep brown eyes looking into my blue ones, he asked, "Do you trust me?"

Still caught up in how beautiful his eyes were, I had the pounding feeling again, this time two soft pounds instead of one. Smiling, I nodded and said, "Yes." And so we made our way back to the hotel.

I felt safe in Elliott's arms as he carried me back to the hotel. It may have just been the fact that a famous superhero was rescuing me, but I felt like he would protect me no matter what. He was such a gentleman for offering to take me back, and then carrying me. All of a sudden, the two soft pounds became three pounds that were no longer soft. I had never felt my heart beating before with anyone, even with Henry.

******

Later, I woke up in my bed, still wearing my mint green tank top and my long flowy white skirt. I would feel the air conditioning running, and I felt so much better than I had before. I looked at my phone for the time: 5:01 p.m. I remembered I had been feeling sick from the sun at the Colosseum and Elliott had heroically carried me back to the hotel, and it was like a fairytale come true. All of a sudden the door opened, and Elliott entered. He looked as hot as ever in his short-sleeve, buttoned down black and ocean blue shirt and his smile.

"Hey Cecilia," he said, closing the door behind him. He had asked me to give him my key in case I needed anything. "How are you feeling?"

Sitting up, I said, "Hi Elliott. I'm feeling *so* much better. Thank you!"

As he was walking towards me, he said, "Thank goodness! We were so worried!"

I asked, "Where are the others?"

"They went to dinner," Elliott replied. "We all decided that you should get some rest tonight. They send their love and thoughts!"

"I think that's probably for the best," I agreed. "But why are you still here? Why aren't you with them?"

"Well," he said, sitting on the side of my bed, "someone had to stay behind to take care of you, so I insisted."

And I felt the pounding of my heart again, this time it was beating non-stop like crazy. "That's so sweet of you Elliott."

A broad smile came across Elliott's face and he winked at me. And the beating wouldn't stop! He then politely asked, "Do you need more water?"

Politely in a fake British accent I said, "Oh, yes please, sir. And while you're at I will also have a Caesar salad to start with, but with just romaine lettuce, croutons, and ranch dressing. Then I would like Sunday roast but with garlic mashed potatoes instead of just plain ones. And for dessert I will have an ice cream sundae but it must be low fat chocolate ice cream and caramel topping please. Thank you!"

Elliott laughed as he got up from the bed and teasingly bowed, "Right away, your majesty!" He winked, and that wink made me smile. The beating kept going on, and now it seemed like some butterflies had started fluttering around in my stomach.

The next few hours were magical. Elliott sat at the end of my bed and we talked for hours and hours about life. We laughed and told funny stories.

"You know what I thought of the first time I heard your name?" he asked me. I shook my head. He responded by singing the famous Simon & Garfunkel song: "Cecilia, you're breaking my heart! You're shaking my confidence daily!"

I started laughing really hard. "You have no idea how many people have told me that! You know what I thought of the first time I heard your name was Elliott?"

"No. What?" he asked.

And I mimicked E.T.'s deep, groggy voice saying, "Elliott!" And Elliott started laughing hysterically. I continued my impression, "E.T. phone home!" Elliott couldn't stop laughing. "Elliott, help me get back!"

Elliott was laughing so hard he collapsed forward on the bed in a fit of giggles. He was the rare man who could giggle and still seem sexy. He briefly touched my feet (which were under the covers, but he still touched them!) When he realized what he had done, he stopped laughing, looked worried and immediately sat up. He looked worried and apologized. "I am so terribly sorry!"

"Don't worry," I assured him. "It's no big deal." I wanted to tell him I was absolutely fine with him touching me, but I didn't.

After a brief moment Elliott asked, "Cecilia can I ask a question?"

"Sure," I nodded. "Ask me anything."

"How old are you?" he asked.

I was in a happy mood, because asking that question clearly meant he was interested. So I happily said, "Guess!"

Elliott thought about it. "Hmmm. Twenty-two?"

I shook my head and said, "Close! Twenty-one!"

Elliott's jaw dropped and teasingly said, "Twenty-one?" Smiling, I nodded quickly. "You look older!"

"Well you play a sixteen year old in *Serpent Boy*," I added. "And you're only twenty-three, right?"

Elliott nodded his head. "True," he said. Then he muttered, almost as if he was speaking his thoughts, "You're so incredibly beautiful!" My eyes widened a little bit, but I secretly liked he called me beautiful. When Elliott realized he had shared his thoughts out loud, he immediately started blushing and said, "I-I'm sorry."

"That's okay," I smiled. I then thanked him for the compliment, and my heart kept beating faster and faster.

Elliott added, "Your boyfriend must be a lucky guy."

"Actually," I told him, "I've never had a boyfriend."

Elliott looked surprised as his eyes widened. "A pretty girl like you? You've never had a boyfriend?"

I shook my head. "Nope. I mean I've been on dates and I've had crushes, but never a boyfriend." Elliott nodded. I then asked, "Have you ever had a girlfriend?"

"I mean, I've dated girls," Elliott said. "Yes, I have had girlfriends." He paused and said, "But I don't have one now."

Smiling, I nodded. We stared at each other for a good minute. I once again looked into his deep, beautiful eyes, and he looked into mine. My heart kept beating faster and faster by the minute. "Don't do this," I kept scolding myself. "He's your friend's cousin." But I started thinking, "But he's so hot and kind and funny and such a smol bean that looks completely---" When I realized what was going through my mind, I told myself to stop. So I quickly changed the subject and asked him, "So, are you ready to go to Pompeii tomorrow?"

"What?" Elliott seemed so caught up in the moment. He finally made it back to the real world. "Oh, right! Hmm..."

"I am," I told him. "Hopefully it will be much better than that stupid movie we watched on the plane."

"What made that movie so stupid?" Elliott asked in curiosity.

I told him, "The whole movie was just bad! The acting, the writing, the special effects. I didn't root for the romance at all!"

"There was a romance?" Elliott asked. I nodded. Then he asked, "Why didn't you root for the romance?"

Then I went on and on about how much I hated the movie's couple. "They were just bland characters! And there was no chemistry whatsoever. I think that a good movie couple, or a good couple in general, need to be there for each other. I mean, honesty, loyalty, and trust are key to a relationship. I mean, I've never had a boyfriend before but those are the keys to friendships so I think it makes sense for romances, too."

"I agree," Elliott said. "And they have to be there to support each other, but they can't constantly be there every single minute of the day so it makes them each uncomfortable."

Then I added, "And it isn't just about sex." I stopped. Why on earth would I say that to my friend's cousin? "I'm so sorry. Why did I just say that?"

But Elliott assured me, "Oh no, no it's fine, really. And I agree. I just don't understand how people can just fool around, have sex, and not have a meaningful relationship. And I don't know about you, but I am definitely a relationship person."

"Me too!" I said, excited that he was one of those people looking for a serious, committed relationship and not just a casual one where it's all about sex. Realizing how excited I looked, I softly said, "Sorry."

"No, it's fine," he assured me, putting his hand on my shoulder, which made me develop a very small smile. When he saw what he had done, he quickly pulled his hand away and said, "Sorry."

I wanted to tell him: "Oh no, it's fine, Elliott! Put your hand on my shoulder, and give me a passionate kiss and a warm hug!" But that was a bit of an unrealistic thing to say to someone you only met a few days ago. So instead I said, "Totally cool."

After that awkward moment, Elliott continued, "Anyway, I suppose I'm not the fleeting type at all."

"Really?" I asked.

Elliott nodded. "It's just—it's not my way of life. I want to be in a serious, committed relationship with a girl, then perhaps someday get married and raise a family with her."

"Yeah," I agreed. "When I was little I had this whole plan for how I wanted my life to turn out you know."

"You did?" Elliott asked.

"Yeah," I told him. "I wanted to graduate college, then sometime along the way meet a guy, date him for about a year, then get married a year after being engaged, and eventually have seven kids with him. I even had names for them and everything!"

Elliott's eyes opened wide as if he had seen something shocking like a pig fly. "Oh my," he said in awe. "Seven children?"

"Yup," I nodded. "And all before I was thirty six too."

Elliott was still amazed by the plan I had created when I was nine. "Is this still your plan?" he asked with curiosity.

"Oh gosh no," I said in reassurance. "I want to get married when I'm in my late to mid-twenties and I want four kids. First a baby boy, then a little girl. And then I'll have another girl so that my daughter will have an ally when playing tricks on her brother. Finally I'll have another boy so my son and his father won't be surrounded by girls."

"That sounds like a better, slightly more realistic plan," Elliott said smiling. "I haven't even thought about things like that."

"That's alright," I said. "And the most important thing is that you find the right woman."

"Yes," Elliott agreed. "And that you find the right man."

Then we looked at each other for a long time. Elliott moved a little closer, and his cheeks were once again crimson red. I took my hand and felt my cheek with it, and my cheek was warm. Elliott kept moving closer, and the closer he got, the faster my heart was beating. He started to move his head closer to mine, and I did the same. I could sense what might happen. A kiss perhaps? "Don't do this, don't do this, don't do this," I kept telling myself. But I just couldn't resist the thought of his lips touching mine.

Just when we were about to lock lips, we could sense the door opening, and we quickly pulled away. I admit I was devastated, but also nervous about how awkward it would be when we had that moment. So we didn't say anything, and Grace walked through the door carrying a large pizza box.

"Hey you guys!" she said in a cheerful voice with a bright smile on her face. "How's it going?"

"Great," I told her. I mean, I nearly made out with your cousin, but other than that everything is splendid!

"It's going fine," Elliott said as he got up from the bed. "How was the rest of your day?" he asked as he walked towards Grace.

"It was great! Thank you!" Grace told her cousin. She then turned to me and asked, "And how are *you* feeling, Cecilia? We were worried about you all night!" She walked over and gave me a big hug.

I told her, "I'm feeling *so* much better! Cooled off and hydrated. Elliott kept me company."

Grace teasingly acted shocked and said, "Really? My cousin? He was *nice* to you?"

"Yes," I assured her. I then turned to him and told her, "He's just lovely!"

"Thank you," he said. Then he jokingly asked, "It's hard to tell Grace and I are cousins, isn't it?"

Grace then got up, crossed her arms, and asked him, "What's that supposed to mean?"

Elliott then told her, "Well all the practical jokes you used to play on me! Such as when I got my wisdom teeth out a few years ago you asked some random girl to help in a prank. I can't remember her name. She was quite pretty though." I felt a pinch of jealousy when he said that. Elliott continued, "So of course after my wisdom teeth were removed, I was on that medication that made me woozy and not able to think. And you had the girl pretend to be my girlfriend, and because of that medication I believed it. When I found out it wasn't true after I tried to kiss her and she said no, I remember I was so angry with you!"

Grace looked slightly embarrassed. Trying not to laugh, I turned to her and said, "You had some random girl pretend to be your cousin's boyfriend after he was put on drugs? That is some serious pranking!"

Trying to think of a more embarrassing story about Elliott, Grace walked towards him and told me, "Well, did you ever hear about how much he loved Rihanna when he was little?"

While I snickered, an embarrassed Elliott blushed and said to his cousin, "Uh, Grace I don't think Cecilia really wants to hear about—"

But I did really want to hear! Interested, I said, "Oh no, I do! What about him and Rihanna?"

Then Grace moved right to my bed and sat on the edge. She started telling the story: "So when he was younger, about nine or ten or so, he would always dress up as Rihanna from her 'Umbrella' video, using what he could find in his mom's closet. Then he'd dance to it relentlessly and committed, full choreography and everything." I was laughing hard and trying to picture a young Elliott dressed as Rihanna, going all out. And with his talent in dance, I'm sure he made a fantastic Rihanna!

Blushing, Elliott walked over and stood next to his cousin. He tried to assure me, "But I was only nine or ten, remember. I would never do that today, I can assure you."

Grace told him, "But what about last year at Christmas when we had that lip sync—"

And before she could finish what she was going to say, Elliott quickly covered her mouth with his hand. "Alright," he said. "That's enough out of you." I was still laughing really hard, and Elliott uncovered her mouth and said, "Well, I used to dance to many songs, not just Rihanna songs. And my mum saw me dancing to them and she soon signed me up to take dance classes."

"Oh," I nodded. "That's cool."

"Anyway," Elliott said, "it's time for me to head off to bed." He started to walk out the door.

"Night cuz!" Grace waved.

"Good night Elliott," I smiled. Oh, why did he have to go? Oh well, at least I would see him in Pompeii tomorrow.

"Good night, girls," Elliott smiled back. "And have fun at Pompeii!"

Wait, what?! Was Elliott not going to Pompeii tomorrow? "But wait a sec," I said. "Aren't you coming with us?"

"Oh, I'm really sorry, Cecilia," Elliott said. He then turned to Grace and asked, "Did you not tell her, Gracie?" Grace shook her head. Elliott turned back to me and said, "The director called at the last minute and said that we have to stay a little while longer to reshoot a scene. So unfortunately we won't be able to make it to Pompeii with you girls. I'm really sorry." My heart sunk. I was disappointed that I would not get to spend more time with him. "But we'll meet you at the Amalfi Coast tomorrow, I just don't know what time. It depends on how long reshooting the scene will take."

I tried to be positive and told him, "Oh no, it's okay. Don't worry about it." But it was *not* okay. I was disappointed that I would not be able to spend more time with Elliott because of those stupid reshoots. And I could tell from the look on his face that Elliott was disappointed too.

"Anyway," Grace said. "Good luck with reshoots and we'll see you soon! Love you, Elliott!"

"Love you too, Gracie," Elliott said. He then turned to me and smiled, "Good night, Cecilia!"

I smiled back and said, "Good night, Elliott. Good luck with the movie!"

And with that, he smiled, and left. While I was sad I wouldn't get to spend some more time with Elliott, at least tomorrow at Pompeii I would get to make up the time I missed with my girls.

Chapter 6: Wishing For A PG-13 Rated Dream

None of us wanted to get up early in the morning. So we decided to sleep in until about nine, meet for some breakfast at a nearby café for breakfast, and then be on our way to Pompeii. While it sucked that Elliott and his brothers would not be joining us, like I said before I was looking forward to some fun with my girls.

Speaking of Elliott, that night I had a dream about him. It was basically what probably would have happened if Grace hadn't opened the door and interrupted us. What happened was that we kissed, rather passionately. I should have known there it was a dream, because knowing myself, my first kiss with someone was always awkward. Then we pulled away, smiled at each other, then moved even closer to each other. Then we continued to kiss even more sensually, but I can assure you that what happened next was *nothing* like a Disney princess movie. I pulled him down by the collar with both of my hands, which were quite sweaty. Now I was lying down on the bed and he was on top of me. We caught our breaths, stared at each other, then he proceeded to impolitely kiss my neck, and I gripped his collar tightly in response. We then proceeded to politely but rather quickly take off the other's clothes, starting with me reaching down to start unbuttoning his shirt. Once it was unbuttoned all the way, his toned six-pack was visible, and it made me sigh in awe. He reached down and started to pull my skirt off. And after that we did some other stuff that I can't talk about further...

Anyway right at the climax of my dream, I woke up startled. I looked around the room. Elliott was nowhere in sight. "Phew," I thought to myself, "it was just a dream!" But then I turned to Grace, who was still sleeping, and she was completely unaware that I had just had an inappropriate dream about her cousin. So when her alarm went off for her to wake up, I kept wondering if I should tell her about it. I worried that she would kill me if she found out about my dream, and I didn't want to have another fight like she had with Esperanza and Nicole at the beginning of the trip. So I decided to not tell her unless it somehow came up in conversation. Fingers crossed, it wouldn't.

When the annoying alarm on her phone started alerting her that bedtime was over, Grace groaned, shut it off, and yawned. Stretching her arms as she did this, she sat up while I just lay there and felt guilty. Then she turned to me and said, "Morning, Cecilia!"

I nodded back and said, "Hi, Grace! How'd you sleep?"

Grace cheerfully said, "Oh I had this *incredible* dream! We had all gone to Disney World together and when we got there it was made of gumdrops and lollipops and marshmallows!" I nodded nervously, thinking about whether I should tell her about the dream I had about Elliott. She continued, "You should have seen it! It was literally in Heaven." Then she added, "I seriously think that gelato was spiked or something. 'Cause we came back in a happy daze, and then I had a dream that was almost like one of those hippie drug trips." Drunk Grace. That's something I never thought I'd see. She changed the subject and said, "Anyway, did *you* have any good dreams last night?"

Now Cecilia, you promised yourself that you would tell Grace about the dream if it came up in conversation, and it just did. So go ahead, tell her! Tell her you had a sex dream about her cousin. Get it over with. I blurted out, "I had a sex dream!"

At that moment, Grace's jaw dropped to the floor and stared at me. "Oh my gosh," she said. "Oh my gosh! Cecilia Hartley, the girl who had at point in her life promised to save herself for marriage, had a sex dream!" I nervously nodded. "Shut up!" she said, shocked. "Shut up!" Okay, maybe she wouldn't ask who it was. You don't have to tell her it was Elliott unless she asks who was in the dream. Then she asked, "So, who did you dream about?" Damn it!

I knew I had to tell her. Even if she would kill me for having such a dream about her cousin, at least I was being honest about it. Just tell her, Cecilia. Get it over with! But of course I just said, "Weird thing was, it was a complete and total stranger." What is wrong with you Cecilia? Way to lie to your friend!

Grace just looked puzzled. "Huh," she said. Then she shrugged and said, "Maybe it's a sign he's your soulmate and you haven't met him yet."

I quickly nodded and said, "Yeah. Maybe it is." Or maybe it's a sign I'm attracted to your cousin!

"Then again," Grace started to think, "dream psychologists say that the people you dream about are *usually* people you've met before or seen before at any time in your life." Was I a goner? Grace crossed her shoulders and questioned me: "What do you think about that, Cecilia?"

I was speechless. "Uh," is all I could come up with. Say something! Say something! "Well, what if it's just a person I saw walking in Rome? No one I knew? Does it have to be someone I knew?"

Grace sat there silently. Had I stumped her? She blew a strand of her hair from her forehead out of her face. She shrugged her arms and said, "Okay. Got me there."

Phew.

"Anyway," Grace changed the subject as she got up from her bed. "We should probably get ready! Pompeii awaits us!"

"Yes," I softly agreed. "Pompeii awaits us!" I knew I was going to have to tell her at some point, but did I really have to?

******

At about ten o'clock we all met in the lobby and went to a nearby café for some breakfast. I got a croissant and tried a cappuccino for the first time. It was okay, just not as good as a Starbucks frappuccino, at least in my opinion. I had been hungry from the night before and all I had eaten was that pizza that Grace brought home for me, and while that was good, it was also cold and I didn't really eat much of it, only about half.

"Man, can I just say," Esperanza hummed after taking a sip of her cappuccino, "I understand you may be homesick, but when we get back to the states, I'm going to be homesick of *Europe*."

"What are you going to miss about Europe?" I asked, taking a bite of my croissant.

"Everything!" Esperanza's voice sounded airy and breezy, as if she was in a happy state. "The lifestyle. The piazza, the wine, the food!"

"I'm going to miss all the hot Italian boys," Nicole interrupted. "I made a promise to myself to get an Italian boyfriend here."

Knowing how boy crazy Nicole was, I sarcastically told her, "Yeah. Of course you did."

"Come on guys, admit it," Nicole whined. She pointed her finger at all of us and said, "You can never go wrong with European boys! Like in high school we had some very attractive boys, they were all just assholes." We all nodded in agreement.

"Speaking of boys," Grace said tauntingly, "Cecilia had a naughty dream last night!"

I nudged Grace on the shoulder and loudly whispered to her, "Grace! Why would you tell them that?"

"Wait a sec," Esperanza held her hand up as if to stop us. She turned to me and asked, "Cecilia, did you really have a sex dream?"

I slowly nodded my head, slowly and embarrassed. Esperanza looked shocked, Nicole looked proud. "It wasn't much," I tried to convince them. "Just making out and fooling around. It really wasn't anything I swear!"

"Yeah," Grace placed her elbows on the table, "it's just you're the last person we ever expected to have that kind of dream about. That's all."

"So," Esperanza curiously asked, "who was the guy that you...you know."

"She said she thinks it was someone from walking in Rome. She didn't recognize him, but I told her that we've seen people in our dreams at least once during our lives," Grace answered for me while trying to show her intelligence.

"Like a one night stand?" Esperanza nearly interrogated me.

"Oh, gosh no!" I said in disgust. I always hated the idea of two people who had just met had sex and then never saw each other again. If you were never going to see them again, then what's the point of having sex with them? I assured them, "It's just that—that I didn't recognize him. Thought it was a total stranger, but when Grace said what she just said, I figured it must of been some random guy in Rome we saw."

Grace and Esperanza looked puzzled, but then pointed her finger at me and confidently said, "You know what I think? I think she's lying!"

Uh oh! Was I busted? I quickly said back, "No I'm not. Why would—why would you think that?" I nervously laughed. I might be busted.

"Ah come on Cecilia," Nicole rolled her eyes. "We've known you since kindergarten! I think we should be able to tell when you're lying!" I bit my bottom lip anxiously and felt a knot in my stomach.

Grace asked her, "Who do you think it is, Nicole?"

"It's obvious!" Nicole exclaimed as if she had figured out who the murderer was at a crime scene. "Your cousin!" I gulped loudly.

Grace scratched her head and asked in confusion, "Elliott?" Nicole nodded.

"What makes you think that?" Esperanza asked in a complete state of disbelief.

"Think about it," Nicole explained. "Who did she spend all night with yesterday as he was nursing her back to health? And did you see them over the past few days? She couldn't keep her eyes off him and he couldn't keep his eyes off her! There's obviously something between them! She's crushing on Elliott!"

I was blushing crimson red and talked at a rapid pace, "Oh come on! Elliott is just a friend!"

Esperanza reminded me, "That's what they all say, Cecilia."

Seeing there was no way out, I admitted, "Fine! The dream was about Elliott!"

Shocked, Nicole and Esperanza said, "What?!" in unison. Nicole seemed as if she didn't actually think it was him until I confirmed it.

Just as appalled and a little bit angry, Grace said, "WHAT?!" I flushed and started shaking like a leaf. Man, I was in the doghouse.

"I'm sorry," I tried to tell Grace. "I wanted to tell you, but I knew you would get mad at me!"

In a frustrated tone, Grace said, "Well you're right, Cecilia! I am pretty mad at you!"

Then Esperanza asked me, "So, how good was he, you know, in bed?" I didn't answer, still staring at Grace's angry face. This seems like déjà vu when Esperanza and Nicole were mad at Grace for lying about Elliott being her cousin. And I must say, I'm starting to understand how Grace felt.

Nicole then got my attention by saying, "Hey, Cecilia!" I turned to her and she asked me, "I know you have ophidiophobia, but were you brave enough to touch his pet serpent?" She and Esperanza started laughing while Grace was disgusted. Still laughing, Nicole said, "Get it? Cause he's Serpent Boy!"

I admit, I didn't understand their joke at all. "What do you mean?" I asked. I only understood what it meant later.

Nicole slyly said, "What do you think I mean?" I wasn't as cultured in sex jokes as my other friends were. I didn't know much about sex at all really. I had only known the basics, as explained to me by my mom and taught to me during Freshman year health class. But when it came to jokes and slang, I wasn't aware. That led to my friends calling me, "Innocent Ears," because I always acted clueless and innocent whenever someone made a sexual joke. Guess I wasn't so innocent after my dream last night...

Fed up with all their laughter, Grace said in a protective but defensive tone, "Hey! Stop it! That's my cousin you're talking about!" And with that, Nicole and Esperanza apologized and, still upset, Grace asked, "So you had one of those dreams about Elliott huh?" I nodded. Then she asked, not as frustrated, "And do you have feelings for him?"

I nodded once again. I tried to convince her, "I'm really sorry, Grace. I really am! But he's just so sweet, funny, and cute! I'm sure it's just a little crush that'll be over in a few days! Please forgive me," I begged.

Grace paused there for a minute. She sighed and said, "I really don't want to have a fight like this again. So, yeah, I forgive you." I sighed in relief, but Grace reminded me, "But if you do decide to go forward with my cousin, know that if you *ever* hurt him, I'm never going to forget that. But, if he hurts you, I will never forget that either. Understand?"

I replied, "Yes, Grace." Then I smiled lightly, and she smiled back.

That was followed by a very brief period of silence. Nicole then broke that silence by saying, "Well, shall we go to Pompeii or not?" And we all agreed and prepared to head to the train station.

******

87

We all forgot about the whole "sex dream about Elliott" thing by the time we got to Pompeii. We took a bus from Rome and arrived in Pompeii at around 1:15 pm. As we walked up to where we got our tickets, we tried to enjoy the shade while we could because in Pompeii you had to worry about the hot sun.

Before we got our tickets, Grace asked me, "Are you sure you're going to be okay? Even after what happened yesterday?"

But I assured her, "Don't worry about me. I'll be fine!" Then I reached into my purse and pulled out a beautiful lavender paper fan with flowers on it I had bought that day in the hotel lobby. I said, "I bought this today in the lobby. Plus I have plenty of water, so I think I'm in good shape!"

"If you say so," Nicole said. "If you say you'll be alright, we trust you!"

After we got our tickets, we started to walk in Pompeii. We looked at the giant map and decided to go to the amphitheater first. It was large and round, with an open ground where the performers stood and then seats surrounding it where the audience sat. It reminded me of a few round theaters where I had been to see plays, such as Colonial Players of Annapolis. One year our high school did a murder mystery comedy play that was theater in the round, although I can't remember exactly what it was called.

"Wait in the movie that we watched on the plane isn't this where they were when the volcano erupted?" Esperanza asked.

"I think so," I said, although I really wasn't sure. "I think they were doing chariot racing when it happened so I don't remember exactly. Could have been."

"I was asleep by that point in the movie," Nicole added.

"I really wish I had been too," I joked, referring to how bad the movie was.

Anyway, after that we walked along the sidewalk. In the road, they had giant, high rocks to walk on. We didn't really feel like treating them like stepping stones when walking, so we just used the sidewalk.

Nicole suggested, "Who wants to race each other using the rocks? It'll be kind of like parkour!"

"I'm in!" Esperanza raised her hand as if we were in school.

Grace crossed her hands to make an x, "Uh, thank you, but no."

"I would," I told Nicole, "but I don't want to break a leg and end up in the hospital!"

"Okay" Nicole sighed. She turned to Esperanza and said, "Well, Esperanza, I guess it's just you and me."

"Maybe later, okay?" Esperanza asked. Nicole nodded. Then Esperanza bragged, "Although, I must say, I've beaten Pilar in races *many* times before, so I would worry if I were you!" Pilar was Esperanza's twin sister, with whom she could be quite competitive on occasion. While they loved each other very dearly, they loved to challenge each other every now and then.

"Well," Nicole started to boast. "Being the oldest of five I've won *plenty* of races! So I think you should worry, too!"

Esperanza shrugged and said, "If you say so..."

We continued walking until we reached a traditional little Roman house. We saw where the bathtub and the kitchen were, and that there was a hole in the ceiling so that they would have light during the day. Nicole talked about how she had learned all about this kind of stuff in Latin, being the proud Honors Latin student she had been all throughout high school.

Next we reached a place where we could see Mount Vesuvius in the background. I had always had a fear of natural disasters. I remember when I went to go visit my Meme's (my grandmother's) hometown of Johnstown, Pennsylvania a few summers ago, I couldn't sleep at night in the hotel because I kept worrying another Johnstown flood would happen. There was also a period where I had a recurring dream where my family and I were vacationing in Thailand, a tsunami struck, and we were all separated from each other. I think I may have had this dream because we had been learning about the 2004 Boxing Day Tsunami in geography class.

"Hey, guys," I asked nervously, "you don't think that volcano is going to erupt anytime soon, is it?"

"No," Grace comforted me, "you don't have to worry, Cecilia. The volcano won't erupt at least while we're here."

"I don't think it's still active," Nicole shook her head.

Esperanza corrected her, "Actually, it still is."

"Uh oh," I muttered.

"I bet you we will be out of Italy by the time it erupts again," Esperanza assured me.

Nicole fanned herself with her hand. "Anyway," she sounded exhausted and out of breath from the heat, "are you guys ready to go? It's so freaking hot out here!"

"Touché," Grace agreed.

******

After we were done with our fascinating but hot one-and-a-half-hour in Pompeii, we went back to the coach bus we had taken from Rome. Our luggage was also waiting there in the bus waiting to take us to Massa Lubrense on the Amalfi Coast. As we were driving up through the rugged landscape that was the Amalfi Coast, we could see the beautiful landscape of bright blue water and green hills. The road we were driving on uphill was so narrow, we were scared we might fall off down the hill and into the ocean.

Grace, who was looking at her phone for updates on when the boys would be arriving, looked up from her phone after getting a text. She gave us an update: "Elliott just texted. He and the boys will be getting here at about eight or nine tonight."

"Great," I smiled. I was excited to see Elliott again because I had been thinking about him all day, but I was also kind of nervous of how awkward it would be after that dream where we...you know.

"Are we meeting for dinner or will we just see them tomorrow when we go to Capri?" Esperanza asked.

"I don't know," Grace honestly said, "might meet in the lobby to hang out after dinner. It totally depends on when they get there and how tired they are."

When we finally reached the hotel, *Punta Campanella Resort*, in Massa Lubrense, I was in complete awe at the sight of the hotel. It was large and exquisite, rustic yet modern. Our room had a beautiful view of the clear blue water reflected by the blinding sun. *Punta Campanella* was right in the center of the small town, which consisted of shops and a marketplace. Esperanza had bought some peaches there, and said they were the best she had ever tasted. I had to say, I liked Rome because of the history, but I think I preferred the Amalfi Coast.

******

After dinner that night, we all were just hanging out at our table, talking about life. We all decided to get dressed up, and I wore a green and white striped strapless sundress that went down to my knees and my golden sandals. We had started to discuss our plans for the future. Nicole wanted to start a career in fashion and Grace wanted to begin a career in medicine.

"What do you think of the name *Essie's*?" Esperanza asked us when she revealed she wanted to start a cupcake business.

"I think it's very cute," I told her. "Cheesy, but I like cheesy.

"Now Esperanza, promise me you're not going to bake poisonous cupcakes like Michael Bernard said you were going to do after you broke up," Nicole teasingly said.

"You promised you weren't going to talk about it!" Esperanza playfully slapped her friend on the arm. When Esperanza caught her junior year boyfriend Michael kissing Vivian Coolidge (who we called "Regina George" because of how much she compared in personality to the character from *Mean Girls*), she told us that she vowed revenge on both of them by baking toxic waste cupcakes. It was a total joke of course! Well Vivian overheard it and told Michael, and they were both dumb enough to think that Esperanza would actually do something like that.

"Anyway, guys," I slowly stood up. "I'm going to go to my room. I think I left something there. I'll be right back."

They all nodded and I left the table to go back up to the room. I didn't tell them this, but I was going to get "dolled up" for when Elliott came. I was so happy at the prospect of seeing him that I couldn't help but put on a broad smile and skip happily through the lobby. But I also wasn't really paying attention to where I was going so I accidentally bumped into someone.

I immediately said, "Oh my gosh, I'm so sorry! I'm so clumsy!"

I didn't really see his face, but in a thick Italian accent he chuckled and assured me, "Oh no, you are fine."

Then I looked up and saw him clearly. He was a young Italian man, around my age, and boy was he hot! He had flowy dark hair, olive skin, some light facial hair, a perfect jawline, and dark green eyes. I was caught up in his hotness, and it seemed as though Elliott was now ancient history.

"Ciao bella," he smirked.

Oh my gosh! He called me beautiful. I replied, "Ciao bello," calling him handsome. "I'm---I'm---I'm Cecilia."

"Bonjourno, Cecilia," he said, taking my hand in his two warm hands. "My name is Matteo," he said as he kissed my hand. I found his kissing my hand very sexy, his light facial hair lightly scratching my skin.

"Are you from here?" I was still caught up in everything sexy about him. But then I realized I should have known he was from Italy. "Wait? What am I saying? You're *obviously* from Italy! That's like if you asked me if I was from the U.S. because of my accent, and it would be so obvious and..."

As Matteo unwrapped his hand from mine, I noticed he was much taller than me, about 6"0. "Do not apologize, Cecilia," he assured me. "I am from Venice. But I am with my family here on vacation."

"Cool," I said. "I'm here with my friends. We're staying here for a few days. Taking a whole trip of Europe in about eighteen days." He smiled at me and nodded. Then there was an awkward silence. I then said, "Anyway, I have to go, nice to meet you, Matteo."

I started to leave to go back upstairs to the room, but Matteo took me by the shoulder and stopped me. He said, "Oh wait, no bella. Don't go yet!"

But I really just wanted to get back up to the room. "I'm sorry, can you please let me go? I have to go get ready for something."

Matteo then took his hands and stroked my hair and talked to me saying, "But you're so beautiful. You don't need makeup."

I was flattered and said, "Awww, thank you. That's so sweet."

He continued to stroke my hair and then took one of those hands and put his hand on my hip, and he said, "Alright, I will let you go, but I just need one more thing from you before you go." Then he pulled me closer and kissed me passionately. My hands were dropped at my side at first, but then I decided to oblige by putting my hands on his back. While the kiss was passionate, it was nothing compared to my dream kiss with Elliott.

Then, after a few seconds of making out with Matteo, I heard a familiar British voice say, "Hmmm. Fancy seeing you here." Then I unlocked my lips from Matteo's and turned to find Elliott standing there with his three brothers, their suitcases in hand. Elliott was *not* impressed. This was really awkward.

Then Ryan jokingly asked us, "Did you guys use tongue?"

Connor then turned to him and scolded him saying, "Hey! That's not appropriate! There's a seven year old baby here!"

"Who are you calling a baby?!" Ollie screamed at his brother.

Elliott scolded all three of them and said, "That's enough boys!"

Matteo, not wanting to be a part of the awkwardness, said, "Anyway, I have to go. Very nice to meet you, Cecilia." I nervously nodded, and he left the lobby.

"Hi, boys," I waved to them. Elliott still had an angry look on his face. Then I asked him, "How was reshooting the movie?"

Elliott, looking down at the ground with his arms crossed, said, "Fine. Simply fine." Then he turned to his brothers, handed Ryan a key, and said, "Boys, take the luggage up to the room, I'll be there shortly, I have to talk to Cecilia about something."

And so the boys quietly and awkwardly took their bags, headed towards the elevator, and vanished. So then Elliott and I were the only ones remaining. And all of a sudden, I couldn't think about the sex dream anymore.

"Who was that?" Elliott asked as he moved closer to me.

"Some guy named Matteo," I told him. "But it was not what you thought it was. He was flirting with me, and he kissed me. It meant *nothing*."

"You had your hands on his back and it looked like you were invested in the kiss," Elliott said. "And he wasn't even that cute." I couldn't believe it. Was Elliott jealous of Matteo?

"What are you talking about?" I asked him. "Matteo was *so* hot! And at least he doesn't..." I was trying to think of something that was imperfect about the way Elliott looked. I couldn't think of anything. Crossing his arms, Elliott waited for me to come up with something. "Have--- have an odd looking nose!" Really, Cecilia? That was the best you could come up with?

Elliott quickly defended himself, pointing at me and said, "For your information, it only looks weird because I've broken it three times. And I like it that my nose looks different. I don't know about you, but I think Matteo's nose is...boring"

"Elliott, are you jealous?" I asked him.

"Me? Jealous?" he asked. He then started laughing. Then he said loudly, "No! I'm just trying to protect you!"

"Well, maybe you can tell me why you want to protect me in a more *private* place because the front desk people are staring at us!" I told him, pointing to the front desk people, who looked very uncomfortable with our arguing.

When Elliott turned to see them, he saw the front desk people's faces and a nervous smile came upon his face and he waved slowly. He then turned to me and said, "Alright, fine. We can talk about this going up the stairs."

So we made our way to the stairs and as we started walking, I asked him, "So why exactly are you trying to protect me?"

"Well," Elliott said, trying to think. "Um." He then said, "Alright fine! I had a dream about you last night and I'm not exactly sure what it means."

He caught my attention the moment he said, "dream." Did he have the same dream I had? Was that a sign? "A dream?" I asked in curiosity. "What about?"

Elliott, biting his lip and taking a deep breath, said, "Well, we were in your hotel room in Rome, and we started kissing and we—and we..."

"Had sex?" I asked him.

"No, we just snogged," Elliott said in disgust. "Or made out," he corrected himself, realizing I most likely wouldn't understand British slang. I flushed red in embarrassment. Elliott didn't dream about having sex with me like I did with him. How could I be so stupid? Elliott was puzzled and asked, "Why would you think we had sex?"

I was speechless. I sort of told Elliott about the dream, and he had a dream that wasn't the dream I dreamed. What do I say? What do I do? I finally said, "I'm sorry I have to go!" Then I ran as fast as I could up the stairs.

Elliott then rushed after me screaming my name. "Cecilia! Wait! Cecilia! Cecilia! Wait!"

But I wouldn't stop. My heart was pounding not only because of my feelings for him, but also because I was so nervous to face him after I told him about the naughty dream I had of him. Then, all of a sudden, I could feel my one shoe, my left golden sandal, slipped from off my left foot. I didn't even bother to go back for it; I just kept running until I got to my room. My face was red from the embarrassment and running, and I felt like I was going to start tearing up because of the stupid thing I said. I took a deep breath, leaning against the front door, and put my hands to my face in frustration.

Chapter 7: Wishing For A Fairytale Kiss

The next morning, we got up at around 7:30 to catch the ferry to Capri. I hadn't really slept well because I was thinking about what happened with Elliott last night. Was he suspicious when I asked him if he had a sex dream about me? And he said he also had a dream about me. But what kind of dream did *he* have? I think I got about a half an hour of sleep last night. I also called my parents at about midnight (6 p.m. their time), to take my mind off of Elliott.

After eating breakfast in the lobby and taking some Dramamine, my friends and I walked to the dock. Elliott and his brothers had gone to breakfast at a café so they met us there. Luckily the dock where the ferry met us was right across from the hotel, so we didn't have far to walk at all. When we got there, the four brothers were already there, wearing summer clothes, matching hats, and sunglasses. They were talking to each other and Grace had to say "ahem," to get their attention. They then quickly turned their heads toward us and smiled brightly.

"Oh, hello girls!" Elliott said. It was so hard for me to look at him without picturing his lips on mine, like in my dream. "How are you?" he asked us.

"Good, thanks!" Grace said. "How about you boys?"

"Quite wonderful, thank you Grace," Elliott grinned.

Little Ollie stepped in and said, "I'm so excited to explore Capri! I've never been!"

"I don't think any of us have," Ryan added.

"Well," I said, "this will be an adventure for all of us!"

We talked and talked as we waited for the ferry to come. While my friends were talking to Ryan, Connor, and Ollie, I was staring down at the transparent, clear blue water. I counted, and I spotted eight jellyfish floating through the water. I had never been bothered by them, but I knew Nicole had a particular fear of them. I was trying to decide whether to warn her or not, but then I figured I wouldn't scare her.

I focused on looking down at the water until Elliott came up and stood right next to me. "Good morning, Cecilia," he said with a smile.

"Hi, Elliott," I replied, smiling back at him.

"I want to talk to you about something," he said. Oh great! He probably wanted to talk about what happened last night. "It's about what happened last night." I was right! Crap!

I was a little nervous about what he was going to say. My heart was pounding, and I started to sweat. But that also could have been because of the heat. But trying to hide my nerves, I calmly said, "Sure. What's up?"

Just as he was opening his mouth to say something, the ferry blew its horn notifying us of its arrival and they began calling people to board. He then told me, "I'll tell you on the ride over." I slowly nodded, and we all began boarding the large ferry.

The ferry had two levels, a shady bottom and a sun-drenched top. We decided to sit on top to get a better view as we made our journey to Capri. The benches sat four to a bench, with Grace, Esperanza, Nicole, and Ryan sitting together. I sat with Elliott so we could talk.

"So," Elliott started to say, "last night when I—," but then he was interrupted by Ollie and Connor who ran up to the bench and sat right next to us.

"Hello!" Connor said cheerfully.

"We're so lucky to be sitting here with you two!" Ollie said, just as happy.

"Are you excited to see Capri?" Connor asked. "I know we are!"

"Um, boys," Elliott told them. "If you don't mind, I need to have a grown up conversation with Cecilia, *alone.*"

Then Connor asked loudly, "Are you going to ask her out on a date like you said you would?" I held my hand to my mouth to prevent myself from laughing.

Elliott was embarrassed, and his cheeks turned as red as strawberries. "Connor!" he said. "What did I say about not telling her?"

Connor sighed and said, "I know. We should let you tell her yourself and wait until after you talked to her to talk to her about it." What a very confusing sentence coming from an eleven year old.

Ollie turned to me and said, "I really like you!" I thanked him and he added, "I hope the two of you get married someday!" I smiled. Ollie was so adorable!

Blushing even redder, Elliott chuckled and said, "Alright, that's enough!" He then got stern and told his brothers, "Now you two, *please* go." The two of them slowly left the bench and sat in the row across from us. Elliott then turned to me and said, "I'm so sorry about that."

"Oh no, it's fine," I assured him. "I'm an only child, but I still understand that little brothers can be a bit of a pain." But then I asked in curiosity, "So, Connor said you were going to ask me on a date, are you?"

"Uh," Elliott said, "yes and no. Well..."

"And please tell me about that dream you had about me the night before," I interrupted him.

"Dream? Oh right dream!" Elliott said. "Well, you know how you asked if the dream I had about you was a sex dream?" I nodded. Elliott went on, "Well, if you recall, I denied having that kind of dream," he admitted nervously, "but I actually did."

My jaw dropped. Did he have the same dream I had about him? "A sex dream? What happened?" I asked in curiosity.

Elliott asked, "You know how we almost kissed until Grace walked in?" I nodded and he continued, "Well, it was basically what might have happened if she hadn't walked in on us."

"Did it start off as a G-rated peck then turn into a PG-13 full on makeout session to R-rated passionate sex with some stripping and tongue involved?" I asked.

"Basically," Elliott said.

"And did you wake up at about the dream's climax?" I asked.

Elliott responded, "I suppose I did."

"Did you leave impolite kisses on my neck?" I asked.

Elliott, looking surprised, asked, "How did you know?"

"Because I think we had the exact same dream," I said.

"Really?" Elliott asked in a mixture of shock and confusion. He was still trying to process it all. "Oh my goodness. What does this mean?"

"Well," I told him. "I don't know if it was just the heat gone to my brain, but I think there might be some kind of feeling I have towards you."

"What kind of feeling?" he asked. "Lust? Admiration? Just a silly little crush?"

"I don't know, Elliott," I said. "I don't know."

"Well, if I'm going to be honest with you," Elliott said, "I think I may be having feelings for you too. I think I like you and I'm not sure what to do about it."

"You like me?" I asked him. "Like you *like* me like me?"

"Why yes," he said. He then took my hands and wrapped both of his hands around them. He told me, "I mean, you're smart, beautiful, funny, and kind. You're a very special person, Cecilia."

My heart began beating really fast once again. I continued looking at him and I started to blush more and more. "Oh my," I said. "I just—I don't know what to say."

"I think we're going to need more time to talk about this," Elliott said with his hands still shielding mine. "Shall we go for a stroll on the beach tonight? After dinner?"

"Sure thing," I said. "I've always wanted to take a romantic stroll on the beach. But of course, this isn't romantic, we're not dating. I mean we could date one day, but I don't know. Let's see how this walk turns out—." I went on for a long time and Elliott looked at me with a wide grin on his face. I then assured him, "I'm sorry, I talk a lot. It's who I am!"

Elliott told me, "Oh no, don't worry, it's fine. I think it is very cute." He winked at me, and I winked back. He then leaned in and gave me a quick, but nonetheless sweet kiss on the cheek, which made a wide smile spread across my face.

I lightly giggled, and I noticed that his hands were still wrapped around mine, but I didn't want to tell him because I didn't want him to let go. Still smiling I said, "Anyway, I think they are about to tell us about the directions—or instructions, or whatever they're called! You know what I mean! And we should probably pay attention."

Elliott was also still smiling and he said, "Alright." We then turned to listen to the man at the front of the boat, but not before Elliott told me, "I can't wait for later."

I responded, "Me too."

The man at the front of the boat's name was Giovanni. He was a rather good-looking Italian man, about late twenties or early thirties. He had tan skin with a dark beard and his dark hair was covered by a sun hat. "Bonjourno!" he said, and we said "bonjourno" back. He continued, "Welcome everybody! I am Giovanni, your tour guide for today! Who here is excited?"

After the crowd cheered, he went on, "After we drop you off at the island of Capri, you will have some free time until about 3 o'clock to walk around the island. There are a wide variety of shops, restaurants, and botanical gardens, but unfortunately you cannot go to the beach here because all beaches have rocks instead of sand." Huh. I noticed that at the beach near our hotel, but I didn't think you would not be able to go in it just because there were rocks in place of sand. "And then after we pick you up at 3, we will take our tour around the island which should take about an hour and a half, and then we will head back and arrive here around 5."

After Giovanni told us all of this, he said the exact same thing in Spanish. Gosh, I wish I could speak another language at any time like him! Anyway, it took us about 45 minutes or so, though I really wasn't counting, to get to Capri. It was so much larger than it looked from a distance, and I was awed by its beauty.

106

As we got to the dock, we quickly stood up to try to be the first ones off. We had a feeling the whole ferry would be crowded and crazy with people trying to get off. Luckily we got there in front just in time to go off the boat, and once we reached the little market area near the boat the whole place was so crowded I got separated from the group at one point.

"Guys!" I shouted. But I was so far behind them that my voice was drowned out by the crowd's voices. "Grace! Nicole! Esperanza! Elliott!" I continued shouting each of their names, but no one could hear me. By this time I had been able to escape from the millions of people and went into a little shop that sold scarves, t-shirts, sunglasses, etc. From the store, I tried to keep an eye out for them, screaming their names.

I was just about to burst into tears because I had gotten lost and couldn't find my way in this crowded place. Then the man who worked at the counter saw me about to cry and quickly came over to me. He seemed like a nice man, Italian of course, and about in his sixties. He was shorter than me, plump, with white hair on a mostly bald head with wrinkles and a kind face.

He came over with a concerned look on his face, put his hands on my arms and told me something in Italian that sounded like it was a voice that was meant to console me. I looked at him, he noticed I couldn't understand, and asked, "English? Yes? No?"

I nodded slowly and said, "Yes."

"What's wrong, mia cara?" he asked. By the way, mia cara means "my dear."

A small tear slowly started to roll down my cheek as I said, "Well, I was walking with my friends, I got lost in the crowd, and now I can't find them." Then I started crying.

The man continued to be nurturing and said, "There, there." He took a handkerchief out of his apron pocket and handed it to me.

I wiped the tears away from my eyes with it and handed the handkerchief back to him and said, "Grazie," or "thank you."

"Prego," he said. Then he asked, "Now tell me please, what do your friends..."

Just as he was about to ask that, Elliott came running in and said, "Cecilia!"

"Elliott," I said back. Looking relieved, he ran towards me and hugged me tight. "I thought I lost you guys," I said. "That was so scary; you have no idea."

"It's okay, it's okay," he told me, looking into my eyes and placing his hands on my arms. "Let's go. We're going to take the incline up to a higher level of the island where we'll get to see the gardens, and get lunch. It'll be fun and will hopefully help you forget this whole scary experience. Let's go!" Smiling, I nodded, tightly grabbed his hand so we wouldn't get separated, and we started to leave until the old man stopped us.

"Wait," he asked Elliott, "are you Serpent Boy?"

Elliott looked at me and then looked at the old man nodded and said, "Yes."

All of a sudden a wide grin filled the old man's face. "Oh my!" he exclaimed. He then took Elliott's hand and shook it uncomfortably uncontrollably. "It's so nice to meet you! We love your movies!"

"I'm glad to hear that," Elliott said. The man then pulled him in for a hug and patted him on the back, and while he did this, Elliott turned his head to me and mouthed, "Help me!" I had a smirk on my face and mouthed the word, "No."

When the man stopped hugging he put his hands on Elliott's back and said, "I am Sergio Mariani! My wife and I are fans of your movies. I'll have to tell her!" He then shouted to a door and yelled his wife's name, "DONNA!"

Elliott and I quickly turned our heads to the doorway to see a short old woman rush through. Must be his wife, Donna! She looked just like Sergio, short, plump, white hair, wrinkled, and had a stern look on her face. After all, they do always say couples start to look alike as they age!

Donna walked over to her husband, still looking stern with her hands on her hips. "Now, Mr. Mariani, what is it now?" she asked. "You know to only call me if it's something important!"

By this time, Sergio had let go of Elliott. He said to his wife, "But amore mia, look!" He pointed to Elliott, who looked very nervous about what would happen next, and Donna's scowl turned into an excited grin.

She quickly ran towards him and exclaimed, "Elliott Parker! Elliott Parker! It's Serpent Boy! It's Serpent Boy!" She ran towards him and gave him a big hug that looked like it was about to squeeze the life out of him. She then took her hands, placed them on his cheeks and pulled him close to her face and said, "Mamma mia! You are not bad looking!"

Elliott was speechless at this point and could only say, "Um, thank you?" When she let go of his face, he had rubbed his cheeks because she had pinched his face so hard.

Then Sergio put his arms on my shoulder and said to his wife, "And look! He even has a girlfriend!"

Donna turned her head towards me, walked away from Elliott toward me, and I was frightened for my life what she was going to do to me. She got closer and closer and examined me. "Oh," she said. She took her fingers and started toying with my hair, twirling it and brushing it out of my face. "I didn't realize Elliott Parker had a girlfriend," she said. She then took her cold, bony finger and started stroking my cheek with it and said, "And must I say, you are quite the beautiful one, my dear."

I shook my head so that her finger wasn't touching me anymore and I said, "Thanks."

"Alright," Sergio said. "Should we have them stay?" He put his hands on Elliott's shoulders. We both looked so uncomfortable.

"Oh yes!" she said, walking back toward Elliott as her husband let go. "I'd love to have a famous movie star and his girlfriend over for lunch! It would be a dream come true!"

Elliott, being the polite person he was, walked away from her and towards me. "Uh, thank you very much Mr. and Mrs. Mariani, but we best be on our way." He then took my hand and said to me, "Come along, darling." Did he just call me darling? In the midst of all this chaos, I felt my heart pounding by the use of that word.

We walked quickly. Just as we were about to make our escape, Donna came running to us and said, "Oh no, no, no, no! You must stay!" she said. "I'll cook a delicious fettuccine for a beautiful couple like you two!" As she said this, she felt Elliott's biceps. Poor Elliott just stood there looking uncomfortable and disgusted.

Getting both jealous and angry at her for doing that to him, I flicked her hand away from him and told her, "Hey, lady! Hands off my boyfriend! Feel your *own* husband's biceps!"

Sergio heard me say this and looked angry. He walked towards his wife and said, "Donna? What were you doing?"

Donna told him, "I'm sorry, Sergio! I just wanted to feel his biceps! He always looks so good with his shirt off in the movies!"

Elliott and I looked at each other like these people were insane, then turned back to the fighting. Sergio screamed, "But you are married, Donna! And he has a girlfriend! He is too young for you!"

"I'm sorry," Donna said. "I just missed having a man with good muscles!"

From there, the two started arguing in Italian, and we couldn't understand a word they were saying. I whispered to Elliott, "Now's our chance! Go! Go! Go!" We then quietly but quickly ran to the doorway and ran as fast as we could to avoid getting caught by the Marianis. And we never saw them again!

By the time we had "escaped" the Marianis' store, the crowd had died down but Elliott and I still rushed quickly to where the others were. Still holding hands, our palms started to get sweaty, and I don't know about him but my heart kept beating more quickly as we touched in this way.

As we were fast-walking I asked him, "So, correct me if I'm wrong, but did you just call me darling back there?"

Elliott was clearly thinking about getting away from the psycho couple and asked, "What?" Then he remembered and said, "Oh right! Well, I had to get them to believe we were boyfriend and girlfriend somehow."

I added, "And I think they believed it! After all, you're a pretty good actor."

Elliott turned to me and jokingly looked disappointed and asked, "*Just* pretty good? Not *very* good?"

I went along and said, "Sorry. You're a *very* good actor. Gosh, don't you get enough praise?" I joked. We both laughed together.

We finally got to where we were supposed to meet the other group: the station where we could get the incline plane tickets. The other six were waiting there, almost impatiently, and as we walked towards them they got up and met us.

"It's about time!" Ryan groaned. "What took you so long?"

"Sorry," I apologized. "We had to escape a psycho, star struck couple."

"Psycho star struck couple?" Esperanza said in disbelief. "That one's going in the books."

"What happened, Elliott?" Grace asked. "Don't you get crazy fans all the time after you? Only this time you brought one of my best friends into it?"

"It's a really, really long story," Elliott said, "We will tell you on the way up the incline."

Ollie couldn't help but notice that we were still holding hands tightly. He pointed to us and said, "Look! They're holding hands!"

Elliott and I turned to each other, looked at our intertwined hands, and quickly broke free, although I think we both secretly didn't want to let go of each other.

"Why holding hands?" Nicole asked jokingly. "Are you all of a sudden the new Hollywood power couple now?"

"Do we have a new sister-in-law?" Ryan asked us sarcastically.

"Did you ask her on a date yet, like you said you were going to?" Connor asked.

"So many questions!" Elliott interrupted. "How about we save them all for *later*?" And with that, we all made our way to take the incline plane up the hill to explore.

******

Once we reached the top, we started to make our way to the botanical gardens. It took us about fifteen minutes to walk there.

Before we began walking Elliott asked me, "Are you going to be alright walking in the sun, Cecilia?" Awww! He was so polite and caring to ask about me!

But I assured him, "Oh, thanks, but I think I'll be fine! I have a fan, and water, and if I survived walking in Pompeii, I think I can survive this!"

Elliott smiled and said, "Alright, I trust you. But if you're ever feeling like the way you did at the Colosseum again, let us know." I nodded as we started to walk to the botanical gardens.

Once we got to the botanical gardens, we were awed by its beauty. There were many types of beautiful, colorful flowers as well as various statues and fountains made of stone and marble. There was even a beautiful view of the blue ocean that would be great for taking pictures and selfies, which we did.

"Come on, girls!" Esperanza enthusiastically said. "Let's take a group photo!"

"Great idea!" Nicole agreed.

"Let's get someone to take it for us!" I suggested.

"Connor! Ollie!" Grace called as she first spotted her two youngest cousins. She asked them, "Will you please take a picture of my friends and me?"

"Certainly!" Connor said as she handed him her phone.

"I want to take it!" Ollie said, taking the phone away from him.

"But she asked me," Connor said, taking the phone back, "and you always get what you want because you're the baby! Give me a turn!"

"I'm not a baby!" Ollie said taking the phone back.

Grace put an end to the fight by taking the phone and saying, "You know what? *None* of you will take the photo! We are going to take a selfie!"

"You're no fair!" Connor pouted, crossing his arms and stomping away.

Ollie did the same thing and said, "Yeah! You're not the boss of us!" And he followed his brother in a similar way.

Grace rolled her eyes and said, "Oh kids! Anyway, let's take a selfie." And so we took a group selfie, one smiling and one silly one. Grace looked at her phone and said, "Awww! So cute! I'll send it to you guys." We nodded and thanked her and continued walking throughout the gardens.

As I was walking and looking at the different flowers and plants, I couldn't help but overhear, "If you like Cecilia so much, then kiss her!" I turned to find Ryan saying that to Elliott. I decided to eavesdrop on the conversation and managed to remain hidden.

Elliott replied, "But Ryan, I just admitted I liked her, I don't want to overwhelm her by kissing her! I think she's still trying to process it all."

"But you like her; she likes you," Ryan said. "She's a nice woman, Elliott."

"I know she is," Elliott said, "She's wonderful! But I don't want to scare her by all of a sudden kissing her." Well, I wouldn't say I'd be scared. Shocked that we kissed after only knowing each other for a few days, but I wasn't scared. "We're going for a walk on the beach later to talk about our feelings, you know."

"So kind of like a date?" Ryan asked.

"Yeah, I suppose," Elliott said. "I hadn't thought of it before as a date." Neither had I!

"Then I guess wait until the end of the date to kiss her," Ryan said. "Just don't let her get away! Because I know she likes you and all, but one stupid mistake you make could drive her away."

"I know," Elliott assured his brother. "I thought I was supposed to be the *older* brother," Elliott said. Then he joked, "Since when did you become more skilled at love and romance than me?"

"Let's face it," Ryan replied, "I've always been better at love and romance than you!" With that, Elliott playfully and lightly punched his brother on the right shoulder and they laughed. I developed a small smile, and my heart began to beat fast once again.

After about an hour at the gardens, we left and decided to head back to town to do some shopping and get some lunch. We stopped at this small pizza place that served Italian food (then again a lot of restaurants in Italy do!). It was small, homey, had carpet and a welcome atmosphere. We ate at a huge table that sat eight. We all decided to get the large cheese pizza to share.

"Oh my gosh," Nicole said. "Look at that hot Italian hunk over there!" She pointed to this young Italian man sitting at the table next to us. He was sitting at a table for two but was by himself, eating some spaghetti. He was good-looking, tan, long wavy black hair, and dimples.

"Here we go again!" Esperanza jokes. "Nicole has found love!"

"What do you think? Should I make my move?" Nicole turned to us and asked us for advice.

"Sure," Grace said. "Go for it, Nicole!"

"You know what?" Nicole asked. "I am!" She then got up from her seat and walked toward the guy and started flirting with him by saying. "Bonjourno!" She then pretended to play dumb and said, "I'm sorry. My Italian isn't very good. How did it sound?"

"Perfection!" the Italian man said. "Luckily for you, my mom works as a translator so she is fluent in English and she taught me at a young age."

Dazed and smitten, Nicole sighed and said, "Fascinating!"

Elliott then turned to us and asked, "Does this happen often?"

I replied, "Too often." Then we all continued to watch the conversation as if it were a reality show.

"I like your smile," Nicole continued flirting. "And your accent is *really* sexy!"

The man looked uncomfortable and said, "Um, thank you." He then changed the subject and introduced himself: "I'm Enzo, by the way."

He reached out his hand and Nicole shook it saying, "I'm Nicole."

Enzo said, "Funny thing! My boyfriend's name is Nicola!" With that everyone either gasped or opened their jaws wide when he said that. Nicole herself looked surprised and her eyes opened wide.

Trying to convince herself she didn't hear what she heard, Nicole asked, "I'm sorry, what?"

"Oh," Enzo said, "Just so you know, I'm gay. That's why I didn't seem to be interested in you."

Poor Nicole just stood there still as a stone. She nervously laughed and finally said, "Oh, good for you!" Still stunned, she might have said a few of the wrong things. "I mean, not good for you. There are a lot of countries across the world who hate homosexuals. I don't, but a lot of people do. There's nothing wrong with being gay, it's just you're so gorgeous, and it's hard to believe gorgeous people really like other gorgeous guys—." Enzo stared at her like she was insane, and Nicole, who had spoken too much, was embarrassed. Blushing, she nervously smiled and said, "Anyway, I think my food is here. Better get back to my table. Bye, Enzo!" Enzo awkwardly waved his hand as Nicole made her way back to her seat.

After a few seconds of silence she said, "Wow. I've flirted with and dated so many guys, and that's *never* happened before."

I almost jokingly assured her, "Don't worry, Nicole. It most likely won't ever happen again. After all, what happens in Europe stays in Europe." With that, everyone laughed, even the still speechless Nicole managed to crack a smile.

By the time we had finished our scrumptious meal, it was time to head back to the dock to be ready for the ferry's departure. We took the incline down, and made our way and waited for the boat. It finally docked, and we got in and sat in the exact same spots we sat before, with me once again sitting next to Elliott.

I turned to him and asked, "So what did you think of Capri?"

Elliott told me, "It was incredible! Beautiful views, adorable small town. And that food was quite delicious."

I kept wondering and waiting to see if he would kiss me or not like he and Ryan had been talking about. I decided to move in a little closer. "I'm sorry," I said. "Do you mind if I move in a little closer?"

Elliott said, "Oh no. Not at all. Make yourself comfortable."

We sat in awkward silence until Giovanni, the tour guide from earlier, came back. He cheerfully said, "Bonjourno people! Welcome back! How was Capri?" The crowd cheered, indicating to him they really liked it, and he said, "Fantastic! Are you all ready for the tour around the island?" The crowd cheered. "Alright," Giovanni said. "Let's get started!" And with that, we left the dock to begin our tour.

It started off with Giovanni talking about the history of Capri. I'll admit, I wasn't really paying attention, as I decided to slowly move my hand towards Elliott. He noticed, and he slowly intertwined his hand with mine. I probably shouldn't have done this, and I admit I later regretted doing it, but I decided to rub my leg against his, slowly. He saw this, gave a small smirk, and pretended to yawn. At first I thought that meant he was bored, but he actually only did it to put his arm around me, which made me smile brightly. Then we turned our heads towards each other, locked eyes. I was breathing slow breaths, and our lips slowly started to move to touch one another's, but Giovanni's enthusiasm prevented anything from happening.

He excitedly said, "Alright! We are now getting to this well known rock called Faraglioni! Anyone know what that is?" Nobody answered, so Giovanni said as he pointed to this large rock that had an archway, "That is it right there! The tradition is that when you go under this rock, you and your romantic partner have to kiss! If you don't have a romantic partner, then oh well! I will put on some music to create the mood, and be ready to kiss!"

As we approached the rock, the music started. Elliott and I turned to one another, gazed at each other once again. We got closer and closer, and I took my hands, cupped his face with my hands, my cold hands touching his warm face. He then took his own hands, slowly moved them down, and finally placed them on my waist, we continued to look at each other and breathe heavily. Giovanni said, "Ready, set, kiss!"

And just as he said that and we went under the rock, our lips locked for the first time. At first it was really awkward, as Elliott and I hadn't kissed each other before. Just a quick peck on the lips. I think I may have even kissed his lips and kissed a little on his chin instead. However, we tried it again, and our next kiss was truly a magical kiss, like something out of a fairytale, that's how it was in my eyes at least. Elliott's lips were soft, and they gently caressed mine. He moved me closer to him, and we continued to kiss more and more. Shivers crawled down my spine. I began stroking his hair and he moved his way up from my waist to my shoulders. It was as if the world had stopped, and we were the only people in the world. It was just like how we kissed in the dream, only much more special. Finally after what seemed like an eternity, our lips slowly separated, and we opened our eyes to look at each other. We both smiled and, based off of his facial expression, I think he enjoyed it too.

After a brief happy moment of finally kissing each other, we turned to see the entire boat staring at us. We looked back and saw we had been kissing even after we weren't under the rock anymore. I turned and saw all the different facial expressions. Grace looked somewhat shocked, although she was aware there was chemistry between the two of us since the beginning of the trip. Nicole looked proud of me for kissing someone like that in public. Esperanza smiled and seemed like she was happy for the both of us. Ryan also seemed happy that Elliott had gone for it and kissed me, and Connor and Ollie also looked happy because they wanted us to get together all along. The other people on the boat, including Giovanni, looked shocked, but also jealous to see Elliott Parker, who was everyone's dream future husband, kissing someone.

Elliott still had his hands on my shoulders, and my hands were still touching his face. Before we could quickly get back to normal, two teenagers, a boy and a girl, from behind snapped a picture of us and said, "We're gonna be the ones who confirm that Elliott Parker is dating someone!" They then were about to post it and then Elliott interrupted.

"Hey, I saw what you did!" he told them. "Delete those photos at once!"

"But we want pictures proving to people we met a celeb in person!" the boy said.

"Yeah," the girl added. "And we want to be the ones who find out and tell people about your new girlfriend!"

"Now look," Elliott told them. "It's one thing to go after me, because I'm famous, but no one knows who she is and I think she deserves her privacy just as much as I do!"

The teen girl muttered under her breath, "She isn't even that pretty."

Elliott was appalled by this and asked, "What did you just say?" I had heard her. And it made me feel bad.

"I said, she isn't even that pretty," the teen girl repeated.

The teen boy agreed and said, "Yeah, all she has to offer are big boobs and decent eyebrows." I was hurt by what they were saying, as it reminded of the bullies during middle school.

All of sudden, that set Elliott off and he pointed to the teens and said, "You have no right to speak about her that way! Not only is she beautiful, but she's compassionate, strong, funny, brilliant, and if you have a problem with her, then keep it to yourself!" I turned to Elliott and felt good that he was defending me like that, but he wasn't doing so with violence or anything physical. The teens were speechless, and Elliott told them, "Now please, delete the photos." With that, the teens showed him that they deleted the photos and they sat there silent. Elliott turned to me, saw I was hurt and put his hand lovingly on my cheek and said, "I'm so sorry about that. Don't listen to them."

I started to tear up a little bit and said, "No, they're right." I then started crying and said, "It's just like middle school. The bullies were right about me in middle school, and those teens are right about me now."

I looked down as I continued crying. Elliott took both of his hands, lifted up my face, and began to wipe away the tears with his thumbs. In a calming voice he assured me, "No you're not! Never say that!" I looked down once again, and he lifted my head up and said, "Hey, look at me!" And I looked straight into his eyes. "You are beautiful, both inside and out. You're so wonderful, Cecilia. Those bullies and teens were just jealous because of how incredible you are. You're kind, you have a good sense of humor, you are the most beautiful girl I've ever met."

I told him, "Thank you, but you don't have to say that to be nice, trust me."

"I'm not saying it to be nice," Elliott assured me. "I'm really speaking from the bottom of my heart! You heard me earlier, love, you're so special!" With that, I slowly stopped crying and Elliott kissed my forehead which caused me to smile. Then I wrapped myself tightly around him and he did the same.

"Oh, Elliott," I told him. "I feel the same way. I really do." After a moment of embracing and cherishing each other I whispered in his ear, "Are we still up for a walk on the beach?"

"Are you kidding," Elliott whispered back in my ear, "I wouldn't miss it for the world!" We both smiled at each other.

After all that, we continued to listen to Giovanni's tour and we finally got off at the dock. As we stepped off, Elliott and I couldn't help but hold hands and walk very close together. And that day, that kiss, would only be the beginning of what at least we consider the greatest love story ever told.

Chapter 8: Wishing For A Date

Until dinner, for some weird reason neither Grace, Esperanza, or Nicole brought up the kiss I shared with Elliott. After we got back from Capri, we all took naps, as the sun made us tired. Then at 8 o'clock, after naps and hanging out at the hotel's pool, we went to dinner at *Un Poi 'di Fantasia*, a fancy yet tiny restaurant near the hotel. It was so close that the walk only took thirty seconds. Unfortunately, Elliott and the boys would not be joining us because Ryan, Connor, and Ollie got sun poisoning (or in other words they got sick from the sun) and Elliott, being the great big brother he was, decided to stay home and take care of them. And unfortunately we had to cancel our stroll on the beach. So it looked like it was just us girls again.

We sat down at the restaurant and ordered. I was in the mood for some lasagna, so I got some. We took our drinks (I was the only one who didn't get wine), and made a toast to a great trip and great friends. Once we set our drinks down, Grace asked, "So, Cecilia, what was it like making out with my cousin?"

As she asked this, I was taking a sip of my water. I spit it back in the cup. I took my napkin, dabbed my mouth, and after placing it back on my lap, said, "Oh, yeah! I was wondering how long it would take you to say that."

"So," Esperanza asked, "which was better: kissing him in the dream or in real life?"

"Oh, definitely real life," I responded quickly. That was so easy!

"Are you in love with him?" Nicole asked me.

"It's too early for that, Nicole," I assured her. Then I turned to Grace and said, "And Grace, please know that if it gets weird for you at any point, we'll stop whatever this is that is happening."

"No," Grace assured me, putting her hand on my hand. "I love both of you, and I want the both of you to be happy. And I don't want you guys to break up because of me."

"Woah, break up?" I asked. "Grace, we haven't even gone on our first date yet!"

"Well, when will you go?" Nicole asked. "Where's he going to take you? Maybe a romantic candlelight dinner for two under the stars!" She said, "Oh, that would be *so* romantic!"

"Well, we were supposed to go for a stroll tonight after dinner, but because his brothers were sick, he had to cancel," I said annoyed.

"Don't worry about it, Cecilia," Esperanza assured me, "you still have plenty of days left in the trip. He'll take you on a date at *some* point."

"I guess you're right," I sighed. "I was just *really* looking forward to the romantic stroll on the beach tonight!" Then I quickly realized something, gasped, and excitingly said, "Maybe if we go on our date while in Italy we can eat spaghetti together, *Lady and the Tramp* style!

And then we end up eating the same noodle and kissing! It works on dogs, do you think it'll work on people?"

My friends laughed, and Nicole said, "There's our girl, loving Disney like she always does!"

Eventually, the food arrived, and my lasagna was so creamy and yummy! Grace asked me, "So, if things go well with Elliott, how are you going to deal with schedules once the trip is over?"

"Schedules? What do you mean?" I asked her.

"Well think about it," Grace said, "when the trip is over you'll be going your separate ways. He'll be going back to London, you'll be back in Maryland. Are you guys going to do long distance? And when are you guys going to find time to see each other?"

Nicole then added, "And he's going to be busy shooting his movies. Apparently he has eight new projects coming up, and according to IMDB, he's supposed to begin filming the new *Serpent Boy* movie in August and some World War II spy movie called *A Spy in Our Midst* later in the year," she said reading from her phone. She then set her phone down.

"And what about you, Cecilia?" Grace asked me. "Once the summer is over, you'll be busy with college. Then once college is over you'll have to get a job, and that job may or may not be far from him."

"Oh, I never thought about it that way," I said. I really hadn't.

"All we're saying is that it's something to think about," Nicole assured me.

"Why do you guys have to be such Debbie Downers?" Esperanza finally said after being silent the whole conversation. "Cecilia and Elliott just shared their first kiss and admitted they like each other. Can't they just have some time to be happy about that? Why shouldn't they wait to discuss their future toward the end of their trip?"

"I see your point, Esperanza," Nicole said to her.

"All we're saying is that it's something to think about," Grace said.

"I totally see what you guys are saying," I told them. I really hadn't thought about what would happen after the trip if things went well between Elliott and me. I sighed and said, "Okay, I'm going to take Esperanza's advice. I won't think about it until towards the end of the trip." All my friends nodded. However, as the trip went on, I would find it harder to not think about how we were going to do the whole "long distance relationship" thing.

******

By 9:30, we had finished dinner and were back at the hotel. I was still sort of bummed I wouldn't get to have my "late night romantic stroll" with Elliott, especially because we weren't going to any other beaches during the night and wouldn't have a chance to during the trip. I was in my pajamas, a black tank top and short lavender and gray shorts, when I plopped down on the bed exhausted. The other three girls were out on the balcony hanging out, and I was about to join them, when I heard my phone ringing, I looked at it to see who it was. It was my mom and dad! Boy was I happy to hear from them!

I answered the phone and said, "Hi Mommy! Hi Daddy!"

"Hey, sweetie," Mom said.

"How are you doing?" Dad asked.

"I'm doing okay," I told them. "We went to Capri today."

"How was it?" Mom asked.

"Oh my gosh it was *gorgeous*!" I said. "Cute little town. And we took a tour around the island, which was truly spectacular! I'm having the time of my life on this trip!"

"Glad to hear that," Dad said. "We were worried about you when we heard you got sick the day before, but it sounds like things are getting much better."

"Yes," I said. "They really are." I started blushing because I was thinking about Elliott, who was part of the reason the trip was getting better. I kept wondering if I should tell them about the kiss we shared and the growing feelings we had towards each other.

"So," Mom asked, "how are Grace's cousins? Are they nice? Well I know the one is because he took care of you after what happened at the Colosseum."

"They're all doing good," I said.

"*Well!*" my father, the grammar police, corrected.

"Even in Europe, I can't escape the grammar police!" I joked, causing my parents to laugh.

"How old are they?" my mom asked, changing the subject back to Grace's cousins. "What are their names?" Any more questions, Mom?

I told her their ages, "Elliott, the one who took care of me, is twenty-three, Ryan is seventeen, Connor is eleven, and Ollie is seven."

"Cool!" Mom responded. I hadn't told Mom about how Grace was related to Elliott Parker, and I figured now would probably be a good time to tell her. But then Mom said, "You know what's funny? I know for a fact that Grace's mom and her cousins' dad are sister and brother. And I know that Mrs. St. Valentine's maiden name is Parker, so that means the cousins' last name is Parker. And the oldest one's name is Elliott, right? So his name is Elliott Parker, like Serpent Boy! That's so funny!"

She had figured it out! *Good for her!* I thought. I then told her, "That's because her cousin *is that* Elliott Parker. And he's the one who took care of me after I got sick."

This caused my mom to laugh. "Is this a story you are writing?" she asked.

"Hey! I'm not making this up!" I tried to convince her. "They just don't really tell people because Grace doesn't want people to bug or tease her about it!"

"Prove it!" Dad finally said after being silent from the conversation.

"Is there a photo?" Mom asked. Actually, there was a photo of the two of us. The one those teen kids took of us kissing that Elliott made them delete. But of course I didn't say that.

"Tell you what," I told them, "later tonight or tomorrow I'll send you a photo to prove it! Okay?"

"If you say so," Mom said.

"Anyway," I said, "I better get some sleep. I've got another big day tomorrow. Good night! Love you both!"

"Love you too!" they said.

"Miss you!" Mom said.

"Good night!" Dad said.

"Give Janie a kiss from me," I said.

"Will do!" Dad said. And with that, they hung up.

I placed the phone by the side of the bed, and plopped my head down on the pillow, my head facing up to the ceiling. After about a minute, I picked up my phone and decided to make a bold and daring search on the internet. I typed in, "Elliott Parker." I figured if I was going to go on a date with this guy, I might want to learn a little bit about him. What first came up was new stories such as, "Elliott Parker Films *A Roman Romance* in Rome," "Elliott Parker Reveals New *Serpent Boy* Movie Will Begin Filming in August," and "Elliott Parker Talks His Love of Dance and Gymnastics, Pressures of Being Famous, and His Relationship With His Family." After scrolling through different news stories, I went to Wikipedia; his entry read:

Elliott Robert Parker (born 1 June 1996) is an English actor and dancer. He first began his career appearing in multiple West End productions before landing his film debut in the disaster drama *Disaster Earthquake* (2011). He went on to appear in multiple films such as *Waiting for Normal* (2012), *Sixteen* (2013), *Chariot Racing* (2015), and *Evening at the Ritz* (2016) before achieving global stardom and critical acclaim for portraying Jimmy Pressman/Serpent Boy in the 2016 film *Serpent Boy*, later reprising his role in *Serpent Boy 2* (2018). His other film credits include *The Edge of Yesterday* (2017), *The Story of How We Met* (2018), and *Perfect Picture* (2019).

I scrolled through and thoroughly read each significant detail on his Wikipedia page. I now knew everything about him. That he was the oldest son of George and Phoebe Parker; that he was of British, Irish, and German ancestry; that he had a background in dance and gymnastics; and so much more. And I watched interviews, read articles, and tried to get a sense of what his character was from what was online. Doing this for about an hour, I lost track of time and realized it was about 10:30. I looked out at the balcony and found the other girls still talking, and I decided to go out and join them.

Just as I was about to go out, I realized something. I saw the one golden sandal, the right one, I had worn last night, but where was the other one? I couldn't quite remember what had happened to it. So I grabbed the sandal I had and started looking around the room for it. After a few minutes of looking, I heard a knock on the door.

Who could it be at this hour? At 10:30 at night? I was still so frantic about losing the one shoe that I didn't think to bother asking who it was. Still holding the one shoe I had, I opened the door. It was Elliott! He had a small smile on his face, with his hands behind his back. He was wearing a burgundy open-collar shirt with vertical black stripes going down it, with dark green pants and white tennis shoes.

I could feel a big smile slowly start to appear on my face as I said, "Hello."

Elliott's smile grew bigger and brighter as he said, "Good evening, Cecilia."

I then asked him in curiosity, "What are you doing here? It's 10:30! And what about your brothers?"

He told me, "First of all, they're feeling much better. They are sleeping." He then slowly pulled out his hands from behind his back and said, "And I believe this belongs to you." He then revealed the left golden sandal from behind his back. I completely forgot! The sandal had slipped off my feet when I ran away from Elliott last night. Man, me losing my shoe while running away from "Prince Charming." Why did this sound so familiar? Just kidding!

Elliott then got down on one knee, took the shoe in both his hands, and said, "Allow me." Then I lifted up my left foot and allowed him to easily slip on the sandal, which caused me to smile because at that moment I was feeling like Cinderella. Elliott then got back up and asked me, "Did I do it correctly? Grace told me how much you love Disney so I was trying to recreate Cinderella." It flattered me so much that Elliott would think to do it. "So," he asked, "did it work for you?"

I put my hand on his shoulder and assured him, "It was *perfect*." As I took my hand off his shoulder, he smiled.

Then he asked me, "And if you don't mind, I think I'll take you for that walk now."

"But Elliott," I said, "it's so late."

"We'll make it quick," he assured me. "And I think I owe you."

"Alright," I agreed. "Can I get changed first?"

"Oh yes, of course," he said. "I'll meet you in the lobby in ten minutes?"

"Sounds like a plan," I grinned. We then said goodbye. As I closed the door, I squealed that I would be getting my walk, and turned to get ready for my date. As I turned around, I saw my three friends, who had apparently been watching the whole time, smiling.

"Awww," Esperanza said. "You've got it bad!"

"I can't believe it," Nicole said. "Cecilia is in love!"

"He likes you, Cecilia," Grace said. "I can tell." This caused me to smile and blush, which Grace pointed out, "Awww! Look she's blushing!"

I then responded with, "Can you blame me?" My friends were happy for me and smiled as I went to the bathroom to get changed.

****

Since I was meeting Elliott in the lobby in a few minutes, I didn't have much time to get ready. So I just put on a peach short-sleeved blouse and a flowy black mini skirt. Esperanza put my hair in a half-up-half-down style which only took ten seconds. After that I was on my way down to the lobby. And, of course, I had the golden sandals on.

I didn't bother taking the elevator, because it always took so long to come. So instead I rushed down the stairs, but as I came closer to the lobby, I walked slowly to make an "elegant" entrance. When I finally reached the lobby, I saw Elliott standing there, by the grand piano, and he looked a little nervous. He was feeling his palms to make sure they weren't sweaty. I couldn't believe he was nervous! He was such a Prince Charming with his charisma, sense of humor, and kindness! Why was he nervous?

I walked over to him and said, "Elliott! Hi!"

Elliott immediately tried to hide his nerves, put on a bright and happy smile, and said, "You're here!" Then after a brief awkward silence he asked, "Would it be weird if I kissed your hand? Or is that too lovey-dovey for you?"

"I like lovey-dovey!" I told him. He then politely took my hand in his and placed a kiss on it, then when he looked up, he smiled, which made me smile. As he let go of my hand I said, "Wow, I was right! You are a real life Prince Charming!"

"Is it just because I placed a slipper, or sandal, on your feet? Or is it because I'm apparently so polite?" he asked grinning.

"A little bit of both," I responded. "Anyway," I said, "Shall we go?"

Elliott then extended his arm and said, "We shall!" Then I locked his arm with mine and we walked out of the hotel towards the beach.

At this point, it was around 10:45, and outside was not busy at all. The moon was shining really bright and reflected on the clear blue water. Millions of stars spread across the nighttime sky, and Elliott and I were astonished by the beauty of that Italian summer night.

"It looks beautiful!" I exclaimed. "The moon, the water, the stars, the peace and quiet, everything! But of course there's the most beautiful thing of all that outshines the moon *and* the stars!"

Elliott turned to me and asked, "What?"

I turned my head to him and beaming I said, "My date!"

At first Elliott was confused and asked, "Your date?" Then I gave him the "Ah come on, you're smarter than that" look and he figured it out and smiling said, "Me!"

Seeing that no one was sitting at the dock, we decided to walk down to the end of it. We took off our shoes, sat at the edge, and dangled our feet over the water.

"I'm so glad this worked out," I said to Elliott, as we stared at the night sky. "And you said you've never been to the Amalfi Coast before?"

"I have not," Elliott said. "But I rather like it. The only places in Italy I've been to are Rome and Venice, but they were all for filming purposes and I didn't get to see too much. That's why when Grace asked me to come along with you guys, I was like 'Yes! Yes! Yes!' And I got really excited."

I laughed at how he sounded so excited about seeing the rest of Europe. We then continued to stare at the night sky, and Elliott reached his arm and wrapped it around my shoulder. I looked at him, gave a smile, and rested down deep into his chest.

"This is nice you know," he said. "In a way it's sort of an escape."

"An escape?" I asked. "What do you mean?"

"Well, being well known by many is not all that fun," he explained. "You constantly have to worry about the paparazzi and the fans at every corner. And you have to be careful with what you say and do, because that could ruin your whole reputation. It's nice to just be here, out in public, and not to worry about what people will do if they see you. You can just sit here, relax, and enjoy a romantic evening."

"Ooh romantic!" I sighed, looking up at his face and taking my head off his chest. With his arm still wrapped around me, he looked at me.

"What? Do you not think this night is romantic?" he started teasing. "The moonlight setting, hand kiss, and Cinderella moment weren't enough for you?" He then unwrapped his arm and continued teasing and said, "Alright, fine. We can leave. I thought you liked me." He then stood up and started to walk away.

I stood up and went along with the joke saying, "Oh no, no, no! It's so romantic! You hear me! It's the most romantic night I've ever witnessed!"

Elliott continued joking and said, "Doesn't seem that way!" He then started walking away again, and I closely followed him and called for him to come back.

Then, Elliott tripped on what seemed to be a rope or a crab net or something. He was about to fall into the water, he let out a small shriek, but I quickly grasped his hand before he could reach the water. I held him there, he smiled, and I pulled him closer to me. Once I pulled him in close enough, I gave him a heartfelt kiss, much like the one we shared before. I placed my hands on his waist as he placed them on mine. We then briefly pulled apart to catch our breaths, and stared deeply into each other's eyes, and just looked at each other for a minute.

Then he took his hand, and placed it under my chin. He pulled me closer in for another kiss, which I obliged by my hands making their way to his back. We briefly unlocked lips and I began to passionately kiss his cheek, and he started stroking my hair. We then pulled apart and stopped kissing. We smiled at how much we enjoyed kissing each other.

"You know something?" I asked him. I flirtatiously told him as I began massaging his shoulders, "You're a *really* good kisser."

Proud of himself, Elliott said, "Thank you! I appreciate that," as he began to put his hands on my waist.

I then asked in curiosity, "What about me? Am *I* a good kisser?"

Elliott developed a huge grin on his face, took a deep breath, and joked, "Eh, you're okay."

Knowing it was a joke, I playfully and lightly smacked my hand on his chest just as he started laughing. I couldn't help but laugh along, and he assured me, "I'm kidding, I'm kidding."

I whispered in his ear, "Now please tell me the truth!"

"You, my darling, are the best kisser in the entire universe!" he exclaimed. "You are magnificent! Superb! Truly talented in the field of kissing!" I laughed at how cute he was when he was polite.

"You're such a dork," I shook my head as I wrapped my arms around the back of his neck.

"A dork who's very much smitten with you," Elliott said, placing his forehead against mine. We stared deep into each other's eyes, and softly but passionately kissed each other again. Our lips moved in perfect sync with each other. We then slowly sunk down to the floor of the dock. I laid down on the dock, and while the dock was really hard, I was too invested in kissing him to notice. I cupped his face in my hands as I started to run my fingers through his curly hair. I lay in between Elliott's arms as he placed both his hands on each side of me. If you think you know where this is going, you would be completely wrong...

After about a minute or so of making out (don't worry, it was dark and nobody was around, so no one saw us!) I pulled my lips away from his and said in shock, "Wait! What are we doing?"

Elliott giggled and replied, "Kissing, you silly goose! Don't you want to continue?" He then went back to kissing me, only this time planting kisses all over my cheek.

I pushed his lips away from my cheek and said, "Wait! Stop!"

Elliott's smile faded to a concerned look. Still on top of me, he asked, "Is everything alright, Cecilia?"

"Yes," I said, still thinking. "I've just—we shouldn't be doing this." I quickly and frantically got up from under him, stood up, and started walking back to the hotel.

Elliott quickly ran after me and said, "Wait, Cecilia! Wait!" He finally caught up to me and stopped me, grabbing my hand and holding it. "If you thought that was going to go any further, I promise I am *not* that kind of guy. And I would *especially* never do anything like that in public! And I'm sorry it made it seem like I wanted to go further, and even if I did I would certainly ask you—"

I interrupted him and said, "No, Elliott! It isn't that at all. It's just, we shouldn't be doing this."

"Doing what?" he asked in confusion.

"You know what!" I told him. "We shouldn't be doing this. We shouldn't be kissing. We shouldn't be on this date. We shouldn't be together."

"What are you talking about?" Elliott asked even more confused putting his hands on my shoulders.

I took a deep breath, and said, "Elliott, we're different. You live in London. I live in Chestertown. You're a huge A-list movie actor. I'm a student at Washington College studying to be a writer. We shouldn't be together."

"Why does this all of a sudden matter to you?" Elliott asked. "You didn't seem to mind before. What changed your mind?"

I sighed, and told him, "At dinner we were talking and the girls were saying about how we might not be able to make this work. You'll be crazy with your movie schedule, and I'll be busy with college. We'll have to work out this whole schedule so that we can find time to see each other, and it will be a lot of hard work! So then what's the point? We should get back to the hotel. Good night, Elliott!" I started walking straight back to the hotel.

I only went a little further before Elliott grabbed my hand once again. "Wait, a minute! Cecilia!" He turned me around so I was facing him. He put his hands on my shoulders and said, "Don't listen to those girls. We may be busy, but we'll find to make it work. Long distance relationships can be hard, but you've got to remember I may be in Los Angeles, or New York, or any other part of the country for filming or promoting a film so I won't be totally far away most of the time. And why are we worrying about this now?" He took one of his hands and touched my cheek saying, "Can't we just enjoy our trip now and worry about how we're going to work long distance after the trip is done."

Looking down, I sighed, and looked up into his eyes and said, "But what if we aren't even right for each other? We barely know each other!"

"Look," Elliott said, placing his other hand on my other cheek. "I've been told I have good instincts. And my mum always told me that when I found 'the one' that I would feel it. And may I say, I can feel it."

"How do you know you can feel it?" I asked.

"Well, um," he was trying to think of how he could prove it to me. "Here," he then took my hands and placed them on his chest, right around where his heart is. "Do you feel that?"

I did. I felt a pounding. "Yes," I replied, looking at where he securely placed my hands. "I think it's your heart pounding."

I looked back up at him as he said, "Well that pounding is for you. Ever since I first met you, ever since you caught me being chased by those fans, I've had that feeling of pounding."

This made me smile. Never had I had a guy say something like this to me, and it sure did feel nice. I replied by saying, "Well let me show you something." I slowly let my hands go from his hands' grasp and took them. I placed his hands close to where *my* heart was. I told him, "Feel the pounding in my heart? It's for you."

Elliott smiled as he heard it. "Wow," he said after being silent for a moment. "That sure is fast!"

"I know," I winked at him.

"And must I say, darling," he said. I blushed red when he used that "d" word. "Your hair is soft like the finest silk," he said stroking my hair with his hands. "And

143

your eyes are like sapphires glittering in the night." I smiled and my heart began pounding even faster. "Now," he finally asked after a little bit, "as a writer did you think that was poetic and romantic?"

I lightly giggled, sighed, and said, "Lots of good similes." I then took my hands and wrapped them around the nape of his neck and said, "When I touch you, I feel like a spark of electricity has hit my body. And my heart is just about to pound out of my chest."

"Wow, Cecilia, you're good at this," he said, leaning in and kissing my left cheek. "And may I ask," he said, "Where did you learn all that eloquent writing language?" He kissed my right cheek and smiled at me waiting to answer.

"Years and years of practice in writing," I told him. "I've been writing since I was six. I've won an award for creative writing at both middle school and high school graduation. Not to mention various writing workshops, camps, and classes. Plus, I'm a student at Washington College, home to the Sophie Kerr Prize. Did I mention it is one of the most prestigious writing awards in the country?"

"Very impressive," Elliott said, putting his hands on my waist. "Very impressive."

"So," I then asked him, "where'd *you* learn *acting*?"

"Are you kidding me?" he asked me trying to be sexy. Smiling, he said, "I was born an actor, darling."

I once again laughed and said, "I mean, if you think that, then that answers one of my questions."

Elliott became curious and asked, "What question?"

I joked and said, "As to why you're not that good an actor. You think you don't need training, but you could actually use a lot."

Elliott knew this was a joke, and he went in on it. His jaw dropped wide and his eyes widened as if in shock. His expression made me burst into laughter. "Alright," he said. "If that's what you think, then I suppose I'm going to have to throw you in the water."

Then he scooped me up, similar to the way he had before, and jokingly started to walk towards the water to throw me in. I just knew he wouldn't do it, so still in a laughing fit, I said, "Wait! No! No! Elliott! No!" He then stopped me before we reached the side of the dock.

Still laughing, he assured me, "Don't worry, don't worry. I'm not going to throw you in. You're too beautiful to get wet."

"I know, I know," I said giggling. "And I'm joking about you being a bad actor. You are very talented."

"I was 98.9% sure you were joking," he said winking. "And I know something *else* you said you thought I was talented in." Still holding me, he leaned forward and kissed me, soft but passionate once again. After this kiss was done, he asked, "So, am I still a good kisser?"

"Uh huh," I nodded. A huge grin brushed across Elliott's face as I leaned in to kiss him again. I placed my hand on his cheek, and set one hand behind his back. We kissed even longer this time, deeply immersed in the kiss. It wasn't very steamy, but it wasn't very chaste either. Sort of in the middle. After kissing for who knows how long, we stared into each other's eyes once again and smiled. Then I asked, "Wait a minute, what time is it?"

Elliott checked his watch. "Oh my goodness! It's 11:15! My brothers are probably worried sick!" he said sort of worried, having totally lost track of my time. "We must be getting back."

"Oh of course!" I told him. "We have a big day tomorrow. Off to Positano and Materdomini!" I then realized he was still holding me and I said, "Um, but you should probably, um..."

"Awwww!" Elliott whined like a little kid. "Do I *have* to let you down?"

"Do you want some person to take a picture of us and have a headline be titled *Elliott Parker Caught Acting Lovey-Dovey Carrying Mystery Red-Head on the Amalfi Coast*?" I asked him.

He sighed and said, "Fair enough. All right." Then he set me down gently. And once my feet were on the ground, he lightly pecked me on the lips, much like our very first kiss only not as awkward. I placed my hand on my lips, the exact spot where he kissed me. A huge smile filled my face, as he leaned in to crash his lips onto mine once again. He held my face with his hands as he continued to kiss me.

I leaned back and pulled away from him completely and, being a tease, said, "Uh uh uh!," shaking my finger and smiling. "There will be plenty of time for us to kiss and show affection on this trip. But right now, you need your beauty sleep, Mr. Handsome Brit."

Crossing his arms, Elliott jokingly pouted and said, "Awww, you're no fun!" This made me giggle. He uncrossed his arms and said with a smile, "At least I like the nickname, Miss Beautiful American." This made me blush and grin. Oh, how charming and sexy and sweet he was! Sigh!

Finally, walking hand in hand, we made our way back to the resort. Our hands intertwined with each other, as if they did not want to be let go. We walked off the dock, through the street, and back to the hotel. We walked up the stairs, since the elevator in this hotel usually took so long. Being the gentleman he was, Elliott walked me back to my room. We didn't say a word the entire walk back to the hotel, as we were too busy reminiscing about the magical night and how much we liked each other.

As we finally made it back to my room, I sighed and said, "So, I guess this is it."

Elliott shrugged and said, "Yeah. I guess so." We still were holding each other really tightly.

"How can I thank you for a lovely night?" I asked him, now leaning against the hotel door.

"No need to at all," Elliott assured me, winking.

"No I feel like I must," I said. "Perhaps a kiss?" Elliott didn't hesitate as soon as I said this, leaning in and kissing me quickly and gently on the lips, then pulling away. As soon as we pulled away, we smiled at each other.

"Well, I do hope we can do something like this again, sometime during the trip," Elliott said, still with a huge smile on his face.

"Which one?" I asked him. "Kissing or the date?"

Elliott shrugged his shoulders, "Why not both?"

I chuckled, thinking of going on a date with him and kissing him again. "Oh, yes! We must!" I said. "Well, good night, Elliott."

We couldn't stop smiling. "Good night, Cecilia," Elliott said.

I took my key card and slowly opened the door. I slowly closed it as Elliott still stood standing there, smiling brightly. I finally shut the door and leaned against it. Everyone was sleeping at this point, but it was 11:26 now and I was still standing there, as if I had just woken up for a dream. I found myself still smiling.

I sighed. *What a day*, I thought to myself. *What a day*.

Chapter 9: Wishing For A Lemon Drink

The next morning, I woke up all happy and relaxed. I had such a wonderful day yesterday (I think you know why!) and I dreamt about Elliott all night! No dreams like the other night though, if you know what I mean... I hummed to myself as I kept my eyes shut and stretched to the side. After a few seconds I finally opened my eyes to start the day, only to find all three of my friends surrounding me, close to my face. I was startled.

"Oh my gosh!" I said, then sitting up. "What the heck? Do you guys *always* wake up people like this?! Smiling right in their faces?!"

"Oh no, of course not," Grace assured, "that would be creepy."

"Thank goodness!" I said. "I was starting to believe my friends were all weirdos."

Putting her hand on my shoulder, Nicole said, "Honey, I think we can all agree that we're weirdos." I nodded my head in agreement.

Nicole took her hand off my shoulder. Esperanza then plopped on the bed down in front of me, took my hands and excitedly asked, "So, how was your romantic Italian evening with the handsome movie star?"

Grace nudged her and said, "You mean *my cousin.*"

"Gosh, Grace," Esperanza said pretending to be annoyed. "Do you *always* have to remind us you're related to a famous movie star?"

Nicole quickly got back on topic and said, "So, anyway, how was the date with Elliott? We want to hear everything! And don't you dare leave out a single detail!"

Part of me really wanted to gush about how wonderful my date with Elliott was last night, but part of me didn't. I don't even know why. I guess probably just because it felt too personal and I wasn't ready to talk about it yet. So, I simply sighed and told them with a smile on my face, "It was very nice."

But the girls wouldn't take that answer. They wanted more. "And..." Grace asked.

Still smiling, I told them, "I said it was very nice."

"That's it?!" Nicole asked in disbelief. I nodded. "You stayed out with one of the biggest movie stars in the world right now until almost midnight, and you only thought it was *very nice*?"

"I think she's lying!" Esperanza said. Pointing, she said, "I see that smile! It was obviously more than very nice! Come on, Cecilia! What aren't you telling us?"

"That's all I'm going to say about that," I said, getting up to go to the bathroom and take a shower.

"Okay, Forrest Gump!" Grace jokingly told me. "What are you telling us?"

"That's not even the line, Grace!" Esperanza corrected. "It's *That's all I have to say about that.*"

"Does it matter?" Grace asked her.

"Uh, yeah it actually does," Esperanza told her. "You know that's one of my all time favorite movies!"

"Really? Since when?" Grace asked in disbelief. "Never have you ever in the how many years I've known you said *Forrest Gump* was one of your favorite movies!" At this point I had gone to the bathroom to take a shower, but I could still overhear their conversation.

Nicole interrupted them and said, "Stop! We gotta figure out what happened on that date! She's not telling us anything! Obviously she had a great time!"

"You don't think we know that?" Grace asked. "She hasn't stopped smiling since they kissed on the ferry."

"And I heard her humming *I Feel Pretty* in her sleep last night," Grace said. Of course she heard that! Grace had always been a really light sleeper, and I did have a dream where I was singing "I Feel Pretty" last night.

"Huh?" Esperanza asked confused.

"I Feel Pretty," Grace told her. "You know from that movie *West Side Story* that you go on and on about how much you hate." That's true. A few years ago Esperanza went on a whole rant about how she thought *West Side Story* was "extremely overrated."

"Oh so you remember the movies I *hate* but you can't remember the movies I *like*?" Esperanza said, bringing up the movie argument once again.

"Ok! We're back off topic again!" Nicole interrupted again. She tried to think of why I was so happy about last night, and after a moment she finally thought, "I think they've declared they love each other!"

"Oh but Nicole, it's too early," Grace assured her.

"Yeah it's only been," Esperanza started to say. Then she used her fingers to count how many days Elliott and I have known each other. She finally came up with: "Five days!"

"So what? Romeo and Juliet declared their love for each other the day that they met," Nicole pointed out. "And they married the next day, not saying Cecilia and Elliott got hitched secretly without telling us."

"Not a good example," Esperanza said.

"Yeah, and you know how Cecilia thinks Romeo and Juliet were idiots," Grace pointed out. That was true too. I thought Romeo and Juliet were the most idiotic characters in all of literature. They knew they couldn't have each other, but they went ahead and got married behind their parents' backs anyway. And they kept saying they loved each other, but if they loved each other then why did they do something that would deliberately upset their families behind their backs and kill themselves just because the person they were attracted to for only a few days had died or "died." I could go on and on about how *Romeo and Juliet* has such a bad message, but I won't.

"All I'm saying is Cecilia and Elliott seem to have a lot of chemistry with each other, and they only *might* have declared their love for each other," Nicole assured them. At this point I was out of the shower and listening by the door, a towel wrapped around my body. I thought and thought. I knew it was really early, but had I fallen in love with Elliott?

******

I still wouldn't tell them about what happened last night, promising to tell them later. We went down to the lobby to have some breakfast before heading to Positano for a few hours. After that, we would spend the night in Materdomini, and head to Assisi the next day. We would spend two nights in Assisi, a day in Florence, take an overnight train from Florence to Vienna and stay there for a day, then take the train to Salzburg and stay there for three nights, head to Germany and go see Neuschwanstein Castle and spend three nights in Munich, and then head home. This trip was going by fast, so I wanted to spend as much time with Elliott as I could, as we would be heading our separate ways once the trip ended. At least we had eleven more days together.

When we got down to the lobby, I saw Elliott and Ryan scrolling through their phones while Connor and Ollie were giggling about who knows what. They were the first ones to see us, and they immediately ran over to us screaming, "Hello!"

We all waved to them, smiling nervously as to what the two British children were going to do, and they asked us four girls to have a group hug with them, and that's what we did. Ryan and Elliott looked up from their phones. Elliott and I immediately locked eyes.

"Hey," he said, smile on his face.

"Hey," I said back, smiling as well.

"Hey," he said again.

"Hey," I repeated. We couldn't stop smiling and we couldn't keep our eyes off each other.

Ryan waved his hand in front of Elliott's face and said, "Uh, hello? Earth to Elliott!" We both immediately snapped out of our trances. The two brothers started to walk over to join us.

We had all separated from the hug at this point. Except Ollie kept his arms wrapped around my waist. "I missed you so much!" he said.

"I missed you too, Ollie," I giggled and patting his back. He wouldn't let go.

When he finally did, Connor ran over to Elliott and began pushing him further towards me. "Oh my goodness!" Elliott chuckled. "What on earth are you doing, Connor?"

"Come on, Ollie!" Connor said to his younger brother. "Push Cecilia together with Elliott so they can kiss!"

"Alright!" Ollie said. He did as his brother asked, and soon started pushing me towards Elliott. They kept pushing us close together.

"Okay, okay, okay," I said.

"You boys are so silly!" Elliott said.

And finally they pushed Elliott and I together so our faces were only inches apart. "Hello, Cecilia," Elliott said smiling as he looked up and down my face.

"Hi, Elliott," I grinned, looking at his soft lips and perfect shiny teeth. There are two British stereotypes proven wrong! Turns out Brits *do* have lips and *do* have nice teeth!

We turned around to the side as Connor and Ollie stood there, arms crossed. "Now what are you doing?" Connor asked.

"Kiss already!" Ollie said.

I turned back to Elliott and said, "Better do what they want."

"Kiss! Kiss! Kiss!" they started cheering, then Ryan joined in chanting, followed by my friends.

After all that cheering, Elliott and I gave each other a quick peck on the cheek.

Ollie's smile turned to frown and pouted, "That was it? What a disappointment!"

Connor turned to him and said, "What did you expect? They can't kiss like crazy in public?"

Ollie then pouted, "But they did it on the ferry! Ryan called what they did French kissing, and I don't even know what that is, but they did it!"

I turned over to Ryan, who had a worried look on his face. He then rushed over to the boys and put his hands on their shoulders, and laughed nervously.

Elliott, knowing what had happened, asked, "What did Ryan call the kissing we did on the ferry?" I was trying not to laugh, seeing Ryan look like he knew he was in the doghouse.

He quickly changed the subject and said, "Goodness, I'm hungry! What do you say we get some breakfast?"

Connor and Ollie quickly forgot about the kissing and ran into the dining room and cheered, "Yeah! Breakfast!"

As soon as they were out of sight, Elliott pointed to Ryan and said, "I'll talk to *you* later."

Ryan smiled nervously and quickly ran after his younger brothers. My friends then came in and crowded around Elliott and I.

"Well hello Elliott," Esperanza said, coming up next to him.

"Good morning, Esperanza," he politely replied back.

Nicole then came up to the other side of him, put her hand on his shoulder, and said, "You are looking very handsome today."

Elliott replied back, "Um, thank you, Nicole."

Nicole then looked at me, smiled, and said, "I know Cecilia certainly thinks so."

"Yes I do," I told her. Then I turned to Elliott and said, "You look handsome every day, Elliott."

Elliott winked at me and said, "Why thank you, Cecilia."

Grace then came up next to me and asked her cousin, "Now Elliott, Cecilia won't tell us *anything* about what happened on your date last night. She only said it was *very nice*. Could you perhaps give us more details?"

Elliott replied back, "Sure. Well you see, we..."

I interrupted him and said, "Okay, I'll tell you! We went down to the dock, kissed, cuddled, looked at the beautiful moonlit Italian night, and talked about life. There you go!" I told them.

"That's it?" Nicole said, sounding disappointed.

"That's it," I replied.

"Nothing special? No crazy fans or declarations of love?" Esperanza asked.

I simply said: "Nope."

"Gosh, Cecilia," Nicole said. "You really got our hopes up as to what you were hiding from us." She and Esperanza walked away into the dining room to join the boys.

Elliott and I looked at each other and giggled. Grace then told us, "Well from what *I* heard it sounded very romantic." She then walked away to join the others as Elliott and I were left alone.

He reached his hand out to me and said, "Shall we?"

I took his hand, intertwined my fingers with his and said, "Of course!" As we walked hand in hand to the dining room, I asked him, "So, how was your night?"

"Oh marvelous!" Elliott said. He decided to tease and said, "I just spent it with the most *beautiful* girl! You would have loved her."

I went in on the joke and was like, "Really? What was she like?"

Elliott continued joking and said, "Well, let's see. She was very, very beautiful, like I said before. She was very sweet, and kind. She was an incredible kisser, not to mention had a good sense of humor. And she kind of looked like you!"

I giggled, and kissed his cheek sweetly, and rested my head on his shoulder. When we walked into the dining room, the whole group was staring at us, in a good way though. We walked to the table and stood there.

Ryan got out of his seat smiling, pulled an empty chair from under the table and said to me, "Please, sit here miss."

I let go of Elliott and sat in the chair and said, "Thank you, kind sir."

He then turned to Elliott with a jokingly annoyed look on his face and pointed to the chair next to mine and said, "And you can sit there."

Elliott laughed and sarcastically said, "Nice way to treat your brother," as he sat in the seat next to mine.

We all eventually got up and got our breakfast from the buffet. I got some fruit and a croissant because I wasn't very hungry. We all sat down after getting our food, and started talking about our day.

"Raise your hand if you're ready for Positano!" Esperanza said. Every single one of us, including Esperanza herself, raised their hands.

"What's so great about Positano anyway?" Connor asked taking a bite of his cantaloupe. "Isn't it just like Capri?"

Grace, who was sitting next to her cousin, turned to him and said, "Well, Connor, Positano has shops, a beach, and is known for having a lot of lemons!"

"Lemons?!" Ollie asked in disgust. "I don't like lemons! They're too sour!"

"Then you can get something like a t-shirt with a lemon on it," Grace said. "And did you know Positano is a village and commune in Campania, Italy?"

"Wow! You're so smart!" Ryan told his cousin.

"Valedictorian right there," I said. "Just like my mom."

"Oh trust me," Grace said. "I don't know how I was valedictorian! There were *so many* smart kids in our grade."

"Because unlike the rest of the kids you didn't slack off during senior year," Esperanza gritted her teeth, annoyed.

Nicole turned to her friend and assured her, "We kept telling you that grades were important senior year! You wouldn't listen."

I turned to Elliott and caught him up: "Esperanza had the highest GPA in our grade. But she got a bad case of senioritis and was salutatorian instead."

"Oh!" Elliott nodded. He then turned to Esperanza and said, "Well at least you got salutatorian. My mate from school, he did the same thing, only he came in late almost everyday and almost didn't graduate."

Nicole told Esperanza, "And at least you weren't Tyler Ludgate."

"Who?" Elliott asked in confusion.

Nicole said to him, "There was this guy, who I dated for a few months junior years, Tyler Ludgate. Such a ass--- jerk. Anyway, every year in May we have a joint Mass in the beautiful gardens on our school property, looking over the creek, where the high school and elementary school come together. As soon as the Mass was done, he jumped into the water."

"Couldn't walk down at graduation," I added.

160

"Oh my goodness," Elliott said.

"I'm surprised he didn't get his scholarship to Yale taken away," Grace said.

I turned to Connor and Ollie and said, "Kids, the moral of the story today is, if you get a special scholarship from a big time school, don't mess it up."

Nicole then asked, "Did you go to college, Elliott?"

"I actually didn't," Elliott said.

"Now please tell me you at least finished school," Esperanza said. "A lot of actors drop out of high school before finishing, and I wasn't sure if you did that."

"Esperanza!" I whispered to her, getting a little annoyed that she said that.

Elliott turned to me, placed his hand on my shoulder, and said, "It's okay, love." He then turned to Esperanza and said, "I actually did finish school for that very reason, Esperanza. I had heard of many actors who had dropped out of school, and later regretted it. I knew I wouldn't want to regret such a thing, so I finished at a performing arts school in Croydon."

"Croy what now?" I asked, never having heard the name before.

"Croydon," Elliott repeated. He turned to me, smiling, and said, "It's in London, darling."

That wonderful word. Darling. I could hear him call me that all day! Darling.

Esperanza gasped. She then turned to Nicole and said, "Did you hear what he just called her, Nicole?"

Nicole nodded and said in a fake British accent, "Darling." Elliott and I were both blushing crimson red, me looking down and smiling.

"Is that your new favorite word, Cecilia?" Grace asked me.

I lifted up my head and looked at her. Before I could respond, Elliott told his cousin, "Actually, I think I know what her *real* favorite word is!"

I turned to him. In curiosity, I asked him, "And what would *that* be?"

He turned to face me, winked, and joked, "Elliott."

I corrected him and laughing said, "That would be my favorite *name*. You're not a word."

Elliott then realized his mistake. "Oh, right," he said in embarrassment.

I wrapped my arm around his shoulder and said, "You're such a dork. And cheesy." Then I paused, smiled, and said, "I love it!" This made Elliott smile as well, and we leaned in and gave each other a very quick peck on the cheek.

Grace decided to tease us and act disgusted. Waving her arms, she said, "Ew, ew, ew, no, no, no!" She then wagged her finger at us and said, "Save it for later, you two." This caused us both, and everyone at the table, to laugh.

After we had finished our breakfast, we went back upstairs to grab our suitcases. A few minutes later we were back down in the lobby and ready to head to Positano. What we were planning on doing was taking a bus that would keep our bags with them, and then take us to Materdomini. But little did we know that Elliott had a special surprise for us.

We looked around and, seeing there was no bus, Ryan asked in confusion, "Where's the bus that's taking us to Positano?"

"Yeah," Esperanza said, "wasn't there supposed to be one of those big coach buses, kind of like the one that took us from Rome to Pompeii to Capri?"

Elliott, with a small smirk on his face, "Actually, there's been a change of plans."

Grace turned to her cousin and asked, "What have you done now?"

Elliott assured his cousin and said, "Don't worry, don't worry, it's a good change of plans."

Just then, he pointed to a long black limo pull up in front of the hotel. When it stopped, the door opened to reveal a man stepping out of the car, closing it after he was outside. He was extremely tall, about 6"4 or even taller, wearing a clean tuxedo with sunglasses. His hair was dark, almost black, and he had his hands behind his back. He looked so stern and serious, almost like a bodyguard. We were confused as to why he was here.

Elliott then took my hand, intertwining his fingers with mine, and used the other hand to motion us to come. "Come along guys!" he said excited. "This is the surprise." Still holding my hand, he rolled his suitcase with his other hand, and I rolled mine with my other while still holding onto him tightly. We all grabbed our suitcases and rolled them down the ramp as we walked toward the limo. All of us were so confused as to what was going on, including me. When we made our way to the limo, we stood there, looking at the tall driver.

Letting go of the suitcase but still holding my hand, Elliott smiled and said to the man, "Lawrence! Thank you so much for doing this!" The man, Lawrence, didn't say anything, he didn't even smile. He just nodded his hand. Not gonna lie, Lawrence was kind of giving me the creeps.

"Hello Lawrence!" Ollie said cheerfully.

"Hi!" Connor said soon after.

"So good to see you, Lawrence," Ryan politely said.

Elliott then began introducing us. "Lawrence, this is my cousin Grace," he said pointing to Grace.

"Hi, Lawrence! So nice to finally meet you," Grace said politely. "I've heard so much about you." Once again, Lawrence just nodded.

Elliott continued introducing us, "And these are her friends." He pointed to Nicole and said, "This is Nicole."

Nicole waved as said, "Hi, Lawrence! I've always wanted to meet a limo driver. I've always wanted to *ride* in a limo!" Still, Lawrence just nodded, not even giving a small hint of a smile.

"This is Esperanza," Elliott continued, pointing to Esperanza.

"Hey, Mr. Lawrence," she waved. "Or should I just say Lawrence?" Once again, a nod from Lawrence.

"And *this*," he said, looking at me and squeezing my hand tightly, "is Cecilia."

I nervously waved my hand and said, "Hey!" Lawrence nodded *again*! I decided to try and get a response from him by saying, "How are you doing today Lawrence?" No answer. Worth a try.

Then Elliott introduced us to Lawrence, "Guys, this is Lawrence. He drives me to premieres, press tour events, and all that other stuff."

"Ok now what's going on Elliott?" Grace asked, putting her hands on her hips.

"Well," Elliott said, "I thought all of you would have fun riding in a limo in Europe, instead of one of those bloody buses. Lawrence will be driving us all over to our destinations." Oh my gosh. This guy! I was squealing inside.

I turned to him and said, "Oh Elliott, you shouldn't have."

"Oh my gosh!" Nicole said with excitement. "We get to ride in a limo?! In *Europe*?!" A bright smile plastered on her face, she said, "How boujee!"

All of a sudden, all grew silent. What kind of word was boujee?

"Boujee?" Grace asked her.

"What kind of word is that?" Esperanza asked.

Before Nicole could respond, I said, "We can talk about that later! Let's get in the freaking limo!" I was anxious (in a good way) to get into the limo. I had never been a limo before, and it was on my bucket list.

And with that, Lawrence helped us put our suitcases in the trunk of the car. As he as doing this, we started getting into the limo. Inside it was spacious, black leather seats all around. What looked to be a mini fridge was set in the middle of the "room," which was mostly room for us to spread our legs. It wasn't much, but I don't think any of us cared.

Nicole was the most excited of us. "This is real freaking cool!" she said in amazement. She was the first to step in, sitting at the far end of the car. "Thank you very much, Elliott," she said, remembering her manners. "This is a dream come true!"

At this point, Elliott was still holding my hand as he said, "Of course, Nicole. Anytime!" He then briefly let go of my hand, which made me pout. When he saw my face, he turned to me and said, "Don't worry, Cecilia, I'm just helping other people in the car." As he was saying this, he assisted Grace going into the limo by touching her back and having her climb in. He did the same to Ollie, followed by Connor, Ryan was next, and then Esperanza.

After everyone had gone in, he helped me in the car, and I slide all the way in so I was sitting next to Esperanza. Finally Elliott got in and sat next to me, holding my hand once again. I quickly turned to him and he asked, "There? Are you happy now?" With a bright smile I quickly nodded, and Elliott said, "Good. Glad to make you happy." And with that, he gave a soft kiss on my cheek, which led me to put my head on his shoulder.

"Awww," Esperanza said. "You guys are so cute!"

"Thank you," I smiled to Esperanza. Then I joked, "Now where's *your* boyfriend?"

Esperanza then gave me an evil glare and said, "You know, if there weren't children here, I would be giving you the finger right now!" I playfully stuck my tongue out at her as I continued to rest my head on Elliott's shoulder.

Meanwhile, Nicole turned over to the window that showed Lawrence in the driver's seat. "Hey, Lawrence is it?" she said to him. "You know what I'm going to do? I'm going to try to get you to talk! Hear that?! I'll get you to talk if it's the last thing I do! I'm going to—." And just as she was talking, Lawrence rolled up the window so that we could no longer see him. Nicole sounded disappointed when she said, "Oh, okay. There's that too."

Ryan chuckled and, as he found two blankets in the compartment for Connor and Ollie who had fallen asleep, said, "Believe me, we've been trying to get Lawrence to talk for years now. He won't say a peep."

167

Nicole looked at the window and said in a dreamy voice, "Lawrence is kind of cute. Isn't he?"

"Sure," Elliott said sarcastically. He then added, "He's also like forty years old or something."

And with that, Nicole snapped out of her dreamy phase and said, "Ew, okay, never mind."

Soon, we were on our way. I briefly lifted my head from Elliott's shoulder to look as we drove away from our hotel. Oh, how I'll miss that place. But of course I was excited to see the rest of Europe. Italy, Austria, Germany, time with my girls, and spend time with Elliott of course! I rested my head on his shoulder once again, as took his hand from mine and wrapped his shoulder around me, pulling me in tightly. His arms were so soft as muscular, he was a well-built guy.

******

After driving for about forty minutes, we had finally arrived in Positano! It was an adorable seaside town, very old-timey. There were hills everywhere, as we noticed when we would walk. Where there weren't hills, there were stone steps to get to the different levels of the town. The buildings were very old-timey, and it looked like something out of a cheesy Italian romance movie. Because they were known for growing lemons, there were plenty of souvenirs with lemons on it. There were lemon purses, lemon plates, lemon perfumes, lemon dresses, anything lemon you could imagine! I wonder if this town ever gets tired of being associated with lemons.

The limo finally came to a stop at a nearby gas station, just at the entrance to Positano. I was still tightly holding Elliott's hand. Connor and Ollie were still sleeping, heads on each other's shoulders. It was so darn cute!

Ryan woke them up by lightly tapping on their shoulders saying, "Connor. Ollie. Psst. Wake up. We're here."

Ollie slowly fluttered his eyes open, whereas Connor opened his right away. "Are we in Capri?" a still sleepy Ollie asked his older brother. Ryan nodded.

"Yay! Finally!" Connor said.

Grace joked, "You two sleepy heads slept the whole way!"

"They must have been tired," Elliott said. "Which I don't quite understand why. All three of you went to sleep at 7 p.m. last night!"

"Well actually—" Ryan started to say, until Lawrence opened the door for us.

"Hey Lawrence!" Esperanza said. "How was the drive?" she asked, trying to get a response from him.

But of course, Lawrence didn't say anything. He just stood by the doorway and waited for us to get out of the car. Elliott dragged me by the hand and helped me get out of the car.

"Thank you, kind sir," I said in an extravagant voice.

"Anything for you, darling," Elliott replied politely, then kissed my hand, which made me grin. Finally, he let go of my hand to help other people out of the car, one by one, which caused me to pout again. Elliott saw my face and joked with a cheeky grin, "Jealous I see?"

I held my fingers slightly apart to show a small amount and said, "Maybe a little."

Once we were all out, Elliott thanked Lawrence, "Thank you very much, Lawrence. Meet you back here at 2:30?" Lawrence only nodded (shocker!), and we all said our goodbyes. As we walked away from the car, we waved to Lawrence, and we were surprised when he waved back.

After we had finally entered the town of Positano, we looked around in amazement at all the old buildings, shops, stone streets, and so much more!

"Who here brought their bathing suits?" Nicole asked. All but one of us raised our hands. We had each brought a little sling bag that contained our bathing suit, in case we wanted to go to the beach. Everyone except Elliott.

"You didn't bring a bathing suit, Elliott?" Grace asked her cousin.

Elliott looked a little embarrassed. He didn't say anything until he finally said, "Actually, um, I forgot to bring a bathing suit on the trip."

"Classic Elliott," Ryan said to himself, "always forgetting stuff."

"That's alright," I told Elliott, putting my hand on his shoulder. "We might not even go in the water anyway, so you don't need a bathing suit." This made Elliott smile. I think I made him feel better.

"Anyway, let's go!" Ollie said, growing impatient.

And off we went! We walked through the streets and stopped in several shops. All us girls pitched in to buy lemon candy at one lemon store. And to be honest, it wasn't very good. We stopped in one store where every one of my friends got something for their mom, all except me. My mom did love lemons, but she always said she would never wear anything with lemons because of how it would look weird with her blonde hair.

Finally, after about an hour of shopping, we went to the beach. We had to pay to use the bathroom to change into our bathing suits when we went to the beach. I was kind of disappointed. It was like in Capri and the Amalfi Coast where the beach was made of rocks. Luckily Connor had brought his big *Serpent Boy* towel (wonder who gave him *that*) and all of us could sit on it. The girls were suntanning, the brothers had gone to explore some more, and Elliott was sitting with us.

And everyone was feeling great, except Elliott. Who was sweating, most likely from having his shirt on. Okay don't get me wrong, I really like Elliott, but who wears a short sleeve black shirt and jeans when in Italy? Or who wears that in the summer in general?

I started to be concerned and asked Elliott, "Um, Elliott, are you hot?"

Elliott decided to turn that into a joke and said with a smirk, "I thought you thought so."

I giggled and said, "No, silly, I meant is the heat bothering you?"

He finally admitted, "Actually, a little I suppose."

I knew one possible way he could be cooler was to take off his shirt, but I didn't want to say that to him, as I feared sounding rude. Instead I said, "You know one thing you might want to consider is—" having to try to give him a hint. "You know..."

"Taking off my shirt?" Elliott asked. I nodded. "Are you sure it's okay?"

"Elliott," I told him, "you are on a beach in Europe and there are shirtless guys *everywhere*. And there are other beaches where the *women* are *topless*. So I think you're okay."

Elliott nodded, and then stood up. Why he was standing up, I don't know? But as he slipped his black shirt over his arms, to me it was like I was watching it in slow motion. I had seen him shirtless in the movies so many times, and now I was actually seeing it with my own eyes. And can I say, he looked *so* good. His chest was toned with a fine-looking six pack, and it was as if his muscles were flexed even more. I could even feel a little drool run down my chin, but I quickly wiped it off. I won't go into more detail about how my hormones were responding, because I want to keep this book rated PG-13!

Anyway, after he had finally taken off his shirt all the way, Elliott sat down next to me, wrapping his huge, muscular arm around me. "I feel so much better now," Elliott said feeling relaxed. But I couldn't keep my eyes off his body.

The girls, who had been laying down finally sat up, and they all turned to face Elliott. Of course, Grace didn't really care much, since he *was* her cousin. But Nicole and Esperanza looked amazed, their jaws dropped and everything. "Was it getting so hot that you took off your clothes, Elliott?" Nicole asked.

"Yes," Elliott replied, pulling me into him while he was still looking at the ocean, enjoying the view. I don't think he could see that I had my eyes fixed on him, and it's probably better that way.

Esperanza, who was fascinated with my fascination with Elliott, jokingly asked me, "Enjoying the view, Cecilia?"

With that, I quickly turned my head to look at the ocean, just as Elliott turned to look at me. "Yes," I stuttered. "It's very—it's very—it's pretty."

Elliott turned to all us girls and asked, "I saw back at the bar they have some lemon slush drinks that looked *delicious*! I'm going to go get one. Anyone thirsty?"

Everyone shook their heads. Esperanza said, "Um, no I'm okay. But I think Cecilia is *very thirsty*."

I quickly turned to Esperanza and said in disgust, "I am not! Shut up!" Then I realized I overreacted, I laughed in embarrassment and turned to Elliott and said in a calmed down voice, "I mean, I am very thirsty. I would love a lemon drink. Thank you."

Elliott smiled at me and said, "Alright. I'll be right back." He then quickly gave me a quick peck on the cheek, stood up, and walked to get the drinks. I turned myself to face the ocean, still in awe of what I had seen.

Nicole, who was sitting next to me, loudly whispered in my ear, "Now that's what I call USDA prime choice. There's certainly going to be no salad in *your* diet, Cecilia." Grace and Esperanza heard this and started laughing, as did Nicole.

I turned to her in disgust and said, "Guys! Shut up!" I then calmed down and started blushing.

Grace pointed out, "With that blush on your face, something tells me that you liked that comment."

"Just as much as you like that bod!" Esperanza added.

"And I thought I saw a little drool come from your mouth," Nicole teased.

I turned to them again and said, "Okay, sure I did. But how can I help it? I'm a female. I have hormones! I can't help it!"

"One of my best friends has hormonal feelings for my cousin," Grace said to herself. "That's a sentence I never thought I'd say."

"To be fair," I said to Grace, "I'm sure he has hormonal feelings too!"

"True," Grace nodded in agreement.

A few minutes later, Elliott came back, carrying two lemon slush drinks. Both of them were in tiny glasses and a tiny white flower inside. Smiling, he handed one to me. "Here you go," he said.

"Thank you, Elliott," I said as he sat down next to me.

"Of course," Elliott said. "Anytime." I looked at my drink, and was about to take a sip until Elliott raised his drink and said, "Cheers!"

"Cheers!" I raised my cup, our two glasses clinking together.

We then turned and looked at the ocean. After a brief moment, Elliott asked, "So, do you like the view?"

"Oh yes it's gorgeous!" I replied.

Elliott turned his to look at me. With a smirk he said, "That's not what I meant."

Confused, I turned to him and asked, "Well what do you mean?" Elliott gave me the, "Oh come on, you know what I mean" look. You know the look your mom gives you when you ask what something means in a movie, but she knows that you know it's a sex joke?

"I think you know what I mean," Elliott said, looking at me smiling.

"No, I actually don't," I say, trying not to crack a smile and blush.

Elliott pointed to me and still smiling said, "I see that smile, darling. You knew exactly what I was talking about!"

I still decided to play along and said, "No, Elliott, I promise I didn't!" Then I decided to give the classic puppy dog eyes and have my bottom lip pop out. In a cute, sweet, innocent voice I said, "Why don't you believe me?"

Elliott sighed and, still smiling, wrapped his arms around me, pulled me close to his chest and said, "I can't stay mad at you!" He then leaned in and kissed me very quickly on the lips. We then pulled away, looking at each other, and he unwrapped his arms from me. Then I pulled him to kiss him once again, rather long and passionately. It was very heated, both the kiss and the temperature.

Nicole noticed us and said, "Uh, wanna get a room?" This caused us to break away from the kiss and laugh at what Nicole said.

For the next few hours or so, we just basically relaxed and eventually we got lunch. Then around 2:30, Lawrence picked us up and we were on our way to Materdomini.

Chapter 10: Wishing For Elliott To Be Sober

The drive to Positano took an hour and a half, which included stopping to go to the bathroom, and by 4:00 p.m. we had arrived in Materdomini. I didn't really know much about Materdomini, except that it was apparently home to the Shrine and Basilica of St. Gerard, the patron saint of pregnant women. I know this because when my mom and dad were having a hard time getting pregnant, they prayed every night to St. Gerard for a child, and the rest is history. I was very excited to see the shrine and basilica for that reason, but I was also going to try my best not to cry because of how much it meant to me.

When we finally came to a stop in a parking lot, I noticed there was no hotel in sight. Looking out the window, I tried to search for it.

I wasn't the only one to notice the missing hotel. Ollie asked, "Where's the hotel?"

Elliott then put a hand on his brother's shoulder, and pointed to a very small building that was hidden, and said, "That right there!"

"I can't see it!" Connor complained, trying to look for the hotel his older brother was pointing out.

"You'll see it when you get there," Elliott assured Connor.

Lawrence finally opened the door to the limo to let us out. One by one, we all exited the limo. Lawrence handed us the luggage from the trunk, and all of us, including Lawrence, began walking towards the hotel. We rolled our luggage down the stone road, the luggage bumping. We finally reached the hotel; it wasn't much, just a white stone building accompanied by two glass doors. We opened the doors, and there were a few small steps in the doorway leading up to the main lobby. So we had to carry, or should I say drag, our suitcases up the stairs. Ryan helped Connor with his and Elliott did the same to Ollie. We finally reached the lobby. There was a little waiting room with a few comfy chairs and a wooden bench surrounding a red wood table, and the front desk was right next to the elevators and stairs. On the other side was a hallway that lead to the restaurant (where we would be eating!) and bathrooms. And it was so stuffy in here, and there wasn't even a fan. *How can people work in this?* I wondered.

Once we had all made our way up the stairs, we walked to the front desk. Standing there was a young man and a woman. The man was tall, very skinny, with slicked back dark hair, and the woman had dark hair pulled up in a tight bun and was very slender. Both had their uniforms on, which were white blouses with black pants and a black skirt.

Grace stepped up to the front desk and asked, "Um, hello, reservation under St. Valentine?"

Elliott then stepped next to his cousin and added with a smile: "And Parker!"

But the man or woman didn't say one word in response. They just stood there, looking at us with blank faces. "Do you not know English?" Grace asked them. But the man and woman just looked confused.

Elliott turned to his cousin and assured her, "Allow me!" He then turned to the woman and man and said very naturally, "Ciao. Abbiamo due prenotazioni, una sotto St. Valentine e l'altra sotto Parker." (If you don't know Italian, that translates to: "Hello. We have two reservations. One under St. Valentine and the other under Parker.") My eyes opened so wide, and I turned to Nicole and Esperanza who were just as shocked. Was Elliott fluent in Italian?

The two workers understood perfectly, and smiling, the man handed him and Grace two keys as the woman said, "Ah sì! Goditi la permanenza!" ("Ah yes! Enjoy your stay!")

Elliott smiled and replied, "Grazie," to which the woman and man nodded. He handed one of the keys to Grace.

"Thank goodness you can speak Italian," Grace said. "I don't know what we'd do if we didn't have a translator on this trip."

"I didn't know you could speak Italian," I said to him.

Elliott looked a little embarrassed by it, blushing and nervously laughing. "Um, yes," he said. "I took it in school and I guess I was good at it. I have no idea how, but I passed."

Ryan nudged me and said, "I think he just wanted to impress the ladies. And, from the way you're reacting, it seems like it works."

Elliott chuckled and said, "That's not the only reason I took it!"

Ryan asked, "Oh really? Then why *did* you take it? Hmm?" We all turned to Elliott and waited for him to respond.

He tried to come up with an answer. "Um, well, uh, you see. Um."

After a little bit, Ryan said, "Ha! I knew it!"

"Anyway," Grace said breaking up the brothers, "let's go to our rooms."

And with that we walked up the stairs to our rooms. We were only up two floors and there weren't that many stairs, so it was easy. The stairs were a boring, dirty white color and the walls were an ugly shade of mustard yellow. We finally reached the top, and I couldn't believe my eyes, but not in a good way. Whereas the last hotel was a gorgeous resort, this was as if I had been transported to a mental institution. There was a long corridor—erm, hallway—that was the same shade of mustard yellow. A closed window was right at the end of the hallway, and three doors lined each side of the hallway.

"Oh gosh," Nicole said sarcastically, "I thought we were checking into an Italian hotel, not the mental institution from *One Flew Over the Cuckoo's Nest*."

"What about a cuckoo nest?" a curious Ollie asked, not understanding the pop culture reference.

Esperanza, who always tries to look at the positive side of everything, said, "It's not that bad. Maybe inside our rooms is better."

"Alright," Elliott said. Pointing to the middle door on the left side said, "I believe this is our room."

Grace pointed the door on the right that was closest to the window and said, "This is our room."

We then separated to check out our rooms. It was similar to the way it was on the Amalfi Coast, where the girls were in one room and the boys were in another. After Grace turned the key to unlock it, she opened the door to reveal our suite of two rooms. The first room had one large bed on the left, with a closet on the side, a window in the middle, and a tiny TV. The next room had two smaller beds with a window on the side, and contained a bathroom with the tiniest shower you had ever seen. The size and amount of everything was no problem, but there was no air conditioning. No fan. Not to mention the room was like an oven!

"Oh my gosh!" Nicole said. "I miss our last boujee hotel! I miss that resort!"

"It's not totally bad," Esperanza said. She pointed to the big bed and said, "That's a nice big bed."

"That's the other thing," Grace pointed out. "There's four of us and only three beds."

I came up with the solution: "Easy! Two can share the big bed, and two can sleep in the two separate beds."

"Who's gonna sleep where?" Esperanza asked.

"Easy," Grace quickly responded. "These beds are tiny. Esperanza and I are the shortest, so we get the two beds, and because Nicole and Cecilia are taller, they get the big one." That was true. Grace was the shortest of us being 5"1, Esperanza was 5"4, I was 5"6 and a half, and Nicole was 5"10.

"Uh, no no no," Nicole said shaking her finger. "Cecilia kicks in her sleep. I know that from sleeping next to her at sleepovers."

I crossed my arms with a shocked expression on my face. "I kick in my sleep and you never told me!" I said.

"I'm sorry, Cecilia," Nicole said. "I didn't want to be rude."

"It's just for one night," Grace told her. "You'll survive."

"Yeah it's okay, Cecilia," Nicole said. "I really don't mind. And I talk in my sleep, so it's a trade-off."

"Yeah, you do," I said, "I noticed that but I didn't want to be rude."

After that, we unpacked. It was hot and stuffy in the room, but we agreed we would figure out that problem later. We met the boys outside in the hallway.

"How is your room?" Elliott asked us.

"Stuffy with no air conditioning or fans, and only three beds," Nicole said annoyed. "How about you guys?"

"Pretty much the same except it's two beds for the four of us," Elliott said. He sarcastically said, "So much fun!"

"What time is it?" Grace asked.

Ryan looked at his phone and said, "4:23."

"Oh Mass is at 4:30!" Grace said, referring to Mass at the Basilica of St. Gerard. "We better get there! Go! Go! Go!" she said quickly, running to the stairs and down. Instead of running, the rest of us walked really fast.

The basilica was right next to the hotel, and by the time we got there it was 4:27, but that was also partially because Grace was making us run. That girl never likes being late!

We walked into the basilica, and it was gorgeous. Almost everything was white with an altar at the front and the uncorrupted body of St. Gerard himself to the side in a glass case. In front of the altar was a shrine made of white stone. It consisted of St. Gerard carrying a brown cross and talking to a crowd of people and a few angels.

Mass was nice, but none of us (except Elliott) could understand the priest because he was speaking in Italian. This caused me to doze off a bit during Mass, and it turned my attention to a statue of St. Gerard on the side. It made me think of my parents and how they prayed to him every night for a year until they found out my mom was expecting me. I started to think of how my parents felt, both while they were praying and when they heard the joyful news, and it caused me to tear up a little. Elliott must have seen me out of the corner of his eye, as he turned toward me and had a sympathetic look on his face.

Starting to stroke my back, he whispered in a calming voice, "Is everything alright, love?"

Still looking at the statue, I turned straight to Elliott and assured him, "Oh yeah, everything is fine." I took a deep breath, wiped a tear off my cheek, and whispered, "It's just that when my parents were having a rough time getting pregnant, they prayed to St. Gerard for a year until my mom got pregnant with me. So he and this basilica are just important to me, I guess. I don't know, it's stupid."

"It's not stupid at all," Elliott continued whispering. "You know how I have a huge family back in Ireland, right?"

"Mmmh," I nodded. "I read it on your Wikipedia page." I realized that sounded stalker-ish and I apologized. "And now you probably think I'm a stalker. I'm sorry."

Elliott chuckled softly and responded, "Oh no, it's fine. Don't worry about it." He continued, "Anyway, in the first two years of my parents' marriage, they lived in Ireland. And every time they'd go to Church, they would say a special prayer to Mary in this one church, I can't think of the name of it, that they would have children and they would be happy and healthy. You see, the doctor told my mum she couldn't have children." Elliott himself started to get a little teary-eyed. He took a deep breath and continued, "And I'd like to think that that was part of the reason why the four of us are here."

I smiled and said, "I guess you also had the luck of the Irish."

Elliott lightly giggled and said, "Now I don't know about *that*."

Just then some old cranky Italian lady shushed us from behind. She put a finger to her lips, had a cross look on her face, and harshly whispered, "Shh!"

Startled, Elliott and I turned around to look at this woman, who gave us an ugly scowl. We inferred she was most likely a nun, based on the clothing (a habit and long robe) she wore. After her face had calmed down and she focused her attention on the mass, Elliott and I turned to each other and laughed, but not too loudly.

It was 5:30 by the time Mass had ended. Afterwards we visited the shrine of St. Gerard, prayed there, and took a walk down to a ledge that had a beautiful view of the Italian landscape. Connor and Ollie got chased by a German Shepherd while trying to befriend it, but the owner stopped the dog and they were allowed to pet him after he revealed his sweet side. We stopped by the market that they had right outside the hotel and looked at the different trinkets, rosaries, foods, etc. I got my Meme a beautiful ice blue rosary. Meme was my grandmother, with whom I had always had a special bond.

Anyway, after exploring Materdomini for about an hour and a half, by 7:00 our dinner reservation was ready. We ate in the hotel's restaurant, but it was as if the restaurant and the hotel were two separate things. Unlike the nearly rundown hotel, the restaurant looked elegant and grand. The room was a crystal clear color with tables that had golden tablecloths. The waiters dressed nicely.

Our waiter was a young man, around Elliott's age. He looked almost like Matteo (you know the Italian hottie I

185

had a thirty-second make out sesh in the lobby with until Elliott walked in and became jealous?), only he had a buzz cut. I've gotta admit, I never was a big fan of guys with buzz cuts. Man, if Elliott ever got rid of his beautiful, curly locks and got a buzz cut, I don't know what I'd do! Unless he did it for a movie role, that would be the only exception.

Anyway, the waiter introduced himself as Leonardo (not like the one Elliott has met). And said in simple English, "To drink?" We could tell he didn't understand English, so we tried to keep it simple for him.

When he was getting our drink orders, everyone had asked for wine, until he got to me. "Um, I will have acqua, prego."

Leonardo for some reason couldn't understand, and so an older waiter, about mid-fifties came up to him and asked him what was going on in Italian. And then the younger waiter explained to him in Italian. All of a sudden the older waiter had a rage of fury come across his face, and he looked at me.

In an angry tone he scolded me: "Signorina, you ought to be ashamed of yourself! It is rude to not order wine at the dinner table! You must be American! Can't you learn to appreciate and accept our customs?"

I was a little stunned and speechless at how rude and aggressive this man was being towards me. I could barely speak. I stuttered out, "Um, um, well—well—you see I-I-I never r-really l-l-liked wine."

"Doesn't mean you shouldn't order it!" he shook his finger at me and waved, "Shame on you, Signorina! Shame on you!"

"I-I-I'm s-sorry," I stuttered out. Elliott saw I was feeling guilty and a little frightened by this guy yelling at me. He reached down under the table and placed his hand on my thigh and squeezed it softly. Not in a flirtatious or sexual way, but rather a way of saying, "I've got you, love."

He told the older waiter calmly in Italian, "She'll have a wine. She's new to Europe so she doesn't know. And every other place we went didn't say anything when she ordered water, so it isn't her fault."

The older waiter didn't say anything. His face was just blank as he walked away. Pretty cool to meet Elliott Parker, but then embarrassing after he had to defend someone else from you. Leonardo took the rest of our drink orders and walked away with a smile on his face.

After he was out of sight, I turned to Elliott, smiled as he said, "Don't worry, Cecilia. I'll drink your wine for you. You don't have to drink it."

"Thank you so much," I told him, blowing him a kiss.

He still had his hand on my thigh, when he winked at me and joked, "If it makes you feel any better, I can give this place a bad review." This caused everyone to laugh.

We got our drink orders and eventually ordered our food. I had veal, because that was the only thing on the menu I wanted to try. It was gross! Then again, even though I consider steak my favorite food, I never liked the idea of eating a baby cow.

187

But the veal was far from my mind now. I was genuinely concerned about Elliott. First of all, he hated his veal just as much as I did, so he didn't really have anything to eat. He had really liked the wine, both mine and his own. He liked it so much that he wanted another one, and another one after that. By the time he had had his fourth glass of wine, Elliott was a little tipsy. Or let me rephrase that. By the time he had had his fourth glass of wine, Elliott was *very drunk*.

"Man! I love a good glass of wine!" he said slurred.

"Do you love four glasses of wine?" Grace asked him, concerned for her cousin.

"Is that how many I've had?" he was slurring. Grace nodded her head slowly. A bright smile came upon his face and he raised his arms up in the air and said, "Then I love four glasses of wine!" We just sat there. Ollie and Connor looked confused, most likely because they've probably never seen Elliott drunk before. Ryan snickered, finding the whole thing rather amusing. Esperanza and Nicole were trying their best not to burst out laughing. Meanwhile, Grace buried her face in her palm. As for me, I found drunk Elliott adorable, but was also concerned for his well-being.

I put my hand on his arm and said, "Um, Elliott, sweetie—"

Elliott interrupted me with a gasp and excitingly said, "Did you just call me sweetie?!" I slowly nodded my head and he all of a sudden pulled me in for a hug and said, "Yay! Yay! Yay! You called me sweetie!" He squeezed me really tight and said, "I love you, baby!" He then sang that song loudly and out of tune, "I love you baby! And if it's quite alright I need you baby!"

At this, Ryan couldn't help but burst out laughing. Grace, who was sitting next to him, slapped him on the shoulder, and scolded him in a whisper: "Stop it!"

I decided enough was enough and Elliott needed to go back to the room. So I took control of the situation and said, "Okay, okay." I stood up and helped Elliott stand up as I said, "Mr. Tipsy here needs to go back to the room."

When I finally got Elliott to stand up, I wrapped my arms under his so I could help him walk. Smiling a huge grin, he turned his head to me and asked with excitement and innocence, "We're going back to the room? Are we going to do the do?" This caused my eyes to widen. Then I started flustering, my face turning red all over.

Poor clueless Ollie, who had no idea what was going on so ever, asked in genuine confusion, "What's the do?"

Ryan had a smirk on his face and asked, "Yeah, *Elliott*. What *is* the do?"

I decided to stop this before it went anywhere, so I said, "Okay, time to head back to the room."

As we walked away, Elliott cheerfully waved back to everyone, "Bye, everyone! I love you all so much!" Everyone nervously waved back as we made our way out of the restaurant. On the way back to the room, Elliott just basically paid you various affectionate compliments such as, "You're so pretty!," "You smell like vanilla. I like vanilla!," "Can I kiss you now? Or do I have to wait till we get back to the room?," just to name a few. I had to admit, Elliott was cute when he was drunk.

When we finally reached the room, Elliott cheered, "Yay! We're here!"

Suddenly, I realized something. "Oh damn it!" I said in frustration. "I don't have the key to your room! Do you have it, Elliott?"

Elliott shook his head. "Nope! Ryan has it!"

I muttered to myself in frustration, "Oh brother." I thought for a minute, but then I remembered that I had the key to *our* room in my pocket. Pulling it out, I said, "Alright, we're gonna take you to my room."

Elliott grinned and his eyes widened as he said, "Ooh! Steamy!"

I shoved at his shoulder and said, "Stop thinking dirty thoughts!" I finally reached the key and started to unlock the door. I hated unlocking my dorm with a key. It was *so* hard. The two previous hotels had keycards you would just have to *swipe* to open the door. How come this hotel room couldn't have had one of *those*?

When Elliott saw I was struggling with the lock, he cheered me on, saying, "You can do it, Cecilia! I believe in you!" Finally, after a minute of trying and Elliott cheering, I got the door to unlock. Elliott cheered, "Yay! Yay! You did it, Cecilia! Yay! I knew you could do it." It was silly but sweet.

Then he took me by the shoulder, spun me around so I was facing him, and started kissing me, passionately, but because of his state, they were rather sloppy. I even think I felt something enter my mouth. I'll let you readers guess what it is...

I think he was trying to push me against the wall, but instead he pushed me against the door and, because the door was open, we both fell, me landing backwards, onto the floor of the room. He landed on top of me. I would probably be able to laugh about it later, but right now I was pretty mad at Elliott for his behavior. We were also probably keeping the neighbors up. But drunk Elliott found it hilarious and started hysterically laughing.

After a little bit, I put my hands on his mouth, and he was silenced. "Shut up!" I whisper yelled to him. Where as before Elliott's eyes looked happy, now they were wide like he knew he was in for it. He had that logic even though he was drunk. "I understand, okay, you're drunk and you really want to kiss me. But this has gone far enough. You could have seriously hurt the both of us, and for all I know, you've woken up the neighbors, now please, SHUT YOUR BEAUTIFUL BRITISH MOUTH!"

I slowly took my hands off his mouth, as Elliott's eyes became sad and, still very tipsy, started to talk in a babyish voice: "Oh no! I'm sorry! Did I make you angry?"

"Yes you did," I nodded. This made Elliott look down in sadness. But then I assured him, "But I forgive you."

This made Elliott look straight back up, and now having a gleeful face, said, "Yay!"

After laying on the floor, both of us got up as Elliott ran to the bed and plopped on it and said, "This bed is *so* comfy! It's like Heaven on a mattress!" A tiny smile came upon my face, seeing him like this. Elliott rolled over on his back and started making snow angels on the bed. "Whee! Look at me! I'm making snow angels!"

"You're so silly," I muttered to myself, still smiling. I went over to the bed, I took Elliott's shoes off for him and placed them by the bed. Once that was done, I sat down. As soon as I hit the bed, Elliott sat up and looked at me. "So," I asked awkwardly looking down at the mattress. I finally looked up and asked him, "What do you want to do?"

Elliott dramatically shrugged his shoulders and said, "I dunno!" Then there was silence. I started to caress Elliott's soft cheek with my hand. I started to lean in to kiss him. "Cecilia," he murmured.

"Yes, Elliott?" I asked in a seductive tone.

But Elliott wasn't thinking about the sexiness in my voice. Instead he said, "I think I'm going to throw up." Just as he said this, he got up and sprinted to the bathroom. I sighed. *Poor Elliott*, I thought to myself.

I quickly ran to the bathroom, and found him, the poor thing kneeling by the toilet, almost violently throwing up into it.

I felt so sorry for him. But at the same time, I was disgusted. But I also remembered at the Colosseum when I was throwing up because of the sun poisoning, Elliott didn't act grossed out, but rather comforted me and assured me it was okay. So I decided to do the same thing, kneeling beside him as he continued to vomit.

"Shhh," I comforted him. "Let it all out, sweetie. Let it all out." After about a minute, Elliott sat up and looked dazed and exhausted. I wrapped my arms around his chest. "My poor baby," I whispered in his ear. "I've got you. I've got you. You feeling better?"

"I think I'm done?" he said, but with a question in his voice. I got up and got a hand towel from the cabinet, washed it with cold water in the sink, and sat back down next to him, wiping away the smidge of throw up on his mouth. "Thank you, darling," he quietly said.

"No problem," I said, rubbing his back as I put a towel on the counter. "Let's get you to bed," I said, helping him stand up. I grabbed a trash can and said, "I'll bring this trash can into the room in case you need it." Elliott nodded and thanked me once again.

I guided him back into the bed. I helped him sit down on the bed. "Now, we can't get into your room, so you can't change into your pajamas. I'm sorry," I told him.

"That's okay," he told me, now sleepy and groggy. "I usually only sleep in my boxers anyway." I raised an eyebrow at him. He saw my reaction and chuckled, "Don't worry, I'm being serious. Besides, I'm too tired to do any of that."

"Okay," I giggled. "I'll help you." He raised his arms and I slipped the shirt over his body, revealing his toned chest that I saw earlier that day. I saw myself smiling as I saw it. That sight never got old. Anyway, his pants were easy to slip off, I just unbuttoned, unzipped, and slipped them off. I folded the shirt and pants and set them neatly on my suitcase. Elliott managed to tuck himself into bed. I walked over to the bed and asked, "Anything else?"

"Yes, actually," he said, his slurred speech coming back. "It's kinda hot in here."

I sighed and said, "I know." I thought for a minute, looking around the room to see if there was anyway to make the room at least a little bit cooler. My eyes caught the window. "Aha!" I exclaimed, "Perfect!" I scurried over to the window and tried my best to open it, which I finally did by pulling it up. And that made the room feel *so much* cooler.

"What if a bad guy comes in?" Elliott said, still sleepy, but in a scared childish voice. Just as I was about to answer, Elliott said something in a dreamy voice that sounded like how I acted when I woke up from my wisdom teeth surgery: "I promise, darling, if a bad guy comes in, I'll protect you! I am Serpent Boy after all!"

I chuckled and said, "Okay, Serpent Boy, anything else you need?"

Elliott, who was getting very comfy on the bed, said, "Yes! Can you come here and cuddle with me?"

My heart started pounding again. This was *so* cute. I found myself blushing once again. "Okay," I grinned. "But first," I said as I made my over to my suitcase and grabbed my PJs and cosmetic bag, "let me brush my teeth and get changed. I'll be right back."

"Okay," Elliott smiled, he started to blush himself. I vanished into the bathroom.

I hadn't even realized what time it was. I looked at my phone and it was only 10 o'clock. And they still weren't back yet. But to be honest, I didn't care. I was going to cuddle with Elliott! I quickly brushed my teeth and put on my pajamas: a pink tank top with white polka dots and matching shorts. After that, I took the messy ponytail out of my face and made it so my chocolate brown curls were down and loose. I checked myself in the mirror one last time, smiled, and left the bathroom to join Elliott in a cuddling session.

When I got back into the room, Elliott had passed out. He was softly snoring. Thank goodness they weren't too loud. At first I frowned that he was asleep, but then I smiled as I watched his sleeping figure. As he breathed, his chest went up and down. I went into bed, laying right next to him. Curling next to him. And then based on what happened next, I had a feeling he was sort of awake. Because as I curled right up to him and placed a hand on his chest, his arm sneaked up behind me and pulled me closer into his side. His warm body gave me warmth, which I kinda needed because opening the window made it very cold. As he did this, I sheepishly smiled.

As I nuzzled my head into his shoulder, I kissed his cheek and whispered, "Sweet dreams, my darling." And after that, I closed my eyes and drifted off to sleep, feeling safety and comfort Elliott held me tight.

Chapter 11: Wishing For Privacy

"Good morning you two lovebirds," a sing-songy voice said.

My eyes were still closed. As soon as I heard the voice they started to flutter open. When I opened them, I found myself still in bed with Elliott in the exact same positions from cuddling the night before. I turned onto my side and saw him still sleeping soundly.

Just as I was about to wake him up, a different voice said, "Um, eh hem." I turned away from Elliott to see who it was. It turned out to be Nicole and Esperanza, standing there in their pajamas with their hands on their hips.

As soon as I saw them I quickly sat up in bed, while Elliott still lay fast asleep. "Girls! Hey!" I yawned. "Where's Grace?"

"She slept with the boys," Nicole answered.

"We came back to find you two sleeping, and we didn't want to wake you up, so we slept in here while Grace stayed with the boys," Esperanza further explained.

"I'm so sorry about that!" I started speaking really quickly. "I didn't have the key, and I had the key to our room, and Elliott was super drunk! So I just came in here and he asked me to cuddle and we fell asleep and—."

Nicole cut me off and assured me, "It's fine, it's fine. Don't worry. But you guys should probably get ready, just so you know."

"We just woke you up early so you could take a shower, pack, the works!" Esperanza said.

"Okay," I said, "Thank you."

I smiled brightly, ready to wake Elliott up. Just as I was turning to him, Nicole said, "Oh, he's gonna be hungover!"

"Yeah, Cecilia," Esperanza said, "don't expect him to act all lovey dovey like he was last night."

"What do you mean?" I asked, turning to them.

"Well, I guess you've never been hungover before," Nicole started to tell me. She continued, "Newsflash: Elliott's probably not going to be in the mood to be affectionate towards you."

Esperanza continued, "Yeah, he's probably gonna need some aspirin. Luckily, I've come prepared! I'll be right back!" She then hurried into the bathroom.

I was about to wake up Elliott when Nicole said, "Oh, and did Elliott puke last night?" I nodded, my face showed disgust at the memory. Nicole had a disgusted look on her face and said, "Then you might not want to kiss him."

She had a good point there. She came near the bed to be beside me when I woke Elliott up. I carefully nudged him and whispered, "Elliott, psst. Wake up."

With his eyes still closed, Elliott just groaned. But I kept trying to get him up, "Honey, it's time to get up."

Then Elliott slowly opened his eyes and groaned once again. When he finally opened his eyes, he looked right at me. He did not have the normal bright, happy smile he had. He looked as though he didn't want to open his eyes. He just looked at me. I could only smile.

"How are you feeling?" I asked him quietly.

Elliott put a hand to his face and muttered, "My head hurts."

I began running my hand through his hair. "My poor baby," I muttered.

Just then, Esperanza came rushing in with water and aspirin, along with what looked to be a cookie.

"Here you go," she said, handing me the water and aspirin.

"Okay, let's sit you up now," Nicole said. The two of us helped Elliott sit up. The poor thing still didn't look like his normal cheerful self.

"What happened?" he groaned.

"You got really drunk last night," I explained to him, handing him the Aspirin.

Taking it in his hand, Elliott asked, "I was?"

"Yup," Nicole nodded. "Drank four glasses of wine. That's why you're hungover."

"I hate being hungover," Elliott murmured.

Still with the aspirin in his hand, I instructed him to take the pill with the bottle of water. I helped him. He put the aspirin in his mouth and held the bottle in his hand as he took a sip.

Esperanza handed him a cookie and said, "Here." Elliott took the cookie as Esperanza explained to me, "He needs to eat something fatty to get the alcohol out of his system.

Elliott took a bite of the cookie. Licking his lips, he said, "That's pretty good. But my head still hurts." He was still holding his head in his hand.

"We should probably get you back to your room," Nicole said. We each took an arm on his side and helped him stand up, for he couldn't walk by himself properly.

"Would you hand me his shirt please, Esperanza?" I asked her. Esperanza did so, handing me Elliott's shirt. Nicole held him while I slipped in on over.

"How about *we* take him back for you, and you can get dressed," Esperanza told me. I pouted my lips, not wanting to leave Elliott's sight. Esperanza chuckled and said, "Don't worry, Cecilia. We'll take care of him. But right now you need to get in the shower, brush your teeth."

"Okay," I said. I was about to leave the room when I turned to Elliott and quickly pecked his cheek. Which made him develop a *very* tiny smile on his face. Then the three of them left and I went to get ready.

******

After showering, getting dressed, and packing, I was ready to head to Assisi. I wore a short, strapless orange red romper accompanied by a black and white wrap. I felt like looking nice for Elliott. He promised me tonight we could go on a dinner date, and I planned to wear one of the cute dresses I brought with me. We all decided to wait about two hours while Grace and her cousins helped Elliott recover from the hangover.

Just as I was getting the last of my suitcases together, Esperanza and Nicole walked out of the shared bedroom. They were holding their phones with worried expressions on their faces.

"Hey guys!" I said cheerfully. As soon as I saw their faces, I asked in a concerned tone, "What's wrong?"

Esperanza and Nicole looked at each other. "Should I tell her?" Esperanza asked.

"Go ahead," Nicole replied.

"You guys are starting to make me nervous. What's going on?" I asked, getting really scared.

Esperanza took a deep breath and asked, "You remember how when you and Elliott kissed on the boat those teens took a picture of you and Elliott made them delete it?"

200

I nodded. "Yeah." I already knew this wasn't going to end well.

"Well," Esperanza said, trying to find the words to say. "I think—I think maybe some more people took pictures of you guys."

I got an uneasy feeling in my stomach. "What are you talking about?"

Esperanza showed me her phone. It was a bunch of pictures. One was of Elliott and I kissing on the ferry after going under the kissing rock. Then there was another one where it was after the kiss, where we were looking deeply into each other's eyes and smiling. Then there was one where we were hugging, after the teens said I wasn't pretty, but you couldn't tell I was crying. I was shocked. The whole world knew about Elliott and me.

Still in disbelief, I covered my mouth and muttered, "Oh my gosh."

Nicole looked saddened. She said, "And that's not even the worst part."

"How can it get worse?" I asked, still trying to process it all.

"Well, I almost don't want to tell you this," Nicole said. "But I think you deserve to know." She was scrolling her phone for something when she finally looked up and me and said, "Somehow, they found out your name and Instagram account."

She then showed me her phone. There was an article that read, in big bold letters that were right in your face. **We Finally Found Out Who The Mystery Red-Head Getting Close To Elliott Parker Was: Her Name is CECILIA HARTLEY**. I scrolled down and read the rest of the article:

*It seems as though Elliott Parker has a new lady. Two days ago, the 23-year-old **Serpent Boy** actor was caught kissing and in close contact with a mystery red-head woman on a Capri ferry. After trying to figure out who the woman was, we finally have a name.*

Elliott Parker's supposed new girlfriend's name is Cecilia Hartley. We know little about her, but we do know that her Instagram account is @cecilia_hartley. Her account is not private, and it seems as though her Instagram is full of photos of her friends, her family, and her puppy named Jane. We even spotted Elliott in one of the pics, and they look so happy.

I couldn't read the rest. I immediately got out my phone and went to my Instagram. First, I saw nearly 1 million people had sent requests to follow me, probably because I was Elliott Parker's supposed girlfriend. I didn't accept any of them. Then I saw that my last post (a selfie in the gardens in Capri), which had previously had 10 comments, now had 10,000 comments. I clicked on the comments and read some of them.

matty_b_g: remind me again why Elliott is with her?

mrs.parker: how did such a hot guy like Elliott end up with a girl like her?

wilcoxgood: r u kidding me? she looks old enough to be his mom

bibi_bibi: tbh, that gurl's not that pretty

robin-bird: i think Elliott could do better than that.

There were so many more. But I couldn't read anymore. I was pretty much exposed in the tabloids. That's one thing, but then to have these people write negative comments about me, that hurt. Everyone knew who I was. I was on the verge of crying.

Nicole placed her hand on my back as Esperanza asked, "Cecilia? Are you alright?"

I couldn't speak. "I–I–I." Those were the only words that came out. I felt as though those harsh words were a knife that stabbed me in the stomach.

Then, the door opened. Grace had her phone out. She looked worried. I guess she knew too. "I just saw!" she said. Then she wrapped me in a tight embrace, and I hugged back. "Are you okay?"

We pulled away, and I lied saying, "Yeah. I'm doing pretty okay." All of a sudden tears started streaming down my face. Grace continued to hug me and tapped my back and Esperanza and Nicole made their way over and comforted me as well.

"Does Elliott know yet?" Nicole asked Grace.

Grace shook her head. "No. The news just came out and he's been in the shower."

Then all of a sudden a bunch of bings started going off my phone. They were all from my mom. I read them.

Mom: Cecilia Margaret Hartley!!!!!!!

Mom: I just saw!

Mom: Those pics of you kissing Elliott Parker!!!! What the heck?!?!?! How did you get with Elliott Parker?!?!?!?!

I put it down. My parents didn't know about us. And that's how they found out.

Just as I put my phone down, someone was knocking on the door, which was slightly cracked open. It revealed Elliott, now fully recovered from the hangover, who was smiling.

"Hello everyone!" he waved. He didn't see me crying. "The other boys are downstairs and we're ready to head off to Assisi!" As soon as he saw my red face with tears continuing to fall down it, Elliott's smile faded away to a worrisome look. "My love, what's the matter?" he asked.

He was making his way over to comfort me, but Nicole was angry. Nicole has a pretty hot temper, and when her friends get hurt, she gets defensive. She made her way toward Elliott.

"What the hell?!" she yelled. "How could you do this to my best friend?"

"I'm sorry," he said, backing up. "I was just asking how she was. She looked upset, and I care about her..."

"That's bull, dude!" Nicole said, backing him up further. "You've only known her for a few days!"

"That's enough, Nicole," Grace, who still had her arms around me, tried to persuade her.

But Nicole didn't pay attention. She kept yelling at Elliott as he backed up into a wall. She pointed at him and said, "You know, you come on this trip with us, pretending to be Mister Nice Sexy British Celeb Guy and you sweep Cecilia off her feet! And you seem like you're the sweetest and most perfect person ever to grace this planet! But then you bring my best friend into your world of paparazzi and jealous fans and do you do anything about it? No! She gets undeserved attention and harsh criticism all because of you!"

"What's going on?" a confused Elliott asked.

Nicole held up her fist and said, "I'll tell you what's going on! I'm gonna punch the living daylight out of you, asshole!" Elliott's eyes widened as he saw her fist close to his face.

Before she could punch him in the jaw, Esperanza grabbed her by the arm and said, "Stop it, Nicole! It's not worth it!"

"It is so worth it! He hurt Cecilia!" Nicole shouted trying to release her arm from her best friend's grip.

"Hurt Cecilia?" a poor puzzled Elliott asked. "What are you talking about? I could never hurt Cecilia! I care about her! And if I hurt her in any way, I would never forgive myself."

"Sure you would! Lies! All lies!" Nicole shouted at him as Esperanza held her wrists behind Nicole's back.

I decided to step in and stand in front of Elliott and defend him. At this point I was still crying, but it had died down by now. "Leave him alone, Nicole," I said. "He didn't do anything wrong." I then turned to Elliott.

He saw the sadness in my eyes. I started sobbing again as I dropped to the floor, collapsing as I continued to sob. Elliott went down to my level and held my hands and asked, "Cecilia, why are you crying, love? Did someone do something to you?"

I looked up at him and tried to speak, but I couldn't, so I just bent my head down and continued crying.

Grace walked over and explained to him what was going on. "Someone, besides the two teens, took photos of you and Cecilia kissing and hugging on the ferry. Now it's all in the tabloids. They even identified her and found her Instagram account and started posting all these hateful comments toward her."

Elliott's jaw dropped in disbelief. He didn't speak. "What—what do the comments say?" he finally asked.

Grace handed him her phone that had the comments on my post. He scrolled through them. His face changed as it went on. At one point he looked disgusted. And then he looked sad. Then he seemed angry. He looked shocked. After a while, he handed the phone back to Grace and looked down, almost as if he was deeply thinking. His jaw clenched at one point.

He turned to me, I was still sobbing in his chest with my arms wrapped tightly around his waist. He started stroking my hair softly and whispered into my ear, "I'm so sorry about this, love. I really am."

"I think we should probably give these two some privacy to talk," Esperanza said calmly.

"Yeah," Grace agreed. "Give them time to process it all."

Nicole sighed and annoyed said, "Okay." Then she pointed to Elliott and said, "Don't you dare hurt her, Parker! You hurt my friend in any way, I will hunt you down and you will pay!"

Esperanza nervously laughed as she ushered Nicole out of the room and said, "Alright, alright, Miss Feisty Pants. Calm down." Grace followed them. Elliott and I were alone.

I freed myself from him and stood up. I went over to sit on the bed, my face buried in my palms. I was stressed. Angry. Upset. So many emotions rolled into one. Elliott made his way to the bed and sat right next to me.

Placing his hand on my shoulder, he said, "I really am sorry about this, Cecilia. But it will get better, I promise. The negative comments are hard, but you'll get through it. Just learn to go with it. And I promise I'll take care of it as soon as possible."

After thinking for a minute, I took a deep breath and looked straight ahead and not at him. "No, Elliott," I shook my head.

"What?" Elliott asked.

I finally turned to him and said, "I really can't do this. I thought I could. If your fans are just going to treat me like trash and not respect me, then what's the point? This was fun while it lasted, but I think this needs to stop."

I stood up and started walking to get my suitcase. Then Elliott grabbed me by the wrist and I turned around. "Wait, wait, wait," he said. "This was just one bad day. It's going to get better."

"How do you know that?" I asked him, crossing my arms. "What happens if they're still attacking me for a long time?"

"Then I definitely will do something about it," Elliott assured me.

"What is wrong with you?" I asked him. "I was just attacked online and all you're saying is that you'll do something about it?!" Then I sarcastically said, "That's very helpful, Elliott. Super helpful."

"Hey, I'm trying to help you here. I've been criticized online every now and then for things I do, but you get used to it after a while."

"Used to it?! *Used to it*?! That's all you're going to say?! That I will get used to it?!"

"I'm only trying to help," Elliott defended himself. I hadn't seen him this mad since he told the teens to delete the photo, and now he looked like he was building up to anger.

"Well, you're not," I said. "My parents didn't even know about us! They had to find out about their daughter having a summer fling with a famous actor through hateful comments on social media!"

Then Elliott looked hurt by the words I had said. "Summer fling?" he asked quietly.

"Yeah, summer fling," I told him. "You really thought this was going to turn into something more than a summer fling? I mean, look at us, Elliott! It's been about a week since we've met and we're already having our first argument! That to me doesn't sound like a relationship that is going to last!"

"Stop it!" Elliott shouted. "Right now!" I shut up. Stared at him. He looked like he had sadness in his eyes. Elliott, took a deep breath and said, "Look, I'm sorry. I shouldn't have yelled. And for the millionth time I'm so sorry you had to go through this. You don't deserve it. And I really like you, Cecilia. I really do. But if you think this is just going to be a summer fling, then what are we doing?" Then I stared at him for the longest time, until he finally said, "I'm going to go downstairs. I'll see you around, I guess." Then like that he walked out the door.

I tried to call him, "Elliott! Wait!" But he was gone. I bit my lip, thinking about how much I had hurt him by calling it just a summer fling. And he *was* trying to help. He did promise me that he would do something about the jealous fans, and he promised that it would get better. Why didn't I listen to him? What is wrong with me? Here I had this really great guy, and I let him get away. But I had to go on. Go to Assisi.

The rest of the day was a blur. Elliott and I didn't really say a word to each other. No one really said a word to anyone. We arrived in Assisi, which was a nice little town.

We stopped in our rooms, went to Mass, and ate dinner. Then we went back to our rooms. It was 9 o'clock. We didn't really feel like doing anything else. I just sat there on my bed, laying down and looking up at the ceiling. My friends all sat near me. Thank goodness we had our own beds this time. They finally came over to me and sat on the edge of my bed.

Nicole gently nudged me on the shoulder with her hand. "Cecilia?" she said quietly.

"You okay?" Esperanza said.

"Leave me alone," I muttered. I still stared at the ceiling, not looking at them.

"Just please talk to us," Grace said. "We can help."

It was then that I sat up and looked straight at them and said, "You can help?! How can you help?! I really liked this amazing guy. The first guy that genuinely cared about me. The first guy I ever felt this way about! And I let him get away! He was trying to help me, but I screwed up. And I called what we were having a summer fling when he wanted something more. And I wanted something more too! But I only cared about what other people thought of me and I let that get in the way of us! And now he won't even look at me! So I don't really think you can help that!" I wasn't crying, but I was very upset. I laid my hand on my face.

After a brief moment I quietly said to them, "I'm sorry."

"You're fine," Grace said, putting her hand on my shoulder and rubbing it soothingly.

"I—I shouldn't have taken it on you guys," I said. "It's not your faults."

"It's no one's fault, Cecilia," Esperanza assured me. "Not even Elliott's fault." She turned to Nicole and said, "*Right*, Nicole?" Nicole looked annoyed but nodded.

Grace added, "If anything, it's those stupid Elliott Parker fans' faults."

"Yeah," Nicole agreed. "And why would they even call themselves his fans if they say negative things about the girl he likes. Those aren't fans. Those are just some people who want to date Elliott Parker and get defensive when he's seen with a beautiful girl."

I nodded. "That's true. I feel awful. I wanna go talk to him, but what if he doesn't want to see me?"

"Well if he doesn't want your forgiveness, it's on him," Esperanza said. "But I can assure you, he'll want to see you. I may have been eavesdropping, which I know is wrong, but I heard him talking to Ryan about how he wishes he would have tried harder to understand why you were upset, and that he should've done something more than assure you it would get better. And he said he was very upset at what happened. That you didn't deserve to have your privacy violated by all those tabloids or be treated harshly by his fans."

"What time is it?" I asked them.

Grace looked at the clock on her phone. "9 o'clock," she read.

"Do you think he's still up?" I asked.

"Are you kidding me?" Grace laughed. "I know Elliott. He'll probably be up till 1 o'clock in the morning. He usually stays up late and he's a very light sleeper."

"And you're a really *heavy* sleeper," Nicole joked. That was true. I could sleep anywhere, no matter the place or if there was a lot of sound and get a good night's sleep.

This made me laugh. "We're opposites in that regard," I replied.

"So go get him!" Esperanza encouraged me. "Go get the guy!"

I slowly sat up. I was wearing the same pajamas I was wearing the night before. So I grabbed my baby blue Myrtle Beach sweatshirt and put it on, and slipped some flip-flops on my feet.

I made my way towards the door, took a deep breath, opened it and turned to my friends and said, "Wish me luck!"

They all waved and said in unison, "Good luck, Cecilia!"

Then Nicole added, "Go get your hot British superhero man with a heart of gold!"

I jokingly warned her, pointing my finger at her, and said, "Hey, back off, Grey! He's mine!" Then I laughed, and they laughed too, and closed the door, off to get my man back!

The Parker boys' room was a floor down from us. When I reached their door, butterflies fluttered in my stomach. I reached to knock on the door, but I quickly pulled away. *I can do this. I can't do this.* I turned around and started to walk away from the door. Then I stood still and realized I needed to do this. So I turned around and quickly walked to the door and knocked. For a little while, there was no answer. Then finally, Ryan answered.

A smile was on his face, "Cecilia! Hey!"

"Hi, Ryan," I said, smiling back. "I came to see Elliott." Then I frowned, bowing my head down, "But I totally understand if he doesn't want to see me."

But Ryan quickly assured me, "Oh no, no, no. *Please* come in! He's been moping all day, kind of a pain in the arse, and I think he'll be happy that you want to see him!" He invited me in and said, "Come in, come in."

I stepped into the room. It was identical to our room. Connor and Ollie lay their on the bed, watching *Little House on the Prairie* (not sure why) in Italian.

"Elliott's in the shower, but he'll be out in a minute," Ryan told me.

I nodded my head. "Thank you," I said. I turned to Connor and Ollie and waved to them, smiled, and said, "Hey Connor! Hey Ollie!"

Their attention was quickly diverted from the TV when they saw me. Smiles lit up their faces as they ran towards me, hugging the life out of me and cheering my name.

Ryan chuckled when he saw his little brothers. He gently pulled them away and said, "Okay, how about we give Cecilia room to breathe, alright boys?" And they did just that.

Ollie grabbed me by the hand and pulled me to the bed and said, "Come on, Cecilia! Watch *Little House on the Prairie* with us!"

And I watched it. A scene with the younger sister Carrie was on, and I don't know why, but she had corn and gravy all over her face, and she was smiling. I could tell the director meant for it to be cute, but it ended up looking creepy and kind of gross.

Connor turned to me and asked, "What do you think of Carrie, Cecilia?"

I shrugged and said, "I don't know. She's cute I guess."

Connor quickly answered his own question, saying, "I think she's really stupid!"

Ryan, who had come over to watch it with us, told his brother, "Now Connor, you don't call people stupid."

I covered both Connor and Ollie's ears and said, "Well you did tell them what French Kissing was!"

Then Ryan made a face that said, "Okay, you got me there." I uncovered the young boys' ears and we all went back to watching.

About a minute later, Elliott came out in a bathrobe and was drying his hair with a towel. It was as if he didn't see me because he told his brothers, "Look, guys, I forgot my clothes to change into while in the bathroom. So I'm just going to grab them and go change in the…"

Elliott stopped as soon as he saw me. It was as if he was in shock, because his towel dropped to the floor. I gave a small smile, as did he. Still at a loss of words he said, "Um, um. Good evening, Cecilia!"

I waved to him and said, "Hey, Elliott."

Awkward silence filled the room. Ryan finally broke it as he got up and said, "Okay, Connor, Ollie, how about we go to Grace and her friends' rooms. We can continue watching the show there. I think we need to give these two some time to talk."

Connor whined, "Awww! Can't we stay here!"

"No," Ryan told him. "These two need their privacy." And so the three boys got up, our on some shoes, and made their way out of the room. Before closing the door, Ryan cheerfully but sort of sarcastically told us, "Have fun you two!" And he left.

But Elliott and I didn't pay attention. We were staring awkwardly at each other the whole time.

Looking down at the floor, Elliott ran a hand through his hair. He looked up at me and asked, "What are you doing here?"

"Well, I uh, I..." I started to say. "Could you come sit next to me, please?" I patted down on the bed next to him, and scooted to make more room for him. As he made his way to the bed and sat down, I turned the TV off.

"What is it?" Elliott asked me.

"I—I wanted to apologize for earlier," I told him.

"Uh huh," he nodded.

"I wasn't being fair. I was sort of blaming you for those negative fan comments, when you didn't do anything wrong. And I said you weren't doing anything to help, but you were trying your best. And the whole thing I said when I called what we have a summer fling. That must have hurt you."

Elliott nodded. "Yeah. It really did."

"Anyway," I continued, "I don't want this to be a summer fling. I want this to be more. I just let a bunch of strangers whose feelings I don't even care about get in the middle of what we have. And I shouldn't do that. Elliott, I've never felt this way about anyone before, and I let you get away. I was stupid. I really was. And I can't stop thinking about it. I really hope you can forgive me, Elliott. And if you can't, I totally respect that. I just want you to be happy." After I said all that, I let out a heavy sigh. I did what I could do. It was all up to Elliott.

I looked at him, and a small tear rolled slowly down his cheek. I put my hand on his shoulder, the first time I had touched him since this morning.

After being silent for a long time he said, "That was really nice, Cecilia. I don't know what to say." He sighed and said, "And I also did something wrong."

"What?" I said in disbelief. "No you didn't."

"Yes, I did," he told me. "I should have tried to have been more understanding. Looking back on it, I thought, I didn't really do anything to make you feel any better. All I did was say that you'd get through it and that it'd get better. I should have tried harder to make you feel better about it. I should have understood that this was your first time receiving bad press, just when you had been introduced to the world."

I admitted, "Well, that *is* what I thought."

He paused briefly, and then said, "And I am really sorry about what you had to go through. I was really upset that you were practically exposed in the tabloids, not to mention criticized by my fans." I nodded my head, and smiled a small smile.

"I just want to say," Elliott said, taking both of my hands in his and placing them close to his chest, "I forgive you. And I'm sorry. Can you forgive me?"

I didn't answer. Instead I just reached in and gave him a heartfelt kiss. We both collapsed on our sides and continued to kiss passionately. We slowly broke our lips apart and opened our eyes.

"Was that a yes?" Elliott smiled.

This made us both laugh and I said, "Yes."

Elliott grinned. He grabbed my back and pulled me closer to him, and we resumed kissing. His lips were so soft and warm, especially after being in the shower. We continued kissing for a while and I slowly climbed on top of him as he lay on his back. I took my fingers and ran them through his hair. The soft feel of his curly, damp hair felt good against my dry fingers.

Elliott parted his lips from mine and asked me, "And I promised you I would do something about those negative comments from my supposed fans. And I will keep my promise." As he slowly started sitting up, he asked, "Could you please hand me my phone?"

But I pinned him down to the bed, preventing him from standing up. "No!" I whined. "I kinda wanted to continue kissing you!"

"Whatever you want," Elliott winked.

I kneeled down so my face was close to his. I ran my finger down his cheek, feeling his soft, warm, rosy cheeks against my skin.

"That tickles, you know," he softly said. This made us both laugh.

But the female hormones got in the way and I whispered in his ear, "You know what I want, hun? I want to just untie that tie on your robe, throw it on the floor, and make love to you like there's no tomorrow."

Elliott's eyes widened when I said that. Then he smiled and said, "Dirty mind, huh?"

Then my eyes widened. I can't believe I just said what I said. "Oh no!" I covered my mouth with my hands and sat up, still in shock.

Elliott sat up with me, and his grin turned into a confused but concerned look. "What–What's wrong?"

"I'm *so* sorry I said that, Elliott!" I told him. "I can't believe I just said that. It's my stupid hormones!"

Elliott chuckled, and placed both his hands on my shoulders and said, "Don't apologize. I didn't think we were going to go there *yet*, seeing as we're so early in this whole thing. But if you want to do it, I'm all for it. Whatever you want is fine by me."

I snapped and said, "No, I can't, Elliott! I don't know how!"

Elliott went silent. "I'm sorry what?" I looked down, flushing with embarrassment. Then he cupped my chin and pulled it up so I was looking into his soft brown eyes. "Hey," he told me. "Is everything okay?"

"No," I laughed nervously. "It's nothing."

Still holding my chin up he said, "You can tell me. What's going on?"

I took a deep breath and said, "Elliott, I–." This was hard for me to admit to him. But I finally said it: "I'm a virgin."

Elliott's jaw dropped. He placed his hands by his side and said, "Oh."

I quickly tried to assure him, "I'm so sorry I told you. It's just, I've never done it before." Then I started nervously rambling on: "I've never really had a boyfriend before. I've gone on lots of dates, but none of them have really led to...you know. And if I led you on thinking I was going to have sex with you, I'm sorry. And if you don't want to be with me because I don't want to have sex with you right away, I completely understand."

I looked down at the sheets, still very embarrassed. But Elliott assured me, as he held my hands in his, "You've got that all wrong!" This made me look up into his sincere eyes and he continued. "I would *never* pressure you into something you didn't want to do. And when you're ready to have sex, that's when we'll do it. I'll wait ten years if that's how long it takes you to be ready. Anything for you."

I took my hands and held his face, caressing his cheeks with my hands. "Elliott, why are you so perfect?" I asked.

Elliott chuckled, smirked, and said, "Trust me, I'm *far* from perfect, darling."

My face lit up at the use of that word. "There's that word!" I excitedly said. "I have my man back!"

Elliott laughed. "You are adorable," he said. We continued laughing as I pulled in to kiss him again, still long and meaningful. When we pulled away, I placed my forehead against his, still holding his face.

"Okay," I said after a while. "I should probably get back to the room. Don't want to kick your brothers out like we kicked Grace out last night."

I started to get up, but Elliott pulled me back in and hugged me tightly saying, "Awwww, can't you stay here and cuddle?"

"No," I said breaking away from him and shaking my finger. "You need your beauty sleep, sweetie." This made Elliott bat his eyes and give puppy dog eyes. I pointed my finger at him and said, "Usually those eyes would work on me, but not tonight. Try tomorrow, Parker."

Elliott stopped doing them, gave up and groaned, "Fine."

I made my way to the door, but Elliott came up behind me and wrapped his arms around my waist. "Come on," he said. "One more kiss?" I turned my head around to face his and gave him one more kiss.

Then I walked towards the door, opened it, and said, "Night, night sweetheart."

Elliott waved to me, smiled and said, "Sweet dreams, darling!"

I winked, and he winked back, before shutting the door slowly so I could see his smiling face for longer. Once the door was shut completely, I leaned my back against the door and sighed. I was falling in love with a wonderful guy!

Chapter 12: Wishing For Three Fairy Godmothers

When the alarm on my phone went off at 7 o'clock in the morning, I was not in the mood. "Ugh," I groaned, as I reached my hand to turn it off.

I wanted to go back to sleep, but when I closed my eyes, Esperanza said, "Come on, Cecilia! Mass starts at 8:30!"

As soon as she said that, I just gave up. I slowly woke up.

"Just so you know," Esperanza said, "Nicole is taking a shower first, then me, then Grace, and finally you."

"How come on I'm going last?" I groggily asked.

Grace chimed in, "Cause you always take ten minute showers."

Sitting up, I said, "Fair enough."

Nicole was already in the shower. I decided to scroll through my Instagram to see if anything was new. To see if there were still any hate comments.

"Oh and by the way Cecilia," Grace said, "you should check Elliott's Instagram."

"Why?" I asked her.

Grace encouraged me, "Go see for yourself."

So I turned on my phone and opened up the Instagram app. Right when I opened it, the first thing on there was a post made by Elliott. It was a selfie that we took in Rome when we were overlooking the city from the roof restaurant of our hotel. It was the day after we met for the first time, and it was of me sticking my tongue out, Elliott doing the duck face, and both of us giving each other bunny ears. I chuckled, remembering the memory. He had tagged me in the photo. I scrolled down and read the caption. It was really long. I read it aloud to the other girls:

elliottparker1996 This here is Cecilia Hartley. I've only known her for a few days, but she is the loveliest girl I've ever met. She's sweet, funny, intelligent, pretty, and I could go on and on. And it has come to my attention that you guys are violating not only my privacy, but hers as well. It's one thing to do it to me, but none of my fans knew who Cecilia was before the news came out and I think she deserves privacy just as much as I do. And then I hear my fans make hateful comments about her. Why would you even call yourselves my fans? What fan personally attacks the person that the person they're fanning over cares deeply about? Now I really like Cecilia, and if I read about anyone hurting her in any way again, you will be blocked. You have been warned. @cecilia_hartley, I am deeply sorry and I will do my best to never let this happen again.

This made me smile. What a sweet guy. Then Esperanza jokingly whined, "I want myself an Elliott Parker."

This made Grace and I laugh, and I put an arm on her shoulder and assured her, "You'll find one someday, Esperanza. You'll find one."

By 7:45, we were all heading down to the hotel's dining room to eat breakfast. There was a little buffet, and we grabbed some food to eat. I was starving, so I had some scrambled eggs and toast. When we were finished, we went over and saw the boys eating at a table. They all waved to us.

Ollie saw me, grinned, ran up to me and hugged me tightly and said, "Yay! Cecilia! You're here!"

He was hugging me so tight, "Good morning, Ollie. So good to see you."

Elliott saw him hugging me and joked, saying, "Sorry Ollie! But she's already taken!"

Ollie pouted and his lips and said to me, "Why do you like Elliott more than you like me?"

Awww, Ollie! I bent down to him and said, "You know something, Ollie? I like all you boys equally." This made Ollie grin happily.

Elliott heard me and pouted, "Hey!" Man, these Parker boys sure like to pout!

I walked over to Elliott and joked to him: "Now Elliott, honey, don't be such a Mister Grumpy Pants!" This caused Elliott to jokingly stick his tongue out at me.

After breakfast, we went to the 8:30 mass at The Basilica of St. Francis. It wasn't far from the hotel, only about seven minutes. The Basilica was gorgeous. It was grand, but still very holy. Colors of gold, blue, and any other color imaginable filled the room. The nicely decorated pillars and arches added to the beauty.

After Mass had ended, we went out to look at the view from the ledge. The view was spectacular, with views of the green, hilly countryside. The sky was the most beautiful shade of blue, so bright and radiant. The view was so incredible I could feel my jaw drop open at one point.

"Girls!" Grace called all of us. "We *have* to get a picture! This view is *gorgeous*!"

We all went together and to take a photo of us with the beautiful landscape.

"Hey Elliott!" Grace shouted to her cousin. He was talking to his brothers, and he turned as soon as he heard Grace's voice. Grace motioned him: "Can you come and take a photo of us!"

"Sure," Elliott said, walking towards us. Grace handed him the phone as we got in our poses, ready to have our picture taken. "It's funny," Elliott said, "people never ask me to take their picture!"

"That's because they want you *in* the picture," Nicole laughed.

"True," Elliott said, "unless it's a selfie then they ask *me* to take a selfie with them. And I usually end up dropping their phones."

Still smiling for the picture, Esperanza asked Grace, "Grace, why would you ask someone who usually drops other people's phones to take a picture?"

"Well I didn't know he did that before," Grace told her.

"Well now you know!" Elliott said. Then he joked and said, "I'm an idiot!"

I went over to him, shook his hand, and teased him, "Nice to meet you an idiot! My name is Cecilia!"

Elliott chuckled and went along: "Hello, Cecilia. Yes, my name is an idiot! I honestly don't know *what* my parents were thinking!"

After some time in the Basilica of St. Francis, Lawrence drove us to San Damiano, right outside Assisi. It was an old-timey church, built in the 12th century. It was where St. Clare built her community of nuns, the Order of Saint Clare. We spent about 20 to 30 minutes in the church before heading back into the city.

By the time we got back, all eight of us were starving! So we got lunch at a cute little pizza place, but it wasn't very good. Oh well! After that we hit the shops! First, we went to a gelato place and got some gelato. I got strawberry, even though I'm not a strawberry fan. I just wanted to try it. I didn't like it. After that we went to the leather markets. I was trying to find something for my mom, but I couldn't find anything. We stopped at a few other stores that sold trinkets, perfumes, clothing, and so much more.

After shopping for an hour or so, we stopped at an ATM because all my friends needed more money. They had spent all their money on shopping! I didn't need to use it because, unlike them, I'm actually careful about how to spend my money. Don't tell them I said that though. They probably wouldn't care though because they've admitted it themselves on a few occasions.

Anyway, they were struggling to get the machine working. So Ryan, who was pretty tech savvy, tried to help them. Connor and Ollie thought it was amusing, so they went over to get a closer look. Elliott and I watched them from a distance.

After a little bit, Elliott turned to me and said, "So, I believe I still owe you a date!"

I turned to him and asked, "A date?"

"Yeah," Elliott nodded. "I was going to ask you last night, but...we weren't speaking."

"Yeah," I slowly nodded. After a moment of awkward silence, I asked him, "But shouldn't we spend time with the others? What are they going to do? I'd hate to ditch them."

Elliott assured me, "It'll be fine. We *have* spent the whole day with them. And we still have eight days left of the trip. That's *plenty* of time to spend time with them. *And...*" He paused, but then said, "And I think I owe you."

"No you don't," I said. "But if you *really* want to do something, I'll do it!"

This made Elliott beam with excitement. A bright, contagious smile plastered on his face. He didn't say anything, he just leaned in for a quick peck on the lips. "Dinner?" he asked.

"Sounds great!" I said. "6?"

"I'll pick you up!" he quickly responded. "Or, meet you outside your door," he chuckled.

"It's a date?" I asked him.

He took my hand and said, "It's a date!"

We both smiled. Finally everyone had gotten the ATM sorted out and we walked back to the hotel to get some rest. The whole rest of the way, Elliott and I held each other's hands.

When we finally got back to the hotel room, it was 3 o'clock. Three hours before my date. As soon as the door shut, I turned to my friends.

Excited and with a huge smile on my face, I said, "Guess what guys? I have my first date with Elliott tonight!"

"What about the late-night beach date?" Esperanza asked in confusion.

"Sorry, my *second* date with Elliott tonight!" I corrected myself.

"You go, girl!" Grace said, giving me a high five.

"I'm super nervous!" I said.

"Why are you nervous?" Esperanza asked.

"What if I mess it up?" I asked. "What if I don't dress right? Or I embarrass myself? Or we run into some fans or paparazzi? Or he..."

Putting her hands on my shoulders, Nicole cut off my ranting, "Cecilia, everything will be fine. Elliott really likes you, and there is nothing you could do to change that. And, plus, you happen to have one of the key dating experts in this room!"

"Who is it?" I asked.

"Why me, of course!" Nicole said. "We're gonna make you look so freaking beautiful that those hating fans of Elliott's will be jealous!"

"Uh," Esperanza sounded like she was hesitating to say something in fear of being rude. But she said it anyway, "I think they're already jealous of her. They seemed pretty upset by their words, ya know? All the hate comments."

"Oof," Nicole scrunched up her face, "you're right, Esperanza." Nicole thought of a better thing to say, and once she did she asked me, "Can I start again?"

"Sure," I chuckled, shaking my head.

Nicole, now with the same energy she had before, said confidently, "We're going to make you look so freaking beautiful that those hating fans of Elliott's will fall in love with you!"

This made me smile. "How?" I asked.

"Well," she said, "this is a Disney princess fairytale after all. And I'm your fairy godmother!"

"Then who are we?" Grace asked in curiosity, gesturing to herself and Esperanza. "Are we mice?" she asked sarcastically.

"The mice are cute," I pointed out to them.

"I'll be Gus Gus," Grace smiled. She pointed to Esperanza and said, "You can be Jaq," which made Esperanza stick her tongue out, but then laugh. Grace turned to me and said, "You're the Disney fan. Their names are Jaq and Gus Gus, right?"

I nodded my head, grinning at how my friends always turned to me about Disney knowledge.

Step one was an hour and a half long nap. We had had a long day of touring and shopping. At 4:30, they started preparing me for the date. Nicole was the "lead fairy godmother," and she did not reveal her plan to us until we woke up.

"Okay people," she said. "We've got an hour and a half until Elliott gets here. And we've gotta make Cecilia look her absolute best. We need to assign some jobs." She pointed to Grace, "Grace, you have good taste in fashion! You pick out what Cecilia is wearing." Grace nodded in understanding. Nicole turned to Esperanza: "Esperanza, you did a really good job doing Cecilia's hair the other evening during her first date with Elliott." Esperanza nodded. Nicole said, "And I will do makeup! While you guys were napping I got all my makeup out!"

"But, Nicole," I said, "you know I don't really wear makeup that much." That was true. I ever wore makeup, except at high school dances, college parties, and a few other exceptions.

"Not much, Cecilia," Nicole assured me. "Just a little blush, lip gloss. Make you look nice. And I promise no eyeliner."

"Thank you!" I told her. I hated putting on eyeliner. It always made me so uncomfortable keeping my eyes open that long.

"Alright everyone!" Nicole clapped her hands together. "Let's go! Cecilia, we'll go into the bathroom and start with makeup!"

We then headed off to the bathroom. I sat down on the toilet while Nicole got out her beauty supplies.

She tilted my chin up with her hand and examined, "Hmmmm," she thought. "Let's see. I'm thinking some base, blush, mascara, and lip gloss should do it!"

As she reached into her bag to pull some makeup out, I said, "Hey, Nicole." She looked up from the makeup bag. "Thanks for doing this."

"Anytime!" Nicole said. She then started to apply makeup. "And you deserve this. You're a good person, Cecilia. You deserve a guy like Elliott who will make you happy." This made me smile, and I felt like I was going to cry at my friend's kind words. She could sense this and teasingly warned me, "Now don't cry! We've got makeup to put on!" This made the two of us laugh like we always did, and she began dabbing some peach colored base on my cheeks.

I don't know why I never wear makeup. I guess because I was never really that concerned with the way I looked. In fact, I was never really concerned about boys in general. Don't get me wrong, I've always wanted to find my true love. But I was never in a rush to get a boyfriend, and I was willing to wait all my life to find the right guy. Unlike a lot of women, I wasn't afraid to be on my own. At one point, during our first year of college, all my friends had boyfriends, except for me. But it didn't bother me. And before going on this trip, all of us were single. Now it seems that one of us would not be by the time this trip ended...

When Nicole was done with my makeup, she showed me it in the mirror. I smiled at my reflection, non-dramatic but nonetheless pretty makeup.

"Oh my gosh," I said, still in awe of how I looked. "I look pretty."

"You're *beautiful*," Nicole assured me.

"Thanks so much Nicole," I thanked my best friend.

"Anything for you," she replied. She gave me a hug, but was careful not to smudge my makeup. When we were done hugging, Nicole said, "Now it's time for your hair. Let me get Esperanza."

She left the room. And I continued to look at myself in the mirror. I felt like a new woman now. I was going on a date with a guy I actually genuinely liked for the first time. On the previous dates, I had thought the guy was cute, but they always turned out to be somewhat of a disappointment. A little surprising considering I've been on a total of twelve dates since my sophomore year of high school. Now Elliott was the thirteenth...

After a little bit, Esperanza came in. "Hey girl!" she said cheerfully. As soon as she saw me, her mouth dropped. "Wow! Cecilia, you look gorgeous!"

"Thanks, Esperanza," I said. "What are we going to do with my hair?"

"Well," Esperanza said, getting out her hair supplies. "Grace and I talked to Elliott to ask where he was taking you and how he was dressing. He's taking you to a nice restaurant, but not *super* fancy. We'll save that hairstyle for a movie or the Oscars or something."

"Okay," I nodded.

"So, I was thinking," she said, playing with my hair, as she mused, "I know your hair is naturally curly, and it's pretty that way. But Elliott hasn't seen you with *straight* hair yet, and you always look beautiful with straight hair. What do you think about that?"

"Why not?" I said, because why not show Elliott what my hair looked like when it wasn't naturally curly like he usually saw me?

"Goody goody!" Esperanza, who was clearly excited, cheerfully said, clapping her hands. She got out her straightener and started to straighten my hair. It took about fifteen minutes, and when we were done, I looked in the mirror once again.

"Do you like it?" Esperanza asked me.

"I love it," I smiled, nodding.

"Great!" she said. "Now we just need one final touch: the outfit."

She took me by the hand and led me to the room. Nicole and Grace were sitting on the beds, and when they saw me they looked amazed.

"Wow, Cecilia!" Nicole said with her eyes wide open. "You look like a total knockout!"

"Thank you," I smiled.

"You look really pretty," Grace said. I nodded. "If those haters could see you now, they'd change their minds *completely* about you!"

I chuckled. "Yeah. What a bunch of losers."

"Now there's just one more thing we need: the outfit," Grace said. "I've talked to Elliott, and he says he's taking you to a nice restaurant, but he's dressing not too fancy, but not too casual." Grace then added, "Oh and he also said to say hi! And that you'd look beautiful even if you wear a sweatshirt and sweatpants."

"Awww," I said. "But I think I can do better than *that*."

"Agreed," Grace said. "Which is why I think this would be the ideal outfit," she pointed to my bed. I looked down upon it to find a spring green sundress paired with a jean jacket and the golden sandals from the night before. "I figured you'd go with your signature color, and a jean jacket in case you get cold, and I think the sandals looked cute with the outfit."

"It looks perfect!" I told her.

"Alright!" she said. "Try it on!"

My three best friends left the room so I could get changed. As soon as they closed the door, I sighed, then carefully started to strip so I could put on the outfit. I easily slipped the dress on, and was especially careful not to ruin my hair or makeup. Next, I put the jean jacket on, followed by the sandals.

Once I finished, I made my way over to the mirror to get the full view of my outfit. I couldn't believe it. I looked quite pretty. My friends had done a great job.

"Girls! I'm ready!" I shouted, still looking at myself in the mirror.

They all came out of the bathroom, and I turned around to show them. I couldn't stop smiling. My friends were absolutely amazed. Nicole put her hand over her mouth. Esperanza's jaw nearly dropped to the floor. Grace smiled brightly, and I could almost see a twinkle in her eye.

"Wow," Nicole had no words. "We did a pretty good job." All of us laughed.

"You look really pretty, Cecilia," Esperanza said. "Now seeing it with everything coming together, it looks really nice."

"Thank you," I blushed.

"Elliott is so lucky," Grace said. She looked as though she might tear up about her best friend and cousin being together.

"I feel lucky to have him," I said. That was true. I was so happy Elliott came on this trip, happy he came into my life.

Nicole then grabbed her green and gold clutch and my phone, and handed them to me saying, "Here." I took them. "It will really bring the whole outfit together."

"I can't thank you guys enough," I opened my arms for a big hug. Everyone came in and we all hugged really tightly.

Once we all separated, there was a knock on the door.

"Must be Elliott," I whispered. Everyone squealed.

"What are you waiting for?" Esperanza asked. "Let him in!"

Just as I was making my way to the door, Nicole grabbed me by the shoulders. "Wait!" she said. Then she started to lead me to the bathroom. "For this, you'll have to make a grand entrance!" When we got to the bathroom, Nicole told me, "Now we'll tell you when to come out. Okay?"

"Okay," I nodded. Nicole gave me one last smile before closing the door. I listened closely to everything going on.

"Can I open the door now?" Grace asked.

"Go ahead!" Nicole eagerly said.

I heard Grace open the door with the click. "Hi," a sweet British voice said. Elliott.

"Hey!" Grace said.

"How is everyone doing?" he asked.

"Fine, thanks Elliott," Esperanza replied.

"Great!" Nicole said. "And you look handsome, Elliott. Cecilia is a lucky girl." I started to get butterflies in my stomach.

"Thank you, Nicole," Elliott politely replied. "Trust me, I don't know how such a wonderful girl ended up with a dork like me. I think *I'm* the lucky one." My heart melted.

"Speaking of Cecilia," Elliott said, "where is she?"

"Yeah, Nicole," Grace said. "Where is she?"

Esperanza joked, "Did you lock her in the bathroom again?" I could hear Elliott lightly laugh.

"Only to make a grand entrance!" Nicole said. "But I think Elliott deserves to see how beautiful his date looks." Then she shouted, "Cecilia! Your date awaits!"

I took a deep breath and slowly turned the door knob. I opened it and stepped out, nervously smiling. When I saw Elliott, I stood still. He looked extremely handsome. He had a black and white striped button-down, collared shirt with black buttons paired with a brown suede jacket and black pants and shoes. The moment he saw me Elliott couldn't stop staring at me. His mouth opened partially, and his eyes were sparkling. His lips formed into a shy, awkward smile.

"Oh my," he said, almost at a loss of words. "W-wow, Cecilia, y-you look st-stunning."

I blushed red, my cheeks feeling warm. "Thank you," I said. "You look very handsome, Elliott."

Elliott smiled, as if he was still amazed by how beautiful I was. "Thank you."

We continued to smile at each other, and just stood there, looking amazed at how the other person looked.

"Now don't just stand there you two!" Grace said, pushing Elliott towards me.

She pushed him so we were right in front of each other.

"Hey," I smirked.

"H-hi," Elliott stuttered, blushing at the close contact. The close contact in front of my friends that is.

Grace whispered to her cousin, "Kiss her already!"

"Yeah, Elliott come on!" Esperanza encouraged him. "She's not going to bite."

With that Elliott slowly leaned in toward me and kissed me. We broke apart after a few seconds.

"So," he asked me with a smirk on his face, "are you ready for our date night?"

I smiled, "As ready as I ever will be!"

Just as we were about to leave, Nicole stopped us saying, "Wait! Wait! Wait!" She then rushed to the bathroom.

"What's going on?" Elliott mouthed to me. I only shrugged.

Nicole came back in with a bottle. It was mint breath freshener spray. I rolled my eyes.

"Now, Cecilia," Nicole said. "Open wide." I did as I was told, and she sprayed it three times in my mouth. Elliott was trying his best not to laugh, even covering his mouth at one time to hide a smile. Nicole turned to him and said, "She gets bad breath sometimes, so she needs this if you guys are gonna kiss!" Elliott, still using his hand to hide his smile, nodded. I flushed tomato red in embarrassment.

"Okay, okay," I nervously muttered under my breath. After blushing, I turned to Elliott and grinned, "I think it's time we go on our date."

"Oh yes!" Elliott said. He checked his watch and said, "Reservation is at 6:15 and it's 6:03!"

"Then I guess we better get going," I said, starting to walk. Elliott put his arm on my shoulder.

"Now you two have fun!" Grace said.

"But not *too much* fun," Nicole joked, causing me to roll my eyes.

"And be safe from all those psycho fans!" Esperanza added.

"We will take all your advice to heart," Elliott winked.

"Bye everyone!" I waved as we neared the door.

"Bye!" all the girls said in unison.

Elliott politely opened the door for us. When we stepped out of the room, everyone was waving at us. As soon as we shut the door, we started to make our way to the steps.

Elliott still had his arm around his shoulder when he asked me, "So, um, are–are you ready for our–for our date?" I think he struggled to have his words come out because he was still taken aback and struck by how beautiful I was.

"With a hot date like you, sweetheart," I flirted, "I'm ready for *anything*."

This caused Elliott to blush and smile. I gave him a quick peck on his cheek, and he did the same to me. Then we made our way to the restaurant, to begin our romantic night in Assisi.

Chapter 13: Wishing For A Spaghetti Dinner

"So," Elliott asked me as we left the hotel, "who was in charge of getting you ready?"

"All the girls, mainly Nicole," I said. "She took over the whole thing!"

Elliott chuckled. "Well, *I* think they did a fantastic job. And I think even without makeup you look beautiful."

"You do?" I asked him. I sighed, then I came to a realization: "You know, Elliott, before you, no guy has ever called me beautiful before."

"Really?" Elliott said in disbelief.

"Yup," I nodded. "I think a few guys have said I look nice, but no guy, besides my dad, has ever even called me pretty."

"Well," Elliott looked at me. "Well–I think they didn't know what they were thinking. Because you're *beautiful*. Not just because of your looks, but I–I think you have a nice personality."

Man, he was too sweet for this world! "You're just saying that to be nice," I told him as we continued to walk to the restaurant.

"No I'm not!" Elliott assured me as we came to a brief stop. He then looked at me in the eyes, his coffee colored-brown eyes sparkling and looking sincere. I've noticed that Elliott often can shift from being very confident and romantic to completely awkward. I noticed this shift as he said:

"Just so you know, Cecilia, that I–I love your personality. You're funny." He awkwardly paused. Then he tried to think of something else, "And you have such a good heart, yeah." He paused again, "And you always put others before yourself. That's good, too." I began to flush a beet red. "And um," Elliott tried to think. Then he thought of: "Oh! And I've seen you with Connor and Ollie. You're really good with kids. And you're very smart. I'm not sure why an awkward, stupid guy like me is with a wonderful girl like you!"

"You're not awkward or stupid!" I said almost in shock. Okay, maybe he kinda was awkward sometimes, but I wasn't going to say that to his face. "I think the same thing about you. You always make me smile. And you're really funny and sweet. You are really handsome, Elliott, but remember that beauty is found within."

Elliott smiled. Then he started to think and asked me, "Why does that sound familiar?"

"Oh, I may have quoted *Beauty and the Beast*," I winked at him.

"Are you calling me the beast?" he asked me, smiling.

"You're the Beast *after* he became the handsome prince," I winked at him.

"Really?" he joked. "I was thinking *I* was Beauty and *you* were the Beast!"

My mouth widened in shock, but I knew Elliott was kidding. "Elliott Parker!" I smacked his chest lightly. "You watch what you say!"

Elliott was laughing, then he assured me, "Hey, hey, I'm joking. I'm joking. You are *definitely* Beauty!"

"Awww," I said, smiling at him.

After an awkward pause, Elliott asked, "Would it be okay if I---can I kiss you right now?"

"That shouldn't even be a question!" I cheerfully replied, leaning in and kissing him. It was a really quick peck, but it was very sweet. After we had pulled apart, we smiled at each other, then we leaned in to kiss again. This time, it was much longer and romantic. We finally pulled apart and smiled at each other once again.

"Now," I said, "We should probably get to dinner. We'll miss our reservation!"

Elliott looked down at his watch and became worried, "Oh no!" he said to himself in a panic. "We're late!" Then he grabbed my hand, "Let's go!" We then began running to the restaurant to make our reservation.

******

"Cheers!" Elliott said, holding up his wine glass. Of course, he had red wine, while I just had water. Thank goodness they didn't give me a hard time like they did in Materdomini.

I held up my glass. "Cheers!" I cheerfully said.

Then there was silence. "Wait, uh, what should we do cheers to?" Elliott asked, realizing he didn't know what to do cheers to.

"Oh, um," I said, trying to think. Then I came up with: "To an incredible trip and an incredible person!"

"Awww," Elliott said. "Cheers to that!" We clink our glasses together. While I took a sip of my water, Elliott immediately set his glass down, causing me to gasp. Elliott thought something was wrong, "Wait! What is it? What is it, darling?"

"Elliott Parker!" I shook my head, pretending to sound angry. "I am very disappointed!"

"Huh?" Elliott asked in confusion. Don't worry, I was just teasing.

I pointed to his glass and said, "You put your drink down after cheers. You're supposed to drink and *then* set your drink down."

Elliott's worried expression faded away and chuckled, "Oh, Cecilia, everyone knows that's just a myth."

I shook my head, "Uh, no it's not. My dad used to point it out to me all the time every time I used to do it. He said the reason you don't set your drink down dates back to the olden days. They clinked their drinks together to assure everyone that they hadn't put poison in the drinks, and if someone did put their drink down without drinking, they would become suspicious that they poisoned the drinks." Elliott nodded, still not convinced that this was true.

I decided to get my point across in a different away. I stared Elliott dead in the eye and said in a serious tone, "Unless, you're trying to poison me. Huh, Elliott?"

Elliott's smiling face turned back into a worried one. "Wait! What?" he sounded nervous. "Why would—why would you think that?"

"I see you're bluffing, Parker!" I continued to look dead serious. "You're hiding something!"

Elliott quickly tried to assure me he didn't poison me. He started talking fast-paced, clearly showing his nerves, "What? What? Why would I do that? I really like you, Cecilia! Why ever would I poison you? Please believe me!"

"You know, Elliott," I said, "Something else my dad told me was that some people talk really quickly when they're nervous. And you seem to be one of those people. You're nervous you'll get caught, that's why!"

Elliott's eyes widened again, as if he thought he was done for. Seeing this I quickly changed from my serious face to a smile. I assured him, "I'm kidding! Don't worry!" I then laughed at myself, proud of myself for making him believe I thought he was trying to poison me.

Elliott then lightly chuckled along. He smirked and said, "Just you wait, Hartley. I'm going to get you back. Just you wait and see!"

"Not if I get you again first!" I teased him. He stuck his tongue out at me, and I stuck mine out at him.

We spent the whole evening just talking and laughing. We shared stories, and shared a plate of spaghetti.

Elliott was laughing when he said, "Oh my goodness! Teddy would *love* you!"

I was puzzled by the name. I had never heard of Teddy before. "Teddy?" I asked. "Who's Teddy?"

Elliott then realized, "Have I not told you about Teddy yet?" I shook my head no. "Oh, I have to tell you!" he said. "Teddy is my best friend. We've been that way ever since we were young lads."

"So kind of like my friends and I?" I asked.

"You could say that," Elliott nodded. "He's so funny! There was this one time where we did a 'How to get in shape like Serpent Boy' video on Instagram about two years ago. And we shot this one bit where it showed me from the top up doing push ups on a bar, and it looked like I was doing it with ease on my own. But in reality, I had my feet on Teddy's back and he was pretty much holding me up."

This made me laugh so hard. "I can just picture that happening!" I couldn't control my laughter.

"You know what, I'll pull up a picture of him for you," Elliott said as he got out his phone and started to scroll through his phone.

I whispered to him, "Elliott, this is a fancy restaurant. You can't have your phone out!"

Elliott looked up from his phone and said, "It will only be a few seconds, love. I promise. Then as soon as I'm done the phone goes away."

I nodded, believing in him. Then he went back to scrolling through his phone and soon found a picture of Teddy. "Here he is!" Elliott smiled, holding up the picture for me. He handed me his phone, and I zoomed in. In the picture there were two young men, one of whom was Elliott, smiling in tuxes. Elliott said it had been taken at the world premiere of *Serpent Boy 2* last year. The other man must have been Teddy! He was slightly taller than Elliott, around 5"10 was probably a guess. He was a good-looking young man (although not as good-looking as Elliott, in my opinion!). He had straight yet unruly sandy blonde hair, a little shorter than Elliott's, and sky blue eyes, with tan skin. While he and Elliott were dressed nicely in tuxedos, they both had goofy faces and made crazy eyes. Even though they were supposed to look elegant, the men decided to let their goofy sides show.

I decided to tease Elliott yet again. I smirked and said to him, "He's cute."

Elliott got jealous and pouted his lips saying, "Hey!"

I looked up and reassured him, "But don't worry. Not as cute as *you*."

This made Elliott smile, knowing he hadn't lost me to his best friend. "You know," I added, looking at the picture, "I think he and Grace would make a cute couple!"

247

"Actually they've never met before," Elliott stated as I handed his phone back to him. He put it away as soon as he had it back.

"He's your best friend and he's never met your cousin before?" I chuckled in disbelief. "Do you not get to see him that often? With your busy schedule and all?"

"Well he works for me," Elliott stated. "He's sort of my assistant I guess. He comes with me almost everywhere I go. And I pay him pretty well. He's a good assistant, except when he asks me to help him impress a lady."

"Oh! Are women just naturally drawn to you because you're famous?" I ask.

"I guess you could say that," Elliott looked down and laughed awkwardly. He titled his head up and shrugged, "Basically I'm always the wingman."

"Wingman?" I laughed. "Elliott Parker is a wingman?"

"It's hard to believe but yes," Elliott nodded. "You see, what happens is that if Teddy sees a woman he fancies we get her to recognize me as Elliott Parker, and that's how we get her attention. Then I'll introduce him as my best mate Teddy and it just goes from there. Ryan asks me to do it all the time too."

I asked in curiosity, "How does it feel to go anywhere, and everyone knows who you are?"

Elliott sighed and said, "Honestly, it's not the best."

"Really?" I asked, wanting to learn more.

"Sometimes it's fun when you see how you touch the lives of so many fans. That makes me feel good," he started. Then he paused, looked down, and continued. "But then there are times where it's the worst."

"What do you mean?" I ask, now *really* wanting to hear more. Elliott paused once again, took a heavy deep breath, and said:

"Well, sometimes I feel like I have no personal life at all. Like yesterday, I realized everyone cares about who I date. And two months ago, in my home, back in London, the paparazzi were waiting outside my house, and I don't even know how they found out where I live. And it can be a little stressful. I like my privacy. I like going out with my friends, I like spending time with my family, I like being with you." I smiled, feeling for Elliott as he told me what he was feeling. "And that's why I'm a very private person. Sometimes I wish I could have two separate lives: my personal one and my professional one. That's why yesterday was a bit of a shock to the system. When all those tabloids came out about us, it upset me not so much that I was exposed, but that you were brought into it all when you didn't do anything wrong. And it made me realize, that this most likely isn't going to be the last time we have an article written about us. But I can do something." Then he took both of my hands in his and set them down on the table, holding them tightly. "I might not be able to prevent it entirely, but I can do a better job of protecting you and making sure you never get hurt like that again. It pained me so much to see you that way yesterday, but I promise to do my best to make sure to not put you, or me, in that situation again."

I found myself tearing up. That was *really* beautiful. I was speechless. "Elliott, I–," I started to say but couldn't find the words to say it.

"Wow," Elliott said to himself. Then he looked back up at me and said, "That was really heavy and serious for our first real date."

This made us both laugh. What was once a serious moment instantly became funny by Elliott making light of the situation.

"Very true!" I laughed. We still continued laughing. We weren't laughing hard or loud, but we were laughing nonetheless. I saw out of the corner of my eye that people were staring at us, and so we stopped.

"Anyway," Elliott said, looking at the plate of untouched spaghetti. "We haven't even touched our spaghetti yet! Shall we eat?"

"I'm so hungry I could eat a horse!" I exaggerated.

"I don't think we can get that here in Italy," Elliott quipped back. This made us giggle once again.

And so, we began to share the spaghetti, we used both our forks to eat. After a little bit of eating, we took our forks and went in for another bite. However, we noticed that we both started to eat the same noodle and were connected by the noodle. Sound familiar?

When we noticed this, we laughed. And I think we both had the same thought because we started to move closer to each other as we began to finish the spaghetti. We leaned closer and closer, and started to lean closer to each other and further across the table. It didn't look very proper, but who cares? We finally were about to reach our lips when the waiter came by.

She was a cheerful middle aged woman, black hair in a sleek bob. "How is it over here young love birds?" she asked in a very perky way.

Just like that, the moment was ruined. Elliott and I hadn't kissed. We had been surprised by the woman. Not only that but we were practically leaning across the table, waiting to kiss. So Elliott and I just forgot about it and slowly sunk back in our seats. Flushing in embarrassment, we took a bite of the spaghetti noodle and that was that. No *Lady and the Tramp*-style kiss for us.

It seemed as though the waitress didn't know what was going on. She cheerfully said, "Any desert for you?"

"Yes!" I said cheerfully.

But at the exact same time, Elliott said, "No, thank you."

Then I turned to him with a confused look. Why didn't he want dessert? But then he mouthed something to me. It took a while to realize what it was, but then I realized what he said: "Gelato."

I nodded my head, understanding what he said. Then I turned to the waitress and said, "Um, no thank you, ma'am. Just the check, si prega."

"Of course!" the waitress said, exiting with a bubbly smile on her face.

I turned to Elliott and said, "I completely forgot about gelato! Thanks for reminding me!"

"Of course," he winked. "We'll only be in Italy for two more days, we might as well enjoy some gelato. When we get to Austria and Germany, there won't be any there."

"Actually," I reminded him, "I remember reading somewhere that they *do* have gelato in those countries."

"Really?" Elliott asked puzzled. As he asked this, he cocked his head to the side. It was cute.

"Yeah," I said, "you can get gelato anywhere, silly."

"I don't think so," Elliott said, by this time he had his head back in the proper position.

"We have gelato in America," I told him. That was true. I've had gelato plenty of times in the states. Although, to be fair, it was never as good as Italian gelato. "Do you not have gelato in England?"

Elliott shook his head. "No," he said. "And even if we did, I've never seen it or had it."

"Wanna make a bet?" I asked him, crossing my arms.

Elliott crossed his arms too and said, "A bet that you're wrong and I'm right? Or you're right and I'm wrong?"

"Uh huh," I nodded my head. "If we get to Austria and we see gelato there, you have to do whatever I say for twenty four hours!"

"Sounds fair," Elliott said. "But if there is no gelato in Austria, *you* have to do whatever *I* say for twenty four hours!"

"You're on!" I smiled. Then I took my right hand, jokingly spit in it, and held my hand out for Elliott to shake, which he did.

"If you don't mind me asking," he asked, "is spitting on your hand before you shake someone's hand an American thing?"

"It can be," I said. "But I mainly just wanted to see if you Brits would react in any way. You guys have a reputation of being a little bit uptight, you know that?"

Elliott sarcastically said, "Sure, Cecilia! We're all like that! Including me, I can be really uptight, you know that?" This made us both laugh. We finished our spaghetti and got the check.

******

As soon as we got our gelato, Elliott and I just walked through the street, heading back to the hotel. I decided to expand my boundaries a little bit and got lemon flavor, while Elliott got chocolate, which was usually the one I ordered.

"How's your lemon gelato?" Elliott asked me, taking a bite of his gelato.

"Delizioso!" I licked my lips. "How's your *chocolate* gelato?"

"Delizioso!" Elliott replied. "Want to try a bite?" he asked me.

"Sure!" I said. "Want to try a bite of *mine*?"

"Absolutely," Elliott said. Then we stopped briefly and turned so we were facing each other. I took a little bit of lemon with my spoon, and Elliott did the same with his chocolate. We each reached our spoons across to give each other a bite, as if we were parents feeding our babies food.

While I got my spoon of gelato perfectly into Elliott's mouth, some of the chocolate was on my lips and in the corner of my mouth.

"Oh!" Elliott pointed out. "You've got some," he pointed to my mouth. "I'm terribly sorry."

"Don't worry about it," I assured him. "Where's the napkin?" I started looking for the napkin, I finally found one and was about to clean off my face.

Then Elliott came in and awkwardly smiled, "Allow me." He seemed to be asking for the napkin, and I gave it to him. He took it in his hand and started to dab the chocolate off my lips. "Now I'm—I'm smudging away your lipstick," he said worriedly. "I'm sorry, Cecilia."

"Don't worry about it," I placed my hand on his hand. "It's nearing the end of the night anyway."

Because we were in close contact, I felt the urge to kiss him. I started to lean closely until Elliott leaned away and said, "Wait, Cecilia."

I was confused as to why Elliott stopped the kiss. "Is something wrong, Elliott?" I asked.

"Oh, n–nothing. I'm so–sorry. It's just—," he started to say. Seeing that he was nervous, I put a hand on Elliott's shoulder, trying to tell him to take his time.

"Do you know how I promised you that I would make sure not to put ourselves in a ferry situation again?" I nodded. Elliott continued, "Well, I think one way to do it is to not be kissing in public. We can still kiss when we're alone, but I think we need to be more careful when we're in public like that."

Not gonna lie, I was kind of disappointed. Elliott tried to tell me, "I'm sorry, love. It's not that I don't—."

But then I realized Elliott was right. We had to be more careful when we were in public. There could be paparazzi or fans at any corner, and we had to be wary.

So I lifted my head, smiled a small smile and nodded, "No, you're right Elliott. We *definitely* have to be cautious. And I respect you for wanting that. I want to be careful too."

This made Elliott feel better, and he smiled when he realized he had not hurt my feelings. "Good," he nodded his head. "That's very good."

And we continued walking. Once we finished our gelatos, we were now walking with arms linked. When all of a sudden Elliott felt a tap on his shoulder. This caused us to turn around to see who tapped his shoulder.

There stood two young girls. One was a teenager, the other looked about a tween. The teenager had strawberry blonde hair pulled in a side braid with eyes the color of emeralds and freckles scattered across her face. The tween looked exactly like the teenager, only she had no freckles, was shorter, and had her strawberry blonde hair in a bob that went to her chin.

"Elliott Parker?" the teen girl asked excitedly with a smile on her face.

"That's me!" Elliott smiled nervously. As he said this, he slowly unlocked his arm from mine and reached toward my hand. He intertwined our fingers together and gave my hand a reassuring squeeze.

"My name's Samanatha," the teen girl introduced herself. She gestured to the tween girl and said, "And this is my little sister Kelly."

"Hi," Kelly, who seemed to be the more shy of the two, nervously waved.

"Nice to meet you, Kelly," Elliott smiled and said to the tween. He then turned to Samantha and said, "Hello, Samantha."

"I'm sorry," Samantha looked down, cheeks flushing the color of her hair. "I'm just such a big fan of yours," she continued, finally looking up at Elliott. I felt as if the girls didn't think I was there.

"Oh really?" Elliott beamed.

"Can I–get a picture, please?" Samantha asked.

"Of course!" Elliott replied.

Before Samantha could get her phone out to take the picture, she pointed to me and said, "Oh my gosh! You're Cecilia!"

I nervously nodded and said, "Yup, that's me." Elliott squeezed my hand again.

At first, it seemed as though Samantha was going to be rude, much like the fans who attacked me on social media. But instead, she developed a concerned look on her face and said, "I'm really sorry about those fans on Instagram. They were being so mean, and you really didn't deserve it."

My nervous smile changed into a sigh of relief. Then I replied to Samantha, "Oh, thank you. That's so sweet."

"I hope you don't mind," Kelly finally piped in, "but I may have looked at your Instagram account, briefly, before you changed it to private." That was true. As soon as the criticism came out, I changed my account to private so the fans couldn't make comments like that on my Instagram posts again.

"Don't worry about it," I assured her. "As long as you didn't post any of the mean comments, you're good with me," I winked at her.

"I didn't, I promise," Kelly convinced me. "And I saw you go to Washington College!"

"That I do," I said.

Samantha said to me, "Washington College is her *dream* school! She won't stop talking about it. She's five years younger than me and she already knows where she's going to college, whereas I don't have a clue!"

"That's good," I said. I turned to Kelly, "Never too young to start thinking about college!"

"What do you study?" Kelly asked me.

"I am majoring in creative writing," I said.

All of a sudden, Kelly got very excited and said, "I want to do creative writing one day!"

"Are you a writer, too?" I asked her. Kelly quickly nodded. I smiled and said, "Well, it's very nice to meet another writer."

"She's *really* good," Samantha told me. "One time, she wrote a research paper I had. And I—," she started to say until Kelly elbowed her. Samantha corrected herself, "*She* got an A!"

I nodded my head, "Impressive," I said. "Pretty impressive."

"You know what," Samantha said. "at first I was kind of upset that Elliott Parker had a girlfriend. But now that I met her and I know what she's like, I'm glad he has you."

"Awwww, thank you," Elliott and I said in unison. We then turned to each other and smiled. Then we turned back to the two sisters.

Samantha asked me, "Do you mind if you get in the picture with us, Cecilia? We can take a selfie with the four of us in it!"

"I'd be happy too!" I said, keeping a smile on my face. Samantha started to hand the phone to Elliott, but I stopped her saying, "No! He can't be trusted, Samantha. Trust me. He always drops the phones when he's taking a selfie."

"That's true," Elliott piped in. He laughed, "I do it all the time and it never ends well."

So Samantha handed the phone to me and I took the selfie. We took two photos: one with us smiling, and the other with us making funny faces. This felt good. It felt good knowing that there were some Elliott Parker fans that were genuinely nice people that weren't jealous of anyone he's romantically involved with.

As soon as we were done, Samantha beamed, "Thank you both so much for taking a selfie with us!"

"Yeah," Kelly agreed. "It was so nice to meet you both."

"Of course," Elliott grinned. "I'm always glad to meet some supportive fans!"
"It was so nice to meet you guys, too!" I said. Like I said before, I was so relieved that these were the nicer and more accepting of the Elliott Parker fans.

"Well, we should probably get going," Samantha said, looking at the time on her phone. "Our mom says we have to be back at the hotel by 9 and it's 8:51!"

After that all of us hugged each other and expressed how happy we all were to have met each other. Just before they left, I stopped them.

"Oh, wait! Kelly!" I said, causing the girls to turn around towards me. "Here, I'll give you my number and maybe one time we can exchange some advice, writer to writer."

This caused Kelly to beam from ear to ear. "Of course, Cecilia!" she excitedly said, taking out her phone to put my number in.

I told her my number as she typed it in: "443-555-6603."

As soon as she was finishing typing in my number as a contact, I asked Kelly, "Where do you guys live?"

"Chicago," Kelly replied.

"Oh, my dad has family who live in Chicago," I said. "We go at least once a year, usually around Christmastime. Maybe the next time I'm there we can meet up!"

"That would be wonderful!" Kelly smiled.

"Thank you so much," Samantha told me.

"Of course," I winked.

And with that, we said our goodbyes once again, and the girls walked away. I ran back to Elliott and we linked arms once again.

"See?" Elliott said to me. "I have some fans who genuinely care."

"Yeah," I looked back, although by now the two sisters had vanished. "They seem nice." I have finally turned back so I was facing Elliott.

"They sure do like you, don't they?" Elliott teasingly said.

"Jealous?" I playfully punched him on the elbow.

Elliott stuck his tongue out, "Wouldn't dream of it." I stuck my tongue out at Elliott playfully.

We continued laughing and talking, and we got back to the hotel around 9:03. We walked up the stairs, and wouldn't unlink our arms. But before I knew it, we were back at my place.

"Okay," I sighed. "I guess this is good night?"

"Doesn't have to be," Elliott shook his head. He looked down at his phone and said, "I got a text from Ryan saying he and the others went out to dinner and to hang out in the piazza. We can go back to my place if you want. Hang out, watch TV, talk some more—"

I cut Elliott off: "Or you come in here. There's two keys for this room, and I've got one of them."

"Are you sure?"

"Positive!"

And with that I tried to look for the key. I eventually did find it, and I unlocked it. I opened the door for Elliott, "Gentlemen first!"

"Thank you," Elliott smiled, walking into the room. As soon as he was in, I closed the door behind me. Then we just stood there awkwardly. I've never brought a guy back into my house, or dorm, after a date. I didn't know what to do.

"Um," I said, trying to break the silence. Very nervous, I just looked down at my feet. "Do you--want to sit down? Make yourself comfy?"

"Uh, sure," Elliott replied. He sat down on my bed.

"And should I come over and sit next to you?" I asked him.

"If you want to, love," Elliott gestured to the space on the bed next to him.

So I went and sat next to him, in the exact spot where he patted on the bed. More awkward silence followed. It was as if Elliott and I couldn't look at each other. I put my palms in my lap while Elliott sat up resting on his palms in the back.

"Sorry," I murmured.

"About what?" Elliott asked in curiosity.

"It's just—" I turned towards him and he turned towards me, with a concerned but eager look on his face. "All the dates I've gone on, I haven't invited the guy into my house or dorm. So in case you couldn't tell, I'm clueless when it comes to *this* part of the date."

"That's nothing you need to apologize for," Elliott assured me. "With my busy schedule and all, I haven't been on a date in a year. So I've forgotten how to do this part of the date, too."

"Oh, okay," I nodded. "So," I dragged out. "What do you want to do?"

Elliott sighed and said, "I don't know. What do you want to do?"

"Don't know," I replied. "What do you want to do?"

"I have no clue," Elliott shrugged. Then he joked, "By the time we figure something to do, they'll be back."

I giggled at this, and Elliott chuckled at himself. Then we went back to awkward silence. Then I muttered, "Kiss me, please."

Elliott didn't hear me. "I'm sorry, what?" he politely asked.

"Would you please kiss me?" I asked, staring at his lips. I longed for them to linger on my own lips. Or anywhere else—

My cheek. My forehead. My hand. That's it...

Elliott smiled and leaned in. He kissed me alright! About as passionate and loving as we've done before. Then I pulled him by the collar so we were on our sides on the bed, continuing to kiss. I snuck my hands behind his back so he would come closer to me. Then we stopped kissing and just embraced. Elliott's warm body kept me warm. He snuck his arms behind my back and rested his head on my shoulder, and then he kissed it. Then he made a trail of kisses down my arm.

"That tickles!" I giggled. Then he held my hand. I could see him grinning as he brought my hand to his lips and kissed it. Then we pulled apart a little bit so we were staring at each other. Elliott had his hands around my waist. I reached my hand and slowly made my way to his hair. I started stroking my fingers through it, feeling his soft curls. I decided to play with it and ruffled it, making it messy everywhere.

When I had pulled my hand away, Elliott chuckled, "Like playing with my hair, do you, darling?"

I giggled and said, "It's just so soft and fluffy! How can I resist it? How can *anyone* resist it?" Elliott laughed.

Then there was silence, we just stared into each other's eyes. Something within me had changed. I took a deep breath, and said softly to him: "Elliott I think---"

Just as I was about to finish what I was going to say, we heard the door unlock. We heard talking and laughter. Elliott and I quickly sat up as soon as we heard them. Then we saw all of them, my friends and Elliott's brothers, talking and laughing with each other. They stopped as soon as they saw us.

"Oh, hey guys!" Grace cheerfully said. "How was the date?"

"We had a blast, thank you," I said.

At the exact same time I said that, Elliott said, "It was a very nice evening, thanks for asking." We then looked at each other and smiled.

"If you don't mind me asking, what was going on in here?" Nicole asked with a little playful tone in her voice.

"Nothing," I said awkwardly. "Just talking and laughing."

"Boring," Nicole said, putting her hands on her hips.

"Well it's what happened," I said. "That's all we planned to do." I sighed, really wanting to be able to tell Elliott what I had wanted to tell him.

Chapter 14: Wishing For A Necklace

All of us were sitting in the limo, anxiously waiting to go to Florence. We were anxious in a good way. We were excited. My parents went to Florence on their honeymoon, and they always told me about the beautiful architecture and all the history that went along with it. They also went to Venice, but we would not be stopping there. We were going to, but then we found an incredible opportunity: to go on the overnight train. That to us sounded like a really fun experience. Only problem was that if we did the overnight train, we wouldn't be able to go to Venice based on the timing of it all. And so we had a decision to make. So we decided to go on the overnight train. I was bummed we wouldn't be able to go to Venice, but I was really excited to go on the overnight train. And the good thing about not going to Venice is that it gave me a reason to go back to Europe.

"What's in Florence anyway?" Ollie asked, leaning his head against Ryan's shoulder.

"So much stuff, Ollie!" Elliott told his little brother.

"Like what?" Ollie asked. It seemed as if he was bored.

"Well---there's---the uh---" Elliott was trying to think of what there was in Florence.

I decided to come in and help him. "Well, you see Ollie, there's a bunch of art. And there's the Duomo where you can go up and see the beautiful view of Florence. And there's this place called the leather markets, like there was

266

in Assisi, where you try to get the best leather for the best prices. Kind of like an auction, if you know what I mean."

"That's cool," Ollie shrugged. "And I bet the overnight train will be fun too!"

"Yeah, I've always wanted to ride in one of those," Connor said.

"Me too," Esperanza said. "Always thought it would be kind of like *Murder on the Orient Express*, you know? But without the murder."

We all laughed at Esperanza's statement. I felt the same way. I always thought it would be fun to ride an overnight train like that. On a train set for a European destination dressed in Victorian clothing. Only no one gets killed. That's close to what I thought the overnight train would be like.

******

We drove for two hours and fifteen minutes. There was so much traffic and Lawrence didn't get a chance to stop for a rest break. Poor Lawrence. By a quarter after twelve, we had arrived in Florence! Lawrence would stay with the car that had our bags in it so we didn't have to carry around our bags for the day. He dropped us off at a bus station and left to park the car in a parking garage. Then we started to make our way toward the city.

"Oh, Elliott!" Grace turned to her cousin. "You remembered the tickets, right?"

Elliott looked genuinely confused. "What tickets?" he asked.

"To see the Statue of David," Grace said. Then he started to sound like a mix of concerned and annoyed. "You *did* remember them, right?"

Elliott tried to think of what he did with the tickets. Then he covered his mouth with both hands. "Oh no! Oh no, no, no!"

"What?" an even more concerned Grace tried to get him to say more. "What's oh no!"

Elliott turned back to her and said, "They're in my suitcase!"

We all groaned. "Ugh, Elliott!" Grace said.

"How could you be so stupid?" Ryan asked, running his hands through his hair in frustration.

Elliott turned to everyone and said, "Hey, guys! I can fix it! I can go find Lawrence!" The car Lawrence was driving was still in sight. "Oh, there he is!" Elliott pointed to the limo. As soon as he saw it Elliott ran after him screaming, "LAWRENCE! HEY! LAWRENCE! STOP! I NEED SOMETHING IN THERE! WAIT!" And Elliott was soon out of sight along with the limo.

Then we just waited there in silence and awkwardness for Elliott to come back. After ten minutes, he finally did, running back with the tickets in hand. As soon as he reached us, he leaned forward with his hands on his knees, panting. Then he held the eight tickets straight up in the air.

Gasping between his words, Elliott panted, "I got the tickets! It took a little bit of time to find Lawrence, but I found him, and I got the tickets."

I rushed over to Elliott and put my hands on his back. "Take a deep breath, babe," I tried to calm him down.

Connor ran over to his brother and handed him his water bottle cheerfully said, "Here you go, Elliott! Have some of my water!"

Elliott, still exhausted from running in the heat, smiled at his brother, "That's sweet of you, Connor but I have my own water." He then stood up, with my hands still on his back. He turned to me and asked, "Cecilia, could you please hand me my water bottle? It's in my sling bag on the back."

"Sure," I nodded. Then I went to the bag Elliott had on his back and opened it. I searched and searched for Elliott's water bottle. Finally, I found it and handed it to him. "Here you go," I said.

"Thanks," Elliott said as he took the water. He took a big gulp of it, and he soon felt better.

"Not to interrupt or anything," Grace said, "but our tickets are for 12:30 and it's 12:25, so---"

And with that, we speed walked to the museum where the Statue of David was. That was an interesting experience. Grace had to cover Connor and Ollie's eyes. Ryan was being immature about the fact that David was naked. Nicole and Esperanza got into an argument about whether David was hot or not. After that we went exploring Florence. The girls and boys wanted to see different things.

The girls wanted to go shopping and the boys wanted to see the different sights. So that's what we did. I went to the leather markets, did some more shopping, took some pictures outside the Duomo, and took a break from the sun in the *Lindt Lindor* chocolate store. I had fun with my friends, but I had to admit, I missed Elliott.

Around 4:30 we met up again in a piazza square. The boys looked exhausted. They looked a little red and sweaty from all the walking and being in the sun. Their fairness must have been the Irish part of the family. They walked over and sat right next to us.

"Hey," Elliott waved.

"Hey," I smiled.

"Hey," Grace replied.

"Hey," Ryan wiped the sweat off his forehead.

"Hey," Nicole looked up from her phone.

"Hey," Esperanza said.

"Hiya everybody!" Connor and Ollie cheerfully said in unison.

"Um, everyone who isn't Cecilia," Elliott said, looking down at his feet and with both his arms behind his back, "could you please go?" My attention was caught when he said my name.

I saw Ryan go next to his brother, put his hand on his shoulder and whispered something in his ear. Elliott turned to his brother, leaned in, and whispered something

270

back. Once he pulled away, Ryan nodded, as if he was giving him approval for something. Approval of something that has to do with me? Curiouser and curiouser...

Grace slowly nodded and bit her lip. I wasn't exactly sure what this meant. Then she changed her mood and brightly smiled. "How about we start to walk to the restaurant," she told everyone. Then she turned to Elliott and I and asked, "Are you guys okay to meet us at the restaurant?" Elliott and I nodded. "Alrighty then!" Grace said. "See you guys soon!" Everyone said goodbye to us as they left and started walking to the restaurant.

Elliott sat me down on a stone bench in the middle of the piazza. He sat down next to me, still with his hands behind his back. "What's up, Elliott?" I asked him.

Elliott started to turn a bright shade of pink. "Cecilia, I---." He couldn't find the words to say.

I reassuringly put a hand on his shoulder and said, "It's okay. Take your time."

With my words, Elliott took a deep breath and said, "Cecilia, I got something for you." I nodded. "But first, close your eyes." I did as Elliott told me to do. "Are you sure you're not peeking?" I heard Elliott tease me.

This made me smile. Still with my eyes closed shut, I tried to convince him, "No, no, no. I promise, they're closed. They're closed I promise."

"Okay, I trust you," I heard Elliott's voice. Then I felt him place something light and cool in my palms. "You can open them now!"

And that's what I did. I opened my eyes wide and looked down. "Oh my gosh," I murmured in disbelief. My mouth dropped wide. I saw what Elliott was giving me, and it was beautiful.

"I saw it, and it made me think of you," Elliott blushed even more.

The gift he gave me was a necklace. A fleur de lis necklace. A beautiful fleur de lis necklace. The chain was a shiny silver with a white gold fleur de lis that looked almost as if there were diamonds in it. It was breathtaking. Elliott really outdid himself.

"Do-do you like it?" he asked me, almost anxiously.

I held the necklace tightly in my palms as I looked up to look at Elliott. "Like it? Are you kidding me Elliott? My mom has one just like it. Ever since I was a little girl I wanted it. Or at least wanted a necklace that was like it. It's beautiful! I love it so much!" My heart was beating. "Thank you, Elliott," I leaned in for a quick peck on a cheek.

As soon as we pulled apart, Elliott smiled and politely asked me, "Would you like me to put it on for you?"

"Yes, thanks," I nodded. I handed him the necklace and turned it around so he could put it on and hook it.

"Turn around," he said. And I did. I looked down at the necklace and lightly touched it. "I love it on you!" he smiled.

"Thank you so much!" I leaned in to hug Elliott in a tight, warm embrace.

We pulled apart, and Elliott asked me, "Shall we head off to join the others?"

"I have Waze on my phone!" I told him. Elliott smiled and took my hand.

Just as we were about to stand up off the bench, we felt two hands on our backs. One hand on my hand and the other on Elliott's. It made us feel really weird. Then we saw who was touching us as she made her way in front of us. I hate to say this, but she was ugly. She kind of reminded me of the old hag the queen disguised as in the *Snow White* movie. She was wrinkly with hair the color of a dirty silver. She had a long black dress on and her hair was ratty. I noticed she had bony fingers and was carrying a silver tin can, to collect money I guess Who knows?

"Ahh, what lovely couple!" the old woman said. She could speak English, but not perfectly. And she sounded as if the old hag from *Snow White* had an Italian accent.

"Oh, thank you," I told her. "Now we must be on our way, really," I sounded like I was in a rush. But I politely said, "Excuse me, ma'am."

I was about to stand up until the old woman lightly pushed me back down. "No, no, no, dearie, don't go!" she tried to convince me. I briefly turned to Elliott and he looked stunned that the woman did that. I squeezed his hand tightly.

The woman reached into a bag she was carrying around her shoulder. As she searched it, she talked to us, "I've got something that might interest you." She turned to Elliott and said, "Now, young man, a beautiful girl like the one you're with needs something special to show how you care about her."

Elliott nervously smiled. "Yeah, uh, well, um ma'am, you see I actually---"

But the woman continued as if she didn't hear him. She finally pulled out what she was looking for. She pulled out a ring. It was golden, that's all there was to it. It was *nothing* compared to the fleur de lis necklace Elliott gave me.

The old lady held the ring up so it glistened in the sun. "This be perfect for your special lady!" she said, examining the ring. "It be 180 euros!"

"Thank you, ma'am," Elliott politely declined, "but we're not interested. Even if we *were*, I don't have that much money." Then he started to stand up and politely told her, "Now if you'll excuse us, we best be going." He smiled at me, "Let's go, love."

Elliott and I started to stand up but the woman sat us back down again. Man, she sure was aggressive! "Oh no, sir, it's beautiful ring," she continued to try to convince Elliott to buy the ring, "and you mustn't pass up opportunity! Perhaps you give me something *else*." She placed her bony finger on her chin as she thought. Then her eye caught something and she grinned enthusiastically, but creepily. "*That!*" she pointed to me. I wasn't sure what she was pointing at, until I looked down. She was pointing to the necklace. The one Elliott gave me. There's no way in a million years I would exchange the fleur de lis necklace for that dull ring.

My eyes were wide open and my jaw dropped wide. "Excuse me, ma'am," I said, I started to get annoyed. "This is *not* for sale."

"I gave that to her as a gift," Elliott told her, starting to defend me.

The woman held the ring very close to my face. "But *this* ring is very special ring," she would not give up! "Don't you want to see beautiful lady wear something *special*." She reached her hand and picked up the fleur de lis on the necklace, before I flicked her hand away with my hand. "Don't get me wrong, this beautiful necklace. But *this ring* very special! It worn by many queens!"

Then Elliott murmured something on his breath. Smiling, and in a somewhat sarcastic tone, he said, "If I was Queen of England herself, I wouldn't even let that thing near my finger."

Then there was a sudden shift in mood of the woman. As soon as she heard Elliott say something, she slowly turned away from me toward him. She gritted her teeth, "I'm sorry, young man. What you say?"

Elliott's smile faded into a worried look. Then a nervous smile came upon his face as he quickly tried to convince her, shaking his head, "Oh, nothing, nothing."

The woman then started to walk towards him, slowly. Still with a creepy smile on her face, she said, "I hear you say something, dearie. What you say?"

Knowing he was caught, Elliott frowned and looked down. He looked back up at the woman and answered truthfully, "I said that if I was the Queen of England herself, I wouldn't even let that thing near my finger."

This caused the woman to change in an instant. It was as if a switch turned on her angry side. She shook her bony finger in Elliott's face and scolded, "Shame on you, dear young man! Not thinking ring beautiful! I could have pick any young couple in city to give this ring, I choose you! You need to learn to be more appreciative when people give you gifts! Shame on you!"

Then what happened next was a sight I will surely never forget. The woman, still angry at Elliott for saying that about the ring, took this time to bring back the tin cup she was keeping her money in. She took the cup in the hand the ring wasn't in and swung it upwards, flicking Elliott's nose with it. Elliott's eyes widened in disbelief. But I also saw the corner of his lips curve up, as if he was trying to resist smiling, thinking it was somewhat funny.

Meanwhile, I thought it was all rather hilarious. But I didn't know whether Elliott felt the same way. So I felt myself slightly smirk, and I felt like I was going to burst out laughing any second now. To hide this, I took my hand and hid my mouth behind, trying not to show the smile I was growing. Elliott pursed his lips together, almost as if he was trying to hide a grin, too.

"Okay, okay," I finally said to the woman. I tried to sound serious and not on the brink of laughter. "We're really not interested in the ring," then I placed my hand lightly on where the necklace was, "and this necklace is *definitely* not for sale."

The woman, with a grimace on her face, nodded. "You making wrong decision," the woman warned me, shaking her finger in my face. "But I respect your decision," she calmly said. Before walking away, she turned to Elliott and warned him, "Do not let her get away. She very special."

"Yes ma'am," Elliott said as if he was taking orders. He slowly nodded. And just like that, the woman walked away as she was putting away the ring in her bag. She vanished and we never saw her again.

As soon as she was out of sight, Elliott and I looked at each other for a brief moment, speechless. What could we say? Elliott's mouth was open wide as a codfish and his eyeballs were about to bulge out of his head. After a moment of just staring at each other, I couldn't contain my laughter. I bent my body forward and was cackling, and Elliott joined me.

"That woman did not want to leave without getting the necklace!" Elliott continued laughing.

I was in a laughing fit as well. "And when you made a joke, she flicked your nose! Your reaction was *priceless*!"

We continued laughing for about a minute or so, and then I saw out of the corner of my eye a few people were giving us dirty looks, and I stopped. I motioned for Elliott to stop as well, and he did.

"What time is it?" he asked me. He looked at his watch. "Oh my, will you look at the time!" he said. He looked up from his phone and said to me, "We should probably head to the restaurant. They're probably wondering where we are." I nodded in agreement, we stood up in unison, and were on our way.

******

We finished dinner by 7 o'clock, because there was a whole thing where we messed up our reservation and had to wait an hour to be seated. Our train was at 10. We walked out of the restaurant. We stood there, lost about what to do next.

"So," I dragged out. "What do you all wanna do now?"

"We could get some gelato," Elliott suggested. "There's one close to the train station."

"How long is the train station from here?" Esperanza asked.

I started to get out my phone, "I'll put it up in Waze." I asked, "What is the gelato place called?"

"I have no clue," Elliott shrugged. "I'm just assuming there are a gazillion gelato places in Florence that one was *bound* to be near the train station."

Nicole crossed her arms, cocked his head to the side, and asked, "Well, what if there *wasn't*?"

Elliott crossed his arms back at Nicole and said, "Then we'd find one near the restaurant."

Nicole further asked him, "What if there isn't one near the restaurant?"

"Then we'd just walk to the train station and see if there are any gelato places on the way there!" Elliott replied quickly.

278

"Guys," Ryan got in the middle of his brother and Nicole going back and forth. He pointed to a gelato place that was literally called *Gelato*. We turned our heads in unison towards it. "We can go *there!*" he suggested.

Ollie tugged on Elliott's shirt in anticipation. Elliott quickly turned his head to face his little brother. "What's wrong, Ollie?" he asked with concern.

Ollie shook his head as he said, "I don't really want gelato."

Elliott nodded in understanding. He put his hand on Ollie's shoulder and assured him, "Don't worry. No one's going to force it if you don't want to."

"I'm still full from dinner, Elliott," Connor piped in. "I don't think I'm hungry for gelato either."

"Alright, Connor. You don't have to get any either---" Elliott started to say.

I interrupted and said with guilt. "Uh, Elliott," I said, "I'm not hungry for gelato either."

"Hmmm," Elliott nodded his head. He said, "Raise your hand if you want gelato." No one raised their hands. "Okay---um. Raise your hand if you *don't* want gelato." Everyone, including me, raised their hands. "Then we don't have to stop and get gelato!" he said.

"But then what are we going to do? We have three hours before we have to be at the train station," Ryan asked.

The eight of us just stood there for a minute, not sure about what to do. Grace came up with the idea: "Let's just go to the train station now! Never hurts to be early."

"You're starting to sound like Granny," Elliott pointed out.

"What does Granny say?" Esperanza curiously asked.

Then, in perfect unison, all four of the Parkers boys said, imitating their Granny in her high-pitched, British voice: "If you're early, you're on time. If you're on time, you're late. And if you're late, then that's just plain rude!"

Esperanza, Nicole, and I lightly laughed at the five's impersonation of their grandmother. Grace giggled, and Elliott stood proud at his spot-on impression. I never met their Granny, but I'm sure they hit her spot on.

Elliott sighed and thought out loud, "Good old Granny Parker!"

"God rest her soul," Ryan said with a little sadness in his voice.

"Oh my gosh, I'm so sorry," I told them with remorse.

"It's okay," Elliott assured me, "it was a long time ago."

"Anyway," Grace said, trying to stop the sadness, "let's go!" And we started walking to the train station.

******

Florence Santa Maria Novella Train Station was an *interesting* place. It was large and crowded, and not the cleanest place I've been to. People rushed to get to catch their train, speaking in an assortment of languages. Loudspeakers boomed to tell passengers about trains being delayed or trains departing. The station was filled with people who weren't the most trustworthy, whether be people trying to sell things like the old woman from earlier or people you would suspect to be a pickpocket. Like pretty much anywhere in Italy, there were pickpockets at any corner. And from what I've heard on traveladvice.com, they were *good*. So we all made sure to be especially careful in the train station, being fully aware that anyone could steal something from your purse or suitcase, and you wouldn't even notice.

So we waited for hours and hours. We sat on the dirty floor, waiting impatiently. There were some shops and food stations all around the station so we got some stuff. I decided to try my first ever cannoli. I should have gotten it earlier in the trip where it was of higher quality, because that cannoli was disgusting. Oh well! Man, Grace was such a genius for saying we should get there three hours early. (That was sarcasm, by the way).

At 9:40, after two hours and forty minutes of waiting and twenty minutes before our train would depart, we went to the ticket booth and got our tickets. The girls went first, followed by the boys. However, the ticket booth lady got a little bit starstruck. She was around her mid-twenties, and looked like all the other Italian women we had seen. She was beautiful with long dark hair and petite in stature.

"Oh my goodness! You're Elliott Parker! *The* Elliott Parker!" she said with excitement in her voice. She may have been around her mid-twenties, but she was *totally* fangirling. I saw her name tag and it read, "Carina."

"That's me," Elliott awkwardly said. He gave a just as awkward wave. "Nice to meet you."

"I'm such a huge fan, I'm sorry, I can't even," Carina fangirled again. I felt a pinch of jealousy as I rolled my eyes. Elliott noticed me do this. He reached for my hand, held it tightly, and started rubbing my knuckles with his thumb. It was as if he was saying, "Don't worry, you're still my girl." This made me feel better and my jealousy started to strain away.

But the jealousy came back when Carina ecstatically said, "Wait! We have a rule here that if we have a celebrity coming on board, we give them the suite room!"

Elliott's eyes widened, then he nervously laughed and assured Carina, "No, no, no, trust me..." he looked at Carina's name tag, "Carina, I don't need a suite room."

"But it's a rule!" Carina reminded him.

Elliott looked down, sighed heavily, looked back up and gave up, "Fine," he groaned. Then he quickly added, "But only if it's for eight people. It's only fair that they come."

"We only have space for three," Carina said, faking that she was sorry. She shrugged and said, "Sorry." But there's no way she was sorry.

"Then I'm not accepting the suite," Elliott crossed his arms.

"But it's protocol," Carina said.

"Is it protocol to reject the offer?" Elliott questioned her.

Carina looked around at us. When she caught my eyes, she gave me an evil glare. She rolled her eyes and groaned, "Oh you." I frowned at how rude this girl was being. She then resumed her evil glare and said, looking straight to me, "I know for certain you're *definitely* not getting to room in the suite."

Elliott came to my defense and said, "Leave her alone. I'll decide whether she rooms in the suite or not. And based on my decision, *no one* is rooming in the suite, including me."

"Man, Elliott," Carina continued to taunt. "This girl got you exposed in the tabloids, *and* she's preventing you from getting a nice suite. Not a good choice for your girlfriend, if I say."

Elliott got a pissed look on his face, looked like he had had it with Carina. He was about to say something, but I put my hand on his shoulder, assuring him I had this. I took a deep breath and said, "And *you're* not a good choice to give us tickets. If Elliott doesn't want to take the suite tickets, then he doesn't want to. *You* can't force him to do anything."

SNAP! That felt good.

Carina just stood there stunned and speechless. She looked so humiliated, looking down at her feet and biting her lip. Elliott smiled at me, placing his hand on top of mine that was on his shoulder. My friends smiled too, as did all of Elliott's brothers. I saw Ryan mouth, "You go, girl!" I grinned at myself, proud for standing up to myself. I don't think I had ever done anything like that before.

After silence, Carina said, "Well, he still has to take it. It's protocol."

Elliott looked ticked off once again. He was about to open his mouth, when Ryan stepped in and told his brother, "Elliott, it says there's room for three. You take Connor and Ollie and I'll stay in the room with the girls." He turned to Carina and said, "If that's okay with your supposed number one fan here."

Carina gave a fake smile and said, "Actually, the girls have two extra beds. There was only one other person supposed to room with them, so you can room with them."

"He's seventeen years old," Elliott told her, being protective of his brother. "I can't let him---"

I cut off Elliott and assured him, "We'll protect him, babe. Don't worry."

"Are you sure?" Elliott asked with concern. "And then there's you girls. You're rooming with a stranger. And I don't want any of you to get hurt." Elliott seemed to be very protective today.

"We'll be okay," Grace tried to convince her cousin.

"Yeah," Nicole promised. She then added, "I also have a black belt in karate so if anyone tries to touch your brother, cousin, Cecilia, or Esperanza," she then got a fake evil death glare and said, "I *will* kill them."

Everyone chuckled at her. Even Carina couldn't help but crack a smile. Elliott went along with the joke and said, "You might not want to do *that*. We don't want you arrested for murder." Everyone chuckled along.

Carina smiled and said, "Alright, it's settled then." It seemed as though Carina was trying to be nice and said, "And the suite isn't far from where you guys are rooming so you can visit each other if you want."

"Thanks, Carina," I thanked her.

"Of course," she smiled at me.

We got our tickets and made our way to the train. Before I left, Carina stopped me, "Cecilia!" I turned around to face her. I got an uneasy feeling worried about what she was going to say. But Carina sighed, and this time with genuine guilt said, "I'm sorry I said that about you. I shouldn't have. And just so you know, I think you're really pretty."

Her words made me relax. I smiled at her and said, "Thank you, Carina. That was very nice of you."

Carina just smiled, and I smiled back. "Have a nice train ride," she told me.

"Thanks," I said. With that, I walked away to join the others.

Chapter 15: Wishing For No More Mean Photographers

Finally, we were on the train! But as soon as we got on, I felt almost claustrophobic. The aisle was really tight and we almost couldn't get our suitcases through. Elliott, Connor, and Ollie's suite was first so they stopped and said good night.

"Be careful," Elliott told Ryan, pulling in and hugging him.

"I will," Ryan promised him.

Then Elliott made his way towards me and hugged me tightly. We pulled apart to face each other. "Good night, love," he said, pecking me sweetly on the lips.

"Night," I weakly smiled at him.

He then told the whole group, "And you guys can visit if you want! I understand if you want to go to sleep because it's late, but you are always welcome."

We all nodded and thanked Elliott as the three went into their suite and closed the door. After it was shut, Grace, Esperanza, Nicole, Ryan, and I all went to find our room. We finally did. Esperanza opened it, and all my excitement about sleeping on an overnight train disappeared with a snap. There were two bunks on each side, each with three levels. The space in between the two was very small, with a small table and charging station on the far end by the window.

"What is this?" Nicole asked in disgust.

"It's our room," Esperanza told her, as if she actually thought Nicole didn't know where we were.

"I know where we are!" Nicole snapped at her friend, causing Esperanza to jump back in surprise.

"It's really small," I pointed out.

"You think?" Ryan asked me.

"Where's the other person?" Grace asked.

"I don't know," Nicole said. She looked upset, "Who cares?! This place makes the hotel in Materdomini look *nice!*"

"It's not that bad," Esperanza tried to look for something positive in it, "it has good qualities to it."

"Like what?" Ryan questioned her.

Esperanza looked around the room, trying to find something positive. She struggled, and couldn't come up with anything. She finally gave up and shrugged, "I've got nothing."

We went into the room and were immediately crowded. The right bunk had Ryan on the bottom, me in the middle, and Grace on top. The left bunk had whoever the other person was on the bottom, Nicole in the middle, and Esperanza on the top. I literally had to squeeze my body to get in. I felt like a sardine. I had to scrunch up my feet so I could fit. Not to mention the mattress was hard.

"This sucks," I murmured under my breath. Just then I got a ping on my phone. It was a message on my phone from Elliott.

Elliott: how is it?

I immediately replied back:

Me: SUCKS!!!!!!!!!!!!

It took a minute to go through because the wifi was so bad.

Elliott: i'm sorry :(do you want to talk?

My face immediately lit up.

Me: Sure. I can stay up late and text.

Elliott: do you not want to come over here and talk in person?

Hmmm. Hadn't thought of that before. Didn't think it was the best idea, so I texted back:

Me: Idk. Kinda tired.

But I sat there, thinking about my text, and I changed my response to:

Me: Actually, sure why not? Where do you want to meet?

Elliott: hmmm my little bros are asleep, that's how tired they are so...

Me: We can be quiet.

Elliott: haha there's a bathroom in the suite we can talk there

Me: Your own bathroom?!?!?! Lucky!!!

Elliott: lol you'll be really jealous when you see the room

Me: I'll be there in a min (;

Elliott: see you soon <3

I immediately tried to get out of the bed. I tried, but I had to swing my legs over and crawl out of the level. I felt like Spider-Man, Spider-Woman, I guess.

"Okay, I have to go, I'll be right back," I told everyone.

"Where are you going?" Esperanza questioned.

"Bathroom," I lied.

Esperanza fell for it. "Okay," protective Esperanza said, "just be careful."

I nodded, "I will."

I headed off towards Elliott's suite room. I reached the end of the hallway where Elliott's suite was. I knocked on the door, softly. Elliott answered it wearing a T-shirt and plaid pajama pants.

"Hello, Cecilia!" he grinned. "Come in," he invited me. But he whispered softly, "but be quiet. Connor and Ollie are sleeping." I nodded.

Elliott took me by the hand and led me inside. The room was pitch black dark, but very spacious compared to our room. I could tell there was a large bed in the middle, where Connor and Ollie were sleeping soundly.

"I can't see a thing, Elliott," I whispered.

"Here," Elliott held my hands tightly, "I've got you." He guided me to the bathroom, and once we were inside, he turned on the light. It was like a bathroom you had on a cruise in your stateroom, with a small toilet and sink, but had much more room. And it was set up nicely and clean.

"Wow," I said in disbelief. "Even the bathroom is nice."

Elliott chuckled. "I know." Then he got serious. Still holding my hands, he whispered, "What's wrong?"

"Oh my gosh!" I nearly shouted. When I realized I still had to be quiet, I talked more quietly, "It's *so* tiny! There is literally no room. Two bunk beds, each with three levels, and no room in between! And the mattress is so hard and I literally had to scrunch up to fit! I felt like a sardine! This is *not* how I expected my night on the overnight train to turn out!"

Elliott looked concerned. "I'm sorry, darling," he said sympathetically. He reached his hands to my shoulders and gently started massaging them to help me feel better. "But remember," he told me, "this is just for one night. Then we'll be staying in three other hotels that I'm sure will be *much* more comfy." This made me smile, Elliott was making me feel better already.

He twirled me around so I was resting the back of my head into his chest. He wrapped his arms tightly around my waist as if he didn't want to let me go. I smiled, sinking back into his chest. He leaned down to my ear and whispered sweetly, "And if you want, we can cuddle all you want in the hotel rooms." His breath and words tickled my ear.

This made my smile grow. "That sounds *wonderful*," I murmured back to him.

I could feel Elliott smiling as he rested his chin on my shoulder. His hands still around my waist, I rested my arms on top of them, feeling his warm, soft, muscular skin.

"And I'm sorry about that girl earlier," Elliott got serious with a more serious expression on his face.

"It's okay," I assured him, "she apologized afterward." This made Elliott sigh in relief. "And I'm sorry that I got defensive and sounded like I was being rude to her."

Elliott quickly assured me, "You don't need to apologize to me." He leaned down and whispered in my ear once again, "I think it's sexy when you're a badass."

With that, I turned my body around to face Elliott. I made my arms wrap around his neck. He kept his arms around my waist as I leaned in to kiss him. I felt his lips, just as soft as ever, gently touch mine. We broke the kiss apart to catch our breaths, and I leaned away to look at Elliott's face. He was breathing heavily, but smiled.

I slowly released myself from his grasp as I admitted with disappointment, "I should probably get back to the room." I started to walk towards the door. I put my hand on the doorknob until Elliott stopped me by placing his hand upon it gently. I turned around to face him, a sly smirk upon his face. He put his other hand on my shoulder, his fingers sinking into my skin.

He whispered in my ear, almost seductively but still tickling my ear, "I thought you said you didn't like your room?"

I smiled and turned around to face him again, my hands making my way behind his neck once again. His hands found their way to my waist once again. "I know we can't—you know. For one thing because I promised I'd wait until you wanted to do it." I nodded my head slowly. "And my younger brothers are in the other room," I nodded my head quickly. "But," he reminded me, "that doesn't mean we can't do *this*."

Without warning, Elliott's lips crashed onto mine. I quickly started to kiss him once again, our lips moving in sync as always. Elliott lifted me up, and I wrapped my legs around his waist. He gently placed me on the counter of the sink, because there was enough room. We didn't dare break our steamy kiss. My legs were still tightly wrapped around Elliott, and his hands were now on each side of me. He slowly moved his lips from mine and made his way to my neck. He started showering quick, chaste kisses all over it. It was so hot yet ticklish at the same time. I could have sworn I heard myself let out some sort of a soft moan. This was the most heated moment I've had with him, or anyone.

Just as I was about to move my hands up his shirt and he had laid a kiss on my collar bone, there was a knock on the door. Just like that, the moment was ruined. Elliott and I snapped out of our trances and quickly turned our heads to the door in worry.

"Who is it?" Elliott's voice became high pitch in worry.

"Elliott?" Connor's soft British voice said from the other side. "I have to go to the bathroom."

I flushed red in embarrassment. What was I going to do now? Elliott buried his face in his palm, as if unsure of what to do. He finally told Connor, "I'll be out soon, Connor."

He turned slowly toward me, I continued to blush a crimson red. Elliott murmured, "I'm so sorry."

"You're fine," I replied, "just—what are we going to tell Connor?"

"I'll think of something," Elliott told me. My legs still wrapped around his waist, he lifted me off the counter and set me down lightly on my feet. We stood there awkwardly, me looking down at my feet and Elliott running a hand through his hair. He turned to the door and slowly creaked it open.

Connor was on the other side, sheepishly smiling. As soon as he saw me, his face turned into one of confusion. "Cecilia? What are you doing here?" Even though he was tired, Connor was trying to figure out what was going on.

"Well you see—she uh—" Elliott tried to think of what to tell his brother.

I came to the rescue and came in saying, "Well, I wasn't too happy about the room and I was talking to Elliott about it." That wasn't a lie. That's what we were *originally* going to do. That's what we *were* doing.

Elliott turned to me, smiled and mouthed, "Thank you." I nodded at him.

Connor believed it. "That's nice," he said. He turned to me, "I'm sorry you don't like your room, Cecilia."

"Thank you for that, Connor," I patted his head, ruffling his curly hair playfully. "I should be getting back. Night boys."

"Good night, Cecilia," Connor sleepily said.

"Good night, darling," Elliott winked.

I turned to him and gave him a *chaste* peck on the cheek, and made my way out the door. I shut it quietly, trying not to wake Ollie and others on the train. I scurried quickly down the tight hallway back to the room. I finally made my way back. When I arrived, I saw the others talking with another woman who must have been our other roommate. She was skinny and looked tall, around her forties. She wore a business jacket and a tight black pencil skirt. She wore light makeup and had her golden blonde hair in a tight bun.

They must not have seen me come in, because I quietly told them, "Hey, guys." And just like that, everyone turned to me, including the mystery woman.

"Hi," everyone said to me.

"Are you Cecilia?" the woman, who had a British accent, asked politely, standing up.

"Yes, ma'am," I nodded my head. For some strange reason, the woman looked strangely familiar.

"I'm Gwen," she reached her hand to mine.

"Nice to meet you," I reached my hand and shook hers firmly. "I'm sorry, have we met before?" I asked.

"No don't worry, I—" Gwen started to say.

"We actually found out she was on the ferry in Capri with us," Ryan told me, sitting up in his bed to look at me.

"That must have been where I've seen you before!" I told her. Just the name Gwen sounded familiar to me.

"You know what's funny?" Gwen said, scrunching her face and looking at me like she was examining me. "I don't recognize your friends from the ferry, but *you* sure do look familiar."

I shrugged. I couldn't put a finger on how I recognized her face and name.

Gwen turned her head around and looked around at the entire group. "I meant to ask you," she said, "did you guys by chance see Elliott Parker on board the boat?" My heart sank.

295

Not wanting to blow our cover, Grace sounded surprised and said, "No way! How did we miss him?"

"Yeah," I was looking down, murmuring under my breath. "How did we miss it? There were all those articles about—" then I got an uneasy feeling. I think I may have realized where I knew Gwen from. I quickly shot my head up and asked more loudly, "What did you say your name was?"

Gwen said confidently and smiled, "Gwen. Gwen Hodges."

Gwen Hodges? I got an uneasy feeling about that name, but I wanted to make sure I was right. "And what do you do for a living, Gwen Hodges?" I asked with almost anger in my voice.

"Oh," Gwen nervously laughed. She grinned and said, "I'm a reporter and photographer for *Celebrity Gossip*. The magazine?"

And then it hit me like a train. I knew how I knew Gwen. She wrote the first ever article about me and Elliott on the ferry. Not only that, but she had taken the pictures of us. I distinctly remember everything. The magazine website page and name. The article title. The name "by Gwen Hodges" paired with her picture with a fake grin on her face. I remembered the articles saying, "Pictures taken by Gwen Hodges." It *was* her.

I slowly backed away from her, feeling as if I was going to be sick. I slowly backed away from the woman who caused Elliott and I so much pain. It was as if she didn't have a clue. Her face looked concerned.

"Is everything okay, Cecilia?" a worried Esperanza asked.

"You don't look so good," Nicole said just as worried.

"Please talk to us," Grace pleaded.

"Do you need to sit down?" a concerned Ryan asked.

I slowly shook my head. It was as if their voices were drowned out by the thoughts of anger and fear I was feeling. I couldn't stop staring at that woman. The woman who not only hurt me, but hurt Elliott as well.

Looking more concerned, she slowly reached her hand to touch my shoulder, "Is everything okay, Cecilia?"

"Don't touch me!" I snapped back, causing Gwen to jump back in shock at my sudden words. Everyone else in the room looked at me with surprise and confusion as to why I was acting this way.

I more calmly asked Gwen, "Did you by chance take pictures of Elliott Parker and that mystery red-haired woman?" Gwen slowly nodded her head in confusion. Then her eyes widened open when she realized something. "Figure it out?" I asked her annoyedly. "I'm Cecilia, the girl in the pictures with him."

Gwen stood there, as if in complete shock, her mouth in an "O" shape. Looking guilty, she shook her head and said, "Oh my gosh, I didn't realize that was you. I'm—"

I shook my head in disbelief, "How could you do this to him? To *us*?"

Ryan spoke up and defended his brother, saying, "That was my *brother* you exposed, lady! How could you?"

Grace stopped her cousin and told him to stop, but politely: "Hey, I promised Elliott we would look after you, and I *don't* think this will help."

Ryan started to get really annoyed and Grace and started to complain, "But—"

"Ryan," Grace gave him the "please, just stop for your safety's sake," and Ryan remained silent but still visibly angry as he crossed his arms and continued to watch the conversation.

Gwen turned back towards me and bit her lip. She genuinely looked scared as to what I was going to do to her. I walked closer and closer towards her and interrogated her, "Why did you do it?" I crossed my arms, trying to look serious.

Gwen tried to prove she was stronger than me, raising her shoulders and puffing out her chest more, and smiling, but laughing nervously, "I had to, Cecilia. It *is* my job to get the personal lives of the stars out there. That's what the world wants, isn't it?"

"You could have at least asked our permission," I felt my voice starting to rise. But when I noticed this, I spoke at my normal volume, still ticked off, "In case you didn't know, a bunch of Elliott's fans practically assaulted me on Instagram, saying I wasn't attractive or good enough for Elliott. As someone who has been bullied, how do you think *that* felt?"

Nicole whispered loudly to herself in disbelief but admiration, "Wow, Cecilia. Damn, you really are a badass."

Esperanza tried to change the subject and offered, "Want us to ask someone to separate her from us?"

"Yeah," Grace said in a motherly tone, "Cecilia, if you're not comfortable—"

"No," I quickly interrupted them. I turned my head to face Gwen. I was talking to my friends but looking straight at her. I gritted through my teeth, "It's fine. Like my mother always said, sometimes in life we have to be with people we don't like. And this is *definitely* one of those times."

Gwen crossed her arms and started to get offended by me and said, "For your information, sweetheart, I almost lost my job. If I hadn't gotten those photos of you and your boyfriend, my boss would have fired me. Those pictures of you two saved my ass!"

"First off," I had calmed down by now, "he's not boyfriend—"

"Then what is he?" Gwen asked, almost evilly. "A summer fling? Friends with benefits?" My blood was really starting to boil at this woman.

Nicole's hot temper started to flare again as she nearly screamed at Gwen: "Hey, that's my best friend you're talking about, you bitch!"

Ryan whined to Grace, "Hey, how come she gets to argue with Gwen and I can't?"

But before Grace could answer, I shook my head and said, "Unbelievable."

"I don't think you understand," Gwen said, trying to look innocent and caring. She walked closer to me, "I don't think you understand, Cecilia." I felt myself becoming scared of her, like she was the Disney villain and she was stronger than me. "There's a system in Hollywood. There are these stars," as she continued speaking with her evil grin, I started to back away as she moved closer to me. "And everyone wants to know these stars' businesses. Who they date and don't date. Reporters like me have to find out that information so people can know more."

By the time she said this, I had backed all the way to the closed train car door, my back flat against it. She came up close to me and pretended to be nice and calmly said, "And my advice to you, Cecilia, is if you really like Elliott, I guess you're going to have to get used to it."

This woman was cornering me and talking evilly to me after she briefly made things miserable for me. I couldn't take this. I was more than a damsel in distress. I may be the princess in my story, but I'm also the hero.

I moved quickly away so Gwen wasn't menacing me anymore and stood up straight, which made her back away slightly. I told her, "You know what Gwen, you're right. If I do enter a relationship with Elliott, I am going to get more and more media attention, and it may be bad at times. But I'm just going to have to learn to deal with it. Because I really do care about him, and I'll do anything for him."

With my sudden change in attitude, Gwen started to get a little scared and started to back away again, like bullies often do. I tried not to be really rude, but to still get my point across: "And I'll also do whatever it takes to protect him, even if it means protecting him from people like *you*."

Gwen was practically speechless. She looked scared, looking down now. I smiled to myself, proud at standing up not only to myself, but to Elliott as well.

Esperanza clapped her hands and said in happiness, "Good for you! Nicole is right! You are *such* a badass!"

"Isn't Nicole *always* right?" Nicole shrugged her arms and said confidently.

"Nicole knows best!" Grace happily pointed out.

"Elliott would be proud of you," Ryan nodded, a proud grin on his face.

Gwen looked mortified. She didn't say a word, just stared at me in shock and horror. After she walked off to find another place to stay the night, I told them, "Uh, yeah, about that—"

"What?" Grace asked with concern all over her face. "Should I be worried?"

I chuckled to myself and said, "Oh no, you shouldn't be *worried*, Grace." My face and voice got serious as I said, "It's just—let's not tell Elliott about this."

"What?" all four of them said in unison, all with just as much shock and confusion.

"At least for now," I raised my arms in front.

"Girl," Esperanza told me, "you *have* to tell him."

"I don't have to," I shrugged.

"Uh, *yeah* you do," Grace nodded with a nervous smile on her face. "He deserves to know."

"What do you want me to do?" I raised my arms shrugging. "Wake him up right now and say, 'Wakey wakey, Elliott! The lady who photographed us smooching in Capri was our roommate!' Do you *really* want to bother him this late at night?"

"Not now," Grace assured me, "Tomorrow. In Vienna."

"No way," I shook my head, making my answer very clear.

Ryan started to get in on this conversation and sided with my friends. He tried to convince me, "Look, I know my brother. And if you don't tell him something and he finds out from someone who isn't you, it really pisses him off. I've learned that many times in the seventeen years I've known him."

I had a quick response, telling Ryan, "Well, no one needs to know." I turned to everyone and said, "Capisce?" I decided to use some Italian.

"What if he finds out from someone who isn't us?" Nicole questioned me.

"I don't think anyone else is going to know," I put my hands on my hips. I thought for a sec,, "Except maybe *Gwen*. But we'll make sure she keeps her mouth shut if she and Elliott cross paths."

"Is this *really* a good idea?" Esperanza asked with almost an uncomfortable look on her face.

"It's *fine*," I told her. I laughed, "It's not like he's never going to know. I'll tell him eventually. When we get to Salzburg."

"Are you sure this is a good idea?" Grace questioned me one more time.

"It'll be fine Grace," I brushed it off. I turned to everyone and asked, "Promise not to tell him?"

My first glance was to Ryan on the bottom bunk, who thought for about a minute. He groaned, "Fine." Pointing a finger at me, he warned, "But if my brother gets mad at me for not telling him, I'm blaming you."

I nodded, "Fair enough." I next tilted my head slightly to Nicole to the middle bunk on the opposite side and asked, "Nicole?" I waited for a response.

Nicole nodded and said. She had a fake smile and said, "Sure, Cecilia. Anything for *you*." I know Nicole. She meant what she said, but she clearly wasn't happy about making this promise.

"Thank you," I smiled at her. Nicole only nodded. I looked up at Esperanza at the top bunk, who was looking down and avoiding eye contact with me. She finally looked up and saw me raise an eyebrow at her. She weakly smiled and nodded her head. "Thanks, Esperanza," I smiled at her. Esperanza kept the same weak smile on her face.

Last was Grace. I scanned all the way across from Esperanza to Grace, who was on the other top bunk. Grace looked like she was the most hesitant of all of them. She sighed, thinking about what was best for me and for her cousin. It was if she was making her decision to keep this promise based on this one factor when she asked, "You *promise* you're going to tell him?"

I nodded my head eagerly, waiting for her to respond, saying, "I do."

Grace looked down and shook her head. She sighed once again and then looked straight at me, right in the eyes, and sincerely said, "I promise."

Chapter 16: Wishing For A Pretzel

At 9 a.m., we arrived at Vienna Train Station. We stepped off the train with our luggage in hand, walking off the platform. We weren't in Italy anymore. We were in Austria. *SQUEAL!* The excitement of being here allowed me to forget all about Gwen. The reason I didn't want to tell Elliott about it was because I didn't want to ruin his trip with it, and I'd be afraid he would do something about it. So I didn't, at least for now.

As we were walking away from the train, Elliott asked me, "So, did you sleep okay last night?"

I turned my head towards him, "Yeah, I did. You?"

"Fantastic," he cheekily smiled. I rolled my eyes, I knew he was trying to tease me and get a reaction out of me. But he asked, "Oh, so how was the other person you were in a train car with? Were they friendly?"

Oh, dang it. He asked me. I didn't think he would ask me. What should I do? Should I tell him the truth? Should I lie? Lying is a sin, as I learned throughout my entire life—and thirteen years of education at a Catholic school. I tried not to panic. He might get suspicious if I panic. So I bit my lip and muttered, "It was—she was fine."

But Elliott knew something was up. He cocked an eyebrow and asked, "Fine? Cecilia, is everything okay?"

I let out a gigantic fake laugh, so fake and loud, I think people stared at us. I crouched over and continued the laughter, I'm sure Elliott didn't understand a single thing that was going on.

He didn't want to be rude, but he nervously chuckled and whispered to me, "Uh, Cecilia, people are staring at you."

I flipped my head all the way back up so I was looking at him, my cheeks hurting from the "laughing." "What?" I laughed. I pointed to myself and made a few Disney references, "I love to laugh, like that old guy from *Mary Poppins*. And like they say on *Splash Mountain*, everybody's got a laughing place!"

"Hee," Elliott briefly had a small smile. Then he went back to concern and asked, "Are you sure you're okay?"

"Elliott," I smiled at him, "I'm fine. Let's just enjoy our trip to Vienna, okay?"

Before he could say anything else, I gave him a peck on the cheek. I pulled back and saw him smile, but I could tell from his face that he knew something was wrong. But I just didn't want to bother him. I saw how he reacted on the ferry when the teens snapped a picture of us, and I'm sure he would be even more furious at the woman that took a picture that was later seen by millions across the world. I would save it for later. Elliott just shrugged it off, and he didn't ask me again for the rest of the day.

As we stepped out into Vienna, we were amazed by everything. By the beauty of Vienna. Rustic and clean, it was a beautiful, old timey city. We were caught up in the charm and feel of the place when Grace all of a sudden asked: "Uh, guys, where's Lawrence?"

Elliott told her, "Oh he's visiting some family in Venice. He'll be in Salzburg tomorrow."

"What time is our train?" I asked everyone.

"5 o'clock," Esperanza answered.

"We have so much time to explore!" Connor said with his hands in the air.

"Then let's explore!" I told everyone enthusiastically.

"But, wait," Esperanza interrupted, "where are we going to put our bags?"

"Right! Dang it!" Grace said, snapping her fingers in frustration.

"Wait, Elliott," Ryan turned to his brother, "What did we do that time when we were staying in San Francisco for just the day and heading to L.A. for the premiere of *The Edge of Yesterday* and we had our luggage with us. What did we do with our luggage *then*?"

"Oh, hmm," Elliott tried to think. His eyes brightened up as he remembered, "Oh, we checked into a hotel room and put our luggage in there!"

"Let's do that," I suggested. "Anyone know a hotel we could check our bags into?"

"Oh! My aunt told me about this gorgeous hotel called the Hotel Regina, very boujee," Nicole chimed in.

"What does boujee even mean?" Esperanza asked her.

"Kind of a cool word if you ask me," Elliott said.

"It's a very *random* word," I added.

Ryan had his phone out and read aloud from it, "According to the internet it's another word for something that is luxurious in lifestyle yet humble in character."

"I say that describes Nicole *perfectly*," I jokingly said. I paused, then added, "The first part at least."

Everyone laughed, thinking it was hilarious. Nicole gave me a teasing evil glare. Grace interrupted and said, "Let's just go put our stuff in the hotel room."

And so that's what we did. With the help of Waze, we found the Hotel Regina. We walked inside, and it was absolutely breathtaking. It was very clean and grand with a diamond chandelier, an old fashioned elevator, a huge lobby, and the hotel walls were red. It reminded me of the lobby part of the Tower of Terror in Disney World, but the not spooky part of it of course.

After that we explored. First we went to St. Stephen's Cathedral, named after the first martyr. It was a gothic style church, like what we had learned about during our gothic literature unit in freshman English class. After that we did some shopping, and I found two beautiful scarves for my mom. And we even found some gelato and, if you recall, Elliott and I made a bet about whether there was gelato in Austria. I could tell Elliott was embarrassed to lose to a girl. So that means for the rest of the trip he had to do everything I wanted him to do.

And the funny thing was that a little bit later in the day, Elliott still seemed friendly, but something about him was off. He could have been grouchy because he lost a bet to a girl, but he wouldn't seem to be the type of person to do that. Perhaps he was just tired from walking around all day? Who knows! It wasn't anything serious, he just seemed hostile, but just a smidge.

At around 4 o'clock we went back to the hotel and got our luggage to head back on the train to Salzburg. The train station wasn't too far away. It was around 4:45 when Elliott and I decided to leave to get a pretzel. Or let me rephrase that: Elliott had to buy me a pretzel because he lost the bet. The pretzel stand was far away from the train, so I don't know why I had decided to wait until *now* right before we had to board the train.

The pretzel line took ten minutes to wait, so Elliott and I had to rush to get back to the train. We were running with our luggage and my pretzel, being careful not to let it fall out of my hand.

Just when we thought we were going to make it on the train, we heard someone shout, "Hey look! It's Elliott Parker!"

Elliott and I quickly turned around in apprehension. Just then a whole mob of people came rushing over to us, crowding and preventing us from going any further. They were all so loud. They were shouting things like, "I love you Elliott!" "Can I get a picture with you?" "You're amazing!" "Stop! We need a photo!"

Meanwhile people were crowding around Elliott so much that I got separated from him. "Elliott! Elliott!" I kept screaming his name, trying to get his attention past the mob of fans. Soon, there were so many people. I found myself being pushed down to the ground.

"Cecilia! Cecilia!" I could hear Elliott screaming my name, as if he was trying to find me. I tried to get up, but the crowd was preventing me. Luckily no one stepped on me or anything, but I felt almost helpless.

Just then a grown man, whose face I couldn't see, grabbed me by the shoulder and pulled me up. I was so overwhelmed by all of it that I was out of it. I could see the man's face, but he was clearly trying to get my attention. I tried to release myself from his grip, but he was way too strong.

All of a sudden I heard a shout, "Let her go!" It was Elliott. I saw the man being pulled away from me. I rubbed my arm, which hurt from the tight grip he put on it. Elliott quickly came to me and put his arm around my shoulder. Our suitcases were on the ground. My pretzel was gone.

"It's okay, it's okay. I've got you, I've got you," Elliott said to me calmly, his grouchy self being gone at that moment. Thank goodness! He then shouted to the crowd, "Back up, everyone! I'm sorry, I really wish I could meet you all, but you nearly hurt her! And I'm sure you hurt some other people as well! So please, BACK AWAY!"

And they did what he said. They left a huge gap in between them. I was trying to catch my breath. I was feeling fine, just kind of shocked by the whole thing. As we picked up our suitcases, Elliott asked concerned, "Are you okay?"

"Mhhm," I nodded. I checked my phone for the time. "4:57! We can still make it!"

"Perfect!" Elliott grinned.

We were right by the ticket booth and we rushed to get there. We handed the man at the booth our tickets, his name was Franco. He was in his forties with long, wavy black hair and pale skin.

"I'm sorry," Franco said, "I can't let you on."

I was starting to get a little annoyed. "I'm sorry what?"

"We're not taking any passengers now," he shrugged.

"But it's 4:57," I pointed out to him, "the train leaves at 5."

"Rules are rules," Franco reminded us. "I'm sorry."

"Well I say those rules are total bullshit if you ask me!" I said, on the verge of losing my temper.

Elliott put a hand on my shoulder and quietly said to me, "Okay, okay, love. Calm down. I'll handle this okay?" I nodded, trusting he would take care of it. He turned to the man and took a deep breath. He looked like he was going to calmly handle the situation, like he told me, instead he said in an annoyed tone, "She's right, those rules *are* total bullshit."

"You're Elliott Parker, aren't you?" Franco crossed his arms.

"Yes," Elliott nodded excitedly. "And surely, sir, you can let us on? Look, I never use my fame to get things I want, but this time I am!" He gestured to me and said, "And we have to get to Salzburg by tomorrow because we're supposed to go on a tour for *The Sound of Music*, which just so happens to be her favorite movie. And if she missed it that would be really bad so *PLEASE* consider making an exception to the rules." I like sweet Elliott so much better than grumpy Elliott.

Franco looked at Elliott, then at me. Then he looked down and smiled. He looked back up at us and said, "I can't get you on this train. But I will see if I can get you two on the next train to Salzburg."

As he went down to his computer to look, Elliott and I cheered.

"Thank you so much sir," I said with relief.

"It's really appreciated," Elliott couldn't stop smiling. He turned to me and said with pride, but not in an arrogant way, "I told you I could do it!"

"I believed in you," I said to him.

"Woah!" he cheered, raising up his hand for a high five. I high- fived him and cheered too.

We turned our attention back to Franco. We looked up from his computer and had a disappointed look on his face. Our faces dropped when we saw it.

"I'm sorry," Franco apologized, "the next available train is in three days at 21:45." That's 9:45 p.m. for those of you who don't read military time.

I had gotten my hopes. I turned to Elliott and reminded him sadly, saying, "We are scheduled to be in Munich by then."

Elliott slowly nodded his head in disappointment. He asked Franco, "Are you sure?"

"I'm sorry sir," Franco said, "I checked. There's nothing I can do."

Elliott and I sighed. I sunk my head low in frustration. Elliott turned to me and whispered, "Let's go outside, love. I've got an idea."

And so we thanked Franco, took our luggage, and left the train station. We went to the bus waiting area. Elliott got out his phone and called Lawrence.

"Uh hi, Lawrence...It's Elliott...How are you?...Well you see, there was a little mishap and Cecilia and I missed our train to Salzburg. Now we're stranded in Vienna...They're fine. They're on the train...So I was wondering if on your way back from Venice you could pick us up...Yes, thank you...8:15?...That sounds great...I think we'll be staying at the Hotel Regina...Thank you again, Lawrence...Say hi to your grandmother for me...Bye...Thanks again." As soon as he said that, we hung up.

"So?" I asked him anxiously, wanting to know what was going on.

Elliott put his phone back in his back pocket. He crossed his arms and looked down, and it was as if grumpy Elliott was slowly starting to return. He looked back up at me and sighed, "Lawrence is picking us up at 8:15 tomorrow morning. We'll have to spend the night. The tour is at 2 so we should be able to make it."

I nodded, "Okay. Okay. That's good. That's good."

"I was thinking we could stay at the Hotel Regina, since the people there already know us from earlier," Elliott uncrossing his arms.

"Sounds like a plan," I smiled. Elliott, however, wasn't smiling like he usually did. I could tell he was stressed. It made me feel guilty. I felt like it was my fault because I wanted to get the pretzel.

Just then, Elliott suddenly snapped at me, "I hope you enjoyed your pretzel, by the way." I was taken aback by it and nearly jumped. That was not the Elliott I knew! What happened to the Elliott who blushed at me whenever we only touched slightly? The Elliott whose smile was contagious? The Elliott who would always protect me?

We decided to take the bus to the hotel, because we were tired of walking. The bus ride was tense the whole way. Elliott and I didn't say a word to each other. It was just like the first day in Assisi all over again.

******

We arrived at the hotel. The people at the front desk insisted they give Elliott a suite. He didn't want to accept it at first, politely declining the offer. However, I admitted to him that I really wanted it, and that he should accept the

314

offer. Because of the bet, Elliott had to do it, which made him groan. I was really getting frustrated with Elliott's behavior.

They gave us the key and we went up to our room. We rode elevator in complete silence up to the top floor. Before we opened the door, we saw the sign read in fancy bold letters:

Honeymoon Suite

Elliott looked almost disgusted when he saw those words. "The honeymoon suite?" he groaned.

"It'll be fun," I said happily.

"Would have been fun if we hadn't missed our train," Elliott muttered under his breath.

I heard what he said and asked in a calm but annoyed voice, "What did you just say?"

"Nothing," Elliott nearly shouted in an angry tone.

"Hey, I don't like how you're doing this," I said, getting defensive. "Look I'm sorry we missed the train, but you can't blame all of it on me. It was *your* fans who practically attacked me."

"You don't have to blame me for *everything*," Elliott gritted through his teeth.

"I wasn't blaming you," I said, starting to get really annoyed with this changed Elliott. "I was blaming your fans."

"Well, if the princess could have asked for a pretzel earlier—" Elliott started to say before I cut him off.

"Thanks for making me feel even more guilty than I already feel!" I said sarcastically. My face started to get red, not because of the blushing, but because I was angry, "And what is it with this attitude of yours? You've been acting like this all day? What in the world is wrong with you?"

Elliott started to get angry too and finally told me what had been irritating him, "How about the fact that the woman who took the pictures in Capri was in the train car with you? And you didn't tell me?"

My eyes widened. Oh crap. I wasn't angry anymore, but perplexed. "W-wait?" I stuttered out, "h-how did you know?"

Elliott crossed his arms, "From Grace."

"I swear—" I muttered to myself in anger, mad at Grace for telling Elliott. She had promised me! Grace, how could you?

"Why didn't you tell me?" he quizzed me. "I wouldn't be mad at you if you had just told me. But I asked you if anything was wrong, and you lied to me!"

I started to get defensive and said, "I thought you would totally freak out. I saw how you acted with the two teens, and I think you would get way too overprotective—"

"I'm just trying to protect you," Elliott nearly shouted, "and you're a Disney fan? You want to be like a Disney princess? Shouldn't you be happy that a man is always saving you?"

With that I just went silent. And Elliott did too. He covered his mouth, realizing he had taken things too far. Taking his hand away from his mouth, he was about to say something, but I spoke first, sounding hurt, which I was: "You know what, Elliott? Nicole was right. You *are* an asshole."

I could tell from his face that Elliott had regretted being so hard on me like that. "Cecilia," he said with an apologetic look on his face, "I'm sorry I didn't mean those words that—"

"I think you meant every word of it!" I shouted at him. I left my suitcases here with him. "I'll come back when you're ready to forgive me!"

"Cecilia don't do this," he grabbed my shoulder lightly, but he still tried not to let me get away.

"Let go of me!" I got defensive, trying to wriggle away from his grasp, my stubborn side coming out.

"You don't know the city very well," Elliott reminded me worried, "you could get lost, or kidnapped, or—"

I reminded him as I finally escaped his grasp, "I can take care of myself, thank you very much. I may think of myself as a princess, but I don't always need a prince to look after me."

I started to walk away, but then I stopped. I reached to the back of the necklace where the clasp was. I undid it, taking off the necklace. I took Elliott's hand, opened it with mine, and placed the necklace in, "And take your stupid necklace back!"

"But Cecilia---" Elliott almost seemed like he was on the verge of tears. "I'm really sorry—"

But it was too late, I was running down the hallway to the elevator, trying to get away from him. He called my name: "Wait! Wait, Cecilia, Wait! Wait! Cecilia!" He took a deep breath and shouted: "Love! Darling! Come back!"

At the use of those words, I stopped. I turned around at him and shouted with as much anger as I had before, "DON'T YOU DARE CALL ME THOSE STUPID NAMES AGAIN! HEAR THAT, PARKER?!"

With that, Elliott stood there, almost helpless and unsure of what to do. I kept running. I went down to the lobby and asked what a good bar was. She told me of one and I went there, wanting to drink my troubles away. I know I'm not much of a drinker, but I had to find a way to get Elliott Parker off my mind.

Chapter 17: Wishing For Some Alone Time

Eight o'clock. I had been at that bar for three hours. Not sure how or why but I was. I really didn't feel like talking to Elliott. I didn't even want to look at him. I was already feeling guilty about missing the train, and he added to the guilt even more. I thought he was a sweet, good-hearted person who would never hurt me. Now I saw I was wrong.

He kept texting me throughout.

Elliott: Cecilia please pick up

Elliott: Where are you?

Elliott: I've called you a million times

Elliott: I'm worried about you

Elliott: i'm sorry for what i said. I feel like such an idiot. Just please call or text me. I want to know you're okay.

Elliott: if not, then PLEASE come back

He called me thirty times in five hours. I never answered. I had twenty seven texts from him. I didn't reply to a single one. The girls called me at one time. I answered them. They told me to respond to Elliott or go back to the hotel room with him. But I couldn't. I wanted to. I missed him. I really was starting to fall in love with this guy. But I can't. After what he said to me I don't want to have anything to do with him, for now at least.

I was also mad at Grace. I blamed her as part of the reason we were fighting, since she told Elliott about Gwen. Ugh! Why are people so frustrating?

I didn't have much to drink. Just a beer or two. They were disgusting, but I didn't care at this point. I also made sure to eat so I wouldn't get drunk. And I wasn't. Maybe a little tipsy, but that's it.

Anyway, it was 10 p.m. I was sitting at a table by myself. Then a familiar face came up to me. It was Franco! He must have been off work and came over to celebrate being done with the day.

"Guten abend (good evening), Cecilia," he smiled. For a brief few seconds he looked scared, not sure why, but he went back to grinning.

"Hi, Franco," I gloomily smiled.

Noticing I was down, Franco came and sat next to me. He was hiding something behind his back, but even when he sat down at the table, he kept it hidden. "What's wrong?" he asked in a concerned voice, putting his hand on my shoulder.

"Nothing," I said, "nothing at all."

Franco looked around the room, and then back at me, "And where's that handsome boyfriend of yours?"

"Oh, he's not—" I started to say. Then I stopped. I noticed a lot of people who didn't know me called Elliott my "boyfriend," when we weren't really. I wasn't sure what we were. But I decided not to get into it with Franco. So I sighed and said, "We're fighting."

Franco grew even more concerned. "Oh my goodness, I'm so sorry my dear," he patted my shoulder. "If you don't mind me asking, what about?"

I shook my head. Still looking down at him, I said, "Oh it's nothing. It's kind of personal."

"Well don't get so glum," Franco continued to try to comfort me, "you still have a few days left in this trip, don't you?" I nodded. Franco asked, "Where are you heading to next?"

I knew I shouldn't have done this since Franco was a stranger, but my head wasn't clear because I was sad and slightly tipsy. Finally looking at him, I told him, "We're heading to Salzburg tomorrow, we'll stay there for two nights, then a few hours in Fussen, Germany, and then three nights in Munich."

Franco grinned and said, "That sounds like fun." Franco revealed what he was hiding: a glass of beer. He placed it in front of me and said warmly, "You want to forget about how you're fighting with your boyfriend? Here, have another drink of beer."

I looked up at Franco, almost disgusted. My parents had never told me to take a drink from strangers. "Uh, no thank you," I told him politely. I also remember they told me to never leave the person you came with. And although Elliott wasn't at the bar, I shouldn't have left him like that in the city.

"I should probably go back to him," I said, almost to myself. "I'm mad at him, but I want to make things right with him." I got up from my chair and said to Franco, "Nice meeting you, Franco, but if you'll excuse me, I've gotta talk to Elliott."

I was walking away, and Franco was shouting at me to come back. But I didn't. I was too focused on walking back to the hotel. And I did. It wasn't a very long walk, but I walked back nonetheless. I finally reached the hotel. I walked up to the suite confidently and knocked on the door without hesitation. I knocked on the door once again. No response. I knocked again. Nothing. I stood there briefly, not sure about what to do. Very confusing. But I remembered something: I had a keycard. So I used it. I swiped it on the grey device outside the room, and the door opened.

I walked in the room, and before I could ask Elliott where he was, I saw the room. My jaw dropped. It was *huge*. There was a hallway with floral grey wallpaper in a room with a mirror that had a golden frame on the side. The carpet was a floral pattern with an assortment of colors. I walked along the hallway to see a breathtaking sight. Let's just say, you could tell it was the honeymoon suite.

The room was a light green, my signature color, almost minty. There were two enormous windows overlooking the nighttime city of Vienna. On one side there was a canopy bed, big enough for the two of us. I ran over to test out the bed. I sunk into the soft creamy white sheets. Right by the windows there was a huge aqua color couch that could fit two people on it. It faced the direction of a TV that was as big as the one at my house, almost like a movie theater. On each side of the bed there were white wooden night stands that had a drawer. I opened one of the drawers, just curious to see what was in it. The only thing in there was a little but thick brown book with a red satin bookmark. In beautiful golden cursive it read: "Bibel," or "Bible." I picked it up out of the drawer. Though it was thick, it wasn't heavy because of its size and the fact that it was a paperback. I flipped through the pages, not able to recognize what passage it was, or even if it was from the Old or New Testament. That was because the book was written in German, which made perfect sense considering I was in Austria. Anyway, right by the couch there was a table, almost like a dinner table, for two, with a vase of beautiful flowers in the center. Right by the TV there was a silver minifridge.

Putting the Bible back in the drawer and closing it, I slowly got up to do some more exploring. I left the "master bedroom" and made my way out to the hallway. On my right, I saw the bathroom. I walked in, wanting to explore every aspect of the room. When I entered, right on my left was the shower, small with stones on the ground and wooden walls. I walked further in. Right next to the shower was the toilet, small and clear. Right in front of me was the sink, hand towels, and a mirror with a silver frame. When I turned to my right, my jaw dropped and my eyes flew wide open. Sitting right there was the largest bathtub I had ever seen in my life. Maybe it was even a jacuzzi! It was white marble, and it felt cold as I placed my hand to touch it. Goodness, whoever has had this suite for their honeymoon was *soooo* lucky.

I had gotten so immersed in the incredible suite that I remembered something aloud: "Oh my gosh. Where's Elliott?"

I ran back into the main room calling for Elliott's name. But that wouldn't do any good. I was smart enough to realize that Elliott must not have been here. Not once exploring did I once say, "Hi, Elliott," so that should have been a sign right here. I started to get worried. So I sat down on the edge of the bed, thinking of what I should do. A lightbulb flicked on, and I reached into my purse and grabbed my phone. I dialed Elliott's number, waiting for him to pick up. Just as I pressed the "call" button, I heard the door open. I diverted my eyes to the hallway, and saw Elliott frantically come in holding his phone up to his ear. He was talking to someone. As soon as I saw this, I set my phone down beside me.

"I just don't know what to do, Grace," he said, panicked into the phone. He spoke very quickly, "I've tried calling and texting her and she won't speak to me...I know what I said was stupid...I'm getting worried. She could be in trouble. And I've looked everywhere all around Vienna and I can't—"

Elliott looked in my direction and saw me. At first he was confused, unsure if it was me, cocking his head to the side and raising his eyebrow slightly. I waved to him, my smile almost out of proportion. He waved back.

"She's here, Grace," he said into the phone. "I'll call you back." He immediately hung up. He just stared at me for a few seconds. Then he smiled, his brown eyes glistening. "Y-you came back," he finally said.

"Of course I came back," I chuckled. I stood up from my bed and Elliott walked quickly towards me. Once we finally reached we shared a warm embrace. I missed the comfort of his hugs. He held onto me tighter than ever.

"Uh, Elliott," I nearly choked.

"Yes, love?" Elliott asked, still squeezing me. He was almost squeezing the life out of me.

"That's-that's too tight," I said trying to gasp.

Just like that, Elliott slowly unwrapped his arms from me, giving my body relief as it became free from his arms. "Oh, sorry," he laughed nervously.

We were just staring at each other. Elliott put his hands on my shoulders, and I did the same with his. "Oh thank goodness," he sighed in relief. "I wasn't sure what had happened to you." He started talking quickly once again, "I called you a million times. I texted you. But you didn't pick up! And I was like 'What the hell is going on?' And so I was looking all over Vienna for you. And I asked the hotel front desk lady where you were, but she wouldn't tell me because apparently you told her not to tell me where you were if I asked. But I kept asking anyway, and she got pissed with me. And then I think she gave the Austrian equivalent of the middle finger, which is *no* way to treat your guests. And then—"

Before he could finish his story, I interrupted his babbling with a quick peck on the cheek. We looked back at each other. I grinned, and Elliott laughed in a cute way saying, "Wow, that's a really nice way of telling me to shut my mouth." I laughed at that too.

I looked down at the ground, and then back at him into his eyes. It was as if the moment had gotten serious, as both our smiles had faded away. "I'm sorry," I breathed. "I should have told you about the photographer. I just didn't want it to ruin our day trip to Vienna. And I was going to tell you the next day."

"It's fine," he nodded. "I trust you. Just please, if something like that happens again, someone who makes you uncomfortable—"

"I will tell you," I finished for him. I added, "And I'm sorry for not asking for the pretzel earlier."

"That's nice of you to say," Elliott said sweetly. He sat down on the edge of the bed as he said, "But I think *I'm* the one who owes you an apology." He patted a spot with his right hand on the bed for him to come and sit next to me, and I did.

"I-I'm sorry," he was looking down at his lap, as if he was afraid to look at me. "I shouldn't have said those things. For one thing about calling you a princess. I know you can take care of yourself and you of course don't need a man to rescue you. And I respect that. And it wasn't all your fault with the pretzel. We-we," he paused, still looking down. But he found the courage and looked back up at me into my eyes. He went on, "We might have made the train, if it hadn't been for my stupid mob of fans. And I was so worried about missing the train that I-that I didn't---you know, ask if you were okay after. What happened was terrible and should *never* happen to *anyone*. And I just made it seem like it didn't happen."

I nodded my head, "It's okay."

"I just—" Elliott struggled to find his words. I put my hand on his thigh and rubbed it softly, in a way to calm him and assure him it was okay. Like he did to me in Materdomini when the waiter was being rude. He found them, "I've had girlfriends—or girls that I—you know what I mean. I've never had to keep a girl that I like out of the paparazzi before."

"I thought you said your privacy gets violated all the time?" I asked in confusion.

Elliott ran a hand through the back of his hair. "*My* privacy gets violated," he reminded me, "but all the girlfriends, or love interests, I've had...they didn't last so long that they were in the public eye. You know what I mean?" I nodded, showing him that I understood. "So I'm new to this whole thing where I don't have to, you know, look after just me. But another person, too. Does that make sense?"

"Yeah, it does," I told him. "But I want you to know, Elliott, that you don't have to worry about me."

Elliott looked shocked. "But—" he started to say.

"Let me finish, please," I politely interrupted. Elliott nodded and allowed me to go on. "I appreciate and admire that you are trying to protect me from all these people in the media. I really do," I paused, trying to find the right words to say. "But—I—but I want you to worry about your privacy, and let me worry about mine." I realized that it came out wrong and I tried to rephrase what I was saying, "I mean—we should worry about each other's privacy, but not too much. I want us to make a deal that we'll help each other deal with paparazzi, fans, and nasty photographers like Gwen Hodges—" I laughed at saying this, and Elliott did too. "But I think we should each try to be responsible in staying out of the spotlight on our own."

Elliott was confused, and sounded a little hurt. "So you're saying we should break up?"

I quickly assured him this was not the case. "No, no, no, no. Not at all. I just think if something happens where I end up in a news story or tabloid, it's on me. If the same thing happens to you, that's on you."

Elliott took a little bit to process it. He looked up at the ceiling, trying to think about what I said and comprehend what it meant. "Ohhh," he said to himself. He looked back at me and waved his finger, "I see what you're saying!" I gave him a thumbs up. But he turned to me and got serious, "And one more thing: *never* walk off in a big city like that and go hours without calling again."

"Fair enough," I nodded.

"I literally felt like I was going to have a panic attack," he remembered.

"I'm sorry I did that," I apologized.

"That's okay," he replied, "as long as you promise to never do that to me again."

I nodded my head and said sincerely, "I promise."

Elliott smiled and pulled me in. I rested my head on his lap, resting my cheek against his jeans. He used one hand to stroke and play with my hair. I felt the urge to look up at him, resting the back of my head on his lap. I stared up at him and he stared back down at me. He snuck one hand to the back of my head to support it and the other stroked my cheek lovingly, cherishing me.

Just like that, the romantic moment was abruptly ruined when he chuckled, "On the plus side, I saw a lot of *interesting* sights in Vienna."

"Really?" I pulled my head up in curiosity. But I wasn't thinking when I accidentally banged my head against his.

"Ow!" we both exclaimed in unison.

I plopped my head back down on his lap, rubbing my forehead to ease the pain. Elliott's head was now flat on the bed. My head felt fine now, after rubbing it. So I slowly sat up to check if Elliott was okay. He was still laying on the bed, rubbing his forehead slowly as he groaned. I crawled over to get closer to him, hovering over him almost.

"Elliott? Are you okay?" I asked him concerned.

Still covering his face with his hands, Elliott began to laugh hysterically. He pulled them away, and I could see his face was red from laughing so much. At first I looked at him like he was insane, but when I saw he thought it was funny, I started lightly laughing along with him. My laughter grew until I was laughing hysterically as well.

Once we finally calmed down I plopped down so I was laying next to him and asked him, "So, do you want to tell me about the *interesting* sights you saw in Vienna?"

"If you really want to hear," Elliott shrugged. And he told me everything, and we laughed.

******

It was 10:30 at night. Elliott was taking a shower and I was comfortably sitting on the couch, watching a movie on TV in a comfy hot pink Washington College T-shirt and really short red shorts. It was none other than *Serpent Boy*, in German of course. It was from back in 2016, when Elliott was twenty years old. Even if it was only three years ago, he still looked so young. His hair was shorter, more straight in this film, and he had a baby face. I smiled at "baby Elliott." When I first watched this movie in 2016, I never would have guessed I would be meeting him, kissing him, and sharing a honeymoon suite in Vienna with him without even being married to him!

Elliott told me he was going to take a shower and then get changed into his pajamas. When he first said this, I found myself smirking because I *know* Elliott's PJs consist of pajama pants or boxers and *no shirt*. Elliott looks so hot without his shirt on, and I'm sure that just coming out of the shower would make him look even sexier.

I heard the bathroom door open and quickly turned my head in that direction, eager to see him. Out walked Elliott, smiling. His curly hair was much more noticeable after the shower, wearing blue flannel pants....and a grey shirt. I tried to keep a smile on.

"Hey, Mr. Handsome Brit," I flirted.

Elliott leaned against the doorway as he winked, "Good evening, Miss Beautiful American." His flirty, sexy side quickly vanished as soon as he turned to the direction of the TV. His eyes widened open and he ran up to me and plopped right down on the couch next to me. "Oh my gosh! It's me!" he said giddily pointing to himself on the screen.

Serpent Boy was in his full-on tight, green and black lycra suit, fighting a bad guy whose name I can't think of.

Serpent Boy eventually took off his mask. Elliott groaned, "Ugh, I look so awkward! I guess I was twenty when I filmed this." Then Serpent Boy started speaking. Only it wasn't Elliott speaking. It was a fast-talking, thick-accented German dub. Elliott laughed, "That's what German me sounds like?" He then said in a terrible German accent, "I sound very good, no?" I continued to laugh.

But I wasn't paying attention the whole time. While Elliott was laughing and making comments about the movie, I was staring at his *clothed* chest the entire time, wishing his shirt was gone.

Elliott noticed something was off and looked down at me, "Is everything all right, Cecilia?"

I snapped back into reality. I shook my head and looked back up at him. "Uh, no. I mean, nothing. Nothing. No. Not at all," I said, embarrassed. I averted my head back to the TV.

I think Elliott knew what I was thinking. Because he casually said, "It's getting hot in here." Wasn't that a song? "Don't you think, darling?" With that, I twirled my head back to look at Elliott. He was reaching for the hem of his shirt and pulled the shirt over his head, revealing his toned chest. He threw the shirt across the room and snaked--or should I say serpented--his arm around the back of the couch. I tried to hide a smirk that was growing on my face. "Is that—better?" he asked me coyly.

I didn't respond. I just stared at his chest, taking in every detail of it. I briefly looked up at him and he awkwardly said, "Uh—you can—you have my permission to—um—you know—only if you want."

It took me a while to understand what he was saying, but I nodded my head and smiled, but not in a creepy way. My attention went back to his chest. I slowly started to reach my hands toward it. I felt my heart pumping faster than ever. Wasn't sure if it was the feelings or nerves. I had never touched a guy in this way before. I finally rested my hands softly on his abs, feeling the warm, smooth skin against mine.

"Wow," I said in disbelief and awe, "That feels really soft!"

"Uh," Elliott smiles awkwardly, "Thank you."

With my hands still on his abs, I asked him directly to his face, "Do you work out?"

"I-I do," he replies. "Not to brag or anything, but I make sure to go to the gym as often as I can, eat food, and—"

Staring back down at his chest, I murmured under my breath but loud enough for him to hear, "It *really* pays off."

Right then, without warning, Elliott crashed his lips onto mine. I kissed him back. I never got tired of his soft lips on mine. It changed from romantic in a sensual way to romantic in a cute way when he slowly separated his lips from mine and moved them to my cheek. He showered kisses all over them. I can't help but erupt into a fit of giggles, feeling more ticklish than ever.

"Elliott, stop it," I giggle more, playfully and lightly slapping his chest trying to get him to stop. But I didn't want him to stop, and I don't think he did either. He finally rested and took his lips off my cheek and stared into my eyes. I asked him, "Don't you want to finish watching your movie?" I teased him, "You seemed so excited to yourself on screen."

Elliott smiled and shook his head. He searched the couch for the remote with his hand, his eyes still trained on me. He finally found the remote, picked it up, and quickly shut the TV off, looking up briefly to make sure it was all the way off. As soon as that was done, he stared at me lovingly, never ending our gaze even as he set the clicker on the table.

"It's alright," he playfully assured me. Brushing a strand of hair out of my face, he smirked, "I've seen it so many times before."

With that, he resumed kissing my cheek. My hands made my way to touch his back, rubbing my hands up and down his hot skin. I used this to pull him down as I sunk down, laying my back on the couch. As I did this, Elliott's lips once again connected with my own. The kiss became more and more passionate. More and more heated. Elliott slowly rubbed his cool hand on my thigh, but not in a comforting way this time.

Realizing something, I broke apart the kiss, "Wait, Elliott!"

This startled Elliott, causing him to break apart the kiss and become worried. "Is everything alright, darling?" he asked as he slowly rose. "Oh, I'm sorry. I'm sure I made you believe I wanted more I'm so sorry—"

"No, no," I tried to convince him as I slowly rose so I was sitting up with him. "I just—I think we should do it."

"Do what?" Elliott asked, for some weird reason not understanding what I meant. I cocked an eyebrow at him, and gave him the "you know what I mean" look. "Oh," he nodded his head. "Are you sure?" he asked again. "Just so you—I'm not going to do it unless you want to. I don't want to force you into something you're uncomfortable with." And then he did the cute babbling thing he does: "And what if I'm not good enough for you? Or something happens? And what if I hurt you? I really don't want to hurt you. Or—"

"Shhh," I silenced him by putting a finger lightly on his lips. I whispered to him, "I *want* to, Elliott."

I took my finger off his mouth and he asked with a sweet look on his face, "You sure, love?"

I nodded and said with confidence, "I think I'm ready."

Elliott grins, slowly leaning his lips back onto mine. I knew he had wanted to do this for a while, but we never did it because he respected me too much to do anything I wouldn't want to. We resumed kissing in the same way again as Elliott slowly made his way off the couch and picked me up. He put his hand under me and I wrapped my legs around his torso. He carried me to the bed, and we didn't stop kissing. We finally made it to the large bed, and he gently placed me on it, briefly ending our kissing. I laid back so my head was against a pillow as Elliott, with a mixture of lust and love in his eyes, stood there looking at me. I smirked, almost mischievously, as he sat on his hands and knees on the bed and started to crawl toward me. Now he was hovering over me, legs at each of my sides.

What I was thinking now was how hot Elliott looked! That, and I wanted to admit to him I was nervous, but I didn't want to back out. It wasn't like I didn't want to do it. I did. I just had never done it before, and I didn't know what to expect. I knew about a lot of things, but when it came to sex, I was clueless.

Before I could share what I was feeling, Elliott bent down and connected his lips with mine in a hungry manner. And all my worries went away—for now at least. I started to stroke my fingers through his curly locks of brown hair as we continued to make out and just enjoy this moment without best friends, younger brothers, rude fans, or press photographers to get in the way.

And let's just leave it at that...

Chapter 18: Wishing For Forgiveness

The Vienna sunshine woke me up. I fluttered my eyes open and looked at the curtains (which almost looked like the ones from *The Sound of Music*, honestly) blocking the sunlight. I squinted at the hidden sun, and smiled as I lay warm under the covers, feeling two hands wrapped tightly around my waist, as if they didn't want me to slip away. A naked chest felt warm and cozy against my bare back. I turned around to make sure it was who I thought it was. Elliott was sleeping there, soundly as a baby, his eyes shut. I smiled at him, examining every little detail about him from his partially open lips to his messed up, ruffled hair.

I won't talk about last night, because it was my first time ever and it was personal. Let's just say this. It was awkward. I kept talking and asking questions because I was nervous and a little insecure, but Elliott made me comfortable and kept on insisting I was perfect in every way, although he ended up being just as awkward and nervous. The whole experience was awkward and not out of a Hollywood movie, but not too bad for the first time. I just liked the feeling *after*, cuddling with the man I cared so deeply for.

I leaned in to kiss his warm cheek softly, hoping he would wake up. But he didn't. He just lay there soundly. I wasn't sure whether he was faking or not, but I went along with it. Seeing myself naked and still tucked in tightly under the covers, I searched for the nearest piece of clothing while still keeping myself fully covered. I found my green hook-in-the-back bra right next to me along with the matching underwear. I grabbed them and, still keeping myself under the covers, I put them on, almost with ease. Once I was done, I leaned in close to try and get Elliott up once again.

After kissing his cheek for the second time, I whispered in his ear, "Wake up, sleepy head." No response. I let myself go of Elliott's grasp on my waist to see if he would respond. But nothing. I was getting a little concerned, so I decided to yell (but not too loudly) in his ear:

"ELLIOTT WAKE UP!" right in his ear.

Although he didn't wake up, I did see a small smile form on Elliott's face, but faded away after one second. So he must have been at least a little awake.

"Ha ha," I fake laugh to myself, "very funny, Elliott." My back started to hurt from the laying down for so long, so I sat up briefly, crossing my arms. "Hmmm," I quietly said to myself. I still didn't get a response, so I said with genuine worry, "Elliott? Elliott?" as I leaned in closer. Starting to crouch down to him again, I got close to his face, only a few centimeters away.

"BOO!" Elliott quickly shot his eyes wide open and I nearly screamed. I hadn't expected that. I jumped back in shock away from Elliott, sitting up instantly. Elliott started chuckling, proud of himself for scaring me.

Starting to get cold from only being in my bra and underwear, I rubbed my hands up and down my arms to keep warm. I was having a terrible laughing fit. I tried to speak my words through the laughter, "Oh my gosh, Elliott, why would you do that?"

Elliott sat up and leaned his head and back against the headboard and answered honestly with a chuckle, "To avoid all the 'cheesy morning after shit' you see in the movies." He turned his head to me.

"I *like* the 'cheesy morning after shit' you see in the movies," I turned my head to him, pouting my lips.

Elliott decided to play with his flirtatious side, as he cocked his eyebrow and smirked, "You like this, darling?"

"I do," I giggled, blushing more than I had ever been.

Elliott took me in his arms, positioning me so that now I was being cradled in his arms, the lower side part of my back placed against his lap. His one arm was placed tightly on my waist and the other was wrapped around the upper part of my back, near where my shoulders were. I looked up into his warm brown eyes, smiling as I watched them sparkle.

Elliott was clearly trying his best to be sexy. "So you like this?" he winked at me. Turning redder and redder, I nodded slowly and giggled. He pulled me closer to his face and kissed me, very chaste. When he pulled away, he continued to act sexy, "Do you like the feeling of us here right now? Cuddling and kissing and wrapped in the sheets the morning after your first time?" I nodded more and more quickly, my smile never fading.

"A little awkward, don't get me wrong," I answered him truthfully, "but I had a nice time."

"As did I," he simply stated, pulling in to kiss you once again, with much more passion and heat (similar to last night) than the previous chaste kiss.

He pulled me in to kiss me again. It was almost desperate, as if it was the last time we would kiss. Which we both knew it wouldn't be. Impolitely kissing each other, we took advantage of a rare moment like this in which we were alone. We finally stopped, then gazed at each other. I was studying every detail of his face, and he did the same with me.

"Elliott?" I broke the silence. Elliott hummed in response, and I asked, "If you don't mind me asking, how many girls have you been with?"

"Getting personal, hey?" he raised an eyebrow.

"I'm serious," I laughed.

"Okay," Elliott smiled. "Including you, three. Both my ex-girlfriends."

"Oh," I nodded.

"Megan and Ella," Elliott unnecessarily said their names.

"Name drop," I teased. Elliott laughed.

"I remember I once told Elle, 'We're Ella and Elliott!' Then she broke up with me a few days later," Elliott explained. This made me laugh. "But I think that was far from the reason we broke up."

That caught my attention. I quickly shot up from his touch so I was sitting up right in front of him. "Why'd you break up?" I asked without thinking. Soon after, I realized it wasn't right, so I nervously laughed and mumbled, "Sorry. I don't know why I said that."

"No, no, it's okay," Elliott shook his head and smiled. He asked me again, "You *really* want to know?"

I shrugged, "If it's okay with you." Elliott took a deep breath and told the story:

"Well, we dated in secondary school, but then we broke up. Then we got back together when we were about twenty-one, but it didn't last. I was gone almost all the time filming a movie, and she didn't like it. Then one day, she slept with someone else."

"Oh my gosh," I muttered in disbelief. How could anyone sleep with someone else when their boyfriend was Elliott? "What about Megan?"

Elliott explained, "Well, I met her while doing a play in the West End, and we started dating after that. As time went on, she said that I was getting all these movie roles while she was jealous that she wasn't getting anywhere with auditions. Then when I got cast as Serpent Boy, she broke up with me."

I felt a combination of anger for his two girlfriends and sadness for Elliott. "What two little—jerks," I said, trying to hide my feelings. I placed my hand on Elliott's cheek and said, "I'm sorry, Elliott."

Placing his hand on mine he said, "It's fine." He removed it and still holding it, put my hand in his lap. "I'm just worried the same thing will happen with you. That's why I get so mad when anyone is cruel to you. I'm afraid that it'll chase you away." I bit my lip in astonishment. I had never known the reason why Elliott always got so protective when I dealt with some of his rude fans or the paparazzi.

"I never knew that was why you were so protective," I shook my head. "But don't worry, I'm not going to leave you just because of a group of strangers."

"Don't let them get in the way of what we have," Elliott advised me.

"Yeah," I agreed. "And just so you know, those girls had no idea what they were missing out on. No one should let other people, or the other person's job, get in the way."

Instead of thanking me for my kind words, Elliott leaned back into me and kissed me passionately, placing his hands on my cheeks. He laid his back down on the bed with me placing my knees on each side of him, never ending our kiss. We eventually departed our lips and looked at each other lovingly, my hands on each side of Elliott's, holding myself up for support.

"You know," I said in a teasing manner with a sly smirk on my face, "It wasn't all bad, just a little awkward. And we can make it less awkward if we practice. And seeing as though we won't really have time for the rest of the trip, we—"

Elliott got impatient, but it was cute. He eagerly said, "Just please kiss me!"

I did what he wanted, kissing his lips once again. His lips slowly caressed mine for what might have been the one hundredth millionth time. We were interrupted by a sound, a ringtone. The ringtone was Elliott's, and the song choice made me laugh: the Serpent Boy theme song. This is how it goes:

Look out! Serpent Boy is coming!
Watch out! He's stopping a crime!
The hero really is something
If he can stop a crime in time
Serpent Boy! There he goes!
Serpent Boy! Quick and sly!
Serpent Boy! Slithering he fights
foes!

Serpent Boy! A very nice guy!

As soon as I heard it, I turned my head quickly, as did Elliott. He looked up to face me with me looking down on him.

Raising my eyebrow and with a smirk on my face, I teasingly said, "Nice choice in ringtone. What inspired your choice?"

Elliott shrugged and blushed. "I guess I'm very committed to my role?" he said, almost as if asking a question.

"I think it's cute," I winked at him. Elliott continued to blush and smile, briefly looking away so he wasn't making eye contact with me. "Are you gonna get that?" I finally asked him.

Being brought out of his daze, Elliott shot up his head and said, "Oh right!" I slowly separated from him so he could have room to get up, which he did. He reached for his phone across to the night stand. He took his phone and looked at it in his hand. He became nervous and looked up at me and said, "Incoming facetime from Grace!"

"Answer it!" I anxiously said, playfully shaking his shoulder.

"B-but what about—?" Elliott started to ask.

"I'll hide," I assure him. "Just make sure she doesn't see me. Just answer!" I didn't want Grace to find out what had happened through the phone, so I would tell them later and, in the meantime, Elliott would try not to say anything suspicious.

A little shaky, Elliott quickly tapped the "answer" button, and positioned the phone at an angle where I wouldn't be seen.

"Hi!" multiple voices said. It sounded like my friends.

"H-h-hey girls," Elliott nervously waved at the camera.

"How's it going?" I heard Grace ask.

"F-fine," Elliott was still nervous he was going to get caught.

"How's the hotel?" Grace asked.

Elliott nodded, "Nice." Smiling, he said, "In Nicole's words it's very boujee."

"Ooooh I wanna see it!" Nicole excitedly said.

"I'll send you pictures of it," Elliott suggested, not wanting to have our cover blown.

"Why can't you just show us now?" Esperanza asked, starting to get suspicious.

"Uh—" Elliott tried to think of a valid reason. I put my head in my palm, anxious our cover would be blown.

Esperanza cut him off and asked, "And where's Cecilia?"

"S-she—" Elliott stuttered out. He thought of an excuse, "She's in the shower!"

"Really?" Nicole was really suspicious at this point. "So, did you guys have fun last night?" she asked, trying to get some answers.

"What kind of fun?" Elliott started bluffing, as if he was a child who had been caught stealing the last cookie from the cookie jar.

"You know what I mean," Nicole groaned.

I could tell Elliott's palms were trying to sweat. "No, I-I don't," he shook his head. "Do you mean dinner? Sightseeing? Drinking in an Austrian bar? Shopping?—"

"Did you guys get acquainted?" Nicole kept trying to get him to spill the beans. I was on the edge of my seat.

"Acquainted?" Elliott tried to use his acting abilities to act as if he wasn't sure what was going on.

I heard Grace, who at this point must have been getting very impatient, screamed, "DID YOU AND CECILIA HAVE SEX OR NOT?"

Elliott looked at me and mouthed, "What do I do?"

Shaking my head, I mouthed, "Don't say it."

But Elliott knew it wouldn't do any good to lie to them, so he looked back at the phone, sighed, and said in defeat, "Okay, fine. We did." My eyes widened and my cheeks started turning red as Elliott's were.

"Ha! I knew it!" Nicole sounded as if she had won a bet.

"You what?" Grace asked in an almost angry tone.

"You owe me fifty bucks," Nicole said to someone. I heard Esperanza groan. My guess is that Nicole and Esperanza made a bet as to whether Elliott and I would have—you know—when we were alone.

I heard Esperanza ask, "Now tell me, is Cecilia here?"

"No, she's in the shower," Elliott lied.

Seeing as I couldn't lie to my friends right there, I finally said, "No. I'm here."

"Can I speak to her?" Grace said annoyed. My guess was that I was gonna get a long lecture.

"Sure," Elliott nodded and handed me the phone. I was holding it so I was looking at my friends. They were all sitting there, and looked as if they were on the bed. Esperanza, with her eyes wide open and her mouth opened wide, looked completely shocked. Nicole had a big smile on her face, as if she was proud of me. Grace didn't look impressed. She had a scowl on her face and her arms were crossed. I gulped.

"So," Nicole asked in a sexy voice. "You were finally deflowered, huh?"

"By my older cousin?" Grace gritted through her teeth.

"That sounds so vulgar," I shake my head.

"So is the image of you two together!" Grace said disgusted. Grace was one of those people who could be cheerful and kind one minute, but then when she lost her temper, she lost it. I looked at Elliott briefly. He sat there helplessly, looking down with his hands in his lap and looked sad as if he couldn't do anything to help.

Esperanza tried to calm Grace down. Putting her hand on her shoulder she said calmly, "Grace, stop. It's not like you didn't know it would happen eventually."

"But they should know better," Grace said to Esperanza, looking at me.

"We just got caught up in the moment," I tried to convince her. "And I promise, this isn't just an attraction thing, I really do—"

"I don't care if it's an attraction thing or not!" Grace snapped back. In disgust she said, "I will have that image burned into my brain for the rest of my life!"

Elliott moved in closer to me to say something. I pulled the phone back so he could be seen. "Hey," he said in defense. "It was both of us. We both made a decision—"

Grace cut him off, "I never said anything about being mad at you, Elliott! But I *am* mad at both of you." I saw Nicole and Esperanza sit there uncomfortably.

I started to get annoyed and said, "Hey, you said it was okay for us to date. And I think you should have known it would happen. And would you have rather had us do it when everyone was there in Salzburg? When you could have walked in on us—"

Grace cut me off and took me a little aback when she snapped, "I'm not mad at you for doing it. I'm mad at both of you for trying to cover it up." I looked at Elliott, and he looked at me. We both had guilty looks on our faces.

But the guilt washed away when I brought up another thing against Grace: "Well you told Elliott about Gwen and I made you promise not to tell anyone!"

Grace's voice started to raise, "Well *I* think it's stupid to not tell the person you really like that the person who exposed you to the whole world was in the same proximity as him!"

"I *was* going to tell him eventually," I fought back, "I told you that."

347

Silence followed. Nicole broke it when she said, "Okay, these two are meeting Lawrence to take them to Salzburg, so we should probably let them get ready."

"Yeah," Grace said sarcastically, "if I were you I wouldn't go for it again. You wouldn't want to keep Lawrence waiting, would you?"

"Okay," Esperanza said, wanting to get out of this conversation before it got even more intense. "Bye guys."

"Bye," Elliott and I said sadly in unison. With that the call ended.

I sighed, and Elliott buried his face in his head in frustration. "Well, that didn't go well," he said quietly.

"I feel so bad," I leaned against the headboard.

Elliott lifted his head and looked at me, saying, "She'll come around."

"We shouldn't have tried to hide it," I pointed out. Then I said getting angry, "But she's also being hypocritical. She's the girl who lied about who you actually were for years and tried to keep it from us until we actually met you."

Elliott nodded, "True. I also think she cares about the both of us. And it's one thing to have your cousin and friend dating, but then it's another thing when they sleep together."

I sighed. "You know what? Let's get ready, have breakfast, and we'll meet Lawrence and we can talk about it in the car."

"Okay," Elliott nodded. I started to get up to take a shower, but Elliott gently grabbed my hand and asked, "Cecilia? Uh---you know how you told Grace that our thing wasn't just an attraction?"

"I remember, yeah," I nodded.

"Well," he asked, "what were you going to say when she cut you off?"

I knew what Elliott was talking about, and I knew exactly what I was going to say. But now wasn't the right time to say it, so I just said with a teasing smile on my face, "That's for another day."

"Come on," Elliott whined.

"Nope," I said, releasing myself from his grip. I got out of bed and started to walk away.

"But I wanna know!" Elliott whined like a baby, but in a teasing way.

Standing there in front of the bed I tapped my chin and "thought." Or more like was teasing him. "Hmmm. Let me think," I said. Elliott's face lightened up and leaned in, as if he was going to get his answer. My smile faded and I bluntly said in a sudden voice, "NO." This made Elliott jump back and his eyes widened, but he smiled when he noticed it was a joke. I smiled too, winked at him, and went off to take a shower.

******

Lawrence had picked us up at 8:15, and we drove and stopped to rest and hit some traffic on the way. The whole car ride had two parts to it. First, Elliott and I talked about what we were going to tell Grace. We decided to apologize for trying to cover up what had happened between us the night before. Second, we slept. We didn't get much sleep last night and we figured now was a good opportunity so we'd be energized for the tour, which made me giddy with excitement. I know I've said this a million times, but I had been a lifelong fan of *The Sound of Music* ever since I was a child. I used to be able to quote every line in the movie, and I know all the songs by heart. I used to make my dad perform "So Long, Farewell" with me, acting it out and everything. That's the one at the party where the children are about to go to bed and are saying good night to the guests. I would play all the girls, and he would play the two boys, and eventually we would argue over who would play the littlest one, Gretl. Ahh, childhood memories.

Elliott and I had woken up by the time we reached Sazlburg. Elliott reached into his pocket. Clearly searching for something, he said, "And I believe *this* belongs to you." He pulled out the silver fleur-de-lis necklace.

"Oh my gosh!" I said excitedly, having completely forgotten about the necklace that I took off after I was mad at Elliott. "I'm so sorry for taking it off in the first place," I said, turning around so he could put it on.

As he was clasping it, he begged, "Please, don't take it off again!"

I turned around and faced him. Putting my hand on his shoulder, I said assuringly, "I won't."

"Good!" Elliott smiled, giving two thumbs up. I gave two thumbs up back to him, and we laughed at how cheesy we were being.

At 11:30 a.m., we arrived at the hotel in Salzburg. It was only two-and-a-half hours until *The Sound of Music* tour. Salzburg was a quaint little town, a typical Austrian one. It had beautiful architecture and nice colors. Our hotel was right outside the downtown area.

Suddenly, we heard the door click and we jumped a little. Lawrence opened the door and held it open for us. We stepped out of the car while Lawrence continued holding it wide open. Our suitcases were waiting there for us. We were about to take it but Lawrence happily got the bags for us.

We went into the hotel, *Hotel Lasserhof*, and went up to our rooms. We walked down the hallway, which was wooden with mustard yellow carpet. Our rooms were right next to each other. Lawrence handed my suitcase to me and Elliott's to him.

"I should probably check out my room and say hi to my brothers," Elliott said, almost disappointingly.

"Don't worry," I patted his back, "we'll see each other in a few minutes."

"I know," Elliott whined, "I'll just miss you!" He wrapped his arms around my waist tightly and pulled me into him.

"It won't be long," I assured him. I placed my chin on his shoulder, wrapped my arms around his waist, and said, "And we'll have to talk to Grace."

"I forgot about that," Elliott said. I took my chin off his shoulder and wrapped my arms around the back of his neck. "Just give me five minutes."

I nodded my head, "Sounds reasonable." I leaned in to peck his lips lightly. We smiled. We turned over to Lawrence to see something I had never seen before.

I pointed to him and in a shocked yet excited tone, exclaimed, "He's smiling! Lawrence is smiling!" Usually, Lawrence had a serious look on his face, almost like a frown. But now he had a smile, not showing teeth. It may not have been the biggest smile, but Lawrence was smiling nonetheless.

"Wow," Elliott shook his head almost in disbelief. "That's a first."

"Anyway," I quickly changed the subject. I slowly backed away from Elliott and grabbed my suitcase. I took out my key as I waved to Elliott, "Bye, Elliott!" I turned to Lawrence and said, "Bye, Lawrence!"

"See you soon, Cecilia," was Elliott's reply. Lawrence, who was still smiling, just waved.

I used the key to open the door and I opened it. I closed the door behind me as I saw the room. There were two rooms. The main room consisted of one big bed for two people to share. That same room had a mini fridge, a tiny TV, and a table set for four. The smaller room only had two beds in addition to a closet. There was also a bathroom, one of the bigger, cleaner bathrooms of the trip.

I could hear murmurs. I walked into the main room to see all three of my friends talking and giggling. Noticing for some weird reason none of them noticed me or even heard the door open, I cleared my throat: "Eh hem."

With that, they all turned to face me, almost in surprise. My attention was on Grace's face. She was smiling, but it was barely evident and it seemed almost as though the smile was forced.

Esperanza and Nicole, on the other hand, had big smiles on their faces. Esperanza quickly stood up, "Hey girl! How are you?"

"Okay," I shrugged, still looking at Grace.

Nicole stood up too and ran over to me, "Now you have to tell us about everything!"

Playing dumb, I asked, "About what?" I didn't really want to talk about this, especially in front of Grace.

Nicole and Esperanza wrapped their arms around my shoulders as they walked me to the table. "You know what!" Nicole said, excited. "I'm so proud of you!"

"For what?" I continued playing dumb as I sat down. Nicole and Esperanza quickly sat in their seats.

"Don't play dumb, Cecilia," Esperanza rolled her eyes at me.

"What's there to talk about?" I nervously chuckled.

Nicole got really excited and said almost too loudly, "Are you flipping kidding me Cecilia?! YOU JUST HAD

SEX FOR THE FIRST TIME with ELLIOTT PARKER, and YOU DON'T WANT TO TALK ABOUT IT?!"

We nearly jumped back when I voice from the other room shouted in shock, "WAIT?! WHAT?!" It sounded like Ryan.

My eyes widened and Nicole flushed beat red in embarrassment. She shouted to the wall and said, "Sorry! Forgot the walls were thin here!" I buried my face in my palms.

We could hear the conversation from the other room:

"Wait, uh, Elliott, did you and Cecilia shag last night?" Ryan asked in confusion. I've always been fascinated by British slang. But British slang affiliated with me in *that* way, not so much.

"Yeah," I heard Elliott laugh nervously. "We did, and we both liked it."

"What does it mean to shag?" Ollie asked curiously.

"Do we need to leave the room?" Connor asked in just as much curiosity.

"No, you don't," Elliott quickly assured them. "Let's just change the subject."

I heard Ryan shout at me, "Wait, so Cecilia, how good was he?"

"*Very* good!" I shouted back.

"On a scale of one to ten---" Ryan started to ask.

"BLOODY HELL, RYAN! JUST SHUT UP!" Elliott shouted.

"Language!" Ollie said, being a cute smart alec.

"You know I'm still mad at you!" Grace finally shouted, after being silent this whole time.

Elliott asked me, nearly shouting, "Should I come over there *now*, Cecilia?!"

"Good idea!" I shouted back.

"Coming!" he replied.

I turned to Grace and almost begged her, "Look I'm really sorry, Grace. We shouldn't have tried to cover up."

"Why did you?" Grace said, sounding almost hurt and betrayed.

"We didn't want you guys to find out that way," I tried to explain to her, "over facetime. Elliott was naked, I was in my underwear---"

"TMI!" Esperanza raised her hands, making a giant "X" with them.

"And, well---" I started to continue.

There was a knock on the door. Esperanza and Nicole quickly stood up, as if eager to answer it and get out of the room before it got intense. They ran and opened the door, revealing Elliott. Nicole grabbed him by the shoulder and pulled him inside, and he stumbled in.

"Bye bye," Nicole waved to all three of us.

"Good luck!" Esperanza said, clearly anxious to get out. And they slammed the door.

Elliott looked at both of us, his cousin and the girl he liked, and flushed red in worry. He paused, took a big deep breath and walked over to sit next to us.

"Continue," Grace put her elbows on the table and folded her arms.

"And it just wasn't the right time," I explained, starting off from where I had left off. "We were going to tell you as soon as we got to Salzburg, I promise."

"I just didn't think you would do it," Grace shook her head. She looked at me and said, "You had always promised yourself to wait until marriage." She looked at Elliott and said, "And you always told me you would never do it unless you really cared about someone."

Elliott sighed, shrugged, and told his cousin, "Well, I really do care about Cecilia." He looked at me smiling as he said this, and I felt a beat in my heart.

Grace turned to me and asked, "He didn't pressure you, did he?"

I reached across to touch her shoulder and said, "No, no. Gosh, no. I told him I was ready, and he even asked me twice before." Grace smiled at this.

She asked, "And did you use protection?"

"You sound like Granny," Elliott teased Grace. She smiled at this.

"You sound like my mom!" Esperanza shouted from the other room.

"And my dad!" Nicole added.

"How about you two stop eavesdropping!" I shouted back.

"Sorry," the two said in unison.

Elliott chuckled, "Anyway," he continued. "Yeah, we did use it. The hotel room had condoms."

"Whoever heard of condoms in a hotel room?" Grace raised her arms.

Elliott shrugged, "Must be an Austrian thing."

We all laughed. After that, we sat silent.

"I'm sorry I was being overprotective," Grace sadly admitted.

"It's okay," Elliott assured her.

"And for breaking my promise not to tell him," Grace added.

"You're forgiven," I said. "I'm sorry we tried to hide it from you. And that I made you promise something I know you couldn't keep." Grace nodded, a tiny smile tugging the corners of her lips.

"Yeah," Elliott added, "we'll try to be honest with you from now on."

"I love you both," Grace stood up, holding her hands out for a hug. Both Elliott and I stood up and rushed over to her and gave her a big hug. It formed into a group hug, kind of like what I do with my mom and dad, and sometimes Jane if she tries to get in on it.

"Love ya girl," I whispered to her.

"I love you so much, Gracie," Elliott whispered to his cousin.

We slowly got out of the hug and looked at each other. Grace turned to me and pointed at me, and said in a tone that was a mixture of seriousness and teasing, "Now don't hurt my cuz, Hartley, or else---"

"I won't," I shook my head. "If I did, I would never forgive myself."

Grace turned to Elliott and did the same thing saying, "And take care of her."

"I will," Elliott nodded quickly, a smile on his face. He turned to me and said, "She's amazing."

As a thank you, I pulled myself into him and without hesitating, I passionately kissed his lips, my hands planted firmly on his waist. Elliott quickly complied, kissing me back with just as much affection, and leading his hands to run his fingers through my hair.

"Oh, and uh, you may want to keep the PDA to a minimum," Grace chuckled.

Elliott and I pulled apart, looked at her, and said in unison, "Fair enough." Noticing we said this at the same exact time, we turned to each other and smiled.

"Now let's get going!" Grace said giddily, clapping her hands together. "We've got *The Sound of Music* tour to get to!"

And we seemed to forget about the whole thing for the rest of the day. I mean, sure, Nicole made a few dirty jokes here and there, but the fight was forgotten. Everyone was forgiven. Everyone was happy. At least for now. But it was great to just enjoy the happiness for now.

Elliott and I, with his arm around my waist, followed Grace out the door to head to Mirabellplatz for the tour. The one I've dreamed of since I was a little girl!

Chapter 19: Wishing For The Hills To Be Alive

Mirabellplatz. It was Salzburg's little town centre. Reminded me of downtown Annapolis. Old timey, classic, clean, only a few people who wanted your money. There was a park filled with green grass and trees that gave shade from the sunlight. We saw a large bus that we assumed to be a bus for the tour. It had Maria and the Von Trapp kids on it, but they looked like they had been painted in watercolor. I heard myself squeal in excitement.

We were walking. We figured we would get something small to eat, since the tour lasted for four hours, because some of the filming locations were a little farther than Salzburg. Elliott intertwined his fingers with mine in one of his hands, and he held tightly onto Ollie's hand in the other. Everyone else was by themselves. They were walking with the group, but I meant no one else was holding each other's hands.

"Look!" I heard Ollie's voice in excitement, "Pretzels!" All of us looked in the direction he was pointing and saw a tiny pretzel stand which sold, well, pretzels! The closer we walked toward it, the more evident the smell became.

Ollie must have really wanted a pretzel, because he tugged on Elliott's shirt and begged him, "Can we get one? PLEASE, Elliott! Pretty please!"

"Alright, alright," Elliott chuckled, "let me get some money." He reached into his pocket for his wallet. He searched for it in his two front pockets. He couldn't find it. A worried, anxious expression slowly built upon Elliott's face. "Oh no," he panicked to himself, "where's my wallet?" His worry started to increase, he asked the group, "Does anyone know where my wallet is?"

"I do," I simply said.

"Where?" he immediately turned his head to me.

I winked, "Check your *other* pocket."

"Other?" a confused Elliott asked. His eyes widened, "Oh," he dragged out, realizing what I was talking about. He went to search his pockets in the back and found it! He pulled it out. His navy blue wallet (which he told me was from a company called Harber London) was in his hands.

"May want to look a little harder next time, Elliott," Ryan playfully teased his brother.

"Yeah," Grace advised him, "and I may want to suggest putting it somewhere safer so pickpockets won't get it."

"Yeah, Elliott," I placed my hands on my hips, "who knows what would have happened if I hadn't been here."

Elliott admitted, "You're right. I'd probably be lost without you."

With my hands still on my hips, I told him, "You're right. You'd be toast."

"I like toast," Elliott pointed out casually.

"But would you want to *be* it?" I questioned.

Almost as if tired from us going back and forth, Nicole said, "Can we please just get some damn pretzels?!"

"Language," I pointed out to her.

"Face it, Hartley," Nicole said, "we all swear here!"

"But not in front of the kids," I gestured to Connor and Ollie.

"I'm not a kid!" Connor defended himself, "I'm a grown up!"

Ollie chimed in, "And I'm a grown up too!"

Esperanza sarcastically said in response, "And I'm hungry for a pretzel!"

We went over to the little cart that was selling pretzels. It was a red oak cart with wheels on it, and was run by a jolly, plump woman around my fifty-something and traditional Austrian clothing: a red checkered dress with an olive green apron with red floral printing on it, and a visible puffy white blouse underneath. A tip jar, which consisted of a silver can like the lady in Florence had, was placed right by the rack where the pretzels were. The dark-haired, but nearly gray-haired, woman with the merry smile was right behind a sign that read the menu and prices associated with them:

Traditionelle Brezel (Traditional Pretzel) 3 euros
Zimt Brezel (Cinnamon Pretzel) 3 euros
Sesam Brezel (Sesame Seed Pretzel) 3 euros

Flasche Wasser (Water Bottle) 1 euro

"Guten tag!" the thick-accented woman greeted with a warm, grin-bearing smile. She spoke, in her best English possible, "What would you like?"

Everyone turned around to look at one another. Our faces were *clearly* asking one another, "Who here speaks German?" I knew for a fact that Grace and Elliott both had German ancestry, and Grace had been trying to master the language for years.

I placed a hand on her shoulder and told her simply, "This one's on you, Grace."

Grace was clearly nervous and started twirling her hair with her pointer finger. "Umm," she murmured. "I'm not very good at it."

"Aww come on," I practically begged her. We each took a different language. We had all taken Spanish in elementary school, but when we entered high school we each decided to learn a different language. I chose Spanish, having wanted to continue the language I already started learning, and I was pretty good at it too, not to brag or anything. Even though Esperanza's mom was my Spanish teacher, and her dad was from Spain, she chose to take French, because, "the language is beautiful! And I want to get married in Paris someday!" Nicole took Latin because she thought it would help her with words on the SATs, and at that time she thought she would go into something medical, until she discovered her love for fashion design. Grace considered taking Latin because she knew she wanted to be a doctor (a career path she is still on), but she eventually chose German to learn a language much of her family spoke.

Grace rolled her eyes and said, "Fine." She turned to the woman, smiled, took a deep breath, and said almost easily, "Hallo! Meine Freunde und ich möchten bitte ein paar Brezeln!"

The minute Grace said this, my eyes widened. Wow! Grace said she wasn't confident in her German, but dang! I'm not fluent in German, but that sure did sound like German to me.

"Woah," Elliott held out in surprise, his eyes nearly bulging out. He smiled at his cousin and said, "Gracie, that sounds *really* good."

"Thanks, Elliott," Grace turned and smiled at her cousin, who turned to his brothers. Ryan's jaw was dropped nearly to the ground. Connor and Ollie were too busy drooling over the pretzels to pay attention. Can't blame them. Those pretzels look pretty tasty!

"Did you learn German overnight?" Nicole shook her head, still astonished.

"No," Grace shook her head. She giggled and answered, "I've been practicing every day for the past seven years. So much so I've been *dreaming* in German. Psychologists say when you think about something constantly, you just start having dreams about it!"

Looking down at the ground, Elliott did the classic, playful pout he does. "Why do *I* never dream in *Italian*?" he whined, but then laughed to himself.

Grace decided to joke with her cousin and said teasingly, "Maybe because you think about *Cecilia*

364

constantly instead. That's why you keep having dreams about *her*!"

Elliott looked up, almost as fast as a cheetah, at her. He was red like a tomato, and bowed his head again to hide it.

A tint of pink visible on my cheeks, I giggled, "Go ahead and order."

"Oh! The pretzels!" Grace had forgotten about the task at hand. She turned back to the woman, but back to us when she realized, "What are all your orders?" We gave them to her and she turned to the old lady and said, "Wir werden vier Zimt, drei traditionelle und einen Sesam haben, bitte!" Basically she ordered a sesame seed pretzel for herself, three traditional for Elliott, Ryan, and Esperanza, and four cinnamon for me, Nicole, Connor and Ollie.

"Wait, Cecilia," Esperanza realized. She turned to me and asked, "Do you need your water?"

I had my green and purple polka dot water bottle behind my back, and revealed it for Esperanza to see. I smiled, and Esperanza didn't say anything, only gave me two thumbs up. With my water bottle still in one hand, I gave her a thumbs up with my left thumb. My dominant hand is my right one, so I was holding the water bottle with *that* hand.

Anyway, we had finally gotten our pretzels. To thank the woman, we said, "Danke," and the woman nodded in reply.

1:30 p.m. The tour started at 2. Thirty minutes to eat our "lunch," which consisted of pretzels. Ryan and Grace had to go and get some money, and because Connor and Ollie were done with their pretzels (the little piggies ate them in ten minutes), decided to go with them. So it was just me, Elliott, Esperanza, and Nicole. My two friends were ogling two hot Austrian dudes from a distance, while Elliott and I were sitting down on a stone wall. Elliott's arm was wrapped tightly around my waist, and the other placed firmly at his side. His pretzel was already gone. I was still eating my pretzel, and I broke it apart and offered him a bite to eat. He happily obliged, taking the piece of pretzel in his fingers and slowly put it into his mouth. He started to chew, rather quietly being the polite English gentleman he was. I had always had a problem with chewing loudly, and my family and friends constantly liked to point this out to me.

But what Elliott did next proved he was *no* polite English gentleman. Still with food in his mouth, he said something. But all I could comprehend was, "Wecilwa, I us wand o to now tat I'm avin a underfu ime on ths ip."

I could see some of the cinnamon pretzel. Gross! Really, Elliott? Really?

I wasn't going to pretend like I didn't see the food. So I just smiled and politely said, "Um, Elliott, just so you---remember to chew with your mouth closed, and then speak."

Elliott must not have realized what he was doing. He covered his mouth and finished chewing, and swallowed. He looked at me, and nervously chuckled, then murmured under his breath, "Sorry."

"It's okay," I laughed at how cute he was. I was still curious about the gibberish he had spoken, so I asked, "So what was it that you were saying?"

He pulled me in closer, with me holding onto my pretzel tighter so it wouldn't fall as I moved closer. "What I *meant* to say was---" he started to laugh. Then he got serious, "I want you to know that I'm having a wonderful time on this trip."

I felt the pounding of my heart again. "Aww," I cooed, placing my chin on his shoulder and looking up at him. He smiled down at me, and I smiled back, lost in those beautiful eyes. Was I falling in love?

I told him sincerely, "I'm having a wonderful time too." My arm, the one that wasn't holding the pretzel, found its way to the small of his back and started to stroke it lovingly. I added to him softly, "And it's all because of you."

Elliott's eyes sparkled at my words, "You really mean that?"

"Mhmmm," I hummed. Elliott lowered his lips on the top of my head and placed a soft, gentle kiss on it. "I was thinking," I quietly said, "maybe later, after dinner, we could go back to the room and cuddle a little bit," I giggled at the word "cuddle." "Whaddya say, Parker?" I asked him again.

Elliott chuckled, looking down at me and replied, "You don't have to ask me twice, Hartley." This made me beam from ear to ear, and Elliott blushing at the sight of me. What I really liked about Elliott was how anything I did could make him blush, which showed how he cared for even the littlest things about me. *Sigh.*

"Only one thing," he said, almost as if with regret in his voice.

I quickly shot myself up, "Oh," away from him.

"I probably shouldn't say this," he shrugged, looking down. He looked back up at me and with hesitation on his face said, "Well, you know I love a good pint, or beer. Austria and Germany are *known* for beer. So, if I get wasted at all in either here or Germany, I apologize in advance."

I brushed it off, "Don't worry."

Elliott raised his eyebrow, "Really?"

"Yeah," I leaned down and whispered into his ear, "I've seen you get drunk before, Elliott. And it's crazy, but it's kind of cute." I leaned away to see him smiling. I also told him, "Oh, and last night I got a little tipsy cause I went to an Austrian bar and had a beer or two."

Elliott's eyes widened, "But you *hate* beer!"

"I don't really like any alcoholic drink," I shook my head. I added, "But many years ago, before I turned twenty-one, at the German pavilion in Epcot, my mom and my aunt tried this grapefruit beer which they said was delicious. I wanted to see if they had it in Austria, and they did! And it was delicious!"

"Grapefruit beer?" Elliott raised his voice with a smirk.

"You should try some!" I enthusiastically told him. "You would like it!"

"That actually sounds really, *really* good," Elliott said, sounding like he was craving grapefruit beer. "I love beer. I love grapefruit. Why not try both of them *together*?"

Before I could respond, two old ladies sat right next to us. One of them had a green flannel shirt with a picture of edelweiss on it, and the other said, "I love *The Sound of Music*." The "love" was actually a giant red heart, and the other words were in bold black letters. These two ladies must be going on the tour! Elliott and I turned our heads to spot them. I was about to say something when I heard Nicole and Esperanza walking back.

"Gosh, Nicole," Esperanza said annoyed, "First the hot gay guy in Capri, now *this*?! Europe is *not* our lucky place to find guys."

Nicole shrugged her shoulders and defended herself, "How was I supposed to know one of them has a fiancee and the other has a wife with a baby on the way? They don't just wear name tags that say that! Plus, they were *our* age. What guy gets engaged or has a pregnant wife at twenty-one?"

"Must be an Austrian thing," Esperanza sarcastically said.

They were walking towards us, when the woman with the "I love *The Sound of Music*" shirt stood up. She slowly, but swiftly walked towards Nicole. She was short and thin, around my grandmother's age. She had short ginger hair with bangs, and plain sunglasses that were just black and nothing else exciting. She had khaki pants on and silver walking sneakers.

She must have noticed Nicole's shirt. It was red and flowy, off at the shoulders, and had a traditional Austrian floral print scattered around it.

"This should be fun," Elliott whispered into my ear. I laughed at his quip, but we kept our attention focused on what was going to happen.

The woman, although much shorter than Nicole suddenly, but not too aggressively, grabbed her by the shoulders. Nicole looked nearly mortified while Esperanza stood there in complete bewilderment.

She pulled Nicole down so she was down to her height. This was a little awkward because Nicole is 5"10 and the old lady was around 5"3 or so.

She told her, almost blandly but with admiration, "This shirt is so *perfect* for Austria." My eyes widened at what was going on. A strange woman doing this?! Who has ever heard of such a thing? I saw Elliott out of the corner of my eye, his hand placed firmly on his mouth and his eyes watering, as if he was trying to prevent himself from bursting into a hysterical laughing fit.

Nicole was speechless. Her emerald eyes wide and her lips making an "O" shape, she pursed her lips into an obviously fake smile paired with an obviously fake laugh. "Uh, thank you, ma'am," she finally said after searching for the right, polite words to say.

The red-haired woman slowly released Nicole from her grip. Nicole stood up straight and looked down at the woman, who looked back up at her. She politely said, "Oh, I'm sorry, sweetheart. My name is Gloria." She gestured over to her friend who was sitting on the bench with Elliott and me. Gloria introduced us to her, "And this is my good friend Sally."

Sally, who seemed to be the more friendly and calm of the two smiled brightly and waved to us. She seemed to be short, around her friend Gloria's height. She had raven dark hair that was almost in a bob, shorter than Gloria's, and tan skin. She had khakis, like her friend, and wore the green edelweiss flannel, and matching sneakers as her friend.

"Hello children!" she piped up, still waving. Children?

"Uh, hey," Esperanza was almost unsure of what to say, "I'm Esperanza."

"Nicole," Nicole waved, but still with a fake smile.

"Cecilia," I waved to both women, trying to appear friendly.

Everyone turned to face Elliott, waiting for him to say who he was. "Hi," he awkwardly waved. "I'm---"

Before he could say anything else, Gloria briskly walked over to him. Standing in front of him, Elliott's instinct told him to stand up out of respect for an elder.

She was wearing sunglasses, but I could tell she was squinting her eyes, trying to figure Elliott out. She took them off, confirming this is what she was doing. I turned to Sally, who was smiling a huge smile at me. I awkwardly smiled back, then I turned to see what Gloria and Elliott were doing. Elliott stood there nervously waiting for a response.

Gloria pointed to him and figured it out, "You're that superhero my grandson really loves!"

"Awww," Elliott put his hands on his chest. He extended his hand and said, "The name is Parker. Elliott Parker."

Gloria reached out and shook his hand, smiling, "Pleased to meet you, Mr. Parker."

Letting go of her hand, Elliott assured her, "Oh, don't worry, ma'am. You can call me Elliott."

"You're handsome," Gloria wiggled her eyebrows, which is something I've *never* seen a woman that age do.

Elliott did his classic awkward laugh and ran a hand through his hair, "You're too sweet." I wanted to roll my eyes about how strange this woman was, but I didn't.

Sally, holding a paper bag, turned to all of us and enthusiastically said, "I got this from the sweet shop on the corner! Do you children want any?"

Nicole and Esperanza, who were walking toward us, politely declined, and Elliott told her, "No, thank you, ma'am. But I've got two little brothers who may want some."

Sally nodded, then turned to me and opened the bag asking, "How about you, dearie?"

"No," I shook my head. I smiled, "Thank you very much---"

"Wait a minute," Gloria interrupted me. She took her hand and placed it on my cheek, turning her to face me. "Oh my goodness, dear," she shook her head in disbelief. "You've got cinnamon all over your face!"

"Oof," I heard Esperanza murmur, Nicole giggled at her comment.

I felt my face, and did notice cinnamon on my chin from the pretzel. Oops. "Does anyone have a napkin?" Gloria looked around.

"Oh-oh," Elliott searched for a napkin. He found one on his lap and started to hand it to me and said, "Here, darling."

I was about to grab it from him, when Gloria impolitely snatched it from his hand. Elliott, who looked at her in surprise, mouthed the words, "O-kay."

Gloria started dabbing, almost violently, the napkin all over my chin where the cinnamon was. "My dear," she shook her head, "you have to be careful. You could have a bunch of bees come and swarm you. We wouldn't want that to happen, now would we?"

"No, Gloria," I shook my head.

She snapped at me, "Call me Mrs. Hangrove." This made me jump back in surprise. How come this woman loved Elliott and not me? Does everyone hate me now because I'm with Elliott? Everyone usually loved me!

Elliott politely stopped Gloria---er, Mrs. Hangrove---and said, "She can take it from here. Thank you, Gloria." *Thank goodness for Elliott freaking Parker. God bless his soul.*

Gloria handed me the napkin. I stood up and leaned to Elliott, saying, "Elliott, a word please?"

"Cecilia, what---" he started to ask, but I politely grabbed his hand and started to drag him away. As I walked him away from them, he politely yelled back, "Pardon us, please!"

As we were walking away, the four who had gone to get money were walking back. Ollie and Connor were running ahead of them.

"Connor! Ollie! Please slow down!" Ryan and Grace called them. They looked like they had been running at one point, sweaty and panting, but now they were walking slowly.

"What took you guys so long?" Elliott asked in curiosity when he saw them.

"Long story," Grace tried to explain, "the machine at the bank wasn't working, and then---"

She was interrupted by Ryan, who was pointing to something, "Who's that lady giving our brothers something?" We all looked to find Connor and Ollie taking candy out of Sally's purse. Sally was smiling at how happy the young boys were.

"And the lady who is making Nicole and Esperanza look like they want to tear their hair out?" Grace inquired.

374

We saw Gloria talking to Nicole and Esperanza (something about her dancing career), and Nicole and Esperanza trying to be nice but dreading every minute of talking to her.

Still looking at what was happening, I answered, "Some old ladies who are going on *The Sound of Music* tour. They *love* Elliott. The one *hates* me."

"You know that's---" Elliott started to say.

I tightened my grip on his wrist and told Ryan and Grace, "Just go and meet them yourselves." The two just shrugged it off and made their way to meet the two old ladies.

Elliott turned to me, and I to him, I let go of him. As he crossed his arms, he asked me, "What's going on?"

"Who *are* these ladies?" I loudly whispered to him. "Giving out candy, warning people about bees! These women are seriously suspicious!"

Elliott shrugged and admitted, "Okay, giving candy to kids and the whole bee business might be kind of strange." But he added and told me, "But they seem really sweet."

"All old ladies seem sweet," I told him. "But then they turn out to be monsters!"

Elliott shook his head and chuckled, "Love, this isn't a Stephen King novel. I don't think they're pretending to be nice to murder Connor or Ollie."

I pointed to them and said, "It *is* exactly like a Stephen King!"

"*Attack of the Old Ladies* by Stephen King. That's a billion dollar idea," Elliott joked.

"I'm kidding about that part," I rolled my eyes. "But don't you see what I'm saying?"

Elliott sighed as he released his arms and placed them at his side, "Well, I hate to tell you, but they are *probably* gonna be on the tour with us."

"Yeah, I know," I groaned.

"They are sweet little old ladies," Elliott tried to convince me.

"It's just," I admitted, "Gloria really seemed to like you, not there's anything wrong with that. But she *hated* me. What if this is going to be like one of your fans all over again, but we're forced to spend four hours with them?"

Elliott took my hands and placed them close to his chest, "I'm not going to let that happen. And I don't think it will. I mean, sure, it's kind of weird that Sally just hands out candy. And Gloria can be a little aggressive. But I do really think they're nice. Just give them a chance? For me?" I was looking down, but he begged, "*PLEEEEEEASE?*"

The sweet, begging face alone made me give up, "Fine. Only for you."

Elliott leaned to me and pecked my lips. He pulled away, but just for a sec before kissing me again, much longer this time. I snuck my hands to place on each of his cheeks. But reality hit. We were in public. We promised to be more cautious. So I pulled away.

My forehead against his, my hands still on his cheeks, I whispered to him, "Save it for later." This made Elliott grin, remembering how we were gonna cuddle back at the hotel later.

"Can't wait," he whispered back. And so I led my hands to his back and him to mine as we made our way back to the others.

******

At 2 o'clock, it was finally time for *The Sound of Music* tour! We all started to board the bus, and it sure was crowded. So many *The Sound of Music* fans were waiting to experience a tour that featured many locations of their favorite film. Among them, of course, were Gloria and Sally. As all of us waited in line, I noticed Gloria briefly caught a glimpse of me. Wanting to be polite, I smiled kindly and waved. But Gloria, with a grouchy expression on her face, went back to talking to Sally. I was a little put off by her behavior, but I didn't say anything for Elliott's sake. He wanted me to give her a chance, and so I decided to.

The ten of us were the last people on board. Ironically, there were ten seats towards the front that were empty. Guess people don't like sitting in the front.

"So, where are we going to sit?" I asked everyone. I was secretly hoping to sit next to someone in my group. *Not* Gloria.

"Uh," Nicole said almost as if she felt bad, "Esperanza and I already talked about sitting together on this bus ride."

"Sorry," Esperanza shrugged. And they went to sit in the most frontward of the seats on the left side of the bus.

"Okay," I said to myself, "No hurt feelings." I turned to Grace and asked her, "Want to sit together, Grace?"

Grace replied with sympathy, "I promised Ryan. We'll sit together next time." And the two of them went to the most backward seats on the right.

"Why are you sitting away from us?!" Nicole shouted.

"Because I hate sitting all the way upfront," Grace replied.

Connor tapped on Elliott's shoulder. As soon as he turned around to face his little brother, Connor pleaded, "Can I please sit next to Sally?"

Elliott put his hands on his knees so it would be easier to talk to his little brother. He told him quietly, "That's up to Sally whether she wants you to---"

"Of course," Sally replied sweetly. Connor cheered as they sat behind Nicole and Esperanza.

The only people left were Elliott, Ollie, Gloria, and me.

Gloria sat right across from Esperanza and Nicole's seats, partially because they were right there. She sat in the window seat.

She tried to look friendly, with a smile that ended up looking really creepy. She held her arms out and said in a "failed" welcoming tone, "Come here, Ollie. Sit next to me."

Ollie obviously looked scared and shook his head, "No," and buried his head into Elliott's arm. I don't really blame Ollie for saying no.

Gloria shrugged and gave up. "Very well then," she grumpily muttered to herself. She turned up to Elliott and with a smile back on her face, asked, "How about you come sit here with me, Elliott?"

"I want to sit next to Elliott!" Ollie pouted. And before Elliott could say anything, Ollie grabbed him tightly by the hand and dragged him to the seat right behind Gloria.

"Okay," Elliott chuckled. "Guess I'm sitting with Ollie."

Oh no. I looked around the bus to see if there were any more seats available. But the bus was full. Except for that one seat next to Gloria. I looked down at her. Inside I was going crazy. I had to sit next to Gloria. The one person I didn't want to sit next to. But I didn't say anything. I had to be polite. So I scooted into the seat right there, next to Gloria.

I turned to her and with a smile said, "Hi, Mrs. Hangrove."

"Hello," Gloria nodded, not even looking at me. She crossed her arms. For some reason she didn't like me, and it was clear as day right now.

I turned behind to look at Elliott. I knew Gloria wasn't probably paying attention to me, so I exaggeratedly mouthed to Elliott, "She hates me." Elliott tried to make me feel better, so he mouthed back, "No, she doesn't."

Before I could respond, I heard a thick female German accent speak into the microphone: "Hello? Can you hear me?" And everyone quickly diverted their attention to the lady up front.

She wore the typical Austrian/German dress (which I later found out was known as a dirndl). It consisted of a full brown skirt, clean white blouse, and pale green apron. Her silvery blonde hair was in a braided bun, and she had a few wrinkles. She was tall and rather plump with a friendly smile.

"Welcome to *The Sound of Music* tour," she said in a friendly voice, "My name is Caroltta, and I will be your guide today." I smiled at Carlotta, she seemed really nice.

Finally we were on our way with the tour. We drove through the town, and Carlotta pointed out some sights. She pointed out the birthplace of Wolfgang Amadeus Mozart, which didn't really have to do with the tour but it was still interesting information to know. We passed a theater that was performing the real story of the Von Trapp family but with puppets. Not like the puppets during the "Lonely Goatherd scene." Thank goodness. Those puppets give me the creeps. We drove past two bridges: the one Maria and the children crossed on the way to the picnic and the other was used during the "Do-Re-Me" scene. Learning all this information was good to know, but I don't think any of the others found it as fascinating as I did.

Finally, after driving for about twenty minutes, the bus stopped at a gazebo. Must have been where they filmed "Sixteen Going on Seventeen!" I was relieved when the bus finally came to a stop. I couldn't bear to sit next to Gloria a minute longer.

People were crowding to get off the bus. I felt like I was being pushed, but it couldn't compare to yesterday when I was nearly crushed by Elliott's fans. Once we finally got off the bus, I felt free. I waited to join my friends as we talked.

"How's it going with Gloria?" Grace asked quietly with concern.

I shrugged, "She doesn't really talk to me. It was clear she would rather sit with Ollie or Elliott because when there were only three of us left she asked them first."

"You okay?" Esperanza asked.

"I'll be fine," I assured them. "We're not really gonna be with them for long."

Nicole decided to add some humor to the situation: "As long as Gloria doesn't turn cougarish on Elliott, I think you'll be fine." We all stared at her, stunned by what she said. "Relax, I'm kidding," Nicole laughed. We all just ignored her and kept walking towards the gazebo.

Once we all reached there, the whole crowd of people stopped to hear what Carlotta had to say. She explained, "Now this is the famous gazebo in the 'Sixteen Going on Seventeen' scene. They didn't actually film here. It was really filmed in Los Angeles, but 20th Century Fox moved it here." Hmmm. Could have read this on IMDB. But I hadn't. And now I'm hearing about it now.

Carlotta talked for a minute of two, and then she allowed us to take pictures. I stood there and took a picture with my phone. As I was putting my phone away in my purse, I felt a pair of hands wrap around my waist.

"Hello there, darling," Elliott greeted me cheerfully. He placed a quick kiss on my shoulder and set his chin on it.

"Hey," I smiled, leaning into his back.

"I have an idea," Elliott unwrapped himself from me.

I turned around to face him. I put my hands on my hips and asked, "Hmm?"

"Whatdya say if we dance the dance they dance in the movie?" Elliott suggested.

Looking back at the gazebo, I said, "I don't think we're allowed in." I looked back at him.

Elliott came up with the solution: "We can dance around it!"

I immediately smiled. Excited, I clapped my hands and cheered, "Yay!"

I took Elliott's hand and ran with him to the edge of the gazebo. After standing still for a minute, Elliott realized, "Wait, do you know how to do the dance?"

"Not really," I shook my head.

We stood there clueless for a few minutes, until I said, "We can just run around and sing."

"I don't know the words," Elliott hesitantly admitted.

"You hum, I'll sing," I quickly responded.

"Deal," Elliott nodded.

And so we began running around the gazebo. I sang the lyrics and Elliott hummed the music. We were pretty in sync. Maybe the two of us should start an a capella group. I leaped in the air at one point, and Elliott did the same. The two of us were very well aware this was not what happened in the movie, but we didn't care. We were having fun.

After about a minute of running around, we stopped to catch our breaths. I was not used to running. As soon as we stopped, I was panting and out of breath. I placed a hand on my chest, right around where the fleur-de-lis necklace rested, and I could feel my heart beating fast.

"You good?" Elliott checked on me.

I nodded, and took a sip of water. "Yes," I drank down the water. "I'm fine."

"Good," Elliott smiled. "That was fun."

"It was," I agreed. "I am twenty-one going on twenty-two."

Elliott piped in: "And I'm twenty-three going on twenty-four."

"Elliott!" a voice shouted. Our heads spun around and saw who was heading toward us. I tried my best not to roll my eyes. Gloria. She was rapidly walking towards us.

"Wow," Elliott quietly said, still looking straight at the approaching woman. "For an old lady, she moves pretty fast." I could only nod in agreement.

She finally reached us. Or she reached Elliott. Went straight up to him. I felt invisible. No one could see me. I was nobody. Thanks Gloria for making me feel this way.

"You're single, right?" Gloria asked. My eyebrows raised up and my pupils dilated when I heard this.

It was so awkward for Elliott who just nervously laughed. "Uh..." he started to speak.

"It's okay to admit it," Gloria assured him as she reached for her phone in her purse. "I've got a special girl who you would be adorable with," she scrolled through pictures on her phone. Elliott immediately turned to me and saw I had an annoyed expression with hands on my hips and glaring at him. Elliott knew I was annoyed, and his smile was disproportionate. "Here, I got it!" Gloria finally said when she found the picture. Elliott leaned down to look at it. I immediately walked over to join them. I wanted to see what the woman looked like.

I saw her. She was pretty. She was at the beach and wearing a blue sundress with white flowers. Her hair was a sandy blonde that was straight and past her shoulders. Her eyes were a stormy grey and she had a creamy complexion. She had a merry smile, and she looked gorgeous. More in Elliott's league than I was.

After staring at the picture, Elliott asked, "Who's that?"

"My granddaughter," Gloria replied. I rolled my eyes. Gloria was trying to set Elliott up on a date with her granddaughter. "Her name is Olivia."

"She's pretty," Elliott thought out loud to himself. I felt a pinch of jealousy, so I elbowed him in the shoulder, causing him to yelp, "Ow!"

"Oh, I'm sorry," I said, faking a sorry voice. "Did I hurt you?"

"She's twenty-two years old," Gloria smiled up at him. "Single, beautiful, smart as a whip."

Elliott nodded. "I'm sure she is."

"You're twenty-two right?" Gloria asked for a reminder.

"Twenty-three," Elliott corrected.

Gloria ignored this and said, "I think you two would make a lovely couple!" Was this lady ignorant? Elliott and I were literally kissing and flirting with each other when she saw us!

"Does she live in England?" Elliott asked. Great, he was probably interested in her!

"No," Gloria shook her head. "She goes to college at Columbia."

"Like in New York?" I asked her.

Gloria didn't answer my question. She just looked at me confused and asked, "Where'd you come from?" She didn't even know I was there!

"I've always been here," I told her bluntly. "You were just too busy bragging about your Ivy League granddaughter to pay attention to the people around you." Out of the corner of my eye, I saw Elliott's reaction. I thought he would be upset that I wasn't giving Gloria a chance, but I saw him look at me with admiration. He smiled at me proudly, nodding his head up and down.

"And I don't believe I told you," Elliott started to say. He walked behind me and pulled me close to him so he was against my back. His arms found his way to waist, and as he wrapped them around me tightly and pulled me even closer, he continued on: "I'm sorry, Gloria. But I forgot to mention there's a girl that's stolen my heart, so I wouldn't say I'm necessarily single." *He's talking about me! I've stolen his heart!* The thought of this had my heart pumping at a steady pace and smirking at Gloria.

She got the message, and did not look pleased about it. She probably wanted to have a new thing about her granddaughter to brag to her friends: that she was dating Elliott Parker. Gloria scowled at me.

"Oh, but don't worry," Elliott added, "I've got a friend back in London named Teddy. He's single and would absolutely *love* a girlfriend."

Gloria didn't respond. She just stood there, still as a statue. Wanting to escape any further embarrassment, she quickly fled the scene. I smiled, thinking about how Elliott was quick to defend me and called me "a girl that's stolen his heart." I was the girl! I was *his* girl! I've never been anyone's girl.

"So," he whispered in my ear with a playful manner, "do you think I should go on that date?"

"Shut up," I murmured, but we both laughed in unison.

Afterwards, we left the gazebo. Our next stop was Schloss Leopoldskron, a palace-turned-hotel used to film the back of the Von Trapp family house. We stopped right across from it, noticing the palace's reflection illuminating the blue water. Trees surrounded the white building, and I squinted my eyes to see if there were really two horse statues guarding the gates.

I took a photo of the palace, then a selfie. Ollie tried to step in the water at one point, but Grace warned him not to.

"Pretty cool, huh?" a voice murmured in my ear. I turned to see Nicole smirking.

"It's amazing," I beamed from ear to ear.

Nicole quickly changed the subject: "So...wanna tell me about last night?"

"Last night?" I asked with genuine confusion. Nicole wiggled her eyebrows at me and I realized what she meant, "Oh! Later."

As I took another picture of the palace, Nicole begged me, "Come on, Cecilia! You're the first one of us who's ever had sex with a celebrity!"

She had said that a little too loudly, so Esperanza came over to us and had to get in the gossip. "What are we talking about?"

Nicole caught her up. "Cecilia isn't telling us anything about what happened last night!"

"I never said that," I reminded her calmly. "I told you guys I would tell you all later."

"You never tell us anything," Esperanza complained. "You wouldn't tell us anything about the late night walk in the Amalfi Coast, now you won't tell us how you lost your virginity."

"I'll tell you later," I promised her. "Now's not the time. We're in the middle of a tour surrounded by who knows how many people. Not to mention his brothers are here."

Elliott walked over to us, a smile across his face. "Hi, girls," he greeted. "What's going on?"

"Cecilia won't tell us anything about what happened last night," Nicole pouted. She put her hands on her hips and gave me a glare.

"For the one millionth time, I—" I started to say to her, getting a little ticked off.

"She was great," Elliott finished for me. I furrowed my eyebrows at him, not sure of what he was doing. "Best night of my life. She was so talented." He wrapped an arm around my shoulder and pulled me close to his side.

"What are you doing?" I whisper yelled in his ear.

"Getting them to shut up about it for the rest of the day," Elliott whispered back. "You're welcome."

Before I could reply, Esperanza laughed, "I'm sure she was a nervous wreck. She's always worrying about how she's not good enough and she'll mess up."

"You little—" I gritted through my teeth.

"Actually," Elliott interrupted me before I could finish, "She *was* a little scared, but she got through."

"You must have helped her to make sure she was calm," Esperanza smiled.

"Yeah," I blushed a little bit. "He did." I hadn't realized it before. Elliott was so thoughtful and asked me at least ten times if I was okay. And he helped me calm my nerves, reminding me that it was just him and I didn't have anything to be worried about. That was a true Prince Charming right there.

"Were *you* scared Elliott?" Nicole asked.

"No, not really," Elliott shook his head. "I don't get scared that easily." A plan started forming in my mind. "It takes a lot to scare me. I say I'm pretty brave. Anyway—"

"Bah!" I yelled right in Elliott's ear as an attempt to scare him. I sure did scare him. His eyeballs nearly bulged out of him, and he jumped back slightly. When he realized it wasn't anything to be scared of, he relaxed and even smiled to himself. Nicole and Esperanza thought it was hilarious, and they started laughing. I smiled to myself, proud I had scared someone who claimed to not be easily scared.

"You'll pay for that one Hartley," Elliott, still smiling, pointed a finger at me.

"Don't care," I shrugged. "It was totally worth it."

We left the palace, which was followed by just driving around to different filming locations. We drove past where they filmed the front of the house though we couldn't really get any good pictures because we couldn't drive right near it. The road was a private road with people walking and riding their bikes near it. We drove past Nonnberg Abbey, where Maria was a nun both in the film and in real life. While the family depicted Maria and Captain Von Trapp getting married in the abbey (which is also where their real-life counterparts tied the knot), the scene was not filmed in the abbey. No scenes were filmed there. Like the inside of the Von Trapps' home, they were filmed on a soundstage in Hollywood. Only the outside of the abbey was used for filming.

Right now, we were heading to the town of Mondsee to visit a church where the wedding scene was actually filmed. None of us had ever been to Mondsee, but

Grace did an extensive amount of research before then. She described it as a typical European-style town with various little shops. The buildings were in a variety of bright colors, from greens to pinks to yellows. The church, St. Michael Basilica, was a Bendictine monastery. From what I had seen in pictures, it was gigantic, a pastel yellow, and very old-timey looking.

The bus ride to Mondsee took time, about an hour. While on the way, Carlotta told us stories about the real Von Trapp family. There were many significant differences between the fictional family and the real-life family. The one that struck me the most was that they didn't actually hike up the mountains and arrive in Switzerland. According to Carlotta, if you were to actually hike over a mountain, you would end up in Germany rather than Switzerland. Not a good idea especially if you're fleeing to escape the Nazis. Instead, they walked to the train station and took a train to Italy, and from there they went to England before arriving in the United States.

Carlotta began to explain to us about the edelweiss. If you are unfamiliar with the flower or the movie, edelweiss is a beautiful white mountain flower found in the mountains of Austria. Carlotta said that men used to risk their lives hiking up to the mountains in search of the edelweiss for their loved ones. Some ended up with broken arms or legs or other injuries, and some have either died. But they did it all for love.

"Hey Elliott," I nudged him. Elliott was now sitting next to me. Gloria and I didn't sit next to each other, for obvious reasons. So now Gloria was sitting with Sally.

"Hmm?" Elliott asked when I had his attention.

"Are you gonna hike up and get some edelweiss for me?" I teased him.

"Sure," Elliott said sarcastically. Grinning, he joked, "I could go buy some edelweiss at a local store, but you need the real deal."

"You know I do," I quipped back.

"But if I get you edelweiss, you have to climb up to the mountains and get some for me too. It's only fair."

"I believe she said the *guy* has to get it for the girl."

"Why not change things up a little bit?" Elliott winked, and I playfully stuck my tongue out at him.

Finally, we arrived in Mondsee. On the way we saw a beautiful lake, obviously called Lake Mondsee. We saw several people relaxing by the side and swimming or sailing in the crystal blue lake.

We arrived in the town, and once we stopped by the church and went inside, we were free to walk around the town.

Us girls were walking together while the guys were doing who knows what. I really liked being with the guys (especially Elliott), but it was nice to have time to just the four of us every now and then.

"Isn't this place gorgeous?" Esperanza spun her body around, taking in every angle of the place.

"Such a cute little town," Nicole inquired. "Very homey." Nicole used her favorite word again: "Though not very boujee."

"There it is," Esperanza pointed out. "That magical word."

"We should come here tomorrow," Grace suggested. "I want to see more of it. Maybe explore the lake a little bit."

"I thought we were spending the day in town tomorrow," Nicole said, a little disappointed.

"Maybe not the whole day," Grace said, looking around and grinning at the adorable little town. "Half a day here and half a day in Salzburg."

"You alive, Cecilia?" Nicole asked me when she realized I wasn't really saying anything.

"I am," I laughed, "just thinking about what you guys are saying."

"Or are you thinking about Elliott?" Nicole teased.

"Oooh," Esperanza joined in. I could only bow my head. Just the sound of his name made we want to blush.

Later on, the four of us were visiting a little toy shop. I know none of us were interested in toys anymore, but it was still fun to look at. I admit that sometimes I like to look at the kids' section of stores. I sometimes find it more fun than shopping for myself or people my age or older.

I was holding up and examining a doll. The rag doll was wearing traditional green and black Austrian clothing, paired with a matching traditional hat. Her blonde hair consisted of string tied together to form braids, and she had black eyes and two red dots to represent her cheeks. I was smiling, thinking about my own American Girl doll when I was little and drawing contrasts and comparisons to the dolls of different cultures.

"Hi, Cecilia," I heard a cartoonish voice from behind me. Startled, I turned around to see what it was, and right behind me in my face was a puppet's face. I backed up and saw it was an exact replica of the boy puppet in the "Lonely Goatherd" scene (though probably not the same one). It was covering whoever's face it was, but I could somehow recognize it was Elliott.

"Hey, Elliott," I replied, trying not to crack a smile.

"I'm not Elliott," he continued in the cartoon voice. "I'm Gustav the Goatherd! From your favorite movie?"

A smile tugged at the corner of my mouth. "Yeah. I remember you."

"Can I ask you something?"

"Sure."

"Who do you think is more handsome: me or Elliott?"

"Oh. Definitely you, Gustav."

"Even if I have a face that would haunt your dreams?"

"*Anything* is better than Elliott's face."

"I think that would hurt his feelings. Maybe you should try giving him a kiss. It would make him feel so much better."

"I'm good," I placed the doll I was holding down on the shelf behind me and started to walk out of the store. I walked out and Elliott ran to join me, without the puppet of course.

"Hey, hey, hey, wait up!" he ran to catch up with me. I finally stopped for him and turned to face him. Luckily, the sun wasn't as bright as it had been on previous days, so we didn't have to squint our eyes at each other.

"Yes?" I asked him. "What's up?"

"I just wanted to say," Elliott took my hands and held onto them in his. "You look really pretty."

I pretended to not hear what he was saying. "I'm sorry, what?"

Elliott caught on to what I was doing and said, "I said that I have to go to the bathroom."

He started to walk away and I caught up to him saying, "Wait, wait. Elliott. I heard you. I'm joking, I'm joking. Thank you for saying that."

"What did you think I said?" Elliott continued the teasing.

"I know what you said!" I pretended to sound irritated, but I was laughing. "And may I say," I flirtatiously said, "you look just as handsome as always."

Upon hearing this, Elliott stopped walking and turned his body 180 degrees so he was facing me. I stopped and looked directly at him. Elliott smiled, created "puppy dog eyes" and asked in a voice imitating mine, "I'm sorry. I don't think I heard you. Could you repeat that again."

I rolled my eyes, but I couldn't help but let out a giggle. Just as I was about to say something else, we heard a voice shout, "Hello, children!" Elliott and I quickly turned our heads to the direction of the sound. We saw Sally, the much nicer friend of Gloria, walking towards us. Smiling, she waved with one hand and was carrying her purse and a shopping bag with the other.

Once she finally stopped in front of us, I greeted her, "Hi, Sally. How are you?"

"I feel wonderful!" she enthusiastically said. "Salzburg is beautiful, and this place is such a cute little town." She was the exact opposite of Gloria.

Elliott, who always had to be polite, asked her, "Would you like me to carry something for you?"

"Oh no, thank you," Sally shook her head, "but I really do appreciate it. You are a nice, handsome young gentleman."

Elliott turned it into a joke, saying, "More like a stupid---" I cut him him off with an elbow to the shoulder. "I mean, thank you," he said as soon as I did this.

"And you," Sally said to me, "you are a strong, independent, confident young woman."

"Oh," I blushed at the compliment. That is one of the nicest compliments anyone has ever given me. "Thank you," I said with genuine appreciation. However, I was kind of confused as to why Sally was saying this. She had only met me a few hours ago. Even then, we barely interacted. But I shrugged it off and enjoyed the compliment.

"Now," Sally changed the subject. She looked back and forth between the two of us and asked, "how long have you guys known each other?" Elliott and I looked at each other, clueless about what to say. Then, we replied with two different answers in unison.

"About two weeks," I answered truthfully.

And for some weird reason, Elliott nervously blasted out with, "A month."

I looked at him, and he looked at me. He looked nervous. I think it was partially because I was giving him an angry glare because he had just told a lie. Luckily, Sally only had heard what I said.

"Two weeks?" she asked. "I remember my husband and I had been dating for that long when he proposed to me." My eyes widened and Elliott looked like he was about to scratch his head in confusion. Sally asked Elliott, "So, does that mean *you're* going to propose to her?"

"Uh, no," Elliott nervously chuckled, "we only just met."

"And we haven't even officially become boyfriend and girlfriend yet," I added. "And we're still so young. I'm not even out of college yet."

"So what?" Sally shrugged. "My husband and I got married as soon as we finished high school." She gestured to Elliott, "And your career seems to be going nicely, so I think you should try and settle down. You seem to be in a good place."

"Maybe in the future," Elliott assured her.

"Okay," Sally nodded. She kept a smile on, but she looked somewhat disappointed.

"You know my fans want us to get married too," Elliott told us. That was true. While a lot of his fans hated me, some were already envisioning what our future wedding would be like.

"I can see why," Sally smiled. "You two really do make a lovely couple."

"Thanks," Elliott and I said in sync and in unison.

"I wouldn't be surprised if I hear wedding bells soon," Sally said cheerfully. She turned to me and asked for clarification, "Now you're twenty-one. Right, dear?" I nodded, a little surprised she had guessed correctly. "That was how old I was when *I* got married. If you're with the right person, you'll be getting married before you know it. And soon, you'll have little children running around. Just hope they don't come first."

Elliott chuckled at what she said, but I found myself a little overwhelmed. When I was little, I always thought you got married to someone after meeting and being in love with them for three days. That's what I had learned from Disney movies at least. But then *Frozen* was right: you can't marry a man you just met. And you should definitely *not* be getting married to someone in your early twenties, when you're still young and immature.

I mean sure, times have changed. Both sets of my grandparents got married in their early twenties, and both couples have been happily married with a family. My parents, meanwhile, didn't get married until they were in their late twenties and they are still happy. I guess it depends on the couple, but I personally believe I am too young to get married.

Elliott shrugged. "I know, but I think we want to take our time. I want us to enjoy being young, and focus on our careers." Elliott shook his head as his eyes dilated. He started to speak quickly, "Not that I'm choosing my career over her. I mean, I want her to finish college and be a writer. And I'm a good point in my career and I like where I'm going. And I want to continue that before I begin a family with her." He quickly corrected himself, "Sorry, I mean I want to get married and start a family with her. I want to marry her before having kids. Because that---"

Giggling at how much of a dork Elliott could be, I placed a hand on his shoulder and said calmly, "Elliott, I think she gets it."

We turned to face Sally. She smiled and shrugged, "I suppose that's fair enough."

******

The other six went out to get some gelato. (Afterall, you can never have too much gelato when you're in Europe!) But Elliott and I were feeling really tired from today, so we went back to the hotel. We were on the couch in his room, cuddling.

Elliott sat his back on the arm of the couch. His arms embraced me, wrapping around my back tightly. I lay my head into his chest, with my one arm wrapped tightly behind his back and my other hand placed lightly on the side of his chest.

"Did you have fun today?" he asked me, placing a light kiss on the top of my forehead. *The Sound of Music* tour and all?"

Sleepy, I yawned and said, "Yeah, I did."

"What was your favorite part?" Elliott asked, trying to keep me awake.

"Hmmm," I thought, "I don't know. I liked the part where I made you promise me to climb up to the mountain to get Edelweiss," I giggled.

Elliott giggled and said, "I remember that, love. I just wouldn't expect it to happen anytime soon."

"I know," I said in a dreamy voice, "but a girl can dream."

Elliott chuckled, "You really are adorable, Cecilia."

"So are you, Elliott," I lifted my head to look at him.

Then there was silence. We stared at each other, but only for a few seconds. It got kind of awkward. Flushing, I looked away and nervously smiled. Elliott placed his fingers on my cheek and turned my head back so I was facing him again.

The silence was gone when he stuttered, "I-I hope you don't mind, but I kind of planned out what we're going to do for the rest of the trip."

I got so excited that I raised myself up backwards, my head losing contact with his chest. Clapping my hands together, I giddily said, "Oooh! What are we doing?"

"You really want to know?" Elliott asked me with a smirk. I nodded quickly, waiting to hear what he was going to say. "You sure?" he teased.

"Uh huh," I nodded, still excited.

"Are you certain?" he continued to tease.

"Of course," I eagerly said, wanting him to stop and just tell me what he planned.

"Positive?" he teased once more with a devilish gleam in his eye.

I got impatient and nearly shouted, "JUST TELL ME!" Realizing my sudden change in volume, I softly whispered, "Sorry. Please continue."

"Okay," Elliott started to say, "but promise not to laugh at how cheesy this is."

"Are you kidding me?!" I shook my head. "I grew up on Disney films."

"Were you going to say you live for cheesy?" Elliott winked.

"How did you know?" I asked, in surprise that he knew what I was going to say.

"Wild guess?" Elliott shrugged his shoulders. "Anyway, do you want to hear it?"

"Yes," I told him, curious to hear what he had planned.

He looked down, took a deep breath, and explained the plan, "So, tomorrow we're going to Lake Mondsee, right?" I nodded. He went on, "So all of us are going to spend some time there. Go shopping, sit by the lake, or something fun. Then we'll leave Salzburg, and Austria, and go to Germany. We'll stop in Fussen, check out the town, and go to St. Mang's. And we'll head to Neuschwanstein, which is as you know---"

"What Cinderella's Castle was based on," I finished, demonstrating my Disney knowledge.

"Good for you," Elliott smiled. "Anyway, we'll go there, take a picture of us in front of the castle, head to Munich, go to dinner, and---"

I interrupted him, "Sorry to be rude, Elliott, but this is just the itinerary we planned to do months and months in advance."

"Wait and see, darling," he quietly chuckled, booping my nose with his finger. I wasn't sure whether to find it adorable or to cringe. But like I said before, I like cheesy, so I just smiled. He got serious with what he said next, "Anyway, so the next day I know all of us had planned to go to Dachau."

I nodded my head somberly, remembering how we wanted to take a day trip to Dachau when in Munich, but to not go on our last day so we wouldn't be sorrowful on the last day of the trip.

"Well, I know we're all going to need something more lighthearted," Elliott said, and I nodded in my head in agreement. "So, I was thinking maybe we could go out to dinner."

"Just you and me?" I asked him, making sure I heard him correctly.

"Uh huh," Elliott replied. "And then the next day we can just spend a day in Munich, maybe some shopping, and maybe another thing too." After a moment of quiet, Elliott said, "And yeah, that's my plan." He looked nervous, as if he wasn't sure whether I would like the plan or not.

"I like it," I smiled at him.

Elliott's eyes softened and a smile started to form on his lips. "You-you do?" he asked quietly, as if in relief.

"I love it," I assured him, "I love it a lot."

A huge grin washed upon Elliott's face as I told him how I felt about the plan. I leaned down to kiss him, and as soon as our mouths collided, he returned the kiss. After about thirty seconds, I slowly parted my lips and lay my head down on his chest, like my position was before. I didn't see it happen, but I felt Elliott's fingers brush through my hair, stroking it ever so lovingly.

"You have really soft hair," Elliott murmured under his breath, sounding like he was fascinated by it, but in a cute way as opposed to a creepy one.

I chuckled at how adorable he was, "Thank you, dork."

"You're welcome, dork," he whispered to me.

"Elliott—" I almost didn't want to say what I was going to ask him. "Can we—can we—?"

"Yes?" Elliott asked, at this point not playing with my hair anymore.

I raised my head up off his chest and sat up straight, moving my legs so they were placed on the ground. Elliott almost squirmed when I sat up, missing me. But he sat up with me in a similar way I did.

I was nervous to ask Elliott my question, fearing he'd say no. "Can we—do what we did last night again?" I finally worked up the courage to ask, only hesitant.

Elliott groaned. Oh no. He didn't want to do it. This is bad. He didn't like last night. And he probably thinks I'm just after him for the sex. Now I'm gonna look like a horny four letter word that begins with "s" that I don't like. This was bad, this is really bad. I know I was being (slightly) overdramatic, but questions raced through my head over what happened next.

Elliott looked at me with a frustrated look, and sighed, "Cecilia, I know it may have seemed reasonable at the time, but I'm not having a fight where you storm off angry into an unknown city again."

The nerves and frustration went away when he said this. He thought I was talking about having another fight. (Why, I'm not sure). I sighed in relief, "Oh thank goodness."

Elliott turned his head in confusion, and I said to him, "Elliott, no, don't worry. I don't want to have another fight."

Now it was Elliott's turn to sigh in relief. But he quickly asked me, "Wait a minute, what did you mean?"

I raised an eyebrow at him, "What did you think I meant?"

Elliott had a blank stare on his face, as if he was clueless. His eyes widened, "Oh!" he dragged out in a good way when he finally figured out what I was saying.

I shook my head. "Oh, Elliott," I rolled my eyes, but playfully. I patted his head and cooed, "You're so pretty."

Elliott laughed, "Forgive me, it's the tiredness. And—"

Before he could finish, I crashed my lips onto his, and he mine. Our lips in sync as always. I stopped briefly and asked in worry, "Wait, what about the others?"

Elliott shrugged and murmured almost desperately, "They're not going to be back for a while."

We resumed making out, with Elliott laying down on his back with me laying on top of him. I interrupted, rambling, once again, "Should we do it here? It's not much space, but I'm fine with whatever."

Poor Elliott, I knew he wanted to continue, but my talking was preventing it. "We can move to the bed in a sec if you want," he told me, quickly.

"I like beds," I told him cheerfully.

"Me too," he smirked, trying his best to look sexy. Next thing I knew, his lips were on mine, almost desperately.

I asked one more time, "One more thing. So you know how—"

But Elliott was getting impatient and just went back to kissing me. I liked kissing him so I didn't have a problem with it. Never separating our lips we stood up almost at the same time. We made our way over to the room. But of course we couldn't see because our eyes were closed and we were invested in each other. So Elliott walked backwards and I followed him, as if he was guiding me. I didn't see where I was going and yelped:

"Ow!" I had bumped into the wall.

Elliott heard this and quickly opened his eyes. "What happened?" he said with fright. He looked back at the wall, then back and me and said, "Sorry about that."

"It's okay," I said softly, "can we just walk the rest of the way and resume when we get inside?"

Elliott nodded and grabbed my hand tightly, "Fair enough." I smiled, happy he understood.

And so he led me to his bedroom, clutched onto the doorknob and slowly turned it to open. Slow like he was trying to build suspense. It finally clicked, signalling the door was open. Elliott pushed it open to reveal his bedroom. It looked just like ours. A small bed (hopefully we will both fit on it) was in the center with a nightstand on the left and a closet and a bathroom on the right. The room was dark. Elliott led me in all the way. As soon as I was in the room completely, my leg against the side of the bed, he walked back over to the door and closed it quietly. He flipped a switch. There were two (and I know this because my room works this way). When you flipped one, the whole room was illuminated and you felt like you were going to burn your eyes out. Then there was one that only turned on the overhead light and gave the room a dim light. Elliott switched on the latter.

I made my way to the end of the bed and plopped down on the edge. I saw Elliott lock the room, for obvious reasons. I saw him smirk as he made his way over to me. I smirked back at him when I saw his smile, and I leaned back further on the bed until I reached it so my head lay just below the pillows. I pulled Elliott down by the arm so he was hovering over me. We were now kissing softly, and continuing our make out sesh.

Just then, we were interrupted again, only this time by the Serpent Boy theme song. Elliott's phone. It was charging next to the nightstand. We stopped kissing as we looked over to the nightstand on our rights. Elliott raised his head up and groaned. I rolled my eyes, annoyed this moment got ruined.

"Who is it?" I whined, still staring at the ringing phone.

"I'll check," Elliott reached his arm across to the nightstand to grab his phone with his hands. I squirmed under him, which indicated to him that I wanted to sit up. He sat up as he tried to unplug the phone from his charger. I leaned against the headboard, impatient that I didn't know who had called.

Elliott looked down at his phone. "It's my agent. Eddie," he moped.

"I can leave the room if you want," I offered politely. I started to sit back up from the headboard.

Elliott just shrugged as he reached back over to the nightstand. "It's alright," he shook his head. As soon as the phone was back where it was before, he looked back at me. "Eddie can wait," he said with a naughty sound in his voice. His eyes had a glint of lust in them. I'm starting to think there were multiple versions of Elliott. Hot Elliott. Silly Elliott. Badass Elliott. Sweet Elliott. Drunk Elliott. Serious Elliott. Thoughtful Elliott. Dorky Elliott. And now I've just discovered *Horny/Lustful Elliott.*

But I decided to be the responsible one in this situation. I said seriously, "No, Elliott. You need to pick up the phone! It could be important!"

"It's going to stop ringing soon," he put his large, smooth hands on the sides of my arms. He started to rub them softly up and down as the phone stopped ringing.

"See?" he cheekily smiled. He started to reach his arms further and further up my arms and to my shoulders. He softly whispered, "Sorry for that interruption. Let me make it up to you by giving you a nice massage."

I still decided to be serious, pointing my finger at him and saying, "No." I felt like a mom by almost ordering him, "You need to call Eddie again *right now*. It could be something about—"

But as soon as Elliott started massaging my shoulders, I lost my train of thought. The hand I was pointing with immediately dropped to my side. "Oooh," I muttered to myself. "This *does* feel really good."

"Thought you'd like it," Elliott smirked. *That sneaky devil.*

I rolled my head back. Elliott continued to leave relaxing pressure on my shoulders with his hands. He moved to my back as I let out a soft moan.

Just then, Elliott ruined the mood when he asked, "Is this good enough for you? I read an article about how to make stuff sexy, because I wanted to make it less awkward than last night."

Just like that, I was out of my trance and tried to convince him, "Oh no, don't worry. You were *really* good. In fact," I looked to the side. I giggled thinking about what I was about to say to him next. I turned back to him and admitted, "I thought you had gotten it as advice from all your Hollywood friends."

Elliott laughed and shook his head, "If I'm honest, darling, my *Hollywood friends* and I talk about all sorts of stuff, except *that*."

My eyes opened wide and said in disbelief, "You call them your friends and they've never given you advice on girls? My friends and I talk about guys *all the time*."

"Well," held out as he rocked his head back and forth. He stopped it as he said, "You've got to remember that most of the times I see them are for filming or movie premieres. Rarely do I get with them outside of filming."

I nodded my head as I agreed with him: "Makes sense."

Elliott clearly wanted to get back to what we were doing as he changed the subject: "Anyway, should we get back to where we were?"

"Yes," I decided to let out my "inner sexy," something I've rarely done in the past. I reached up and whispered into his ear lustfully, "You get ready to show me more of what you can do. I am ready to—"

Before I could finish I felt Elliott's hand cover my mouth. He turned his head so he was facing me all the way. He slowly moved his hand away from my mouth and placed it gently on my cheek. As I leaned into his touch and closed my eyes, I felt his lips reconnected to mine desperately, as if he wanted more. It was slow and sensual. Romantic and passionate. But of course it had to be ruined. By the phone. *AGAIN*.

I opened my eyes as Elliott disconnected our lips and bowed his head down to the bed. He shook his head.

I touched his hand that was still on my cheek and started stroking his knuckles with my thumb to comfort him. "You should answer it," I told him sincerely.

He looked back up at me with soft eyes, "But, I wanted to give you a better experience than last night. I—"

"It's okay," I interrupted him, trying to assure him it was fine. "We can do it afterward."

"But what if when I'm done with the call, they all come back?" he asked.

"Then we'll do it Germany," I replied. "We can try to get them out of the hotel. I know that sounds mean but I'm just—" I wanted to say more, but the Serpent Boy theme song was really starting to annoy me. Fed up with it all, I said, "Just answer the damn phone."

Elliott didn't say anything; he just reached for the phone. He answered it. "Hello Eddie." Pause. "It's wonderful, thanks for asking." He looked at me and said with a smile, "I've met someone who I like," this made me blush profusely. Elliott took his other hand and reached out to touch my cheek in the same spot as before. I leaned into his touch again, and I closed my eyes because this was really nice. I continued to listen in on his conversation with Eddie.

"So, what's up?" Pause. "Right now?" Pause. "Can't it wait till tomorrow?" Pause. "Alright one sec."

I knew he was speaking to me when he said with regret, "I have to take this."

I opened my eyes and assured him, "It's fine, Elliott."

"I'll be back as soon as I can," he promised me.

"Take your time," I told him.

Elliott smiled as he leaned me close to his face. He said with affection, "You are so sweet and that's one of the many things I really like about you."

I smiled and continued to blush red as a tomato as Elliott pulled me in for a quick, soft kiss. He pulled away and I noticed he was a blushing mess as well.

I shooed him away and giggled, "Go, go. Talk to Eddie."

Elliott winked at me as he slowly slipped off the side of the bed and separated his hand from my skin. I almost squirmed as his touch left mine. He walked to the door and unlocked it.

As soon as it opened, he turned around to me and smiled at me. He started to close the door, and continued grinning as he started to talk to Eddie: "Sorry about that, Eddie. What's up?" He shut the door, but not all the way, he left it slightly cracked open.

I couldn't hear anything, just mumbling. As I continued to try to decipher what they were saying, I lay down on my back, waiting almost impatiently. My fingers tapped on the scratchy covers, as if I was counting down the seconds the call would be done. I was hoping it would be quick.

Finally, after what was actually three minutes but felt like an hour, I saw the door start to open. It finally did, and I saw Elliott. I beamed from ear to ear when I saw him, only for my smile to fade when I realized it was not the Elliott from a few minutes ago. This Elliott had a sad look in his and his head was dropped down to the ground. He walked to the bedroom, but only got right about the doorway when he crossed his arms and sighed. My mouth opened wide and I felt my eyes turn soft and sad like his. What had happened? Did he not get a role in a movie he wanted? Did he have a fight with Eddie? Why did his mood just change like that?

I wanted to find out more, but I just asked with concern, "Hey, how did the call go?"

Elliott looked at me. Still with his arms crossed he said, "Fine."

Now I was really starting to get worried. I slipped off the bed and started to walk towards him. "Did something happen? What was the call about?"

"Something about a movie," Elliott replied quietly.

I took his face in both of my hands and asked him with more concern than ever, "Hey, sweetie, what aren't you telling me?"

Then, something happened in Elliott that just clicked. It set him off. He backed away from me so I wasn't touching him anymore. Then, he said with frustration, "Stop asking all these questions, Cecilia. Okay? Can you leave now? I just want to go to bed." I looked at Elliott with both shock and confusion. Why wasn't he telling me what was going on? "Good night," Elliott simply said.

"Elliott," I tried to reach out to him. "Please tell me what happened. I can help you. If you only just—"

"I said good night," Elliott snapped at me. I jumped back again at how grumpy Elliott was, he looked stressed. But I really didn't want to deal with this anymore, so I just left his room. I didn't even want to look at him.

Chapter 20: Wishing For An Answer

"So let me get this straight," Nicole tried to understand as us four girls were sitting down to eat breakfast the next morning. "You and Elliott were about to do the dirty again until he got a call from his agent. Then after the call, he came back into the room and his mood had completely changed?"

I nodded, "Yeah. Haven't talked to him since."

"Have you even *seen* him since then?" Nicole knew what my answer was as she leaned in and asked, trying to get the answer out.

"No," I shook my head. I sadly admitted, "That's why I wanted to get down to breakfast early so we wouldn't have to wake up with them."

"You can't ignore him forever, Cecilia," Esperanza advised me. "You have to talk to him."

"And if you want us to not do anything with the boys today, we can just do something with us girls," Grace told me as she took a bite of her sausage.

"It's fine," I told them. "I *want* to talk to him."

Esperanza pointed behind us and said, "Oh look, here come the boys now."

I turned around and gulped. I saw Elliott, wearing a blue and white plaid shirt with sleeves rolled up, a white shirt underneath, and tan khaki pants. He was walking with his brothers, all of whom seemed to be happy, except for him. He looked at me as if he felt guilty, demonstrating his adorable puppy dog eyes.

"Hello everyone!" Connor and Ollie cheerfully waved to all of us. We waved at them back, but I was mainly focused on Elliott, who looked down on me.

I noticed Ryan lightly slapped Elliott on the arm. "Hello, Elliott," I said politely with a fake smile. It was my way of telling him, "Eff you."

"Look, Cecilia," Elliott started to speak with genuine remorse written all over his face and clearly in his voice. "I really am sorry for last night. I shouldn't have treated you that way. You were only trying to help."

I nodded and lied, "I accept your apology." The truth was, I would not accept his apology unless he would tell me why he was upset. "Would you like to tell me what made you upset last night?" I questioned him.

I could hear Ryan lean to Elliott and whisper to him, "You promised you would tell her, Elliott."

Elliott whispered back, "I don't think she's ready."

"Not ready?" I said, fed up with it all. "Pfft. Not ready? Not ready for what?" I stood up from my seat to show just how angry I was. I tried to not yell, because that would be awkward in public. "Not ready to get attacked by your fans online? Because that's happened to me already. Don't worry about that, Elliott! Or am I not ready to meet your parents? I actually don't think I'm ready to meet them yet considering I just met you a few days ago. And I don't really think you're ready to meet my parents either. They both love me and can be *very* picky with the guys I date."

"Okay," Grace nervously laughed. Still sitting down, she took my hand and said, "How about you sit this down and we can---"

However, I shook her hand away and pretended as if she wasn't there. I started to walk to Elliott. He just stood there as if he didn't know what to say. I really started to go off: "Why did you not tell me? You basically lied to me. My friends can tell you that I want a relationship that's honest. And if you can't be honest with me Elliott, then I guess you'll have to lose me."

Elliott didn't say a word. He just stood there in silence. He was speechless. Didn't know what to say or how to say it.

"What's wrong?" I felt like I was taunting him. He looked to the side, as if he couldn't even look at me. "You know what would make me feel so much better, Elliott? If you tell me why you were upset last night. That way I know you can trust me. If you don't want to tell me, then I guess I have my answer."

Elliott looked back at me and stood up straight and puffed out his chest, trying to display that he was brave. Was he ready to tell me what had happened?

But I noticed Elliott had gotten sad. He said with sadness in his voice, "I really wanted to tell you what had happened. I really did. But the truth is---" I was waiting for him to finish, crossing my arms and tapping my foot as if to show him I was "patiently" waiting for him to tell me.

And he finally did. "Eddie called. Before I went on this holiday he promised me reshoots wouldn't take place until two weeks after. But now because of a personal issue with the director of the movie I was working in Rome, reshoots are rescheduled to begin on July 6."

"That's tomorrow," I said to him. My eyes grew large and my mouth dropped wide open when I realized what was going on. Elliott would be leaving for Rome...tomorrow.

"I'm sorry for not telling you," Elliott said sincerely. "I'll be leaving tomorrow morning."

Part of me was sad. Elliott was going back to Rome. I thought I had all this time with him. But I didn't. I only had today. We had a whole plan. We were going to spend as much time together as we could. *This is not fair*, I kept telling myself over and over again.

But part of me was angry. Angry that Elliott didn't tell me about it last night. Instead he chose to tell me now. In front of everyone. If he had told me last night, I wouldn't have been mad because at least he would have been honest with me and I would have had time to process it.

But I didn't want to make a scene. So I blunty said, "Let's go to Lake Mondsee. We'll talk about this later." Elliott looked deep and hurt that I didn't display an ounce of sadness. I should have. Should have shown him I was sorry and truly upset that he was going back to Rome and our time on this trip together was cut short like a knife. So

418

we just finished up breakfast and started to head to the bus station to Lake Mondsee.

******

The hour-long drive to Lake Mondsee was the most awkward hour of my entire life. No one said a word to each other the entire ride. Ollie and Connor tried to get us to speak, but when they noticed we were responding they just talked and played games with each other. Then they would try to get us to talk again. Elliott and I couldn't even look at each other the entire ride. We tried to look in directions so it would be impossible for us to make eye contact with each other. I really didn't want to speak to him and I know he really didn't want to speak to me.

The bus finally stopped in Mondsee. We were there yesterday for *The Sound of Music* tour.

"Oooh you know what would be so fun?" Esperanza piped up, "We should take a boat along the lake! In Nicole's words it would be so boujee!"

Nicole chuckled at what Esperanza said, but then spoke, "Only one problem." She had to ruin the fun, and it sounded like she didn't want to. "No one here can drive a boat! Even though some of us grew up in the sailing capital of the world and some of us grew up in a city near the River Thames!" That was true. All of us lived in Annapolis for eighteen years, and none of us even owned a boat. Maybe the Parker brothers knew how to drive a boat?

My question was answered when Ryan spoke up: "I know how to drive a boat! Have my own boating license and everything!" Ryan seemed cocky, but you couldn't help but think his pride was adorable. You could tell he was Elliott's younger brother.

"Can you drive too, Elliott?" Grace asked him.

But Elliott responded coldly, "Yes, but I do not want to go on a silly old boat ride."

I rolled my eyes and groaned, "Don't act like a jerk just because you're mad at me."

Elliott turned to me and crossed his arms saying, "I'm not mad at you. I'm mad at myself. Why do you have to make everything about you, princess?"

My eyes opened so wide they almost popped out. My jaw dropped almost to the stone ground. "You know what, I always used to think you were like a Disney prince, but with *your* attitude you're clearly like a Disney villain."

"Why are Elliott and Cecilia fighting?" Ollie asked disappointedly, tapping on Grace's shoulder.

Connor pouted his lips out and shook his head at Ryan, saying, "I don't like it."

"Neither do I," Ryan told Connor, looking at both Elliott and me.

Grace decided to calm the situation, saying in a gentle tone, "Maybe you guys *should* sit this one out. We'll give you some time to talk it all out."

I put my hands on my hips and started walking towards Grace. Annoyed, I reminded her, "But Elliott said," and I mocked him in his British voice, "I don't want to go on some silly old boat ride!" Elliott, hands still crossed, shook his head with an angry expression on his face. I returned to my normal voice when I pleaded with Grace: "But *I* really want to go and see the view from the lake! Please, Grace! Please!"

"I hate being the bad guy," Grace sighed. "But this is silly. If you *both* go on the boat, you'll be fighting the whole time and no one will have fun. I know you, Cecilia. If *you* go on the boat without Elliott, you'll complain and mope about him the whole time, and we'll *still* have no fun." I sighed, knowing she was right. But she said, "But if you guys just stay alone for an hour or so, while we're on the boat, maybe there's a chance you could make it up and have fun together the rest of the day."

Elliott started to walk toward his cousin again, saying in frustration, "But Grace---"

Nicole interrupted him. She pointed to him and said with a bossiness in her voice, "Do as she says, Parker." With that, Elliott just stood there, speechless.

I wanted to get out of this situation. I placed the bag I was carrying in my hand over my shoulder and said, "I'm going to change into my bathing suit."

Walking towards the bathroom, I made sure to bump my shoulder into Elliott's. And I didn't apologize. I didn't even look at the other people. I just headed straight to the bathrooms. They were clean for bathrooms, but they smelled like the ocean and I noticed sand in the showers. I opened a stall and changed into my bathing suit. It was a green and white striped one-piece, with two pieces of the fabric crossed at the front and I tied the strap in the back.

I finished changing into my suit in about fifteen seconds. But I stayed in the bathroom for fifteen *minutes*. I wanted to be alone to process everything that just happened. By myself. No Elliott. No Grace. No Connor. No Esperanza. No Ryan. No Nicole. No Ollie. No one. I also wanted to work in my mind what I was going to say to Elliott.

After fifteen minutes, I stepped out of the bathroom, ready to talk to them. I was going to try to reason out with Elliott. Then maybe they would allow me to go on the boat ride and Elliott would be more in the mood, and we would all have a perfect day. A perfect end to Elliott's vacation---or holiday as he would say. But alas, not every aspect of your life is going to plan out perfectly, like it does in the movies.

When I came out of the bathroom, I walked to where the group had been standing. They were nowhere to be found. I scratched my head. Where did they go? It was then that I saw out of the corner of my eye Elliott sitting at a cafe table. All by himself. Just him. He had his elbows on the table---which would not make my grandmother happy---and looked stressed. So I went over to him to go see what it was about. I walked over to where he was sitting, pulled out a chair, and sat right in front of him.

"Hey," I quietly mumbled to him. In a way I kind of hope he didn't hear me.

But I know he did when he looked straight up at me, then immediately back down again. After a brief moment of silence, he slowly raised his head up to look at me. Very softly, he replied, "Hello." Then he finally looked at me in the eyes. Did he want to make peace? Was he just being polite so he wouldn't make a scene? Was he still mad? Did he want to beg for forgiveness? I couldn't tell.

Instead of asking for the answers to any of the questions mentioned above, I asked, "So where are the others?"

"They left," Elliott answered.

"What?" I said in absolute surprise. "Already?"

"Yeah," Elliott nodded. "The line wasn't very long so they asked for the boat right away. And the people had a boat ready for them, and they were on their way. They said to say goodbye."

I shook my head to myself and said, trying to understand what was going on, "But I don't understand. I know I was gone for fifteen minutes but---"

"You knew you had been gone for fifteen minutes?" Elliott said in shock. "I was worried about you. I was---"

"You're *always* worried about me," I pointed out, a little annoyed. "What am I, your pet?"

"I didn't say---" Elliott started to speak, but I barked back at him:

"I'm still mad at you, you know!" At this point, I had my arms crossed, I was looking down at the table away from Elliott, and I was *not* in a good mood. Probably because I really wanted to go on the boat ride and now I couldn't.

But Elliott, despite my grumpy and somewhat rude behavior, kept talking politely, "I'd like to apologize for what happened. I really wanted to tell you last night, and I really regret it---"

I interrupted him again and let all my anger out on him, "You know what's funny, Elliott? I remember Ryan distinctly said on the train that you *did not* like it when people kept secrets from you. And when I didn't tell you about Gwen, you made me feel so bad about it. And here you are right now and you kept a secret from me and you expect me to forgive you like that?"

"Okay, so I'm a hypocritical asshole," Elliott dramatically shrugged, starting to get a little annoyed. But when he realized he might lose his temper soon, he reverted to a more calm, collected state. He put his hands back on the table and sincerely told me, "But I really am sorry, Cecilia. You're right, it wasn't right of me. Especially how I got mad at you in Vienna for the very same reason. But I really want to put this all behind us and just enjoy our last day together."

But because I was stubborn, I couldn't forgive him that easily. "I may forgive you for that, but you're still leaving me tomorrow," I angrily said. Then I really lost it and said, "We had all these plans. Why did you and your gosh darn movie have to screw it all up?"

Elliott was slowly starting to get annoyed. "Hey, it's not my fault. I was so disappointed when Eddie called me and said I was going to have to leave this trip early. I was so excited to do everything we had planned to do."

"So I was I," I softly admitted to him and to myself. My mood shifted back to frustration, "But you could have

424

talked to the director and asked him to move the date of reshoots? You're the star. Don't you always get what you want?"

"I really tried," Elliott nearly shouted. "I begged Eddie to talk to the director about rescheduling. But it was because of the director's issues with his family that we had to change them so they start tomorrow. There's a lot in movies that you don't understand---"

That was where I really lost it. "Let me guess? I'm going to have to get used to it? Just like how I'm going to have to get used to your fans being rude? Is this what you expect my life to be like now, Elliott? Changes in our plans because of your movies and fans being rude to me? Do you really think *anyone* wants to have a life like that, Elliott?"

With that Elliott was speechless. His mouth in a straight line, he bowed down his head and ran his fingers back through his hair. I knew I had gone a little too far. And I needed to be by myself.

I lowered my voice. "Uh," I couldn't speak. "I need to calm down a little bit. I'll be right back." I started to get up out of my chair, and Elliott raised his head so he was looking at me. Then I pointed to the dock and said, "See that dock? I'll be over there, where you can see." I figured I'd tell him where I was going, and go to a place he could see me. Elliott didn't say anything, he just nodded and gave a small smile. I waited a second to see if he would say anything, but when I realized he wasn't going to, I left to go to the dock.

As I walked over, I tried my best to contain my tears. I did. For now at least. I would not make a scene. I quickly walked over to the tiny dock where no one was sitting. It was near the bathrooms, but it was still out of the way so no one could see you. I sat on the edge of the dock, which wasn't that far from the shore. My feet dangling on the edge only a few feet above the water, I debated about whether to go for a swim. I decided not to for two reasons: one, I shouldn't be swimming in strange waters I don't know by myself and two, Elliott would probably freak if he saw that. Instead, I took the opportunity to take in my surroundings. I looked around at the lake. It was absolutely breathtaking. The water was a clear, sparkling blue, but not too clear that you could see under it. The land surrounding it was green and full of trees, with some houses or other buildings here or there. A large mountain stood at the center, it may or may not have been the mountain for *The Sound of Music*. I sighed, then took a deep inhale of the fresh saltwater. In a way, it reminded me of Annapolis. I felt a pinch of homesickness. I hadn't been homesick the whole trip but then, when I found out Elliott wouldn't be here for the rest of the trip, I was starting to wish I was home.

I almost jumped when I felt a hand placed lightly on my shoulder. I turned around and felt a wave of relief when I saw Elliott, crouched down and a twinkle in his eyes. He looked sad, but he still smiled. I smiled when I saw him.

"Mind if I sit down with you?" he asked politely.

I nodded my head, "Sure." He was about to sit on my right side. So I scooted to my left to allow more room for him. He sat right there. He took off his sneakers, placed them behind him, and dangled his feet. While they were a little closer to the water than mine were, they weren't completely dipped in.

We didn't say anything to each other. We just took in the moment and looked around the lake. The sun wasn't shining, so we weren't squinting our eyes. It wasn't cloudy like it was about to rain, but I wouldn't say it was the sunniest day of the whole trip.

"It's beautiful," Elliott was still looking at the landscape.

"Uh huh," I nodded. "I actually really love Austria."

We still didn't look at each other, but Elliott asked me, "Which do you like better: Vienna or Salzburg?"

"They're different," I shrugged. "Vienna is a really beautiful city, and Salzburg is a simple but cute little city."

"Fair enough," Elliott replied.

We didn't say anything for a few minutes. But I turned to Elliott and told him sincerely, "You know I know it's not your fault." As Elliott turned his face to me, I continued, "I'm sorry if I made you think that. I understand you can't really control that. And I appreciate you trying to get Eddie to talk to the director to reschedule."

Elliott tried to convince me, "I really did try. I offered to send him a list of dates that work and everything."

I chuckled, "You're sweet." Elliott bit his lip and nodded, a small smile on his face and laughing nervously. I told him, "And I'm really gonna miss you."

Elliott's smile turned into a frown, "I know. I'm going to miss you so much." I leaned down so my head was resting on Elliott's shoulder. He snaked both his arms around me like he was hugging me. He kissed my head, and leaned his forehead against my head.

The rest of the day was kind of quiet. Elliott and I went back up to the town to check out the shops, where I got my dad a royal blue wallet with an edelweiss embroidered on it. We didn't talk about him leaving tomorrow, but we weren't smiling as we had the whole rest of the trip. When the others got back, we shopped some more, and we took the bus back to Salzburg. After getting dinner at a pizza place, we went back to the hotel. We still had fun, but it was not as boisterous as the previous days of the trip had been. Partially because I had one thing stuck in my head: *Elliott was leaving.*

******

That night, I took a shower to calm down. I think I was getting hormonal or something, but when we got back to the hotel, I just started breaking down in tears again. A good cry out in the shower always helped me. No one could hear or see me crying, and I pretended that the tears streaming down my face were only droplets of water. When I was being bullied in middle school, I would do it all the time. Other than writing, it helped me escape the real world and let me get out all the tears and sadness.

In the many years I've cried in the shower, I've only cried over a boy once. Henry. Before junior year started I made a personal promise to myself that I would tell Henry how I felt. Then when I got to school, I found out that he had moved back to England in the middle of the summer. I was devastated. So I shed a few tears in the school bathroom, walked out, and carried on with the rest of the day. As soon as I got home I ran into the shower and sobbed for about ten minutes. When I heard Henry had moved, I felt like a piece of my heart had been taken away from me.

But when I found out Elliott was leaving I felt as though my heart had shattered into a million tiny pieces and was now empty. I know it sounds cliche and extreme for a guy I've only known for fourteen days, but it was true. The funny thing was that I felt more heartbroken over a guy I had known for two weeks than a guy that I knew all throughout my first two years of high school. I think that was because Henry was just a silly little crush that I only thought was true love. Elliott was a guy who I deeply cared for a lot and felt a special connection with, AND he felt the same way. Call me crazy, but this moment in the shower makes me look back on that day when I cried over nothing. Henry was just a guy who I barely had the guts to talk to. Elliott was different. Different from Henry. Different from any of the guys I had been on a date with.

When I finally calmed down, I shut off the water, reached for the towel, opened the glass door, and dried off. As soon as my entire body and hair was dry, I put on my pajamas. It was a short cotton knit white nightgown. It had no sleeves, was a cream white, and had pink roses with some green and blue on it too. I put my hair in two side pigtails, something I do often but had not yet done on this trip. I put the towel back on the shower rod and walked out of the room.

I didn't pay attention as to what was going on so I just said, "Hey girls. So I'm out of the shower if anyone---"

I stopped in my tracks when I saw all three of my friends standing there with someone else. It was Elliott, who had an awkward, disproportionate smile on his face.

"Hello, Cecilia," he waved awkwardly.

"Hi," I smiled back. This was followed by awkward silence. I finally asked, "If you don't mind me asking, what are you doing here?"

The next thing Elliott asked was, "Can we talk in private?" I nodded my head, saying it was okay. But being as polite as he was, he turned to all my friends and asked the same thing: "Do you girls mind if we talk in private?"

"Sure," Grace nodded.

"We can go to my room," I gestured ahead to where my bedroom door was.

I started to walk to my bedroom, and Elliott followed behind me. Nicole, of course, had to make a joke: "Don't be too loud!" I just rolled my eyes playfully.

"Wouldn't dream of it," Elliott grinned.

We made it all the way into my room. I turned on the lights and closed the door completely behind me. Leaning against the door I asked him, "What's up?" I was sleepy, but still had a dash of energy in me.

"Mind if I sit down?" Elliott asked as he stood near the edge of the bed. I nodded, indicating it was okay. And Elliott sat down. I decided to go over and join him. I might as well. And so I sat on the edge of the bed with him. He went on.

"I just wanted to check and see you were okay," Elliott said as he set a hand on my thigh and squeezed it lightly. "I really am sorry about everything. I'm sorry for not telling you. And I'm sorry I have to leave."

I took a moment to think about what he just said. "First of all," I finally spoke, "you don't need to apologize for last night. I've already forgiven you for that." I admitted, "Though I do like how you keep reminding me you've made a mistake."

Elliott chuckled at me. "Well, I sure have changed and made many mistakes since you first met me," he chuckled at himself. Using his sometimes-used-self-deprecating humor, he teased himself, "Then again I've always been a real dick."

I playfully and lightly punched him on the shoulder and told him, "You're not a---." Then I whispered in a low voice, "dick."

Elliott laughed at me, but not in a mean way. He said, "You can swear if you want."

"Oh I do swear sometimes," I proudly said. But then I shamefully admitted, "More times than I'd *like* to anyway." But I went back to proud as I said, "I just usually don't use *those* kinds of swear words."

"What kinds of swear words?" Elliott tried to ask seriously as if he sincerely didn't know. But the smile he cracked upon his face gave it away.

"You know," I laugh.

Elliott, still bearing that cheesy, adorable grin, shook his head, "No, I don't."

"Yes, you do," I nodded. I myself started to smile.

"No, I don't," Elliott continued shaking his head.

"Yes, you do," I continued to nodd.

We did this a few more times before we collapsed on our backs giggling. We couldn't help but laugh. We made each other smile, crack up, and have a good time. We were laying down, staring at the wooden ceiling, and laughing our butts off. Then, I don't know what it was, but my mood shifted. Instead of bursting out in laughter, I was bursting into tears. Non-stop. I guess it was the fact that Elliott was leaving and we would never share moments like this for the rest of the trip. And who knows when I'd see him next? I had no idea what he was doing after reshoots were done. Would he be free the rest of the summer? And when summer ends, I would be back to finish college and he'll be back in London or shooting some movie in Hollywood or wherever. We would never see each other. And after college was done, who knows where I'd end up? I could be working at a job that was nowhere near him! All of that made me cry.

As soon as Elliott could hear me sobbing, he immediately stopped laughing. He turned his head to me with a concerned and sympathetic look on his face. He sat up and looked down at me. I could see his angel face, though it was blurry through the never-ending tears.

"Hey, hey," Elliott reached his hand to my cheek and started rubbing the tears away with his thumb. He scooted back all the way so his back was against a pillow and patted next to himself to signal me to come sit with him. I sat up and compiled.

As soon as I got next to him, I buried my head deep into his shoulder. Elliott stroked my hair and hushed me. He took both my legs and swung them over his lap. Now he had a hand on the small on the back and the other still stroking my hair.

"Shhh," he whispered to me. "There, there. It's okay. I know. I feel the same way. But right now, I'm here."

I didn't look at him, but I said through my sobs, "It's not fair! We had this whole plan! Now it's cut short and ruined!" I finally got the courage to look him in the eyes. His face was sweet and understanding, searching my face and wishing he could help. I went on: "And after you're done reshoots and the trip ends, who knows what will happen to us? When summer ends, I'll be back at Washington College and you'll be filming a movie gosh knows where! We won't see each other! And I just---I just---"

I couldn't take it anymore. I collapsed my head into his shoulder again, unable to continue on. Elliott rested his head on top of mine. And I noticed something. I could have sworn I heard him crying. Here was this guy, who plays one of the most famous superheroes and always acts so heroic, crying. I felt a teardrop hit my head lightly, and he sniffled a little bit. And he didn't say anything. He wanted to say something, but he couldn't. He was too heartbroken to say anything.

"Please stay with me tonight," I let out softly. "I don't want to be myself."

"Of course," I heard Elliott speak through tears. He then softly whispered, "Anything for you."

******

Now it was eleven o'clock. Elliott and I cried into each other for about ten minutes before I was laying in bed. Elliott had gone out to talk to his brothers before he spent the night. They would be taking an uber to the airport tomorrow morning before we left to go to Neuchswanstein, and Lawrence would be our driver the rest of the way. It would just be us girls for the rest of the trip, as we had planned.

I lay in bed silently, comfy and cozy under the covers, thinking about the days to come. I was disappointed in Elliott leaving, but at the same time I was happy it would be just us girls. For one thing, I felt bad because I felt as though I had been abandoning them to hang out with Elliott. And I really liked Elliott, I really did, but now I'm starting to see what my friends were saying about wanting to have a break from boys. In the midst of my thinking, I heard a soft knock at the door.

"Come in!" I shouted. The door opened to reveal Elliott still in his clothes he just wore.

"Hello, gorgeous," he grinned and winked at me.

"Hey, dork," I teased him. "Are you wearing those clothes to bed? No offense, but you've been wearing those clothes all day and they might be---"

"Oh, bollocks," Elliott cursed under his breath. He shrugged and said, "Oh well! Guess I just have to wear what I *usually* wear to bed." He unbuttoned his plaid shirt,

434

folded it and gently placed it on the end of the bed. My ears grew red as I had a feeling of what he was going to change into. Next to go were his khaki pants, which he unbuttoned, unzipped, and pulled all the way down. Once he was done with that, he placed it with the shirt. He placed one foot on the bed, took off one sock, and did the same with the other.

"Picking up the clothes he had discarded he realized he had nowhere to put them: "Umm." He turned to me and asked, "Where would you like me to put these?"

I pointed to my suitcase and said, "On my suitcase is fine. Just remember to take them."

Elliott nodded, walked over to my suitcase, and put his clothes on it. "Thank you," I turned to me.

"Yeah. No problem," I nodded politely, but secretly wanted him to come and cuddle with me.

As he was making his way over to the bed, I said, "Hey, Elliott, can I tell you something?"

"Sure, what's up?" he asked as he crawled under the covers next to me.

I turned to face him, and he did the same resting on his elbow.

"Well," I started to say, "before we met, I have to admit, I didn't think you were that cute." I was a little embarrassed to say this.

"Don't be embarrassed," Elliott chuckled. It was like he knew what I was feeling.

"Well," I held out. I told him honestly: "There was *one* thing I liked about you."

"Oh?" Elliott started to get curious. "Which was?"

"Uhh---" I was trying to decide whether I should tell him about this or not. I finally told him. Hesitantly, I said: "I thought you had a really cute butt."

Elliott's eyes widened at first, and he blushed a little bit. Then he started to laugh. I know I had mentioned this before, but before I met Elliott and had seen him in the movies, I didn't think he was that attractive. The one thing I did notice about him was the Serpent Boy suit made his butt look really big. And I thought it was kinda cute.

"You thought my arse was my only redeeming quality?" Elliott chuckled. "Honestly, you're probably right."

"It was the Serpent Boy suit," I told him the reason, smiling.

"Aww," Elliott smiled, "it's fine. Don't worry about it."

Elliott hesitated to say what he was about to say, and then he decided to be honest, "Well, if we're sharing first impressions, when I first met you I thought you had a nice bum."

I laughed and teased him, "No offense, but that sounds wrong."

Elliott raised a hand in front of him and giggled, "Hey, I thought we were sharing."

"I'm kidding," I winked. In a fake, somewhat mocking British accent, I teased, "I always thought I had a nice bum myself."

"You have a nice *everything*," Elliott smiled.

"Thank you," I smiled at him. He leaned in to kiss me, and his lips captured mine. As we continued this, his hand started to stroke my hair, running his fingers through my soft auburn locks. Once we stopped kissing, he pulled apart, eyes open, our faces a few centimeters apart. He still stroked my hair, and we smiled. I wouldn't be looking into this guy's eyes for much longer. I probably wouldn't be able to be this close to him for a long time. I cherished every second of this moment. Before I knew it, it would be tomorrow. And tomorrow, he will be gone.

"Just so you know," Elliott softly reminded me, "this is *not* the end of us."

"I know," I whispered. "I don't know what I'd do if it was."

Elliott sat up, I wasn't sure why at first, but then I saw he was going to turn off the lamp at the side. I had turned off the lights and the table lamp at the side was our only source of light. I thought we were going to bed, but I could see Elliott was hovering his head over me, even through the dark. He moved his head closer to me and attached his lips to mine. I started kissing him back, enjoying this special moment. I felt the same heartbeat I had always felt for him.

437

Chapter 21: Wishing For Him To Be Beside Me Again

The very next morning, we all stood outside as Elliott and his brothers waited for their uber. We were saying our goodbyes and Lawrence was watching their suitcases. Our suitcases were already in the trunk of the limo, and we would leave for Neuschwanstein as soon as the boys left for the airport.

I crouched down to Ollie and Connor to get down to their level, and they gave me the tightest hugs ever known, nearly squeezing the life out of me.

"We will see you again, won't we?" Ollie asked as if he was about to tear up.

Noticing how upset he was, I pulled away and looked at them. Ollie had tears pooled in the corner of his eyes, and Connor was frowning. I put my hands on their shoulders, and told them, "Of course you will. Don't worry." Then I pulled them in for another hug.

I stood up from them and smiling down at them, I ruffled their hair, making their frowns turn upside down. I moved over to say goodbye to Ryan. He saw me walking towards him, making him smile. I enveloped him in a hug.

Patting him on the back, I said, "See ya, Ryan."

"See ya," Ryan said. When we pulled away, Ryan smiled at me, and I smiled back.

When we were done, I saw Elliott make his way over to Grace. She was the first to hug, and she hugged him tightly. She was around where the lower part of his chest was, because she was so tiny.

They looked at each other and Grace said, "It was really good seeing you, cuz."

"You too, Gracie," Elliott replied, smiling. Grace weakly smiled back. And Elliott made his way over to Esperanza and Nicole and hugged them both at the same time. "Nice to meet you girls."

"You too," Esperanza and Nicole said in unison. When they separated, the three of them smiled at each other.

Knowing I was next, I lowered my head down to the ground so as to not be seen. Within a few moments, I could sense Elliott's presence because his feet were right in front of mine. And I mumbled to myself in a somewhat joking way, "Of course I'm the last one you say goodbye to." This made Elliott and me chuckle together.

Next thing I felt was his hand softly placed under my chin. Elliott tilted my head up to face him. He didn't have to tilt very far, as he was only taller than me by one and a half feet.

"Let me know when you get there, okay?" I reminded him.

Elliott smiled, "Of course." We already said much of our goodbyes last night to each other in private, so I quickly wrapped his arms around him. I tightly squeezed him, and he did the same thing to me.

The moment was ruined when a voice said, "Uber is here." Elliott and I looked at each other in the eyes.

I mumbled to him, "Bye bye, Serpent Boy."

Elliott chuckled, "Goodbye, darling." I backed away and smiled as I let him go, and he nodded at me.

He turned his back and started to walk to the uber with his brothers, but suddenly he just stopped right there. I was puzzled as to why he did this. Until he turned back around to face me. He quickly started to walk back towards me, and before I knew it his lips were on mine again, his hands cradling my face. I didn't react at first, but I got caught up in the moment and wrapped my arms around his torso and held onto it tightly, as if to try to keep him from leaving. We kissed for all of a few seconds, but it felt longer. He slowly departed his lips from mine, and we opened our eyes. His forehead was now against mine, and mine was against his.

"I'll miss you," he whispered to me.

"I'll miss you too," I whispered back, smiling.

We unwrapped ourselves from one another as Elliott gave me one smile before walking to get his suitcases. We helped them load up their belongings, they got in the uber, waved to us as they drove away, and just like that they were gone.

******

It was a few hours later. My friends and I were on the trail up to Neucshwanstein. I was reading a text in the group chat for the people on the trip. It included me, Grace, Nicole, Esperanza, Elliott and Ryan. Their plane was about to take off. I looked blankly at the text, not sure what to think.

Grace could sense something was up. "Is everything okay, Cecilia?" Grace asked, looking over my shoulder as we continued to walk up the trail. I quickly put my phone back in my pocket, feeling like I was being rude in having my phone out and looking at texts. I had it out to take pictures, but I was curious when I saw a text from Elliott.

"Yeah," I nodded at her, trying to convince her I was fine.

Nicole had her phone out and said out loud, "Their plane is taking off."

I looked down at the ground in sadness as I was reminded of the text. The news that they were heading off to Rome. That Elliott would be what felt like worlds away. I held this feeling inside of me but tried to hide it. We kept walking, but my friends were concerned about me.

"Girl, you okay?" Esperanza asked as she put a hand on my shoulder.

My head rose up and turned to face her. She was looking at me with a sympathetic look on her face. "What do you think?" I asked sarcastically, though visibly upset. I'm not gonna cry. Not here. Not now. Now was not the time for that.

"Want to talk about it?" Esperanza tried to help.

"Later," I responded. I tried to show her I appreciated that she wanted to help, but I wasn't really in the mood for talking about it right here and now. But then I realized something. I stopped right there where I had been walking. My friends realized this and stopped with me.

"What's wrong?" Nicole frantically asked. "Why are you stopping in the middle of the trail to walk up to Neuschwanstein?"

Taking a deep breath, I said, "I need to tell you guys something."

"Oh no," Esperanza looked frightened. I gave her a questioning look, and she said right away, "Elliott has another girl!"

"What?" I said startled. "Oh no, that's not it all."

"You're not pregnant are you?" Nicole asked in a state of panic.

Disgusted that she had thought this, I quickly assured her, "Oh my gosh, no!"

"It takes four weeks after sex for pregnancy symptoms to start show, and she and Elliott have known each other for less than that," Grace corrected her. "And they only had sex three days ago, and a baby isn't conceived until---"

"Guys," I calmly interrupted. They showed me they were giving me their full attention by silencing themselves and looking into my eyes. I went on: "Thank you. I'm gonna try and forget about Elliott for the rest of the trip. I'll

443

still text him and facetime him, but I'm gonna focus on the last days of the trips with you guys."

"You sure?" Grace asked.

"Yes," I nodded. "Let's just forget about it and go to Neucschwanstein, okay?"

"If you say so," Nicole shrugged. Smiling that they understood, we continued walking to the castle.

Finally, after twenty minutes of walking (or should I say hiking) we reached the castle.

It was a large, Romanesque palace upon a hill. It was white with a grey roof and several small towers with grey on the top. It did look like Cinderella's castle. Or Sleeping Beauty's. Whoever's castle it looks like, it looked like something out of a fairytale. This made my inner child come through.

Just as I was taking in the beauty, I felt a tap on my shoulder. I turned around to see Grace ask, "Did you drink your water?"

I didn't respond. I just took a large gulp of my water. I respect and admire how Grace was trying to protect me, but why did she have to be so bossy. She wasn't my mother.

"Want us to take a picture of you in front of the castle?" Esperanza offered. "You can caption it on Instagram as 'Living the Disney dream.'"

I would usually be excited about the prospect about something like that. But I just simply said, "Sure." I could tell I was being grouchy. Hopefully they didn't notice.

Esperanza either didn't notice anything or just didn't want to address the way I was acting. "Do you want to take it on your phone or do you want to use my phone and send it to you?"

"I think my phone would make more sense considering it's *my* picture," I snapped at Esperanza. She nearly jumped, and looked slightly taken aback by it.

"Whoa, what's with the bitchy attitude?" Nicole said disgusted. She crossed her arms, looking at me with anger. Esperanza looked sympathetic, and Grace was trying to figure out what was going on.

"I do not have a bitchy attitude!" I said offended.

"Then what do you have?" Grace asked, but she clearly knew what was going on. "Missing a certain British boy?"

I softened at the mention of Elliott. I looked at all my friends. I immediately felt guilty for being so rude when they were only trying to help.

"I'm sorry, Esperanza," I said softly with genuine guilt. "I'm sorry to all of you. You were only trying to help."

"Don't worry," Esperanza shook her head. "We're here for you girl."

"I just miss him," I sadly admitted. "We had this whole plan to spend more time together, and it all got ruined because of a stupid movie."

"It really is sucky," Grace nodded her in agreement.

"Want to talk about it?" Nicole offered, rubbing her hand up and down my back.

"No," I tried to fight back tears. "We can talk about it later. I just want to enjoy the castle."

"I understand," Grace said. "Whenever you're ready."

Esperanza quickly changed the subject, "So, you want that picture or not?"

I smiled an authentic smile for the first time that day. "Absolutely!"

Neuschwanstein was fun. We learned all about King Ludwig, the architecture, and the significance of each room in the house. Nicole was complaining about how the rooms were hot, and she was sweating and the sweat was ruining her clothes. I thought it was funny how much of a drama queen she was being, though I didn't let it show.

When we came out of the castle and started walking back down the trail, we were laughing. I don't even remember what we found so funny, but we were having a good time. Then, of course, something caught me off guard.

I saw a little boy around three years old. He was wearing a shirt that had no one other that Serpent Boy on it. *Of course. Had to be Serpent Boy.* I looked at the shirt, and my smile faded. I was usually happy and smiling whenever I thought of Elliott, but now I was sad simply because he was not here with me.

Nicole was the first to notice something was wrong. "You okay?" she asked. Then as soon as she saw the little boy's shirt, she already guessed what was wrong.

"What's the matter?" Esperanza asked. Nicole gestured to the little boy, and Esperanza nodded.

As Grace looked at it, she said, "I'm sorry, Cecilia." Then she immediately grinned as she came up with an idea, "How about we call him?"

"Yeah," Esperanza agreed. "I'm sure he's missing you just as much as you miss him."

"I think he's still on the plane," I said quietly. "You can't call on the plane." I remembered that time when I was eleven and my dad called me, "the airplane mode police," because I was worried when a woman sitting next to me on a flight was looking on her phone. She didn't have her phone on airplane mode, and it was during the safety announcement.

"I don't think so," Grace said. "It doesn't take that long to get to Rome from Austria by plane, and we've been here long enough.

"Then he's probably already on set," I added. "He did mention that they would get to work on reshoots as soon as he got there."

"So screw it!" Nicole said with annoyance. She gave an inspiring speech with passion in her voice, "You never know what he's doing. He could be done for the day or taking a break for all we know. Like Grace said, I really think he wants to hear from you. And he could be available to talk now. You never know until you try and take that risk."

"Can we please just not talk about Elliott right now?" was all I said. "I just want to have a fun day with my girls."

Nobody said a word. Nicole finally said, "Okay. Whatever you wish." Then we continued to walk down the trail.

******

It was later that night. We were in our hotel room. We stayed at a Marriott and got adjoining rooms. Like Rome, Grace and I were in one room and Esperanza and Nicole in the other. I was taking a shower, not because I was crying, but because I felt like it. I needed to just relax in peace and the shower was the way to do so.

I turned off the shower all the way, opened the sliding glass door, and stepped out of the shower with a towel tightly wrapped around me. As I started to dry off I could hear all the voices laughing and talking. I couldn't tell what they were saying, but it sounded like they were having fun. So I quickly dried off my hair and body and rapidly changed into the pajamas I had laid out to wear: the same nightgown from last night. I wrapped my wet auburn hair with a scrunchie in a tight bun so in the morning it would make my wavy hair look curly for a change. I opened the door and could hear my friends and what sounded more clearly.

I found myself nearly glowing when I heard a familiar British voice: "And then Ollie goes like, 'What in the world is a twinkie?'" When I realized who it was, I beamed from ear to ear. All my friends immediately looked up and saw me.

"Oh! Hey Cecilia!" Esperanza said cheerfully.

"Cecilia? Is she there?" Elliott asked excitingly.

"She is," Grace said, turning the phone around so it was facing me. There he was in all his glory. He was clearly shirtless, but a thick blanket covering him up. He had a cheerful smile on his face, but I could tell he was tired. His eyes looked droopy, and he was laying down, comfortable in bed.

"Hey, babe," I said, happy to see him.

"Hey," Elliott raised his hand up. "How are you?"

"I'm fine. How are you?" I asked.

"I'm fine," he shrugged. I walked closer to him so I could talk to him.

"Where are your brothers?" I sat on Grace's bed with my friends to talk to Elliott.

As Grace handed me the phone, Elliott answered, "They're tired, so they're in bed."

"Then why are you talking so loudly?" I asked.

"Good point," he pointed. He continued to whisper, speaking with his mouth moving exaggeratedly: "I will talk like this, if that's okay." Giggling, I nodded. Elliott went back to speaking normally, but quietly, "I heard Neuschwanstein was fun."

"It was," I nodded. "I wish you could have been there."

"I know!" he whined. "I really wanted to go too! I wanted to tell people I had been to Cinderella's castle."

"Actually," Grace joined in, "it was the *inspiration* for Cinderella's castle. It isn't *actually* Cinderella's castle."

"Isn't that what I said?" Elliott asked, though I think he knew that's not what he asked.

"Sure," Nicole said sarcastically. She said to me, "Cecilia, your boyfriend is really dumb." What's it with calling him my "boyfriend?"

"I have ears you know," Elliott sounded annoyed, but we could tell he was saying this in the nicest possible way. In other words, we could tell he was joking. Then he admitted, "But it is true, I am not the sharpest tool in the shed."

"How's filming?" I asked, changing the subject.

Elliott sighed, and then shrugged. "It's fine I guess." He let out a yawn, saying, "I am pretty knackered though." Hearing this word, I cocked my head to the side and gave him a questioning look. "It's how us Brits say tired or exhausted, love," he answered, as if he was reading my mind.

"Makes sense," I said.

"Want to go to bed, Elliott?" Grace asked, clearly seeing her cousin was tired.

"What? No," I complained, "I just started talking to him."

Grace started acting like a mother and said, "But Elliott's had a long day. And he's in for a long day tomorrow. And we have to get up at 7:45 to go to 9 o'clock mass tomorrow. Then to Dachau. And all of us need sleep."

"We can talk tomorrow, darling," Elliott promised, "I promise." We both knew he was making a promise he might not have been able to keep.

"Okay," I said, though I only pretended to sound like I was fine with it.

We all said our goodbyes and hung up. After that, things got really silent. No one said a word about Elliott the rest of the night.

Chapter 22: Wishing For Grace's Advice

The final days of the trip weren't the best. I mean it wasn't all bad. I found Dachau to be very moving and it made me understand how horrible the Holocaust really was. There were lighter moments too. We went shopping in downtown Munich and saw the Glockenspiel. The Glockenspiel was a giant clock in Marienplatz, a town square considered to be "the heart of Munich." It would ring every day at 11 a.m. or noon (and sometimes at 5 p.m.) and put on a little show of wooden dolls.

Anyway, I still had fun, but I missed Elliott so much. I would stay awake late at night thinking of him. And every time I tried to call him, he wouldn't answer. Then every time he tried to call me, I wouldn't be able to pick up. This was making me really sad. And the fact that there were debates on social media about "if Elliott Parker and his girlfriend broke up or not," didn't help. And I felt empty without him being near me. Like I couldn't eat or sleep or even sometimes think. What was this feeling?

It was the night before we had to leave to go back home. We had a fun final night, filled with talking and walking around Munich one last time. I was exhausted and, because I wasn't busy, was thinking of Elliott. I lay there in a grey Disney World T-shirt and black pajama shorts, staring at the ceiling.

I turned my attention to the bathroom door as it opened. Out walked Grace, who had just gotten out of the shower. Her blonde hair soaked, she was drying it off with a towel and wearing her pajamas: a lilac-colored top with matching shorts.

"Hey," Grace waved. "I'm just done with the shower if you wanna head in."

"I'm good," I shook my head. "Thanks though."

Grace plopped down on the bed and laid down. She stretched herself so she was all over the bed. "I can't believe this trip is over. Seems like just yesterday we were in Rome."

"Yeah, crazy."

"I guess all good things must come to an end. I wrote all about the trip in my journal. They say that's one of the many ways you remember an experience. As you get older you start to forget things and you..."

But Grace stopped when she turned to look at me, still laying still as a statue on the bed.

Sitting up, she asked me, "What's wrong?"

"Just sad the trip is over," I said to her. "It all happened so fast."

But Grace was not having it. She knew there was something more to what I was saying. "I know you," she stood up from the bed and walked over. She stood in front of me and crossed her arms, "This is about more than the trip being over." She sat herself on the edge of my bed, causing me to sit up straight. "Is it about him?"

I nodded, knowing we were talking about the same person. I sighed and leaned back so my back was against the headboard of the bed. "You guessed correctly."

"You know we never did talk about him and everything," Grace scooted closer to me. "Want to tell me what you're feeling *now*? My siblings call me, 'Dr. Grace' for a reason you know."

I chuckled and she laughed at the nickname. It suited her so well. Grace was the mother of the group, but she was also the doctor. She knew everything and would always give us advice and try to help solve our problems. That and she was planning on becoming a doctor.

"Yeah, sure. We can talk," I said.

Grace scooted closer. I sat up so now we were knee-to-knee. "Go ahead. What's bothering you," she said.

I told her everything I was feeling: "I just miss him so much. That and it's making me rethink things."

"What kind of things?" Grace asked.

"About whether we should be together or not. I can't help but think this will be how it's going to be from now on. We make plans, then something with Elliott's work comes up, and we both end up hurt and disappointed." Grace nodded to tell me she was still listening. "It's just gonna be so hard," I felt tears start to pool in my eyes. "With our busy lives and living on different continents and everything. Not to mention those stupid fans of his will probably still be a problem. And I didn't even think about people at school. They're gonna judge me and be jealous of me just because I'm dating a celebrity. And everything is just so..."

I couldn't take it anymore. At this point I was bawling and my face was red. I covered my face with my hands and continued to sob. I felt a hand on my shoulder and looked up to see Grace. She was sitting there, a warm yet worried look on her face. I felt a little relieved that she was here, comforting me and listening to my troubles.

"That's not even the worst part," I continued to cry.

"What is?" Grace asked.

I sobbed out loud, "I'm on my period!"

When I realized how ridiculous this sounded, I started laughing. Grace started to laugh with me once she knew I thought it was funny.

"Could explain all the crying and hormones," Grace suggested.

"Gosh, being a woman is so hard," I loudly whispered.

"Tell me about it," Grace replied.

I had stopped crying, but my face was still still red and blotchy from all the tears. Once we had stopped laughing, Grace got serious again.

"Is there something you want to do?" Grace asked me, continuing our little "therapy session."

"I'm thinking about ending this thing," I told her, which was what I was thinking over the past few days. "If we can't make this work, and if I'm gonna be a baby about it, maybe this isn't going to work. Maybe I was right. Maybe this was just a summer fling."

"Okay, I have a few things," Grace said when I finished pouring out my feelings. "One: you're not a baby. You're far from it." Using my wrist, I wiped a remaining tear from my cheek. "Two: please don't use summer fling again. I know the both of you. You're definitely more committed-relationship-type people. You would never just have a fling for the summer and then break up when you part ways."

"But what if I *am* one of those people? I've never really had a relationship with a guy last this long. Before I just had dates."

Grace sighed in defeat, "Good point." She continued, "I refuse to believe it though. You've always dreamed about finding true love since you were a little girl."

"I guess so," I shrugged.

"And did you ever think about why you and Elliott have lasted for more than just one or two dates?" Dang. She had a pretty good point.

My eyes widened when I realized this. Grace was right. I've only ever been on one---or two if I was lucky---dates with a guy. Twelve guys in my life. And then there was Elliott. Lucky number thirteen.

"Well, what about the conflicts? And living in different countries?" I came up with more problems.

"You guys will figure it," Grace seemed confident. "You two are smart and responsible people who will work hard towards a goal. If you both work hard, you can do it. I believe in you guys."

I was starting to feel a little bit better. Grace was really helping. "And the..."

"Fan girls?" Grace finished me, clearly annoyed. I nodded and she said, "Who cares about them, honestly? They're only teenagers, and they're probably never going to marry Elliott. And I've seen they've already started to warm up to you."

"I guess," I smiled, thinking about all the fans making posts and supporting Elliott and I as a couple. People apparently made tik toks and other social media posts of us and gave us words of encouragement. There were still a few petty ones, but the good ones outshined the bad ones.

"You can do this," Grace pulled me in for a hug. She patted my back. As we pulled away she told me, "And Elliott really likes you. He would be heartbroken if you ended things. Two of his girlfriends ended things with him because he was famous, you know."

"Yeah, I know," I frowned. "He told me." The fact of someone breaking up with poor Elliott just because of his star status really broke my heart. I touched the fleur-de-lis necklace as I thought of him.

"And you know what he told me his favorite part of the entire trip was?"

"What?" I asked. I started to guess in my head. The kiss? The beach? Getting drunk? The gelato? Our night together in Vienna? The tour?

"When he got chased by the mob in Rome," Grace finally answered. When she saw I gave her a questioning look, she explained the reasoning. "Two reasons. He got a lot of exercise running like that." We both laughed. I could picture him saying something like that. "And it led him to you."

My hand still touching the necklace, I felt my heart beating. I can't believe Elliott remembered. I admit *I* had forgotten our first meeting with all the other stuff that happened the rest of the trip. If he hadn't come running into the lobby to hide from his fans, I may never have met him.

Oh, wait. I would have met him anyway. He was Grace's cousin and supposed to be going on the trip with us. Silly me. I guess what I *meant* to say was we might have never shared that special connection. And most likely he wouldn't have known me enough to invite me out to dinner when he thought I felt lonely when the girls were still fighting. And who knows, we may never have connected in such a deep way at all. You never know.

"Awww," was my response to Grace. "I remember thinking he was so weird for running and hiding behind a plant like that. But that was before I knew who he was."

"Hey, I would have thought the same thing," Grace laughed.

After a few seconds of silence, I thanked Grace. "I really appreciate you talking to me about this."

"Oh, no problem," Grace gave me another tight hug. We pulled away and smiled at each other. I was so lucky to have a friend like Grace.

"I do have one more question." Grace listened in as I asked, "Could you give me a reason as to why I'm feeling this way?"

"What do you mean?"

"The past few days, almost all I've ever thought about was Elliott. I lay in bed awake at night just thinking about him. And I feel so empty when I'm around him. Like I can't sleep, eat, or even think. I can't stop thinking about him, and when I'm around him, I feel so wonderful. I just want to be with him, and all I care about is his happiness. And I feel so many other emotions! I think it may just be the hormones, but it's something else. And I keep feeling a beating in my heart whenever I think about him or am around him. And..."

Grace cut me off from my rambling. "Okay, okay," she laughed, "I think I know what it is."

"What?"

Grace opened her mouth to speak, but didn't say anything. Smiling to herself, she said, "I'll let you figure it out on your own."

I furrowed my eyebrows at her. "Why?"

"You'll see," Grace winked. Still smiling she said, "We should probably get to bed. We have to get up bright and early to go home tomorrow."

I was too tired to say anything else. I got a really good night sleep, despite the fact we had to wake up at three in the morning tomorrow. Talking to Grace really helped. I felt more relaxed about everything going on and more confident that Elliott and I could work this out.

Chapter 23: Wishing For Love

The trip from Munich to home was very tiring. I know we didn't really do much except sit on a plane for nine hours and thirty minutes, but that didn't mean it couldn't make us exhausted.

For one thing, we had to get up at three in the morning. This was something that all of us (especially Nicole) weren't particularly thrilled about. Then we had to go through baggage and customs and all that fun stuff. Plus we had a really long flight. I slept most of the way, though I did wake up and watch *Serpent Boy 2* just to see Elliott's cute face. I felt a pinch of jealousy when Elliott had to kiss Isla Tinsley, the actress playing his love interest in the movie. I know it was just acting, and Elliott had told me the two were just friends, but I couldn't help but feel protective. Not in a possessive way I promise.

When we landed, it was around two in the afternoon. I was jet-lagged, and it would take a while for me to get back on-board with the Annapolis time difference. When we stood up, my legs felt sore, and I wanted to take a nap. We took a shuttle from the plane to the main building. By the time we were at baggage claim, we were happy to be home.

"Europe was fun," Nicole said as she grabbed her suitcase off the luggage carousel, "but I'm happy to be home."

"When I get home," Esperanza exclaimed giddily, "I'm gonna bake, sleep, and spend time with my family."

"I'm gonna take a long hot bubble bath and watch a movie in *English*," Nicole said. "Maybe even go to the bar and hope I meet a hot guy."

"Of course you will," Grace laughed. "I'm gonna catch up on my sleep and go back to binge-watching *Grey's Anatomy* after not watching it for two weeks."

"What about you, Cecilia?" Esperanza asked me. "You must have *something* you want to do."

"I don't really know," I said. I guess I hadn't thought of it. Probably spend time with my family, play with Jane, get some American food, and maybe try to facetime Elliott.

Grace muttered something under her breath: "I think you'll have something to do pretty soon."

"I'm sorry what?" I asked her confused, as to what this meant.

"Nothing," Grace quickly replied back. I just shrugged it off.

Once we all had our luggage with us, we went straight to the side to meet our parents. They were all standing there, smiles on their faces and waving, happy to see their daughters return. As soon as I saw my parents, my heart exploded. They were standing there in all their glory, still looking the same as when I left him. I ran to them, my luggage dragging behind me and my backpack bouncing on my back.

"Mom! Dad!" I exclaimed in happiness as I ran straight into their arms.

"Sweetheart," my mom mumbled, "we missed you so much."

"And you're back in one piece!" my dad quipped, causing me and my mom to laugh.

I pulled apart to look at them. My parents had proud smiles on their faces.

"Oh my gosh, you have no idea how much I missed you two," I beamed.

"We missed you too," my mom placed her hand on my cheek and stroked my cheekbone with her thumb.

"I'm surprised," Dad jokes. "I would think all you would be thinking about is that Snake Boy."

Chuckling, I corrected him, "*Serpent* Boy. And of course I missed you both. I thought about you guys every day. And I love you guys."

"We love you too," my dad smiled. "And I've gotta say, I wasn't sure about that *Serpent* Boy. But now that I met him, he seems like a really nice guy."

"He sure is," I gushed about Elliott. But I shook my head when I heard what my dad had said. "Wait, what?!" He had said something about meeting Elliott. But he's never met Elliott.

My mom turned to him and lightly hit her husband on the arm. "Patrick," she whispered in anger. "You spoiled the surprise."

Dad turned to her and held his hands up in defense. "I'm sorry, Kate. But she was going to find out eventually."

"Wait, wait," I tried to see if I had heard them correctly. "You've *met* Elliott? How is that possible?" I tried to think, and I came up with an idea. A smile on my face, I said in realization, "You visited him in Rome, didn't you?"

"No, not exactly," Mom chuckled and shook her head. She pointed behind me and said, "Look."

I turned all the way around. I saw a short, muscular man with brown curls talking to someone. My eyes grew wide, then I squinted to see if I was right in who it was. The man was talking to a young girl, singing what looked like an autograph. When he was finished, he gave her a warm hug and smiled at her. Then the girl asked him something else, and the man nodded. He looked anxious, but did what she wanted anyway. The girl's mother took a picture of them together, and at that moment I knew exactly who it was.

Elliott Parker.

My mouth dropped open wide. What was he doing here? How did he get here? What happened to the movie in Rome? What was going on?

As Elliott waved the girl and her mother goodbye, several other people came crowding towards him. I'm not sure what had happened exactly as I was still in a state of surprise and confusion, but Elliott politely dismissed the crowd. He looked so sorry, and the crowd left disappointed. They walked away, and Elliott felt guilty. I know how much he cared about his fans. I think he cared more about them than they did about him. He briefly turned his head to face me, then looked the other way. Then when he realized who was there, he turned his full body to me. His frown changed into a happy smile with a friendly wave.

I walked toward him, slowly. Was I dreaming? He was certainly beaming from ear to ear at the sight of me. I got closer and closer to him, and as I did I reached out my hand to make sure he wasn't a ghost. As soon as I got close enough to touch his face, his face felt smooth against my skin.

To make sure I wasn't going crazy, my other hand touched his shoulder. To triple check both of my hands touched his cheek. I felt tears in my eyes.

He finally spoke. "Don't worry, it's me. I'm not a ghost."

We laughed in unison, as a tear of pure joy rolled down my cheek. "It *is* you!"

With that, Elliott pulled me into his warm embrace. I hugged him back tightly, so happy to be in his arms again. My heart was pumping faster than ever. We wouldn't let go. We refused to let go.

"I missed you," he murmured.

"I missed you too," I said back. When we finally pulled apart, I asked him, "What are you doing here?"

"I finished up the movie early," he explained. "And when Grace told me how sad you were, I had to come and see you."

My smile faded as I asked, "Wait...she didn't tell you...?"

"She told me everything," he nodded with concern in his voice. When Elliott saw how sad I was, he pressed his forehead against mine. "Listen, we can work this out. I lo-I really like you, and I want to start a relationship with you. Long distance relationships can be hard, but we can make this work. I know we can. I want to do this for you, because I..."

I shut him up by pressing his lips against mine. He seemed a little surprised at first, but started to kiss me back. We had not kissed nor touched each other in what seemed like an eternity. Our noses now touched, our noses were pressed together. We stopped kissing briefly, our foreheads still touching and our eyes closed.

"I'm happy you still like kissing me," he murmured, and I laughed along with him. He kissed me again. I had missed everything. The way his lips felt against mine. The way smelled. His smile. His accent. His adorkable charm. *Everything.*

"Eh hem," we heard a throat clear. We quickly pulled apart and saw Nicole staring at us. Her hands on her hips, her foot tapping on the floor, a serious look on her face. Then she smiled and pulled me in for a hug.

"I'm so happy for you, girl," she whispered.

"Thank you," I smiled.

"You deserve it," Nicole said as she pulled apart. I felt Elliott's hand wrap around me, his hands wrapped around my waist and his chin on my shoulder.

"But if I were you," Nicole winked, "when you're with your parents keep the making out to a minimum."

Elliott laughed at this, and I came up with a comeback: "Shut up, Nicole. Don't be a hypocrite." Nicole's eyes widened, but then she laughed.

Elliott then became prideful in a very cute way. He cheerfully said, "That's my girl. Always having a good comeback."

The three of us started to walk back to meet our parents again. Elliott and I were walking hand-in-hand, our fingers intertwined when Esperanza came and engulfed the both of us in a big hug. Elliott and I hugged her back.

"You guys are *so* cute," Esperanza gushed about us. Reuniting our hands, Elliott and I smiled at her. Esperanza said glumly, "Makes me feel single."

"You'll meet someone," I put my hand on her shoulder. "Just you wait."

Elliott offered, "I can set you up with one of my famous friends if you like."

"No offense, but I don't think I'd want to date a celebrity," Esperanza said honestly.

"Not even if it's Miles Albright," Elliott casually mentioned his name just to get a reaction from her.

"You're friends with Miles Albright?" Esperanza said in a mixture of shock and excitement.

Miles Albright was this actor that Esperanza had been crushing on for years. I had mentioned to Elliott that Esperanza liked him, and he mentioned he was one of his closest Hollywood friends. But I'll save that for another story.

"Okay, okay," I patted him on the shoulder. Just as I said that, Grace came running up to us with the biggest smile on her face. She hadn't looked this excited since she found out she was going to be Valedictorian of our high school class.

I shook my head and smiled, "You sneaky friend."

"I just had to," Grace shrugged. "If I really want something to happen, I have to make it happen. I'm very much a goal-setter."

Elliott bent down and said to me, "It's true. She is." I nodded my head in agreement.

I walked closer to her and hugged her. Elliott came in for a group hug, until I snapped at him (though not in a mean way): "Hey, Parker back off. You've gotta wait your turn."

"Sorry," Elliott said quietly. When Grace and I were done, she gave Elliott a huge hug. When they were done, I saw Elliott whisper something in Grace's ear, and she whispered something back. I never found out what they whispered to each other.

As soon as everyone was done hugging, we went off to join our parents. Elliott and I locked hands once again, and I felt joy in my beating heart.

The next evening, Elliott and I were on the couch in the living room watching *Harry Potter and the Sorcerer's Stone*. I had promised to watch all eight movies with him, and we were starting at the beginning. I had to admit, they weren't as bad as I thought they were going to be. I saw why Elliott and Grace liked them. But I knew Grace would probably be mad at me, because she's been trying to get me to watch them *and* read the books for years. Oh well. She would probably be over it in a day or so.

Elliott was lying so he was facing the TV, and his feet were resting on the ottoman in front of him. He had his arm wrapped behind me, and I was leaning into him with my head on his shoulder and my hand on his chest. Jane was curled up by my feet, just barely awake. My parents were watching it with us too, but they had fallen asleep. My parents really liked Elliott. My mom was a little hesitant at first. She had watched a few interviews and red carpets with him, but she wasn't sure if his personality was the same when he wasn't posing for the cameras. Then they got to know each other, and she told me he was, "Every mother's dream boyfriend for their daughter." My dad, he was being his normal funny dad himself. For one thing, he would not stop teasing him about playing a superhero named "Serpent Boy." And he kept teasing him about a lot of other stuff too, as if he was trying to scare him away. But Elliott grew up one of four brothers, so I think he's used to it.

The movie had just ended. The school year was over and all the students were leaving Hogwarts. As soon as the credits started rolling, I became nearly surprised that that was where it ended. It seemed like there were so many plot holes that needed to be solved.

"That's it?" I sat up and gestured to the screen in disbelief. I turned to Elliott and tried to convince him what happened next. "What's going on? I'm so confused! What happens next?"

Elliott rubbed his eyes and said, "You'll have to wait till the next movie."

"But I'm really confused!" I whined.

"About what?" Elliott asked.

"Everything!" I exclaimed. I was quiet so I wouldn't wake my parents up.

"Don't worry," Elliott tried to explain to me. "There's seven more movies."

"Seven!" my eyes widened. "I thought there were like *four* other movies! I have to watch *seven other movies* for my questions to be answered?"

Shrugging, Elliott suggested, "You could just look it up on the internet if you're that desperate."

"No," I shook my head. I curled up to him so we were in our same positions as we were before. I assured him, "I liked this movie. It was really good. I liked watching it." I could tell I was getting tired because of all the random fluff I was saying. "I liked watching it with *you*," I winked at him.

"Thank you," Elliott smiled. "Not to brag or anything," Elliott said as if he were proud, "but I think I know more about *Harry Potter* than J.K. Rowling."

"That's a pretty bold statement," I pointed out. "Saying you know more than the creator."

"It's true," Elliott nodded. "I went to a *Harry Potter*-themed pub quiz one time with my mates, and I smashed it." Elliott sounded like he was being a little cocky in his *Harry Potter* knowledge.

"What's a pub quiz?" I curiously asked.

"You don't have pub quizzes here in the States?" Elliott asked confusedly.

I shook my head. "We don't have many pubs. Mainly bars."

"Bars are nice," Elliott nodded. "Anyway, a pub quiz is basically a quiz held in a pub. You're on teams and they give you questions and you have to answer correctly to earn points," he explained. Laughing to himself, he added, "It's both fun and informative at the same time."

I started to connect a pub quiz to something else in American culture: "That sounds like trivia night. That's something we have here in America."

"Oh, that's right!" Elliott realized. "I've been to a thousand trivia nights when I'm visiting! I guess I could have just told you it was the British version of a trivia night. Oh well!" We laughed at how Elliott wasn't thinking.

I yawned, still tired and trying to get back on the American time zone. "What time is it anyway?" I sheepishly asked Elliott, too tired to look at either the clock on the fireplace mantle or the clock on the TV. The mantle clock wasn't digital, and I wasn't in the mood for reading a traditional clock. And the TV clock seemed too far away.

"I don't know," Elliott replied, just as he was reaching into his back pocket to grab his phone and look. "Woah," he whispered in surprise. He immediately shot up from laying down, and I sat up with him.

"What?" I asked, trying to figure out what happened.

"It's 11:27!" he frightfully whispered. "Aunt Charlotte and them are probably worried."

"Did we lose track of time?" I asked, trying to figure out how it ended up being so late.

"Well, we did stop a few times to get popcorn," Elliott pointed out. "And take bathroom breaks. And when Jane was barking at the TV. We really did stop a lot!" Elliott stood up and looked back down at me, "I've got to go."

He started to grab the popcorn bowl to help clean up, as it was the polite thing to do. But I firmly yet gently grabbed his wrist, and he immediately met my eyes in response.

"Please," I tried to convince him. "Stay the night."

"But my family will be terribly worried," Elliott told me as if he was sorry.

"Text them," I rapidly responded. "You can sleep with me." Elliott raised an eyebrow at me, but I quickly assured him, "Not like that. Just---we can sleep in the same bed." But I muttered under my breath in realization: "But my parents probably won't like it."

"See, I'll just go," Elliott gestured his thumb back.

"They don't have to know!" I told him almost too loudly.

My dad had heard, and he immediately woke up from sleeping. My mom was just still snoozing away peacefully on the chair. That was a surprise, considering my mom was a light sleeper. She most likely would have woken up right away from how loud I was speaking.

"What?" my dad said, still sleepy. He turned to face me. Not seeing Elliott, he warmly but sheepishly smiled, "Oh, hey honey. How was the rest of the movie?"

"It was good," I nodded. "I liked it."

"Good, Mom thought you would," my dad yawned. He looked up at Elliott and asked, "Still here, Serpent Boy?"

"You don't have to call him that, Dad," I gritted through my teeth.

"I actually like it when people think of me as Serpent Boy," Elliott turned to me and smiled. I rolled my eyes, but was secretly loving how much he loved playing the iconic superhero. He turned to face my dad. "And yeah, I was just leaving now," Elliott nervously said. He started to walk away, worried he would get in trouble for being here at 11:30 at night.

"No, no," my dad stopped him. He looked at the clock, "It's 11:30," then he suggested to Elliott, "Why don't you just spend the night?"

"Oh, but sir," Elliott started to say. He corrected himself, "Mr. Hartley. You don't need to---"

My dad interrupted him, "It's no trouble. Just text your aunt that you're spending the night."

"Is this a good idea?" I asked dad, trying to seem as though I didn't think it was a good idea. But I actually really wanted Elliott to spend the night. "I don't think Mom will like it."

That was true. One time in high school, Esperanza and I were working on a project and she was staying for dinner. Afterwards, we decided to watch a movie, and it was over by 10:15. I tried to convince my mom to let her spend the night since it was so late, but she insisted on taking Esperanza home. I doubt this time would have been any different, especially if it was a man.

"It'll be fine," Dad brushed it off. "I'm the parent too, you know."

Maybe Dad would allow Elliott to sleep in my room? I thought I'd take a chance and ask. I got up from the couch, walked over to where Elliott and my dad were, and offered, "He could sleep in my room."

"Absolutely not," my dad responded immediately and surely. "I don't want little Elliotts or Cecilias running around the house." I rolled my eyes, but Elliott snorted, causing me to lightly smack his shoulder. "Elliott can sleep in the guest room. It's cleaned up and the sheets are washed." So much for late night cuddles with Elliott.

"Are you sure about this, Mr. Hartley?" Elliott asked. "I can go home. It's no big deal."

"It's no problem," my dad assured him. "Just text your aunt and I'm sure it will be fine."

Elliott nodded, "Okay." Reaching for his phone in his pocket, he said, "I'll text her now."

******

At 1 o'clock in the morning, I was still wide awake. Wrapped under the sheets with Jane curled up in a ball, sleeping at my feet. I was thinking about Elliott. He was only a few doors down the hall, and I missed him desperately. This is how it was on the last days of the trip. Missing his touch and comfort so much. Wanting to be with him. Not being able to sleep at night because of my thoughts of him running through my mind. I had contemplated these feelings over and over again over the past few days. But now I had come to a conclusion, and I needed to tell somebody.

My eyes immediately went to Jane, sleeping so peacefully. I hated to wake her up, but I couldn't wait any longer, or else I'd go crazy. I reached her towards the end of the bed, and brought her to me. She was lying beside me. It was dark, but I could tell she was awake.

"Sorry, Janie," I whispered to her. "But I need to tell you something. If I don't tell someone, I'll go crazy."

Jane immediately sat up as if she was listening, and I giggled at how smart she was.

I rubbed her soft head and kissed her forehead. Then I started talking: "Elliott is amazing, girl. He's so sweet and caring towards everyone he knows. He gets along so well his brothers. He has such a good sense of humor. He always makes sure I'm okay. He has the best smile. The cutest dimples, even if they're just barely there. I love everything about him."

Unable to contain it anymore, I said almost a little too loudly, "I love him!"

Just as I said that, there was a knock at the door. I immediately jumped and faced the door. Jane seemed surprised, too. She tilted her head to the side, then looked at me to see how I would respond.

"Come in," my voice cracked.

The door creaked open slightly. My heart was beating in anticipation. I saw Elliott peek his head in. Uh oh. He started to open the door wide and he stepped inside. It was dark, but I was able to pick out little details. His curly hair was messy and he was wearing his boxers and the T-shirt he had on before. He probably didn't want to be shirtless while sleeping over at my parents' house.

"Hi," he sleepily, but almost alarmingly, said. "Mind if I come in?"

"Sure," I nodded. "Close the door though."

Elliott did as I said, and I turned on my bedside lamp so I could see better. I saw him standing there in all his glory---though it was obvious that he had just woken up from sleeping.

"What are you doing here?" I questioned him. "My parents will kill us if they know you're in here."

"They're on the third floor," Elliott reminded me as he began walking toward me.

When he stopped so he was on the side of my bed, I asked him, "You didn't hear anything, did you?"

I was still laying down when Elliott leaned on the side of the bed, moving his head so his face was right in front of mine. My eyes dilated, worried what would happen next. He was gazing down at me, his eyes sparkling and his mouth slightly agape.

"You really love me?" he said in quiet disbelief.

He heard. Dang it. Quick! Recover!

"Um..." I tried to think. Still staring at him, I could tell he was eager for an answer. "I may have, but I completely understand if you don't love me---"

"Shhh," Elliott shushed me and placed his hand on my mouth. I was freaking out. He was probably going to say he didn't love me and that it was all just a summer fling. I waited for him to say it. I was prepared.

"I-I love you too," Elliott's face started to heat up as he grinned.

When he took his hand off of my mouth, I asked him, "You do?" I wanted to make sure I was hearing him correctly.

"I do," Elliott nodded. "I've known since my first night back in Rome. I couldn't sleep that night. I was thinking about you and how hurt you were. I kept wanting you to be here with me. Then the next day at work I kept messing up my lines during one scene. That's when I knew!" He sounded confident and happy he was saying this, I even noticed a single tear roll down his cheek. He seemed so happy to finally get it out in the open.

"Really?" I grinned, happy he felt the same way. Smiling, Elliott nodded quickly. Sitting up so we were at the same level, I told him, "I love you so much."

Next thing, Elliott connected his lips to mine. We hadn't kissed alone like this in ages, and it felt nice. He climbed onto the bed so now he was on top of me, and we continued to express our love for each other.

"I love you," Elliott whispered against my lips, causing me to hum. It felt so nice to hear someone say they love you in a romantic way. No one has ever told me they loved me in that way. I've never even been in love myself.

Elliott planted a soft smooch on my right cheek and whispered again, "I love you." He did the same to my left cheek and chuckled, "I love you so much!" He lovingly gazed into my eyes. Caught up in my love for this man, I reached my hand and started to stroke his cheek. I cherished him, knowing that now that he loved me, I was his. And he was mine.

Elliott leaned his lips close to my forehead, and adoringly kissed my forehead. He muttered against it, "I love you, darling."

The romantic moment of course was ruined by Jane, who I thought was asleep. But she wasn't. I tried to contain my laughter when I saw Jane licking Elliott's cheek.

"Awww," I cooed. "Jane likes you."

Elliott smiled, then turned to face Jane, who continued to kiss him. It was as if she wanted to be a part of it too.

"I thought *I* was Jane's favorite," I jokingly pouted.

"Jealous?" Elliott teased me, but he was still caught up in the affection Jane was showing for him.

"Okay, that's enough," I chuckled, pulling Jane apart from Elliott when I realized Jane had been kissing him for about a minute. "Wait," I just realized to myself out loud. Elliott was now sitting at the end of the bed, Jane curled up on his lap. He was petting her back, running fingers through her soft brown fur.

"What?" he asked in curiosity.

"Why were *you* in here?" I smirked at Elliott.

"Honestly," Elliott shrugged, "I wanted to tell you how I felt."

"Really?" I said in disbelief, thinking he was making this up.

"Yes. I couldn't sleep. I got all of twenty minutes. But I woke up because I couldn't stop thinking about you and how much I loved you and how I needed to tell you how I felt!" he said the last part a little too loudly, so I shushed him.

Elliott must have noticed something next to my part of the bed, because his eyes squinted. "Wait a minute, is that?..."

"What?" I asked in confusion. Elliott gently lifted Jane off his lap and placed her to the side. She was asleep by now. He crawled over to the bed, his smile growing wider. He was on his hands and knees when he picked up what he was looking at: the Serpent Boy beanie baby from fourteen years ago.

Elliott examined the toy, and chuckled as he held it up. "You got a beanie baby of me?"

"Of Serpent Boy," I corrected him. I was flushing a little. I was kind of embarrassed.

"I am Serpent Boy," Elliott pointed out, grinning. "It's so nice to see the girl I love has a plush toy of me." He bends over and kisses my cheek tenderly.

"I won it at a fair when I was seven," I admitted.

"You did?" Elliott smiled. "How come you never told me the story?"

"Well..." I wasn't sure whether I should tell him that I once hated Serpent Boy and nearly threw a tantrum when I won the toy. "How about I tell you another time?"

"Why not now?" Elliott crawled so he was hovering over me again.

"Tomorrow?" I asked.

"Later today," Elliott reminded me it was already the morning.

"Yes," I promised him.

He leaned down and kissed me once again, with as much love and passion as all the other kisses had been. We finally stopped to take a rest, and he flipped so now he was next to me, his head laying on my chest. He almost didn't want to leave me. He wanted to stay. But I had something else going through my head.

"Are we gonna work?" I asked him, breaking the silence.

"What do you mean?" Elliott asked with his head still on my chest.

"Are we going to be okay?" I asked him, almost looking for comfort. "With the living in different countries and the crazy fans, will we make this work?"

"I think we can," Elliott said confidently. He sat up and leaned his head against the headboard. I responded by laying my head across his lap, looking up at him. He told me, "I believe we'll be okay. Long distance relationships get hard, but we can make this work. I'll always find time to visit you, and you can come to London or Los Angeles or New York or wherever I am any time I want. And when you graduate, it will be easier. And we have one thing for each other that I know will keep us strong."

"What?" I asked in curiosity.

"Love," he smiled. I smiled too, never getting tired of hearing how much he loved me.

I sat up in front of him. My heart beat fast as lightning. I leaned into him and kissed him with everything I had. He snaked his hands to my back and pulled me closer. I placed both hands on his face, deeply immersing myself in the kiss. My heart was beating fast, and I heard his heart pump faster and faster against my chest. I always wanted to find true love. Someone who would make me happy. And now I was with Elliott. And Elliott made me happy.

Now, I would say "and we all lived happily ever after," but I can promise you one thing: this is *not* where the story ends.